Tycho Brahe's Path to God

AGM COLLECTION

AVANT-GARDE & MODERNISM

Tycho Brahe's Path to God

A Novel

MAX BROD

Introduction by Stefan Zweig
Translated from the German by Felix Warren Crosse
Introduction to the new edition by Peter Fenves

Northwestern

University Press

Evanston

Illinois

Northwestern University Press
www.nupress.northwestern.edu

Northwestern University Press edition published 2007. Copyright
© 1928 by Max Brod. Introduction to the new edition copyright
© 2007 by Peter Fenves. First published 1928 by Alfred A. Knopf
under the title *The Redemption of Tycho Brahe*. All rights reserved.

Printed in the United States of America

10 9 8 7 6 5 4 3 2 1

ISBN-13: 978-0-8101-2381-6
ISBN-10: 0-8101-2381-9

Library of Congress Cataloging-in-Publication data are available
from the Library of Congress.

♾ The paper used in this publication meets the minimum
requirements of the American National Standard for Information
Sciences—Permanence of Paper for Printed Library Materials,
ANSI Z39.48-1992.

To my friend Franz Kafka

KAFKA: "Somebody must have been telling lies about Joseph K because one fine morning he was arrested . . ." [*Turns the book over to look at the title. There is a moment of shocked silence, then he shouts:*] MAX! [*Nobody comes. KAFKA rushes off the stage and comes back with some of the books taken out of the bookshelf, looking at them and throwing them down as he comes.*] Kafka! Kafka! Novels, stories, letters. Everything. MAX!

[BROD *creeps on to the stage.*]

BROD [*Faintly*]: Sorry.

KAFKA: Sorry? SORRY? Max. You publish everything I ever wrote and you're sorry. I trusted you.

BROD: You exaggerated. You always did.

KAFKA: So, I say burn them, what do you think I mean, *warm* them?

　　Alan Bennett, *Kafka's Dick*

Introduction to the New Edition

The Kafka-Werfel-Einstein Effect

PETER FENVES

It is without a doubt the most famous scene of betrayal in modern literary history. Not only does Max Brod (1884–1968) fail to burn the papers of Franz Kafka, as he had been asked to do in two separate documents; he moves in the opposite direction, publishing almost everything of Kafka that falls into his hands. Although it is unlikely that Brod foresaw the magnitude of the phenomenon that would gather around the name of Franz Kafka—a phenomenon that would soon eclipse his own—he was keenly aware of his friend's literary talents, having praised him in print even before he had published a single word.[1] When Brod and Kafka were young, they occasionally traveled together, and they even planned on writing a travel novel together.[2] Except for an isolated chapter, this plan faltered; but in a larger sense—until recently, when new editions of Kafka's works began to appear—the two went hand in hand. Wherever there was Kafka, so there was Brod. Just as Sancho Panza accompanies Don Quixote, so does Brod accompany Kafka, including in the publication of Kafka's "The Truth about Sancho Panza," which Brod first published and which presents Don Quixote as Sancho's consoling fantasy.[3] Beyond the occasional specialist in modern Prague-German literature, or in the genesis of German expression-ism, or in the history of the Prague-based Zionist movement, or in the dis-semination of Leoš Janáček's operas, or in the popularization of Jaroslav Hašek's *Good Soldier Švejk,* or in the founding institutions of Israeli theater —for Brod was involved in all of these—few readers come across his name except in connection with that of his friend. And in this connection, the fol-lowing thought can never be altogether suppressed: Brod betrayed him.

Of course, Brod had his reasons. His postscript to Kafka's *Trial,* first published in 1925, discloses several, albeit not all, of them. Among the most compelling of these reasons is perhaps the best-known one: Brod had made it clear to Kafka that under no condition would Brod destroy any of Kafka's writings; if, therefore, Kafka had really wanted all of his papers to be destroyed, he would have found someone else to carry out this dismal task.[4] As Walter Benjamin convincingly argued when accusations of betrayal were first being leveled at Brod, the work of Kafka that Brod edited and published reveals the paltriness of his accusers, who condemn him on the basis of moral concepts that are altogether foreign to the work in ques-tion—categories such as "inner conflicts" and "ethical maxims."[5] The con-troversy generated by Brod's decision to ignore the documents in which Kafka requested that his papers be turned into ashes has itself died out. But the story of Brod's actions lives on. Indeed, it is so widely known and so much a part of Kafka's image and legacy that it can almost be counted among the unfinished tales he left behind.

What is far less widely known—more exactly, almost completely forgot-ten—is the fact that, years before Kafka contracted the illness that would take his life, Brod had conceived of a novel that culminates in a scene of betrayal that, in certain circles and among a few scholars, is almost as widely known as the one in which he would later play a leading role. This novel literally begins with the name of "my friend" Franz Kafka, to whom it is dedicated. The scene of betrayal around which it revolves is likewise associated with the city of Prague. In exile from his Danish home, the great astronomer Tycho Brahe (1546–1601), having fallen hopelessly ill, entered into a state of delirium and "was frequently heard to exclaim that he hoped he should not appear to have lived in vain ('ne frustra vixisse videar')."[6] The German astronomer Johannes Kepler (1571–1630) was at Tycho's bedside, and he understood the dying words of his benefactor to mean that he, Kepler, should henceforth use the astronomical charts that Tycho had painstakingly prepared to confirm the Tychonic system of planetary motion. According to this system—which is remembered today largely as a scientific curiosity[7]—the planets revolve around the sun, while the sun, along with the planets, rotates around the earth. In this way, the new astronomy of Copernicus is granted a degree of validity, while the principle of the old Aristotelian-Ptolemaic astronomy remains firmly in place: human beings still occupy the center of the cosmos. Had Kepler followed Tycho's deathbed instructions, as he himself understood them, he would have disappeared into the obscurity of Franz Tengnagel, Tycho's son-in-law, who inherited the Tychonic system along with the right to dispose of his father-in-law's papers. In some broader sense, Kepler can be said to have shown that Tycho did not live in vain; but the discovery of the elliptical path of the planets, which Kepler announced in his *Astronomia nova* of 1609, made the Tychonic compromise between Ptolemy and Copernicus—or, more generally, between old and new, ancient and modern—into a thing of the past.

The twelfth and last chapter of Brod's novel *Tycho Brahes Weg zu Gott* culminates in Tycho's dying request that Kepler demonstrate the truth of his system. First appearing in the pages of the prestigious monthly *Die weißen Blätter* (*The White Pages*) during the winter and spring of 1915, the novel was published in book form a year later by the innovative publishing house of Kurt Wolff. It received largely favorable reviews, sold exceptionally well, required numerous reprints, and was translated into a number of languages, including English in 1928.[8] The translation prepared by Felix Warren Crosse and published by Knopf—which is reproduced in this volume—relies on a slightly antiquated diction and does not always render the German in an entirely faithful manner; but it is largely successful in capturing the swift tempo of Brod's text. Only in one place has Crosse's translation been altered. The 1928 version appeared under the title *The Redemption of Tycho Brahe*. It should have read: *Tycho Brahe's Path to God*. The difference between the two titles is slight yet important: whereas the former assumes that Tycho Brahe reaches his goal, the latter does not.[9]

The following remarks do not attempt to provide a broad overview of Max Brod's tumultuous life and massive oeuvre. Suffice it to say, for now, that he was born in Prague into a middle-class Jewish family, became involved in the Zionist movement shortly before he began the Tycho Brahe novel, fled from the Nazis in 1939 on the last train out of Prague, and settled in Tel Aviv, where he lived out the rest of his life. During this time, he wrote more than eighty books alongside hundreds of articles, reviews, prefaces, and postscripts. Stefan Zweig's foreword, which follows this introduction, reflects on Brod's career at its midpoint and is of continuing interest not only for what it says about the special qualities of his work but also for what it positively leaves out: Zweig emphasizes the methodical character of Brod's development as a novelist without ever alluding to the fact this development revolves around what Brod describes as his "struggle with—and for—Judaism."[10] English-speaking readers who are interested in a more complete overview of Brod's work, which sharply contrasts with Zweig's purely aesthetic treatment, would do well to consult the Leo Baeck Memorial Lecture that Robert Weltsch published under the title *Max Brod and His Age*.

This introduction goes in a direction that is opposed to both Zweig's foreword and Weltsch's lecture, for it seeks to illuminate only a single novel and its age. But it should not be forgotten that the novel in question is itself an indirect reflection on Brod's own struggle to affirm his Jewishness, and its age is redoubled as a result: while recounting certain elements in the scientific and religious atmosphere of early seventeenth-century Bohemia, it indirectly reflects on corresponding elements in the literary and religious atmosphere of early twentieth-century Prague. This reduplication of the place and redoubling of the age is only a preliminary indication of the extraordinarily rich range of elements that enter into the work that Robert Weltsch, for one, considers Brod's best.[11]

"To My Friend Franz Kafka"

Not only does *Tycho Brahe's Path to God* culminate in a scene of betrayal but it is premised on one as well. Years before the event depicted in the novel, which revolves around the last years of Tycho's life, an astronomer named Nicolaus Raimarus Bär, otherwise known as Ursus ("bear" in Latin), had entered into Tycho's company, caught a glimpse of his notes, made some copies, and published a rudimentary version of the Tychonic system, for which he then proceeded to take sole credit. To make matters worse, Ursus mercilessly disparaged Tycho in a series of broadsheets. The novel takes its point of departure from these events, which threaten to deprive Tycho of the pleasure of knowing that his name will be spoken whenever the structure of the heavens comes under discussion. After enticing Kepler to become his assistant in his castle at Benatky, which lies about twenty-five miles from Prague, Tycho assigns him the task of preparing a formal refutation of Ursus's slanders. Within the context of Brod's novel, however, the assignment of this task to the newcomer has a paradoxical result, for as long as the *Apologia Tychonis contra Ursum* remains incomplete, Tycho cannot be sure that Kepler is, as it were, entirely on his side. Kepler might secretly be in league with Ursus, in which case he would be nothing more than a "paid enemy"—to cite the memorable words that Kafka's father applied to the assistants in his shop.

From the first page of the novel onward, then, Tycho's relation to Kepler is marked by ambivalence. Viewing Kepler "as a weary father looks upon a growing son, with mixed sentiments of anguish and joyous expectation" (3), he finds it almost impossible to disentangle the two competing emotions. The opening scenes of the novel play out the consequence of this ambivalence, which affects everyone within Tycho's circle. The fiancé of his daughter, the aforementioned Tengnagel, becomes intensely jealous of Kepler, who has displaced him in his master's affection and whom he considers, for this reason, a traitor-in-waiting.[12] And in a compelling description of the chaotic character of Tycho's castle—which includes a deformed court jester who, as another adopted son, functions as an inverted image of Kepler—Tengnagel demands that Tycho choose between his two assistants, with the result that he, the dull but steadfast "Junker," is promptly driven out of the castle by Tycho's sons and surreptitiously ensconced in the sacristy by Tycho's daughter, Elisabeth, who, as it turns out, has betrayed her father by becoming pregnant—and thereby inadvertently repeated a decisive moment in his own early life, when he impregnated a servant girl and thereupon took her as his wife, to the great consternation of his noble family. Everything in Tycho's circle, in short, revolves around betrayal.

And the world of Kepler, as depicted in the novel, is not entirely different, for he is betrayed by his friends, who publish his papers without his permission. His response to this situation is different from that of his new employer. Instead of worrying about the origin and consequences of this dubious action, Kepler simply shrugs it off, as if it were of no concern to him. The friends of Kepler justify their actions with reference to the fact— which, it should be noted, is sheer fiction—that the talented young astronomer would never publish anything that was not absolutely perfect, and the only absolutely perfect text would be one that solved the riddle of the heavens. The words that Brod uses in his postscript to Kafka's *Trial* could be directly transferred to the novel he published ten years earlier— in this case, as a description of Kepler's astronomical endeavors: "admittedly without ever saying so, he [Kafka] applied the highest religious standard to his art."[13] Or, to the same effect, one could quote from Brod's review of Kafka's first book, *Betrachtung* (*Contemplation;* 1913), which owes its publication in no small part to Brod's prodding: "Wherever he [Kafka]

cannot attain perfection, the most ecstatic happiness, he gives up altogether."[14] Perhaps in recognition of his friend's prodding, Kafka placed the
following cryptogram at the beginning of his book: "For M. B." Brod is
doubtless relieving himself of a debt when he dedicates his own novel to
Kafka.[15] Since, however, the two writers do not relate to their respective
work in the same way, as his review of *Contemplation* states more or less
openly, the word "reciprocity" cannot entirely capture the meaning of gesture that takes shape in the apparently simple phrase with which the novel
opens: "To my friend Franz Kafka." Without friends, a Kepler or a Kafka
may escape the eyes of a wider public. The dedication of *Tycho Brahe's Path
to God* not only gets Kafka's name into print once again, it also associates
the author of this novel with the friends of Kepler, who are responsible for
the small degree of visibility the self-effacing perfectionist enjoys.

And Kafka, for his part, sees little trace of reciprocity in the novel's dedication. On the contrary, he sees a series of discrepancies, beginning with
the disproportion between Tycho's vitality and his own and concluding
with the imbalance between Brod's generosity and his own unworthiness.
Having been sufficiently immersed in the drafts of the novel to adopt the
term "Tychonic"[16] in his correspondence with Brod, Kafka delights in the
news that he will be included in the novel. Thus he writes to Brod in February 1914: "Do you know what such a dedication implies? That I am raised
to the same level as Tycho, who is so much more vital than I. And even
though this is only semblance, some gleam of light from this semblance still
warms me in reality. How small I shall be, orbiting this story! But how glad
I shall be to have a semblance of property rights in it. As always, Max, you
are good to me beyond what I deserve."[17] Finding himself a part of a
Tychonic system, Kafka responds in an appropriately Tychonic fashion. The
"semblance" (*Schein*) of ascending to Tycho's level of vitality is double:
Tycho's life is mere semblance, whereas his is real enough; but he is not
really as alive as Tycho. Which is to say: he is not nearly as tempestuous.
The resulting "shine" (*Schein*) that emanates from "Tycho"—both the fictional character and the real book—affects him in two ways: he is already
warmed; and he will soon be seen as small. The only form of reciprocity
that Kafka acknowledges can be found in the "property rights" he is able to
exercise as a result of having his proper name inscribed into every copy of
the book. But these rights, too, are irreal: he has no right to the royalties
and, indeed, no right to anything in the book—not even the inscription of
his own name, which, as the very first element of the novel, not only
obtains a meaning beyond a "proper" one but can even be called its enig-

matic principle. Brod puts Kafka in his debt, without Kafka having asked for something—not even by dedicating *Contemplation* to M. B. The result is a kind of strange double gratitude, in which Brod cannot find Kafka anywhere in the novel except where he literally is, and Kafka, in turn, discovers a semblance of life there on the dedication page.

"This Kepler, That's You"

In one further sense, Brod's novel revolves around an act of betrayal. With reference to Kepler, the narrator notes matter-of-factly: "His wife and stepdaughter he left behind in Graz" (6). In the absence of his family, Kepler does not engage in extramarital affairs. When, for instance, he finds himself alone with Elisabeth Brahe in his bedroom at the stroke of midnight, there is no chance that their struggle—to quote one of the aphorisms of Kafka that Brod will later publish—"ends in bed."[18] Kepler is far too invested in his studies to concern himself with such mundane matters as erotic entanglements. His betrayal of his family is purely negative: he is simply not very interested in them. Indeed, he is not even very interested in himself: "He was endowed with a happy blindness for everything which diverted him from his scientific aims" (95). In so portraying the man who discovered the laws of planetary motion, Brod can be seen to have committed an indiscretion of sorts. Among those who knew something about the turbulent state of physics at the time of its publication, the novel was immediately recognizable as a portrait of its most promising representative. After reading the novel, the Nobel Prize–winning chemist Walther Nernst said to Albert Einstein, "This Kepler, that's you."[19] The very form of this statement is noteworthy: it sounds as though it were an accusation. And this is far from surprising, given the fact that the figure of Kepler is almost demonic in his devotion to his study of planetary motion. Nernst's statement is also credible, given the fact that Brod became acquainted with Einstein in the sixteen-month period during 1911 and 1912 when the physicist was a professor at the German University in Prague. It was in Prague, moreover, that Einstein's marriage to his first wife, Mileva Maric, finally collapsed. Mileva, along with their two sons and her mother, reluctantly moved with Einstein from Zurich, where he held a position of instructor at its polytechnic, and they all moved back with him to Switzerland in 1912 after the polytechnic offered him a professorship; but no member of his family accompanied him to Berlin, where he settled in 1914 and remained until the Nazis took power.

The German University in Prague was certainly fortunate in attracting Einstein to its faculty, and he was publicly welcomed as a major addition to the university.[20] But he was by no means a world-famous figure. In 1905, without a university position, he had revolutionized physics by publishing four papers, two of which were soon called "the special theory of relativity." The theory is "special" because it is concerned with a specific case of the "electrodynamics of moving bodies," to cite the title of Einstein's first paper, namely, bodies in uniform motion. The basic principle of this theory is that there are neither privileged places in the cosmos nor privileged perspectives from which things can be viewed. A general theory of relativity would preserve this "equivalence" principle under all conditions, including in the event of acceleration and within a gravitational field. After 1905, and for the next ten years, Einstein was concerned with a large number of problems; but none was as important to him as the development of a general theory of relativity, which would constitute a new, non-Newtonian theory of gravitation. And as Einstein himself notes in the Czech preface to his popular book on relativity, it was precisely in Prague that he first came up with an insight into this theory that could be astronomically verified: "In the quiet rooms of the Theoretical Physical Institute of the Prague German University in the Vinicna ulice, I discovered in 1911 that the equivalence principle demands a refraction of the rays of light at the sun of a sum that can be observed."[21] When, in 1919, an eclipse of the sun—and an exhausted peace among warring states—allowed for the confirmation of this insight, Einstein became almost overnight a mythical figure of modern genius and, it should be added, a major target for anti-Semites. But in 1911 he did not yet see how the theory implied by this insight could be mathematically expressed and was free to pursue his studies without consideration of mundane matters of world politics: "While Einstein was in Prague, his development of the theory [of general relativity, that is, gravitation] got stuck in [certain] mathematical problems, in particular the derivation of the laws of motion."[22] Similar language could be used to describe the situation of Kepler when he first arrived in Prague.[23] Brod's interest as a novelist does not lie in the problems per se but rather in the combined feelings of expectation and frustration that arise from the absence of a solution. Just as Kepler around 1600 cannot quite grasp the laws under which the planets move, so Einstein around 1911 cannot get a handle on the mathematics that would allow him to determine the electrodynamics of moving bodies under any and every condition.

It was not every Prague-based writer who would have taken an interest in the phenomenon of Einstein. Kafka records something of note in this regard: "As a boy I was as innocent of, and uninterested in, sexual matters . . . as I am today in, say, the theory of relativity."[24] Here, however, Brod stands in a different position—not necessarily with regard to his early experiences of his own sexuality (although there is evidence that he was unlike his friend in this area as well) but rather in terms of his interest in Einstein's theories. It is not as though Brod seriously studied modern physics; but he was interested in the strand of contemporaneous academic philosophy that enthusiastically welcomed Einstein's theories, namely, the version of neo-Kantianism that developed out of Hermann Cohen's work and generally goes by the name of "the Marburg school."[25] One of the less-prominent members of the Marburg school was Felix Weltsch (Robert's cousin), who belonged to Brod's inner circle of friends. In 1913, Brod and Weltsch together published a monograph that announces its relation to neo-Kantianism in its very title, *Anschauung und Begriff* (*Intuition and Concept*).[26] For Kant, the faculty of intuition and the faculty of concepts are the two sources of knowledge; for the members of Marburg school, conceptuality is the sole source of knowledge. Thus the problem that Brod and Weltsch address: Can intuition, which is "unscientific" by virtue of its immediacy, contribute to knowledge, which only expresses itself in concepts? The last chapter of their monograph links their solution to this problem with the one proposed by Ernst Cassirer, who, for his part, made the second edition of his major epistemological study into a reflection on the philosophical significance of the general theory of relativity.[27] As a result of his discussions with Weltsch, in short, Brod found himself in an auspicious position to encounter Einstein.

The discussions between Brod and Weltsch that resulted in *Intuition and Concept* did not take place simply as a consequence of their friendship. Both of them were accustomed to engaging in philosophically inflected conversations at the Café Louvre; but the so-called Louvre circle was under the direction of Franz von Brentano's students and disciples, for whom, as Brod notes, a number of topics—especially Kant and relativity—were "taboo."[28] An offshoot of the Louvre circle, however, found a place of refuge in the house of Berta Fanta, the wife of a prominent pharmacist, whose Zum Einhorn occupied a central position in the old city. Brod dubbed these gatherings "Kant evenings," since they were largely devoted to discussing the major epistemological works of Kant and his successors. In addition to Brod and Weltsch, the inner circle of the Fanta circle included Berta's son-in-law, Hugo Bergmann, who played a leading role in the Zionist youth organization Bar Kochba and held a position as a librarian at the university; and Baron Christian von Ehrenfels, the founder of Gestalt psychology, who also published, among many other books, a version of post-Kantian, dualistic metaphysics under the title *Cosmogony* (1916). Kafka—who as a boy argued with Bergmann about the existence of God—was a more sporadic participant in these evenings. As he notes at the end of the letter to Brod that revolves around the dedication of the Tycho Brahe novel, he would go the meetings at the Fanta residence "without pleasure."[29] Some of the other participants in the "Kant evenings" delivered impromptu lectures about recent scientific advances: the mathematician Gerhard Kowalewski, for example, discussed Cantor's transfinite mathematics; the astronomer Erwin Finlay-Freundlich, who later helped confirm the general theory of relativity, spoke about quantum theory; the assistant whom Einstein brought with him from Zurich, Ludwig Hopf, delivered a two-part lecture on the new sciences of psychoanalysis and relativity; the physicist Philipp Frank, who replaced Einstein at the German University, discussed the relation between causality and probability. And as for Einstein himself, he entered into the Fanta circle at a point where the discussion had just moved away from Hegel's *Phenomenology of Spirit* and returned to Kant. There is no record of a lecture he delivered; but during at least one of the evenings, he entertained the participants with a violin sonata, with Brod accompanying him on the piano.[30]

Walther Nernst was certainly not the only reader of *Tycho Brahe's Path to God* who noticed a striking resemblance between its Kepler and the Einstein he or she knew. As Philipp Frank notes, "It was often asserted in Prague that in his portrayal of Kepler, Brod was greatly influenced by the impression Einstein made on him."[31] Soon after the novel was published, Hedwig Born, the wife of the physicist Max Born, wrote to Einstein in Berlin and inquired whether he had had a chance to read it. His reply is eloquent both in what it says and in what it leaves unstated. "I've read the book with great interest," he writes. "It is without a doubt interestingly written by a man who knows the cliffs of the human soul." Applied to the author of the letter, this can only mean that Brod captured something of his own soul, surrounded as it is by dangerous cliffs. Those who get too close to these cliffs fall off—or get shipwrecked. Although Einstein does not quite concede that he sees himself in Kepler, he reluctantly admits that he is acquainted with the author: "I do believe that I met the man in Prague. He seemed to belong to a philosophically and Zionistically infested circle there, loosely grouped around the university philosophers, a small host of world-distant [*weltfernen*] men, reminiscent of the medieval ages, with whom you, too, have become acquainted by reading this book."[32]

Einstein's analysis of *Tycho Brahe's Path to God* is short but incisive. The novel is not really about Tycho's time, in his view; rather, it is about the time of its author, who projects the characteristics of his own circle onto those of Tycho's. And the decisive characteristic of Brod's circle of friends consists in its detachment from the world. It is therefore no surprise that the novel is historical; it cannot fail to be historical because the milieu from which it originates is itself a matter of history. The distance between 1916 and 1600 is a function of the distance that separates the author and his circle from the world they have left behind. In saying all of this to Hedwig Born, Einstein establishes his own distance from the "world distance" he discovered in old Prague. In other words, Einstein presents himself as someone who remains in contact with the world, and the proof of this proximity lies in his distance from philosophy, on the one hand, and from Zionism, on the other. On the hither side of metaphysics is, of course, physics. It is less clear, however, what lies on the hither side of Zionism— perhaps realpolitik, which Einstein, already a committed pacifist, generally repudiates. At any rate, in 1916, Einstein places himself squarely at odds with the "world distance" that characterizes Brod's circle, which readers of his novel can get to know by getting to know Tycho Brahe's circle. Whether it is intentional or not, Einstein thus associates himself willy-nilly with the figure of Kepler: just as Kepler retains his distance from Tycho's circle, so does he keep his distance from Brod's—so much so that he barely retains any memory of the author of the novel, despite the fact that he took part in the "Kant evenings" only a few years before.

Gerhard Kowalewski includes the following remark in his memoirs of the period: "An altogether regular and very interested participant in these meetings [of the Fanta circle] was the writer Max Brod. During one of these evenings I told him about Dreyer's biography of the astronomer Tycho Brahe, which offered him the factual basis for his famous novel *Tycho Brahe's Path to God*."[33] If Kowalewski can be trusted—and there seems no reason to dispute his account—the origin of the novel lies in one of the "Kant evenings" during which the life of Tycho Brahe came under discussion. A scientist of Kepler's stature may have been in attendance; but even if he were not, his presence was still palpable. And yet, despite all of this, in his later reflections Brod tends to downplay the importance of Einstein in the genesis of his novel. Soon after the Second World War, Philipp

Frank published a biography of the physicist whose position he inherited at the German University in Prague. One section of Frank's biography consists of a dozen or so passages from *Tycho Brahe's Path to God* and is appropriately entitled "Einstein's Personality Portrayed in a Novel."[34] Under certain circumstances, Brod might have been flattered by this kind of reception, for it is a tribute to his great powers of perception. But Brod was not flattered in the least; on the contrary, he considered himself misunderstood, if not altogether wronged. In the autobiography he published in 1960 under the Tychonic title of *Streitbares Leben* (*Combative Life*), he not only rejects Frank's biography but also contrasts its author with its subject. Whereas Frank, in Brod's view, showed himself to be a strict Einsteinian, Einstein did not. It would be difficult to formulate an odder remark. To say that Karl Marx was no Marxist, as Marx apparently did, makes a certain degree of sense, insofar as there are putative Marxists who are so "doctrinaire" that they refuse to look beyond than the pages of *Capital.* By contrast, to say of a physicist around 1912 that he is more Einsteinian than Einstein means almost the opposite: such a physicist would be able to see beyond the special theory of relativity and grasp the manner in which its principle could be generalized to all cases of motion. Obviously, Brod wishes to convey something very different:

> [Einstein] seemed to take a complete delight in exploring all the possibilities of the scientific treatment of a subject, and he did so with tireless daring: he would never tie himself down; with virtuosity and humor, he never avoided any complexity along his path, and he thereby retained a secure and creative grip. In my Tycho-Brahe novel I modeled the figure of Kepler on this quality of scientific courage, which consists in always beginning anew; in Tycho Brahe himself, by contrast, I wanted to sketch an obstinate scholar who props himself up on the basis of his system.[35]

As Brod proceeds to explain—on the basis of conjecture, as he admits—he must have told Frank something about Einstein's minor role in the genesis of the novel. Unfortunately, in his view, Frank misunderstood this remark and drew the erroneous conclusion that he had discerned an "egocentric" trait in Einstein's personality. Brod's *Combative Life,* then, seeks to set the record straight. In doing so, however, Brod mischaracterizes Frank's rationale for including passages of his novel in his biography of Einstein. The point is not that Brod spoke to him about the origin of the novel; indeed, Frank declines to take a position on whether Brod consciously or unconsciously thought of Einstein as he was portraying Kepler. The resemblance, in Frank's view, is striking in either case. And in *Combative Life* Brod similarly mischaracterizes Frank's assessment of Einstein's personality. The point of Frank's reflections on this matter is not that there were limits to Einstein's openness or generosity; rather, he simply wants to supplement this impression by adding a further dimension: "[Einstein] was averse to entering into very intimate personal relations with other people, a trait that has always left [him] a lonely person among his students, his colleagues, his friends, and his family."[36] Brod obviously reads this remark as an indictment of Einstein for which his novel might be held responsible. Although he admits that it is impossible to remove an impression once it has been entered in popular consciousness, he nevertheless commits a few passages of *Combative Life* to this quixotic purpose: "I have never noticed such an egocentric trait in Einstein; on the contrary, I have always found him gracious, benevolent, and astoundingly open."[37] It is not difficult to identify a reason for Brod's defense of Einstein against the accusation that he resembles the figure of Kepler. In his letter to Hedwig Born from 1916, Einstein distances himself from Zionism. Three years later—and partly at the behest of Hugo Bergmann—Einstein publicly associates himself with the project of establishing a Jewish homeland in Palestine.[38] From 1919 onward, he championed the Zionist cause. And in 1947, when Frank's biography first appeared, this cause had, of course, reached a critical juncture. The otherwise innocent claim that Einstein resembles the figure of Kepler could be interpreted to mean that he is not only inaccessible to his colleagues, friends, and family but is also, at bottom, detached from the Jews in Palestine. Far from involving himself in this highly emotional issue—so the suggestion would go—the great scientist cares only about the laws of motion in the end. Tycho finds Kepler's inaccessibility unnerving; Brod simply denies that Einstein is detached.

What Brod wrote about Einstein in his autobiography was probably a repetition of what he wrote to him in private. In 1948 Brod sent him a copy of his recently published sequel to the Tycho Brahe novel, *Galilei in Gefangenschaft* (*Galilei in Prison*). It is highly likely that Brod included some critical remarks about Frank's biography, to which Einstein replies by dismissing the whole affair, apparently without informing his correspondent of the fact that he had already written a favorable preface to the work in question. "There have already been published by the bucketsful such brazen lies about me," Einstein writes to Brod, "that I would long since have gone to my grave if I had allowed myself to pay attention to them."[39] By a strange coincidence, however, Einstein's posthumously published preface to Frank's biography is largely concerned with Galileo's imprisonment. Public interest in Galileo's work, according to Einstein, is entirely comprehensible, for this work undermines the church-sanctioned conception of the position that human beings occupy in the architecture of the cosmos; by contrast, the interest taken by the general public in his own work is perplexing, for the theory of relativity is little more than a "purification of basic physical concepts."[40] In his response to *Galilei in Prison,* Einstein praises Brod's insights into the "driving force of human beings, which are embodied in what we call 'history,'" but he then turns his attention to a corresponding perplexity: he cannot understand why a scientist of Galileo's stature would willingly go to Rome and get involved in a futile struggle to win over priests and politicians. He, for his part, would never have done anything similar for the theory of relativity: "I would think: truth is incomparably stronger than I am, and it would seem ridiculous and quixotic to want to defend truth with sword and shield."[41] Not without a trace of irony perhaps, Einstein thus reiterates the comparison in dispute: just as the figure of Kepler has no interest in the machinations of the imperial court in the years preceding the Thirty Years' War, so does he remain unaffected by the political frenzies that will soon solidify themselves into the cold war.

A Name Game

From Brod's retrospective perspective, in sum, Einstein played a negligible role in the creation of his Kepler. And Brod passes over in silence the question of whether Kafka played any role in the novel at all—beyond its dedication. Whereas Brod is reluctant to associate Einstein with the figure of Kepler, presumably because this association suggests that the most famous Jew in the world is ultimately unconcerned with the cause of Zionism, he is reluctant to bring Kafka in conjunction with this figure for a congruent reason: it would imply that ultimately their friendship was traversed by a certain distance. Soon after Brod's biography of Kafka appeared in 1937, Walter Benjamin wrote a devastating review that takes its point of departure from precisely this question. Brod claims in his biography that Kafka "found himself on a path to holiness," but, as Benjamin points out, the utter lack of distance he shows with respect to Kafka discredits this claim, since everyone who is holy—or even only on the path to holiness—

is fundamentally unapproachable.[42] Kafka may not have been unapproachable in principle, but at the time in which Brod completed *Tycho Brahe's Path to God,* he no longer felt so close to its author. "Of course Max and I meet—every day, in fact," Kafka writes to his fiancée, Felice Bauer, as he describes his reaction to the news that Brod will dedicate his new novel to him:

> On thinking it over, however, I don't believe we are as close as we used to be, at least at times. (At no time were we as close as when we were traveling together. . . .) It is my fault that we (to be on the safe side, I repeat: Max and I) are no longer as close; he in his innocence is not acutely aware of it, has even dedicated to me his latest novel, *Tycho Brahe's Path to God,* one of the most intimate of his books, a story of positively painful self-torment. But even this fault of mine is not really a fault, at least only to a minor degree. Max does not understand me, and where he does, he is wrong.[43]

Kafka is characteristically precise in his formulations: it is not as though Brod is unaware of the distance that now separates them; his awareness of this distance is only less acute—or more repressed—than Kafka's. Hence the importance of the dedication of the Tycho Brahe novel: it is a sign of his innocence, which is to say, his lower degree of awareness. The greater the awareness, the higher the degree of guilt; but then again, the greater the awareness of distance, the lower the culpability, for the friend in question, namely, Brod, does not really understand Kafka, which means that he (Brod) *cannot* know how far away his friend may be, and the other friend (Kafka) cannot be held responsible for his friend's lack of understanding. So, in conclusion, whenever Brod understands Kafka—*really* understands him and sees through his own misconceptions—"he is wrong." Applied to the novel in question, this means that Brod's failure to note the resemblance between Kafka and Kepler confirms the suspicion that, in his eyes, his friend is indeed Kepler-like.

Of course, anything can be proved in such a manner. And this game of discovering who lurks behind the characters in the novel would be of little interest if it were not for the fact that Brod invites his readers to participate in it—while at the same time rigging the game so that only a single outcome emerges. The outcome is as follows: behind the figure of Kepler lies the expressionist poet Franz Werfel (1890–1945), and behind the figure of Tycho there is Brod himself. The first chapter of Brod's *Combative Life* revolves around his troubled relationship with Werfel, as if this relationship—and not his familial ones—marked the onset of the combat into which he was fatefully drawn. Six years Brod's junior, Werfel created a literary-cultural sensation with the publication of the poems that were collected into *Der Weltfreund* (*The Friend of the World*, 1911). According to Brod—who clung to this conviction with great tenacity but without much philological support[44]—Werfel drew the inspiration for his early poetry from the "more personal" mode of poetic communication with which the older poet had experimented in *Tagebuch in Versen* (*Diary in Verse*, 1910): "The rare case thus occurred in which the teacher falls at the feet of his student. A few years later I took up this remarkable relationship as the basic impetus for my novel, *Tycho Brahe's Path to God*."[45] In short, Brahe is to Brod as Kepler is to Werfel. And an Ursus crystallizes this analogy: the contemporaneous counterpart of the slanderous astronomer is named Karl Kraus. The particular incident that superimposes one literary era onto another can be formulated as follows: Werfel managed to get some of his early poems into Kraus's *Die Fackel* (*The Torch*). Considered in itself, this youthful achievement could not be considered an act of betrayal, but it certainly reminded the older writer—who was still quite young—that, despite all his efforts, he had not been similarly recognized. The whiff of betrayal comes in the form of a witticism that the mischievous Kraus places alongside one of the poems of Werfel that he publishes in *Die Fackel:* "When you smear intellect on bread [*Brod*], you get lard."[46]

One thing is therefore certain about the genesis of *Tycho Brahe's Path to God:* the figure of the Ursus corresponds to Kraus. If all the terms of the analogy can be maintained, then one can deduce that Kraus must have published Werfel's poem in the same underhanded manner that Ursus published a letter from Kepler—which is highly implausible, to say the least. The *only* thing that is certain about the genesis of the novel, therefore, is that Kraus is similar to Ursus. The reviewers of the novel who were conversant with the literary controversies of the period—Paul Adler and Otto Pick, in particular—made this conclusion a matter of public knowledge: according to Adler, Brod wrote the novel in order to express his loathing for Kraus; according to Pick, this loathing found a medium for the creative transformation of the historical material.[47] Yet neither Adler nor Pick mentions Werfel. And Brod, for his part, does not *simply* say in his autobiographical reflections that his relationship to Werfel is reproduced in Tycho's encounter with Kepler. Instead, he affirms something far stranger and more interesting: the novel both captures and prefigures his relationship with Werfel, who—at least as a young man—enjoyed a noncombative life. Not only did Werfel gain early success without much exertion; because his family was wealthy and wished to support him, he did not even need to struggle for his "daily bread." Not so Brod, who includes the following remark in his biography of Kafka: "The years I spent as an official in the post office, and during which I wrote, among other things, in the afternoon and evening, my *Tycho Brahe,* remain so dimly in my memory that I can hardly see a single detail any more. It has all been forcibly crammed into the maw of the subconscious."[48] Nowhere in *Combative Life* does Brod indicate that he had in fact been able to recapture what had been forced into his subconscious; but in conjunction with his assertion that the novel uncannily contains all of his struggles with Werfel—both those before and those after its publication—he provides a schematization of its principal figures:

In Kepler I wanted to represent the young genius favored by luck, who is driven by his own capacities and is little influenced by outer circumstances, including the obligations of friendship, whereas Tycho represents the older man, who is constantly besieged by the blows of fate, because he let himself get involved with fate, because he does not disdain it and does not know how to vault beyond his perniciousness unconsciously and without a clue as to what he is doing. Out of pure conscientiousness he becomes the stepchild of life, whereas Kepler knows no conscience other than the needs of his work. I thereby strongly diverged from historical reality out of artistic reasons of structure—not in Tycho himself, whom I rather exactly created on the bases of the reports I read; very much so, however, in his counterpart Kepler, who I constructed simply as a counterpart to Tycho, completely according to the laws, immanent to poetry, of opposition. In historical reality Kepler was much more like Tycho as I represented him; both suffered from closely related scholarly fates, that of being misunderstood—nevertheless with characteristic deviations, which, one day, came to me as an idea for the entire novel and made the basis of this work clear to me suddenly, as it were, in a single lightning bolt as an encounter with myself and my own fate.[49]

There are reasons to doubt certain aspects of Brod's reconstruction—not the contention that *Tycho Brahe's Path to God* captures its author's conflict-laden life nor the claim that idea of the novel appeared to him as an unrepeatable event of self-illumination. No, the doubts are generated by the analogy on which the self-analysis is based: Brahe is to Kepler as Brod is to Werfel. At the very moment in which the serialized version of the novel was completed in the summer of 1915, Brod and Werfel fell into a bitter dispute over the relative merits of Judaism and Christianity. A few years earlier, Brod had come to the conclusion that he, as a Jew, should reassert his Judaism and that a certain version of humanistic Zionism was the proper form of this reassertion. By contrast, Werfel, who was born Jewish and never had himself baptized, favored the spirit of Catholicism and recommended the total dispersion of the Jews.[50] Regardless of the details of the dispute—which give shape to all of Brod's later religiophilosophical reflections, including his discussions of Kafka's religiosity—one thing is immediately apparent: at a certain point, the governing analogy goes awry. For, if Brahe is to Kepler as Brod is to Werfel, then Werfel's *doctrine* must be considered superior to Brod's, inasmuch as Kepler's theory of the heavens is superior to Tycho's. The turbulent *life* of the Danish astronomer may be vindicated; indeed, it may even be redeemed. And something similar may be said of Brod with respect to Werfel. But vindication and redemption are accomplished, at least in part, only in light of the fact that the lives in question lend support to alien doctrines: in the case of Kepler, a modified version of the Copernican world system; in the case of Werfel—well, there's the rub.

The doubts about Brod's retrospective interpretation of the novel are only intensified when his last remarks on the subject are analyzed in detail. There is no question these remarks cry out for such an analysis, moreover, since they are about the basic elements of literary meaning, namely, letters. Brod wants to demonstrate that the analogy "Brahe is to Kepler as Brod is to Werfel" emerged from the depths of his unconscious life, about which he is generally silent. This silence is broken when he suddenly sees himself in the names of the characters he once tried to bring to life:

> Much later it occurred to me that there was something in the *names* of my two heroes that predisposed me to make them into symbols of the conflicts between myself and Werfel, which went on for so long and were so painful. One may consider it a game [*Spielerei*], indeed a game that has much in common with a similar reflection that Kafka makes about "The Judgment." In fact, however, it is articulated differently, and as I will soon show, it is also independent from Kafka, for I became acquainted with Kafka's diary notations much later, after his death. Now out with this name game, although (as a genuine game) there is also something ridiculous about it: the historical names are like, or are

reminiscent of, the life-relationships that incited me—*Brahe* has the same initial sound as *Brod,* and in *Tycho* one can find in the unusual letter *Y* an analogy to the *X* that adorns my name. Kepler was called "Johannes," thus "Hans," which is reminiscent of Franz (Werfel), and the two *E*'s, as well as the placing of the consonants are very similar in both the surnames *Kepler* and *Werfel.* . . . In Kafka's diary, the analogy between the name *Bendemann,* to which he gave the protagonist, and Kafka is shown; yet this is not so strange as in my case, for Kafka had, of course, freely constructed the name *Bendemann,* whereas I had to retain the names provided to me by history.[51]

If Brod wants to align himself with Brahe by distinguishing himself from that type of inspired artist who is favored by luck, he has gone about this task in a wildly inappropriate way, for, at least in the case of *Tycho Brahe's Path to God*—which may be a singular occurrence in Brod's long literary career—the two qualities with which he defines the *other* type of artist apply to him: *unbewußt* and *ahnunglos,* "unconscious" and "without a clue." And even as Brod emphasizes the degree to which he struggled with Werfel, his description of this struggle is expressed in terms of a struggle with *another* writer, who, as it happens, wrote an early set of stories entitled "Description of a Struggle," which Brod helped get into print in part and posthumously published as a fragmentary whole. And because this writer shares his first name with Werfel, Brod is forced to place the latter's last name in parentheses; otherwise readers may think that he is writing about the wrong (Jo)hannes-Franz. Added to this, of course, is the fact that a similar procedure produces a different result. Just as the name "Brahe" corresponds to "Brod," with the addition of a vowel, so does "Kepler" correspond to "Kafka," with the addition of a consonant. And it cannot be denied that the letter with which both "Kepler" and "Kafka" begin plays a prominent role in the novel that the eventual survivor of the friendship would publish without its author's permission. It was by no means foreordained that Brod would be the survivor, and the Tycho Brahe novel can be read as a semirepressed reflection on what would happen to his own literary legacy if Kafka outlived him and, having overcome his indolence, published the literary equivalent of Kepler's *Astronomia nova.* Brod, at any rate, completed his account of Johannes Kepler at the very same time Kafka was abandoning his account of Josef K. And what Kafka says about Brod's novel is equally applicable to his own J.-K. novel: "a story of positively painful self-torment."

Tychonic Revisions

Whereas "somebody must have been telling lies about Josef K."—to cite the famous opening sentence of *The Trial*—somebody is definitely telling lies about Johannes Kepler. Readers of Brod's novel even know his name: Franz Tengnagel, whom Kepler inadvertently wronged by entering into Tycho's circle. Readers also know that Johannes Kepler will not fall victim to the religious strife that issues into the Thirty Years' War but will instead write the *Astronomia nova*, which, as its title indicates, marks the beginning of a new and fully modern science of astronomy. Remove all extratextual knowledge, however, and the novel becomes considerably more problematic. Of course, this knowledge cannot be removed entirely; but it is possible to do something similar: make a historical novel "feel" unhistorical, especially in the case of Kepler, whose life, as is fairly well known and Brod admits, was almost as combative as Tycho's. It was not an uncommon occurrence among the reviewers of Brod's novel to note, with a greater or lesser degree of disapproval, certain unhistorical aspects of the novel.[52] But none of his reviewers, to my knowledge, noticed that in the novel itself, Tycho makes a similar comment. It occurs when Tycho—alone and without any arms, in an act of undiplomatic surrender—suddenly decides to reconcile with Tengnagel, whose fortress had been set ablaze by an army under the loyally rebellious leadership of his sons. This reconciliation can take place only under the condition that Kepler be dismissed. As he informs Tengnagel of his decision to get rid of his most promising assistant, Tycho declares, in effect, that this assistant is extrahistorical:

> Kepler is purer than either of us. His immaculate purity is the very thing that causes offence to us sinners, and so we are very glad to make him the scapegoat for our faults. But now I really think that we have overestimated the excellent Kepler. We have exaggerated him beyond all conceivable limits. Kepler is really no longer a man at all, but a phantom. As I understand things now, Kepler does not exist *outside* of us; no, indeed, each of us has his Kepler within him, and it is in facing him, in facing his own Kepler, that he has to endure his sharpest spiritual tests. (228–29)

"Kepler does not exist": this is a remarkable statement to come across in a novel about the relationship between Tycho and Kepler. The level of literary self-reflection is such that a character in a historical novel declares that another character in the same novel is equivalent to a character in another kind of novel altogether, as if the novel were itself a Tychonic compromise between two kinds of novel: one that revolves around historical facts, another that goes its own way. By diverging from the historical record—especially in its portrayal of Kepler, about whom readers could be expected to know a fair amount—the novel engages in a form of novelistic self-reflection and, at the same time, establishes its distance from a prevailing paradigm of the era. Imagine what would have happened if Brod had focused his attention on the historical Kepler, who was abused as a child and whose mother was charged with the crime of witchcraft when he was an adult. Obviously a very different novel would have emerged—a novel, moreover, that would stand in closer accord with the basic paradigms of German expressionism. Under these contrafactual conditions, the son would be at the center of the literary cosmos; the son's consciousness would illuminate the world, to the degree that it can be illuminated; and the injustice done to the son would come to light, perhaps in the form of a shock—that his mother was a witch, for example. If the expressionist replacement of the perspective of the anxious bourgeois "paterfamilias" with that of the desperate-hopeful son can be called a Copernican revolution in the arts, then Brod's novel represents a Tychonic revision of this aesthetic revolution.[53]

The basic structure of *Tycho Brahe's Path to God* is thus doubly Tychonic: on the one hand, the novel represents a combination of a historical novel and a purely fictional one; on the other hand, it consists in a recentering of the expressionist novel onto the figure of the father, who, as he admits, struggles with a "phantom" son. When Tycho recognizes the phantom-character of this son, however, he is not relieved of his troubles; instead they immediately intensify, for not only must Tycho convince the satellites of his struggle—Tengnagel, for instance—to see that the struggle is really about nothing but he must also struggle with *himself* to remember what he now recognizes. Hence the scene that quickly follows upon the scene of reconciliation: Tycho wants Kepler to write letters to him after he departs from his castle, but Kepler, who promises nothing, reminds him of his "terrible indolence [*Trägheit*]" (233). Upon hearing Kepler describe himself in such self-deprecating terms, which imply that he is indeed phantomlike, "Tycho fell back a step. . . . It was a decisive moment. All at once it was clear to him that he was well on the way to that 'exaggeration' and 'overestimation' of Kepler with which he had reproached his son-in-law an hour previously, down in the fortress" (233–34). By recognizing that his opponent is merely a "phantom," Tycho turns his "combative life" into a struggle with himself over the knowledge that he is, at bottom, struggling *only* with himself, for the supposed antagonist is his own creation.

Several years after the appearance of Brod's novel, Kafka invents a character about whom something similar could be said: "K." of *The Castle*. This is not meant to suggest that Brod's story of the castle at Benatky is the "key" to *The Castle*—as if there were one. Nevertheless, certain aspects of K.'s character can be plotted in relation to the opposing poles of Brod's narrative. K. leaves his home to enter into an alien land that is dominated by an obscure and apparently arbitrary power. In this way, he resembles Kepler, who fails to find his bearings when he first enters into Tycho's castle. From the beginning of K.'s entrance into a foreign land, moreover, he launches himself into a series of struggles with a form of power whose very existence is questionable. In this way, he resembles Tycho, who tries to convince himself, with limited success, that his opponent is only a "phantom." Upon entering into the territory of the castle, K. claims to be a land surveyor. Both Tycho and Kepler are brought to Bohemia in order to survey the heavens—which, however, they are unable to do: "It must be difficult to study the stars here" (50). To add one further element to this already overloaded schema, the character who first accompanies Kepler on his way to Tycho's castle and who in the course of the novel outdoes the Danish astronomer in the complexity of his machinations—namely, the "court physician" Thaddäus Hagecius—is said to have been a land surveyor who triangulated the area around Prague for a map that has since been lost.[54]

A Comparison and Its Disavowal

In his biography of Kafka, Brod presents the K. of *The Castle* as a seamless unity of universality and particularity. The story of the would-be land surveyor, in Brod's view, captures the plight of humanity in general as well as the fate of Jewish existence in particular—and this despite the fact that, as Brod notes, "The word *Jew* does not appear."[55] Brod, for his part, was not so reticent to include this word in his publications. On the contrary, the novels immediately preceding *Tycho Brahe's Path to God* display this word in their very titles: *Jüdinnen* (*Jewish Women*, 1911) and *Arnold Beer: Das Schicksal eines Juden* (*Arnold Beer: The Fate of a Jew*, 1912). And in a curious postscript to *Arnold Beer*—which is printed in a different script, as if it were intended for a different readership—Brod responds to the critics of *Jewish Women* by promising more of the same. These critics have identified three failings in his Jewish-oriented fictions: he creates no "sympathetic" characters; he does not include enough dramatic incidents; and above all, he has "no decisive tendency, no ethos; despite their titles, [the novels] express no actual opinion about the essence and future of Judaism."[56] In response to these accusations, Brod does not so much plead innocent as beg for more time. He admits that he has created only certain "types" of Jews, who are representative of corresponding "groups." But at no point has he tried not to identify "the" Jew—not even in *Arnold Beer*, which, as he insists, concerns "the fate of *a* Jew." Vindication of his method will therefore come in the future, as he creates "a cycle of further novels" that ascends to a point where a "higher type" of Jew either appears or is deemed "forever unthinkable."[57] Brod, in short, promises to produce a *Comédie judaïque* in which the multiplicity of Jewish life is captured in its "typical" forms.

Given Brod's postscript to *Arnold Beer*, one would assume that his next novel would be about further "types" of Jews. But it is actually about Tycho Brahe's path to God. Brod thus breaks his promise—unless, of course, the new novel responds to the question posed by the postscript: Is there, after all, a "higher type" of Jew? If the novel does indeed respond to this question, it can do so only indirectly, for—this scarcely needs comment—Tycho Brahe is not Jewish. He can appear to be *like* a Jew, however, in which case the question of the "higher type" enters into the problem of comparison. And this is precisely what happens in the course of the novel. At a critical point in the novel, when the castle is threatened with destruction, Tycho prepares to deliver a lecture about his life that no one wants to hear: "Originally I had intended to choose as a title: 'Ahasuerus, or the Life of the Wandering Jew,' or 'Failure and disquiet.' But I have abandoned that, just as I intend to abandon every kind of poetic comparison [*dichterischen Vergleichen*], every kind of elegant and precious language" (213). Tycho, in other words, sees that his life is like that of the Wandering Jew, and yet, on reflection, sees that it is not—or refuses to view it this way. By comparing his life with that of someone else, he could be guilty of falsely redeeming it. And for this self-reflective and therefore "higher" reason, he may be like the "higher type" of Jew, who appears in the form of a non-Jew in the course of seeing himself as a Jew.

This situation is Tychonic in the extreme. It could be called a "compromise formation," to use a term of Freud that applies to the system of planetary motion that Tycho proposed: Brod wants to extend his cycle of Jewish novels; but having seen his "combative life" mirrored in Tycho's, he constructs a novel in which he abandons the search for Jewish "types" for the sake of creating a comparison with the Wandering Jew or the "eternal Jew" (*der ewige Jude*)—and immediately disavows this comparison. The question, then, is this: How did Brod find himself in this complicated situation? Whatever the answer to this question, it is certain that the stakes of the comparison are very high indeed. The epigraph to the novel, drawn from the thirty-second chapter of Genesis, suggests that the novel is concerned with the rebirth of Judaism out of the spirit of struggle: "*And there wrestled a man with him until the breaking of the day. . . . And he said, Let me go, for the day breaketh. And he said,* I will not let thee go, except thou bless me" (1). Jacob wrestled for an entire night with "a man"—if this is the right word—and thereafter was renamed "Israel." Such is the struggle between Tycho and Kepler, by way of comparison. And the twelve chapters of the novel record one long night of struggle, which—when it is finally over—may yield a new Israel.

Four Landmarks on the Path to a Comparison

The path by which Brod comes to write a short series of Jewish-oriented novels in contemporary settings, abandons his plans for an expansion of this series, and turns instead to the life of a Danish nobleman who compares himself to the Wandering Jew cannot be reconstructed in detail—for at least two reasons: it would occupy far more space than is available in this introduction; and certain potentially important documents, especially Brod's diaries of the period, remain in private hands.[58] Only a few landmarks on this path toward this comparison can be marked.

Brod did not begin his career as a writer with any particular interest in Jewish types or topics. If his earliest work refers to a Holy Writ, it is certainly not the Hebrew Bible but, rather, Arthur Schopenhauer's *World as Will and Representation.* And this is the *first* of the landmarks on the way to the comparison between Tycho and the Wandering Jew. Far from seeing himself as a Jewish Balzac, Brod wanted to experiment with the aesthetic consequences of Schopenhauerian doctrine, which denies that there can be any breaks in the nexus of causality. By the time Brod was eighteen, he was a "fanatical" Schopenhauerian, having spent several years absorbing the master's works.[59] The result of Brod's immersion in Schopenhauer was a philosophicoaesthetic doctrine of his own invention, which he dubbed "indifferentism." Nothing in the world "moves" the indifferentist, and for this reason, nothing can be considered intrinsically admirable. Because nothing is admirable, however, the indifferentist is ironically "free" to admire anything in the world, including and especially "the beauty of ugly images," to cite the title of a collection of essays Brod published in 1913, which includes, among other items, a remarkable reflection on the already outmoded phenomenon of the panorama.[60] Brod's first collection of stories describes itself in terms of the doctrine it expresses: *Tod den Toten! Novellen des Indifferenten* (*Death to the Dead! Stories of the Indifferent*, 1906). "The dead" are none other than the artists, who have inherited the exalted—and therefore mendacious—position of spiritual authority that was once occupied by priests and other exponents of religious doctrine. Once the "the dead" are dead, a kind of shimmer of life emanates from everything, regardless of its origin. Life is not exactly justified, to be sure, much less redeemed; but it is made buoyant, even uplifting, despite its utter pointlessness.

Brod's first large-scale work of fiction, *Schloß Nornepygge* (*Castle Nornepygge,* 1908), carries a similarly formed subtitle: *Der Roman des Indifferenten* (*Novel of the Indifferent*). For Walder Nornepygge, the archindifferentist, there is "no path to God" for the tautological reason that such a path would have to be different from others. Whereas, according to Schopenhauerian pessimism, the best thing in life is not to be alive at all, according to Brod's revision of this dour doctrine, the best life lies in avoiding all paths and movements, *alle Wege und Bewegungen.* Translated into an imperative, this means: go back to bed. Such is indeed the nonpath adopted by Brod's most amusing proponent of his doctrine, a character named "Little Lo," who first appears in a story from *Death to the Dead* entitled "Indifferentism." Little Lo is lame and for this reason is excused from the demand that he get up and get going. Walder Nornepygge, by contrast, curses himself for having the good luck of being healthy. Because of his physical strength, he cannot simply remain bedridden. But the very act of getting out of bed and choosing a path out of the bedroom is impossible to sustain for long. As Walder recognizes—and these are his last words—"movement is a lie, a misunderstanding."[61]

Robert Weltsch places the following claim at the center of his memorial lecture: "A mirror of Brod's own inner struggle in his early period during the years 1909–1915 is the novel *Tycho Brahe's Path to God.*"[62] The year 1909 was the one in which Brod began to repudiate the doctrine of indifferentism that *Castle Nornepygge* elaborates in meticulous detail. Defeating indifferentism is no easy task, however. The battle against an indifferentist—to use an image drawn from Kafka—is more like combat against a wily insect than against a noble foe.[63] Indeed, indifferentists are incapable of engaging in real struggles, for they are, by definition, indifferent to their outcome. A "frontal assault" on indifferentism is therefore out of the question. And Brod does not go about the struggle in this manner. On the contrary, the terms of combat came to Brod as something of a surprise. After finishing *Castle Nornepygge,* he returned to a love story he had once published and expanded it into a novel entitled *Ein tschechisches Dienstmädchen* (*A Czech Servant Girl,* 1909). This short novel—and the short-lived controversy it engendered—represents the *second* landmark on the path that led Brod to the comparison between Tycho and the Wandering Jew. The plot of *A Czech Servant Girl* revolves around the attempt to combat indifferentism; in this case, the driving force behind this battle is a Jewish father who wants his son to take an interest in something, no matter what. Having been forced by his father to leave his circle of friends in Vienna and travel to Prague, the son falls in love with a lower-class Czech woman, with whom he has an affair—and whose brutal husband eventually kills her. To put this in shorthand: love cures indifference while simultaneously contributing to the solution of the problem posed by differences among the nations. In a review of the novel in the Zionist weekly *Selbstwehr,* its editor, Leo Hermann, made a cutting comment that Brod recalled almost fifty years after it first stung him: "The young author seems to believe that national questions can be decided in bed."[64]

Hermann's comment is of a piece with a major motif in Brod's early literary career. From the lame Lo to the dying Tycho, the bed serves as a scene of action—or the absence thereof. One of Kraus's admirers, Leopold Liegler, published a "technical critique" of Brod in which he accuses the author of, among other errors, composing his love poems in bed.[65] In response to Liegler, Brod bitterly attacked Kraus in the preface to the collection of stories he edited under the nonpolemical title of *Arkadia* (1913)—a collection, incidentally, that contains Kafka's story "The Judgment." And in response to Hermann's bed-centered comment, Brod threw himself into the "national question," with particular attention to the nation to which he himself belonged. Out of his outrage came *Jewish Women* and its sequel, *Arnold Beer.* If the former can be faulted for providing little more than a catalog of Jewish "types"—which is precisely what Kafka accuses his friend of doing[66]—the same cannot be said of the latter. To be sure, *Arnold Beer* provides no "solution" to the "Jewish question," but it creates a memorable scene in which the question of Jewish difference assumes an acute form. Leaving Prague to visit his dying grandmother in the Bohemian provinces, Beer finds the remnant of the once magnificent and still vital nation from which he descends. Lying in bed, the tiny grand-mother suddenly emerges as a giant.[67] Acknowledging *Arnold Beer* as one of the literary sources for "The Judgment," Kafka reverses this scenario: the father of his protagonist, Georg Bendemann, lies in bed and, like Beer's grandmother, suddenly becomes gigantic; but whereas the father con-demns the son to death, the grandmother unintentionally gives the grand-son an insight into a path of life that is unquestionably different, even if it is—and this is its appeal—at the same time also his own.[68] Beer thus over-comes his indifferentism without having been forced to take up a new position—under the pressure of a domineering father, for instance. Beer *can* defeat indifferentism precisely because he has no intention of doing so. The sight of his grandmother in bed comes to him by accident and, for this reason, determines his "fate."

The distance between the Bohemian provinces, where the grandmother lives out her poverty-stricken yet experience-laden life, and Prague, where the grandson conducts his futile business adventures, marks the fault line of European Judaism. From the father in Vienna, through the son in Prague (*A Czech Servant Girl*), to mothers and daughters at fashionable spas (*Jew-ish Women*), on to the grandmother in the provinces (*Arnold Beer*)—this is the spatiofamilial trajectory that Brod's truncated series of Jewish novels tra-verses. And the encounter with the "other side" of the fault line that sepa-rates the "Western" from the "Eastern" Jew represents the *third* landmark on the path to the comparison between Tycho and the Wandering Jew. It is even possible to specify the location of this encounter: Prague's Café Savoy, which provided a makeshift stage for troupes of Yiddish actors.[69] In the early 1910s, Brod and Kafka shared an enthusiasm for Yiddish theater, and for both of them, although in different ways, this enthusiasm gave direc-tion to their future work. For Brod in particular—and this is perhaps the source of the growing distance between the two friends—the discovery of a difference internal to the difference called "Judaism" solidified into a new doctrine, which represents the overcoming of indifferentism. Because Judaism is itself split, the assertion of Jewish difference—especially in the form of Zionism, which calls for *some* separation in its very designation—is no longer a more or less open form of self-assertion; rather, it is the asser-tion of an other. And this other, which is here called "the Eastern Jew," is comparable to, and therefore representative of, whoever finds himself or herself downtrodden and oppressed. Because particularity is divided against itself, in short, it can accord with "universal humanity." Zionism can then be, for Brod, a vehicle for universal humanism.

Another major writer of the period could also be seen to be at work on a similar project, namely, Martin Buber. For Brod—as for an entire generation of German Jews who had lost contact with the "insignificant scrap of Judaism" inherited from their parents, to quote Kafka once again[70]—Buber's translations and transformations of the legends of Hasidic sages made a "hidden" experience of the Eastern Jew widely available to a Western audience for the first time.[71] And this marks the *fourth* landmark on the path to the Brahe novel: the excavation of what Buber calls "underground Judaism."[72] This term appears in one of the three lectures that Buber delivered in Prague under the auspices of the Bar-Kochba Youth Organization from 1909 to 1911. The very title of this lecture, at which Brod was present, indicates the degree to which Buber was also interested in establishing an accord between particularity and universality: "Judaism and Humanity." This accord can be discovered, according to Buber, only on the condition that "underground Judaism"—which is neither "reform" nor "orthodox"—be brought into view. All of this resonates with Brod, whose return to Judaism never had much to do with synagogues or temples. But Brod cannot therefore be considered a disciple of Buber. In one of his early diaries, Gershom Scholem amalgamates Max Brod and Martin Buber into a single misguided bungler named "M. B."[73] But this is unfair—and not least because Brod sought to distance himself from Buber in the some fairly exacting terms. Under the title "Vom neuen Irrationalismus" ("On the New Irrationalism"), Brod attacked Buber for promoting precisely this: a new irrationalism, which, unlike the irrationalisms of the past, actually celebrates the absence of reason.[74] The connection between "On the New Irrationalism" and *Tycho Brahe's Path to God* could hardly be closer: the essay appeared in *Die weißen Blätter* in the spring of 1914, and the novel began to be serialized in the same periodical a few months later.

Help Comes in Two Forms

Brod distinguishes the new irrationalism from its predecessors with reference to their assessments of "the path." Older forms of irrationalism, such as Schopenhauer's, fully recognize that despite its best efforts, human rationality can never go so far as to overcome nonreason. Nothing can "rationalize" the data of sensation, for example, and nothing can uproot inclinations and passions, regardless of whether such an operation is considered desirable. But the earlier forms of irrationalism, in Brod's view, at least acknowledge that the path of reason is justified. Not so the new irrationalism, which claims that the path of reason is wrong and another path should be forged instead. For Buber, this other path lies in the sphere of "lived experience" (*das Erleben*), which is wholly incompatible with the "experience" (*Erfahrung*) to which the natural sciences appeal: "the new irrationalism wants to make it so that all *ratio* is undignified, all dignity free of *ratio*," Brod writes: "In Buber, every science, every working with concepts (except for something like heuristic moments) is characterized as anxiety and longing for security, as 'clever economy, whose cleverness stinks to heaven, because it only saves up and does not renew' [Buber]. This seems to me, however, as if one wanted to found the meaning of astronomy in the refutation of the fear of comets."[75]

At least one conclusion about Brod's forthcoming novel can be drawn from this critique of Buber's philosophy of "lived experience": the path of Kepler will not be despised. Kepler's attempt to determine the nature of planetary motion will not be grounded in a repressed fear that the sky is falling. According to Buber, the path of scientific experience arises out of, and results in, nothing more than "orientation" in a scattered world; the path of "lived experience," by contrast, testifies to, and consists in, what he calls "realization"—making oneself who one is as one gains a stance vis-à-vis an equally actual other. Adopting this vocabulary for his essay in *Die weißen Blätter*, Brod concludes his critique of Buber by postulating an "ideal" in which both "realization and orientation" appear "in the form of their highest purification, in which they are, according to the object, one and the same."[76] This obscure remark can be illuminated with respect to the forthcoming novel. The "object" in question is "the sky" or "the heavens" (*der Himmel*). For those who "orient" themselves in the world, *der Himmel* means one thing; for those who "realize" themselves, it means another. Because the synthesis of the two cannot be solely a matter of contemplation, "realization" takes precedence over "orientation"—regardless of whether contemplation is understood in terms of astronomical observation or mystical insight. But "realization" cannot be accomplished without some relation to the world in which one orients oneself. Brod thus proposes, with a certain trepidation, that the synthesis of "orientation" and "realization" can be accomplished "only in the ethical act." In the essay Brod goes no further. In his correspondence with Buber, however, he promises a supplement. "What more I have to say about the postulated synthesis," he writes at the beginning of 1914, "will be found, in part, in my Tycho Brahe."[77]

Tycho Brahe's Path to God will be therefore oriented around an "ethical act." Which one, however? And what is the relationship between this ethical act and the difference called "Judaism"? Obviously, for Buber, "underground" Judaism represents a path of "realization," whereas its "official" counterpart is nothing more than "orientation." This schema can perhaps be carried over to other religions, but the potentially universal applicability of the schema is of no help in determining the ethical act that would be the synthesis of the two terms. Help, however, comes to Brod in two forms: one that emphasizes the universality of its answer, the other that insists on the Jewish character of the question. By a strange coincidence—but this shows, once again, the peculiar capacity of Brod's novel to absorb and reproduce the environment from which it originated—both formulations of the ethical act can be traced to the "Kant evenings" in the house of Berta Fanta, where Brod first heard about the struggle between Tycho and Kepler: a non-Jewish participant in these evenings, namely, Christian von Ehrenfels, determines the universal-human form of this act, while a Zionist participant, Hugo Bergmann, reflects on its specifically Jewish character.

The two formulations of the ethical act, moreover, yield an identical imperative: act so as to help God. According to Ehrenfels, God needs our help in creating the cosmos. Without such help—so says the inventor of Gestalt psychology—the formative capacities of the world cannot overcome the counteracting convulsions of chaos. Achieving *any* clarity of consciousness is a small victory over these convulsions and, for this reason, lends assistance to God. Thus the sixth and last "dogma" of the "new dogmatism" that Ehrenfels proposes reads as follows: "We human beings—at all events, with at least a part of our consciousness—are part of the divine inner life and therefore co-laborers with God in his works."[78] And Bergmann agrees with this proposition, while adding an important caveat: Jews in particular are called upon to be God's collaborators. Such is Bergmann's interpretation of the famous passage from Leviticus, which serves as the proof text for an essay he published in 1913 under the title "Die Heiligung des Namens" ("The Sanctification of the Name"): "You shall not profane the Name of My holiness, that I may be sanctified in the midst of the children of Israel. I am Jahwe, who sanctifies you."[79] Given certain metaphysical notions inherited from ancient Greek philosophy, there is nothing perplexing about the image of a divine being sanctifying its mortal counterpart; but the reversal of this formula, according to Bergmann, sets Judaism apart. It is the sanctification of the Name. During the Middle Ages, this phrase acquired a dreadful connotation: it referred to the act of committing suicide rather than submitting oneself to forced conversion. More recently, as Bergmann explains, the phrase has been degraded to such an extent that it is used to designate such trivialities as the visit of a high-ranking official to a synagogue. But originally—and for the sake of the future—"the sanctification of the Name" should be understood to mean that Jews, who set themselves apart from others and from themselves, are enjoined by God to help God, so that creation can be cocompleted.[80]

The Comparison Redux

In his essay for *Die weißen Blätter,* Brod recommends Bergmann's essay as a major advance over the "new irrationalism" advocated by Buber; but he goes no further in his discussion of the essay. The advance over the formulations in the essay takes place in the final pages of the novel. The movement traced in these pages is both a reversal and a repetition of the movement with which *Arnold Beer* concludes. Beer leaves Prague for a Bohemian province, where he encounters a tiny-gigantic figure; Tycho leaves the Bohemian provinces for Prague, where he encounters a tiny-gigantic figure. Of course, Tycho does not encounter a grandmother; rather, he stumbles upon the great "father" of Prague Jewry, namely, Rabbi Judah Löwe ben Bezalel, otherwise known as the "Maharal."[81] All of the oppositions Buber had enumerated intersect with this singular figure: he is both "Western" and "Eastern" Jew, and he is both a representative of "official" Judaism and one of the last great sources of its "underground" currents—so much so that, according to a legend that had just been revived in Prague, to great acclaim, Rabbi Löwe was in command of the secret formula for the creation of a golem. The very issue of *Die weißen Blätter* that begins with Brod's essay "On the New Irrationalism" concludes with an installment of Gustav Meyrink's *The Golem.*[82] Once Meyrink's novel appeared in book form, it became an instant best seller and was immediately made into a movie—and remade a few years later into one of the classic films of German expressionism. Meyrink, moreover, was not an incidental figure in Brod's own career as a writer. Just as Schopenhauer gave direction to his philosophicoaesthetic doctrine, so was Meyrink his first literary "master."[83] And just as the climactic moment of *Tycho Brahe's Path to God* decisively breaks with Schopenhauer's "pessimism" and "fatalism," so does it silently repudiate Meyrink's representation of the central figure in the legend of "mystical Prague." Instead of creating a golem for the protection of the Jewish people, Rabbi Löwe inadvertently reawakens Tycho's awareness of the likeness between himself and a people to which he does not really belong:

And now the Jewish people, homeless and fugitive like himself, the butt of perpetual hostility like himself, like himself misunderstood in their doctrine and yet clinging to it, despoiled and wounded like himself, this people of misfortune, really seemed to him a veritable symbol of his own lot in life. It struck him that he had already once, at some earlier time, compared himself to Ahasuerus, the Wandering Jew. But today the enigma must be solved; that he felt. . . . He cried out in vehement tones: "But tell me, how is it possible to endure so much suffering? How is it possible to support all this? And all for nothing, for a few letters?" (263)

Franz Rosenzweig is doubtless referring to this passage when he asserts that *Tycho Brahe's Path to God* should be considered a "Jewish book."[84] It would be more accurate to call it a "Jewishlike book" or, even more accurately, a likeness book in general and a being-like-a-Jew book in particular, for everyone is invited to see himself or herself reflected in Tycho: suffering so much for the sake of so little. The solution to the enigma of this kind of suffering does not lie in indifference; but it does not therefore lie in indifference to indifference, which would amount to a kind of sheer activism. Rather, the solution can be found in the character of the Rabbi, who, by virtue of his ideal synthesis of "realization" and "orientation," through no will of his own, can make those around him Rabbi-like:

So here in the service of God a dim inward fervour had united with a clear consciousness, those two selfsame opposing tendencies which tore Tycho's soul in twain. They had united to form a living unity, which immediately passed over into Tycho and by the very intonation of the words convinced him of its kinship with him. "Is God, then, not almighty?" asked Tycho in trembling tones, "Does He need our help, our words of blessing?'"

Rabbi Löwe continued: "It is just to this that Rabbi Tarfon refers when he quotes the words of scripture. . . . From [this], however, it may be seen that the Eternal, praised be His name, not only commands our help, but even complains if it is not rendered." (264)

Having come for help, Tycho unexpectedly learns that he is called upon to help. But—and this is crucial—the doctrine of help is not entirely unprepared; on the contrary, he learns only what he has taught himself and what he has himself taught. If the characteristic trait of Kepler is indolence

(*Trägheit*), then that of Tycho is deferred action (*Nachträglichkeit*): he learns about what he learns only after he learns it yet again.[85] Thus, he sees what he meant when he called Kepler a "phantom" only after Kepler describes himself as phantomlike. Thus, he recognizes himself as Ahasuerus only after he had already called himself Ahasuerus—and then disavowed this comparison. Thus, he learns that God needs our help only after he declared that Jesus's last words, as they are recorded in the New Testament, are wrong: "'No, no!' he cried. *"It is not finished"; thus the text should run"* (217). The Maharal simply draws a conclusion from this contra-Christian premise: because "it is not finished," we are called upon to help finish it—which Tycho begins to do by correcting the text of the New Testament so that it revolves around the words of the Old. This is among the last of the Tychonic revisions that can be found in the novel. This revision, however, helps neither Brod nor Brahe answer the question at hand: it champions Judaism over Christianity, to be sure, but it does not let anyone know how God can be helped. If the argument Baron von Ehrenfels developed in his *Cosmogony* were convincing, the answer would be relatively simple: everyone can assist in creation simply by gaining a clearer consciousness of the forces that order the cosmos. Einstein would under this condition be the greatest helper of the era. If, however, this merely contemplative solution is deemed inadequate, as Brod declares in "On the New Irrationalism," then the question is considerably more complicated: Whom, in particular, should one help, given the fact that God cannot be helped directly and we cannot help everyone?

One thing is certain about the question: there is no *direct* answer. And this means that the question cannot be answered in a purely expository form. When Brod writes a letter to Buber and says that only in his "Tycho Brahe" will he be able to represent the "ideal" he postulates, he is not simply signaling his preference for narrative over argument; he is also responding to the exigencies of the question that arise out of his reflections on the arguments of Ehrenfels and Bergmann. Brod may not have been altogether familiar with Søren Kierkegaard's conception of "indirect communication" when he opted for fiction as a medium for the articulation of the "ethical act" of helping God under the condition that he cannot be directly helped.[86] But a theory of indirect communication is nevertheless at work in the making of the novel. And *Tycho Brahe's Path to God* can be seen to suffer, in any case, from one of the weaknesses of Kierkegaard's pseudonymous work, namely, the absence of a fully realized fictional world—an absence that, in Brod's case, expresses itself in the form of a historical novel that is deficient in authentic historical material. The underlying dilemma is Kierkegaardian, however, regardless of whether Brod was familiar with Kierkegaard: in helping God, someone other than God must be helped, and this "someone" cannot be directly identified. "Poetic comparison" is therefore irreducible, and yet it must be disavowed, for the act of helping someone other than God is based on the premise that God is altogether different: specifically, he is the one who cries out for help but cannot be helped directly.

The War—When Helping Is Barely Distinguishable from Betrayal

If the one whom we are called upon to help is seen as similar to God, then it is fairly certain whom Tycho should help: the one who must be seen as God-like. His name in the novel is "Rudolf II, the Emperor of the Holy Roman Empire." And the principle upon which Rudolf appears to be God-like is the basis of all political theology: the sovereign is like God, God like the sovereign.[87] If this principle is justified, then the "ethical act" for which Brod searches would consist in helping the one who is more God-like than any other, for this comparative quality defines his very being. Soon after Tycho speaks with the Maharal, Tycho is ushered into Rudolf's chambers and immediately notices the comparison: the Emperor is indeed like God, as he has now come to understand God, for he is so very weak. The earthly sovereign is comparable to his heavenly counterpart, in short, because both are in need of assistance. The assertion "it is not finished" applies both to the work of God and to that of the Emperor. In the case of the God, it means that Jesus is wrong. In the case of the Emperor, it means that his collections of beautiful and curious objects will never be completed. It may not be immediately evident what it means to help the Emperor around 1600, but it is altogether certain what it means in 1915. It means joining his faltering army or, if that proves to be impossible for certain physical reasons—Brod, for instance, suffered from curvature of the spine—contributing to the war effort with pro-Imperial propaganda.

Brod, however, had not the slightest intention of doing so. Not only did he show no enthusiasm for the war that erupted in August 1914 but soon after it began, he sought to create an international organization of writers and intellectuals for the purpose of promoting peace among the nations in conflict. He even coaxed Werfel into codrafting a proposal for such a union of nonbelligerence, and he was disappointed when some of those he had convinced to meet and discuss this proposal—Max Scheler, in particular—published glorifications of the German warrior ethos.[88] About the beginning of the war, Brod writes the following: "Who would have thought about the possibility of war in 1914! A few specialists perhaps, strategists, diplomats. . . . One thought of war as something with which history had finished, something fantastical, something in which earlier races of human beings (the unlucky ones!) had believed—not, however, us realists, who were endowed with reason."[89] The time before the war and the time after the war were in a strict sense incomparable, and it is for this reason that "poetic comparison" assumes such a high degree of importance in *Tycho Brahe's Path to God:* two times are made comparable, even though they are traversed by a hiatus in human affairs that, as it turns out, was not a hiatus at all. For this reason, among others, the First World War was a "decisive turning point in life": it showed that two eras that appear to be incomparable were comparable after all.[90] The dreadful consistency of history is an uncanny presupposition of the novel: despite all of our "realism," nothing really happens, for the reality of war is still with us. The uncanniness of this presupposition struck Brod fifty years after the fact, as the following ungrammatical remark in *Combative Life* demonstrates: "I believe that the strong power of attraction that historical material exercised over me afterwards [after the First World War] in large part derives from the fact that I, to my horror, found myself in the decisive year of 1914 without any feeling for world-historical contexts. (Not completely right, since I had already begun, in 1913, to write *Tycho Brahe* in premonition [*in Vorahnung*])."[91]

Brod had no idea what the word "war" meant when he began the novel, and yet it was written in 1913 in premonition of the coming war. When Brod says in his biography of Kafka that much of what happened around the time in which he wrote the novel had been thrown back into his subconscious, he does not mention his premonition of war; but this lacuna is perhaps justified under the assumption that the premonition scarcely rises to the level of consciousness, even as it takes shape in a parenthetical remark. And in any case this premonition could never be directly expressed. *Tycho Brahe's Path to God* is not only the indirect expression of Brod's answer to the question "whom to help," it is also an indirect expression of his sense that the past, as Faulkner famously said, is not past: war comes again, despite our "realism" and "rationalism." The two forms of indirection converge on the figure of two weak and withdrawn emperors, each of whom desperately needs help: Rudolf II and Franz Josef I. Brod refrains from engaging in propaganda in service of the latter, and Tycho betrays the former by helping the anti-Astrologer, Johannes Kepler.

Rudolf II is concerned with nothing so much as signs and portents, and the only passion in which he indulges, beyond the futile efforts to collect all kinds of strange and wonderful objects, lies in the field of astrology. Kepler, by contrast, is passionately opposed to astrology. From the beginning of the novel onward, he is so completely contemptuous of astrological humbug that he undiplomatically expresses this disdain in the presence of certain characters, especially Hagecius, who might betray his attitude to agents of the imperial court. The discourse of astrology is comparable to that of war propaganda, insofar as they both serve as mendacious support for empires bent on disaster. And when Tycho recommends Kepler for the post of court mathematician, he is himself courting disaster, since he is associating himself with the kind of suspicious character of whom the Emperor does not approve:

> "Kepler, then, upholds your theory, and my information is false?" asked the Emperor, full of interest.

> "False and not false. There are difficult questions involved. In some we are not in agreement and I, too, have objections to oppose to him. But these are not of the kind that his traducers allege; they are of a kind that could not arise at all unless he were accorded the fullest recognition." Tycho hesitated. Suddenly the inner voice which had already brought him to this point cried: "Now or never is the time to testify, now or never, to testify and to withhold nothing." And so he continued firmly: "As regards the question of astrology, we are of course entirely of one opinion. One must certainly admit the existence of a general affinity and a divine operation within the cosmos, but it is not enshrined in the naïve prophecies of the horoscope—"

> "That is my opinion as well," interrupted the Emperor, speaking more vivaciously than at any time during the whole conversation. (278)

In this, the crucial conversation of his life, Tycho speaks truth to power. Or so it seems. But he does not *exactly* speak "the truth," for he knows that Kepler cannot suppress his disdain for astrology. And Tycho does not *exactly* speak "to power," for he knows that the Emperor is weak. As if to prove the point, the Emperor instantaneously capitulates to Tycho's request despite his misgivings about Kepler: in the face of a firmly formulated statement, he is helpless, and there is no one in his chambers who is in a position to help him. It would not be an exaggeration to say that Tycho takes advantage of the Emperor's weakness, the full extent of which he recognizes as a consequence of his conversation with the Rabbi. Yet Tycho does not take advantage of the Emperor's weakness in order to promote his own affairs; rather, he promotes the career of one who openly denounces the system of thought that gives the Emperor the minuscule strength upon which his life rests. Enter Kepler, exit astrology, good-bye Emperor.

Who Is Johannes K.?

Who, then, is this "Johannes Kepler," whom Tycho helps? A possible approach to this question lies in the acceptance of the premise that Tycho is a stand-in for Brod and that Kepler corresponds to someone in his circle of acquaintances. On the one hand, this approach can be pursued by reflecting on those whom Brod actually tried to help, in which case the answer is satisfying but ambiguous. It is either of the two (Jo)hannes-Franzes—Werfel or Kafka. On the other hand, the approach can be pursued by considering the manner in which the figure of Kepler engages with the enigmas of the cosmos. In this case, the answer is unambiguous but unsatisfying, namely, Einstein, whom Brod could not have helped even if he tried. Nevertheless, the result of this approach is not wholly negative. The fact that a number of plausible answers emerge from a procedure of this kind says something about the figure in question. In colloquial terms, Kepler is difficult to pin down. In less-colloquial terms, borrowed from the letter Kafka wrote to Brod in which he expresses his appreciation for the dedication, Kepler appears to be comparable; but this appearance is "semblance."

Another approach to the question of Kepler runs directly counter to the first one. Instead of following Brod in his reflections on the people and incidents that drove him to create this character, one could examine the novel solely in terms of the ethicotheological problem it seeks to answer. "Kepler" in this case is the name of the one who is directly helped whenever one helps God. This cannot mean that "Kepler" means "genius," for under this condition the act of helping Kepler cannot be considered an ethical act at all; it is at best an aid to contemplation—whether contemplation takes a theoretical or aesthetic form. Furthermore, Tycho's assistance to Kepler cannot be understood simply in terms of the application of an "ethical maxim," which might read as follows: one should overcome one's "inner conflicts" so that one can give help to others, even though this help may be at the expense of one's own happiness or renown. For Kepler is neither a name for genius nor an indifferent "someone." He is, above all, the passionate opponent of astrology. Helping Kepler means betraying a sovereign who stakes his life and governs his state on the basis of an ideology that consists, at bottom, in the exaltation of "higher powers." Kepler—being who he is—will contribute to the destruction of this ideology. By showing that all of the planets, including the earth, move in elliptical paths, he helps us become aware of our responsibility for the decisions we make, including and especially the decision to launch a disastrous war.

An interpretation along these lines may have been at the forefront of Brod's mind as he reflected on the difference between the era in which he began the novel in 1913 and the era in which the novel was completed a mere two years later. But this interpretation also begs the question, for it assumes that we know who Kepler is. And it relies on a further assumption, which Einstein succinctly formulated in his response to Brod's novel *Galilei in Prison:* "truth is incomparably stronger than I am."[92] In the theological terms spoken by the Maharal, Einstein's statement is false. If God is truth, then I cannot assume that truth is stronger than I am; on the contrary, truth may be weaker and, in any case, it cries out for help. In less-theological terms, expecting that the progress of scientific insight into the structure of the cosmos will eventually resolve earthly conflicts is no better than relying on astrologers to identify the dates of upcoming disasters.

A final approach to the question of Kepler can be found in the other major thesis with which Brod, in later years, sought to elucidate the murky intentions behind his novel. According to this thesis, Kepler is little more than a cipher, whose basic function consists of being different from his Tychonic counterpart. By means of his counterpart Tycho approaches God. In other words, as the counterpart to Tycho, he is his "way" or "path" (*Weg*) to God. In still other words, the title of the novel, *Tycho Brahe's Path to God,* mentions Tycho but denotes Kepler. If the act of helping God is called "the sanctification of the Name," then the act—or rather, the indolent abstention from action—that characterizes the counterpart to Tycho should be called "the desanctification of the name." Whenever the Name is sanctified, according to Bergmann, it returns to God, whose Name it is. The desanctification of the name goes in another direction altogether: the name is stripped of the thing it names. Apropos of his former assistant, Tycho tells the Emperor, "'He is simply perfection itself, pure, fruitful, inviolable perfection'" (277). Tycho thus raises the status of his former assistant beyond that of God, whose work isn't finished and who, for this reason, cannot be called "perfect." The Kepler about whom Tycho speaks to the Emperor is, in short, a name in name only: a name that singles out a "no one" that lies beyond both creation and the Creator; a perfect "thing," in short, that, by virtue of its perfection, can come into being only at the end of time, when the collaboration of Creator and creatures finally reaches perfection.

And in calling Kepler "perfect," Tycho is perfected as well: he reveals himself as *a perfect fool,* which is to say, he is incapable of learning anything. It would be an understatement to declare that, in his conversation with the Emperor, Tycho once again "overestimates" Kepler; he over-overestimates him to such an extent that all talk of "estimation" is mistaken, for the status of him about whom he is speaking is beyond measure. *Tycho Brahe's Path to God* does not track Tycho's "learning curve." Still less is it a bildungsroman. If it is said that Tycho learns that he should help God rather than beg for help, then it should not be forgotten that this learning is predicated on a corresponding unlearning: he forgets that the one through whom he helps God—namely, Johannes Kepler—"does not exist." Saying "namely" in this context is, however, misleading: "Kepler" functions as a pure name, which can refer to something only when everything in creation becomes Kepler-like, that is, "perfect." If Tycho were capable of learning, he would distinguish between "Kepler" as a proper name and the pure name "Kepler," which means, in the end, "whatever is beyond our help." He alone is the one whom Tycho needs to help. His name might as well be "John Doe" or—to keep a few elements of the historical name in accordance with Brod's decision to keep a few elements of the historical figure—"Johannes K." Tycho indicates that he understands this when he calls his assistant a "phantom." The first book that Brod published is entitled *Death to the Dead!* The work that Weltsch, among others, considers Brod's best could be called *Help the Dead!*

Deathbed Acquittal

In June 1938, Walter Benjamin wrote a letter to Gershom Scholem, the first part of which reproduces verbatim his annihilating critique of Brod's recently published biography of Kafka. Fearing that Brod's work is so weak that it would not allow him an opportunity to develop his own thoughts, even if only indirectly, Benjamin adds some further comments on Kafka. These supplementary comments were first published in English in abstraction from the critique of Brod's biography,[93] and they have become incomparably more influential than anything Brod ever wrote, with the possible exception of the postscripts to Kafka's novels, in which he explains why he failed to carry out his friend's written request. Near the conclusions of his supplementary reflections, Benjamin writes:

> Folly is the essence of Kafka's favorites, from Don Quixote through the assistants to the animals. . . . Of this much, Kafka is sure: first, that to help, one must be a fool; and secondly, only a fool's help is real help. The only uncertainty is whether such help can still work for human beings. Perhaps it works only for angels (see p. 171 [of Brod's biography], about the angels that are given something to do)—and they could do without it anyway. So, as Kafka says, there is an infinite amount of hope—only not for us. This statement truly contains Kafka's hope.[94]

It is unlikely that a more accurate précis of *Tycho Brahe's Path to God* could ever be formulated. And it is not entirely out of the question that Benjamin's comments on Kafka, which are supposed to be separate from his critique of Brod's biography, absorb a faint trace of his novel, for they begin by describing Kafka's work as an "ellipse" and include a long quotation from one of the major expositors of the theory of relativity.[95] Kepler and Einstein are thus subtly inscribed in Benjamin's letter, even if Brod's novel was far from his mind.[96] "Tycho Brahe," in any case, is the name of Brod's favorite. And Tycho is a fool.[97] Not only does he assist his own assistant but his assistance consists in making sure that his assistant is in a position to destroy his system to the point where it will be remembered as nothing more than a clever—which is to say, foolish—compromise. And when Tycho assists his assistant, he does so by compromising himself: he speaks truth to power by speaking half-truths to a weakling. Added to all of this is the certainty that the helper whom Tycho helps has no need of his help, since he is perfect. Benjamin—following Brod, who cites Kafka, who quotes Kierkegaard— calls those whom the helper might actually be in a position to help "angels." And Brod indirectly does the same. The epigraph to the novel describes the nocturnal struggle between Jacob and an unnamed "man" who, so the commentators say, was in reality not a man but rather an angel of the Name. His name in the novel is, of course, Johannes K.

In the final chapter of the novel, which briefly stages the famous scene of Tycho's death, Kepler is acquitted of the accusation of betrayal. The basis of this acquittal lies in Tycho's realization that the Tychonic system is not *his*. This, after all, is what Ursus wanted to do: deprive Tycho of *his* system. At the end of the novel, therefore, Ursus apparently triumphs—and this, despite the fact that Kepler, finally reunited with wife and child, delivers the completed version of the *Apologia Tychonis contra Ursum* to the bedside of the dying Dane. In reality, as Dreyer notes, there is no evidence that Kepler ever completed his "Defense of Tycho against Ursus," much less delivered a copy to Tycho.[98] But in the economy of the novel Tycho's *Apologia* must be finished, otherwise Kepler would not be perfect. And the Kepler of the novel must be perfect; otherwise he would not be Kepler. More exactly, the name "Kepler" comes to mean "perfection," and the completion of the *Apologia Tychonis*—this could be the title of Brod's novel—is a sign that creatures and Creator will have in the end collaborated in the completion of creation. In the eyes of posterity, however—which is to say, in the eyes of those who are not themselves perfect—Kepler still appears to be slightly imperfect: he knew that Tycho wanted him to use the Tychonic charts of the heavens to demonstrate the truth of the Tychonic system, and yet he failed to do so. The end of the novel opens the eyes of posterity to what Tycho actually meant when, at the end of his combative life, he spoke of "his system": "by his system he naturally no longer meant those earthly experiments, but the all-comprehensive, divine certainty of the true law wherein he now felt himself a blissful participant. . . . But his strength did not suffice for him to make this clear, and so Kepler inevitably misunderstood his words" (288).

Weakened to the point of silence, Tycho, like both God and Emperor, is in need of help. Specifically, he needs help to say that "my system" does not mean "my system," for "my" is no longer rooted in "I." Brod does not exactly resurrect Brahe; but he gives Tycho a chance to say something that he was too weak to say. The epigraph to the novel suggests that the novel takes place during a single night of struggle after which the protagonist is given a new name: Israel. The final scene of the novel suggests that all of the preceding events constitute a long prelude to the few words that Tycho wanted to say: not "It is finished," as Jesus is reported to have said, but rather "Finish it." Brod helps him in this endeavor. Tycho does not then receive a new name, as Jacob did; rather, he ceases to identify himself with his own name. "Tychonic" no longer means "Tycho's," and "Tycho," in turn, no longer means someone in particular: it, too, is a name in name only, a name for the helper, who helps anyone who is, strictly speaking, beyond help.

By helping Tycho say what he was too weak to say, however, Brod also betrays himself. Kafka and Einstein were certainly not the only readers of *Tycho Brahe's Path to God* who noticed that Brod sees his own struggles mirrored in Brahe; indeed, Brod admits as much. By helping Tycho Brahe express his final thoughts, Brod is only helping himself. And this, too, follows from the demands imposed on the "ethical act." There is no one other than the self who *can* be directly helped: Kepler cannot, because he is perfect, and God cannot, because he is God. All help is only self-help. Or, more exactly, in the course of Brod's novel, help betrays itself as self-help. The very weakness of the novel—and perhaps the weakness of Brod's entire literary production—can be understood accordingly: the author of the novel helps someone else speak, but this "someone else" is none other than the author himself, who, always on the verge of death, is too weak to speak for himself. *Tycho Brahe's Path to God* recounts this paradox and is worth reading for this reason.

An even better reason can be found in one of Kafka's letters to Felice Bauer: "Soon I will send you Max's new novel, which I like very much."[99]

Notes

I would like to thank Julia Ng for her help in preparing this introduction.

1. Max Brod, review of Franz Blei's *Der dunkle Weg* in *Die Gegenwart* 6 (February 9, 1907): 93; Kafka is said to belong to a "sacred group" of writers.

2. Malcolm Pasley has brought out an edition of the texts that Brod and Kafka wrote in collaboration with each other (volume 1) as well as their correspondence (volume 2); Max Brod and Franz Kafka, *Eine Freundschaft,* ed. Malcolm Pasley (Frankfurt am Main: Fischer, 1980).

3. For a succinct and sympathetic reflection on Brod's activities as an editor, see Osman Durrani, "Editions, Translations, Adaptations," in *The Cambridge Companion to Kafka,* ed. Julian Preece (Cambridge: Cambridge University Press, 2002), esp. 206–14.

4. See Max Brod, postscript to 1st. ed. of *The Trial,* by Franz Kafka, ed. Max Brod, trans. Edwin and Willa Muir, rev. trans. E. M. Butler (New York: Vintage, 1964), 326–35.

5. See Walter Benjamin, "Kavaliersmoral," in *Gesammelte Schriften,* 7 vols. ed. Rolf Tiedemann and Hermann Schweppenhäuser (Frankfurt am Main: Suhrkamp, 1972–91), 4:466–68.

6. Quoted from the source of Brod's knowledge of the relation between Tycho and Kepler, namely, John Louis Emil Dreyer, *Tycho Brahe: A Picture of Scientific Work in the Sixteenth Century* (Edinburgh: Black, 1890), 309. A German translation of Dreyer's biography was first published in 1894. Gerhard Kowalewski identifies Dreyer as the source (see note 33 below). As the editor of Brahe's collected works, Dreyer was a reliable source. His work has since been surpassed by that of

Victor Thoren (with contributions from John R. Christianson), *The Lord of Uraniborg: A Biography of Tycho Brahe* (Cambridge: Cambridge University Press, 1990). For readers interested in the events reflected in Brod's novel, two recent studies are worth noting: Kitty Ferguson, *Tycho and Kepler: The Unlikely Partnership That Forever Changed Our Understanding of the Heavens* (New York: Walker, 2002); Edward Rosen, *Three Imperial Mathematicians: Kepler Trapped Between Tycho Brahe and Ursus* (New York: Abaris Books, 1986). A more speculative—and melodramatic—version of the same events can be found in Joshua Gilder and Anne-Lee Gilder, *Heavenly Intrigue: Johannes Kepler, Tycho Brahe, and the Murder Behind One of History's Greatest Scientific Discoveries* (New York: Doubleday, 2004).

7. But not wholly so: in the 1980s, a Tychonian Society was formed in hopes of reviving the geocentric conception of the cosmos. Its journal is entitled the *Bulletin of the Tychonian Society*.

8. By 1925, the novel had sold more than fifty thousand copies; see Max Brod, *Max Brod: Hamburger Bibliographien,* ed. Werner Kayser and Horst Gronemeyer, intro. Willy Haas and Jörg Mager (Hamburg: Hans Christian, 1972), 67. The English edition reproduced in this volume was first published as Max Brod, *The Redemption of Tycho Brahe,* trans. Felix Warren Crosse (New York: Knopf, 1928). Page numbers cited in parentheses in the text refer to the 1928 version here reproduced.

9. One further correction has been made. The phrase "poetic comparison" replaces "poetic composition" on page 213. The German word *Vergleich* is unambiguous; it means "comparison," not "composition." Later in this introduction I discuss the significance of the specific "poetic comparison" to which Tycho is referring: he views himself as the Wandering Jew.

10. See Max Brod, *Im Kampf um das Judentum* (Vienna: Löwit, 1920). It should be obvious that this short book was written before Zweig's assessment of Brod's literary career. For an analysis of Zweig's blindness with regard to his own Judaism, see Hannah Arendt's review of Zweig's *World of Yesterday: An Autobiography* (1943), in Hannah Arendt, *Reflections on Literature and Culture,* ed. Susannah Y. Gottlieb (Stanford, Calif.: Stanford University Press, 2007), 58–68.

11. See Robert Weltsch, *Max Brod and His Age* (New York: Leo Baeck Institute, 1970), 15. Another succinct and sympathetic account of Brod's work as a whole can be found in Heinz Kuehn's essay "Max Brod," *American Scholar* 62 (Spring 1993): 269–78. For the most complete account of Brod's life and work yet produced, see Margarita Pazi, *Max Brod: Werk und Persönlichkeit* (Bonn: Bouvier, 1970); subsequent translations of quotations from this source are mine. For a study of Brod's religious thought from a Catholic perspective, see Anton Magnus Dorn, *Leiden als Gottesproblem: Eine Untersuchung zum Werk von Max Brod* (Freiburg: Herder, 1981). There are also several collections of papers on Brod, including Festschriften, and an interesting book-length essay by Berndt Wessling, *Max Brod: Ein Portrait* (Stuttgart: Kohlhammer, 1969). In my estimation, however, the most incisive investigation of Brod's work can be found in Claus-Ekkehard Bärsch, *Max*

Brod im "Kampf um das Judentum": Zum Leben und Werk eines deutsch-jüdischen Dichters aus Prag (Vienna: Passagen, 1992). For a wide-ranging and well-researched investigation into Brod's city, which discusses many of his works (but not the Tycho Brahe novel), see Scott Spector, *Prague Territories: National Conflict and Cultural Innovation in Franz Kafka's Fin de Siècle* (Berkeley and Los Angeles: University of California Press, 2000).

12. Frans Ganser Genaamd Tengnagel van den Camp (1576–1622) was not—needless to say, perhaps—the doltish character whom Brod creates; for a brief account of his life, see John Robert Christianson, *On Tycho's Island: Tycho Brahe, Science, and Culture in the Sixteenth Century* (Cambridge: Cambridge University Press, 2000), 301–5.

13. Brod, postscript to *The Trial,* 327.

14. Quoted in Franz Kafka, *Kritik und Rezeption zu seinem Lebzeiten, 1912–1924,* ed. Jürgen Born, with the assistance of H. Mühlfeit and F. Spicker (Frankfurt am Main: Fischer, 1979), 25, my translation. For an inquiry into Kafka and his publishers, see Joachim Unseld, *Franz Kafka: A Writer's Life,* trans. Paul Dvorak (Riverside, Calif.: Ariadne Press, 1994).

15. Thus does Brod represent the motivation for his dedication, while getting the dates a little wrong; see Brod, *Franz Kafka, A Biography,* trans. G. Humphrey Roberts and Richard Winston (New York: Schocken, 1963), 130–31.

16. Franz Kafka, *Letters to Friends, Family, and Editors,* trans. Richard Winston and Clara Winston (New York: Schocken, 1977), 100.

17. Ibid., 105.

18. See the eighth aphorism in the text Brod published under the title "Reflections on Sin, Suffering, Hope, and the True Way," in Franz Kafka, *The Blue Octavo Notebooks,* ed. Max Brod, trans. Ernst Kaiser and Eithne Wilkins (Cambridge, Mass.: Exact Change, 1991), 87.

19. See Philipp Frank, *Einstein: His Life and Times,* ed. Shuichi Kusaka, trans. George Rosen (New York: Knopf, 1947), 152–53; Philipp Frank, *Einstein: Sein Leben und seine Zeit* (Munich: List, 1949), 152: "Dieser Kepler, das sind Sie."

20. See the press accounts of Einstein's arrival in Prague, as quoted by Jozsef Illy, *Isis* 70 (March 1979): 79.

21. Quoted (in English translation) in John Stachel, "The Genesis of General Relativity," in *Einstein Symposium, Berlin,* ed. H. Nelkowski (New York: Springer, 1979), 432. The Czech translation of Einstein's book on the theory of relativity appeared in 1923.

22. Albrecht Fölsing, *Albert Einstein: A Biography,* trans. Ewald Osers (New York: Penguin, 1997), 313.

23. For Einstein's own explanation of the mathematical problems that Kepler had to solve—problems, incidentally, which he may have discussed at the meetings of the Fanta circle, given the obvious connection between Kepler and Prague—see "Johannes Kepler," in Albert Einstein, *Ideas and Opinions,* ed. Carl

Seelig, trans. and rev. Sonja Bargmann (New York: Three Rivers Press, 1982), 262–65.

24. Diary entry dated April 10, 1922, in Franz Kafka, *Diaries: 1914–1923,* ed. Max Brod, trans. Martin Greenberg and Hannah Arendt (New York: Schocken, 1949), 227.

25. Kafka writes that upon visiting Brod, he found his friend immersed in "an immensely complex book by [Hermann] Cohen—*The Logic of Pure Knowledge*" (Kafka, *Letters to Felice,* ed. Erich Heller and Jürgen Born, trans. James Stern and Elisabeth Duckworth [New York: Schocken, 1973], 185; translation slightly modified).

26. See Max Brod and Felix Weltsch, *Anschauung und Begriff: Grundzüge eines Systems der Begriffsbildung* (Leipzig: Kurt Wolff, 1913). In a certain sense, Brod represents the side of "intuition," Weltsch that of "concept," but the treatise shows no lack of unity—as if it were written by a "philosopher of life" (Brod) in uneasy collaboration with a "neo-Kantian" (Weltsch). The treatise received a respectful review in one of the major English-language philosophical journals of the period; see the review of Harry Watt in *Mind* 25 (January 1916): 103–9; see also the extensive review in *Kant-Studien* 24 (1920): 321–25. At this point, it is perhaps worth commenting on the characterization of this book in Scott Spector's *Prague Territories:* "a derivative and often stilted text with [a] pretentious title" (212). With respect to Brod's reception of Schopenhauer, Spector is similarly dismissive: "Brod drew from Schopenhauer a coarse notion of the arbitrary role of destiny, but Brod's indifferentism is optimistic, even lighthearted, beside Schopenhauer" (61), the evidence for which is a single passage in Brod's first collection of stories. Is there a "refined" notion of the "arbitrary role of destiny," and if so, can it be found in Schopenhauer? More generally, is Brod and Weltsch's *Intuition and Concept* less philosophically sophisticated than Deleuze and Guattari's study of Kafka, in which every differential term is mapped onto the distinction between "re-territorialization" (read: Apollinian) and "de-territorialization" (read: Dionysian)? My own sense is that Brod and Weltsch are a little more "derivative" and slightly less "stilted" than Deleuze and Guattari. There may be good reasons to look down on Brod's philosophical reflections, but one must establish a perspective from which this view is justified.

27. See Ernst Cassirer, *Substanzbegriff und Funktionsbegriff,* 2nd. ed. (Berlin: Cassirer, 1923), which includes *Zur Einstein'schen Relativatätstheorie: Erkenntnistheoretische Betrachtungen* (Berlin: Cassirer, 1921); the English version combines the two: *Substance and Function* and *Einstein's Theory of Relativity,* trans. William Curtis Swabey and Marie Collins Swabey (New York: Dover, 1953).

28. Max Brod, *Streitbares Leben: Autobiographie* (Munich: Kindler, 1960), 252. All English translations from this source are mine. A posthumous version of the autobiography was published in 1969 and includes a number of notes about Brod's last years.

29. Kafka, *Letters to Friends,* 106; translation modified. For his argument with

Bergmann, see his diary entry dated December 30, 1911, in Franz Kafka, *Diaries: 1910–1913*, ed. Max Brod, trans. Joseph Kresh (New York: Schocken, 1948), 205.

30. See Brod, *Streitbares Leben*, 253; with respect to Ludwig Hopf, see Klaus Wagenbach, *Franz Kafka: Eine Biographie seiner Jugend, 1883–1912* (Bern: Francke, 1958), 174.

31. Frank, *Einstein: His Life and Times*, 85.

32. Albert Einstein, *Briefwechsel, 1916–1955*, ed. Max Born (Frankfurt am Main: Ullstein, 1986), 21.

33. Gerhard Kowalewski, *Bestand und Wandel: Meine Lebenserinnerungen zu gleich ein Beitrag zur neueren Geschichte der Mathematik* (Munich: Oldenbourg, 1950), 249, my translation.

34. Frank, *Einstein: His Life and Times*, 85–89.

35. Brod, *Streitbares Leben*, 314–15.

36. Frank, *Einstein: His Life and Times*, 89. Fölsing notes, incidentally, that after returning to Zurich, Einstein complained that he was lonely in Prague, having found no one with whom he could discuss the topics that mattered to him most (see Fölsing, *Albert Einstein*, 278).

37. Brod, *Streitbares Leben*, 315.

38. Bergmann notes that he never spoke about Zionism with Einstein during the latter's short stay in Prague; see Hugo Bergmann, "Personal Remembrances of Albert Einstein," in *Boston Studies in the Philosophy of Science*, vol. 13 (Boston: Reidel, 1985), 390. For Bergmann's letter to Einstein, asking him for support in establishing a Hebrew University in Jerusalem, see Fölsing, *Albert Einstein*, 492; as Fölsing notes, Bergmann's letter calls Einstein "the greatest Jewish scientist," although it was written before the astronomical confirmation of the general theory of relativity turned into a public spectacle.

39. Einstein, letter to Max Brod dated February 22, 1949, quoted in Albert Einstein, *The New Quotable Einstein*, ed. Alice Calaprice (Princeton, N.J.: University of Princeton Press, 2005), 13–14.

40. See Einstein's preface, written in 1942, to the German edition: Albert Einstein, "Vorwort," in Frank, *Einstein: Sein Leben und seine Zeit*, n.p., my translation.

41. Albert Einstein to Max Brod, 4 July 1949, quoted in Carl Seelig, *Albert Einstein: Leben und Werk eines Genies unserer Zeit* (Zurich: Europa, 1960), 209–10, my translation.

42. See Walter Benjamin, "Review of Brod's *Franz Kafka*," in *Selected Writings*, ed. Howard Eiland and Michael Jennings, trans. Edmund Jephcott (Cambridge, Mass.: Harvard University Press, 2002), 3:317. This review was unpublished during Benjamin's lifetime. It should be noted that Brod was himself attracted to the idea of distance in connection with the "national question." Hence, he proposed the idea of "love of distance" (*Distanzliebe*) in his novel of 1933, *Die Frau, die nicht enttäuscht* (*The Woman Who Does Not Disappoint*); see Pazi, *Max Brod*, 76–80. Even Felix Weltsch found this idea disappointing, however, as Pazi notes in her

discussion. Brod sent Benjamin a copy of the book; but as Benjamin indicates to Scholem, he has no intention of reading it (see Walter Benjamin, *Gesammelte Briefe,* 6 vols. ed. Christoph Gödde and Henri Lonitz [Frankfurt am Main: Suhrkamp, 1995–2000], 4:358).

43. Kafka, *Letters to Felice,* 392–93; translation slightly altered.

44. On the publication history of Werfel's early poetry, see Karl Guthke, "Wunderkind und Impressario in eigener Sache: Franz Werfel's Anfänge," in *Das Abenteuer der Literatur* (Munich: Francke, 1981), 295–309. For Brod's own account, see especially his "Wie ich Franz Werfel entdeckte," *Prager Montagsblatt* 52 (December 27, 1937).

45. Brod, *Streitbares Leben,* 15.

46. Karl Kraus, "Selbstanzeige," in *Die Fackel,* 326–28 (July 8, 1911): 34–36, my translation; Werfel's poem is entitled "Natürliche Kahnfart."

47. See Paul Adler's review in *Die Rheinlande* 26 (1916): 376; Otto Pick's review can be found in *Die neue Rundschau* 27 (1916): 862–64. According to some unpublished notes of conversations with Alma Mahler-Werfel, Pick was partially responsible for the conflict between Brod and Werfel; see Peter Stephan Jungk, *Franz Werfel: A Life in Prague, Vienna, and Hollywood,* trans. Anselm Hollo (New York: Grove Weidenfeld, 1990), 253.

48. Brod, *Franz Kafka,* 81.

49. Brod, *Streitbares Leben,* 315–16. In a letter Brod wrote to the Czech translator of his novel, Jan Wenig, Brod made an interesting comment in this regard: having engaged in further study of Tycho Brahe, he was surprised to see the degree to which his image of the astronomer, which was formed on the basis of mere intuition and empathy, nevertheless corresponded "completely, down to surprising details," with the figure found in the historical sources; quoted from Pazi's translation of the Czech, my translation into English; see Pazi, *Max Brod,* 155.

50. See Franz Werfel, "Die christliche Sendung: Ein offener Brief an Kurt Hiller," *Die neue Rundschau* 28 (1917): 92–105. Brod's furious response appeared in the first issue of Martin Buber's new journal; see Max Brod, "Franz Werfels 'Christliche Sendung,'" *Der Jude* 1 (1916–17): 717–24. Brod expanded his case for Judaism, and against Werfel, in the "confession" he wrote near the end of the First World War and published in 1921 under the title *Paganism, Christianity, Judaism,* trans. William Wolf (University, Alabama: University of Alabama Press, 1970); see esp. 84–85, which briefly discusses the Brahe novel.

51. Brod, *Streitbares Leben,* 316–17. It is worth noting that Brod did have *some* leeway with regard to the spelling of "Kepler"; it is not uncommon to find his name spelled "Keppler," even in contemporaneous discussions.

52. The most emphatic of these objections can be found in the review by Kurt Pinthus, *Beiblatt der Zeitschrift für Bücherfreunde* 9 (December 1916): 458–59; in this context, see Gabriela Veselá, "Das Rudolfinische Prag in der deutschsprachigen Literatur um die Jahrhundertwende," *Philologia Pragensia* 29 (1986): 131–42, esp. 137–38.

53. In his autobiography Brod asserts, with a certain degree of naïveté, that he always loved his father, never experienced anything like an Oedipus complex, and therefore occupied a "lonely, isolated position" with the expressionist movement (Brod, *Streitbares Leben,* 26).

54. Kafka, incidentally, would probably have been aware of the fact that Brod's image of Tadeáš Hájek (1525–1600) departs significantly from the historical sources. At least two of the reviewers of the Czech translation (published in 1918) objected to Brod's portrayal of Hájek; see Veselá, "Das Rudolfinische Prag," 138–39. The same objection resurfaces in Peter Demetz's discussion of Prague during the reign of Rudolf II (see *Prague in Black and Gold: Scenes from the Life of a European City* [New York: Hill and Wang, 1997], 188).

55. Brod, *Franz Kafka,* 187. See also the remarks of Hartmut Binder, *Kafka Kommentar zu den Romanen, Rezensionen, Aphorismen und zum Brief an den Vater* (Munich: Winkler, 1976), 287. Binder draws on a passage from Kafka's letters to Milena Jesenská in which he asserts that, as a "Western Jew," "nothing is granted me, everything has to be earned, not only the present and the future, but the past too—something after all which perhaps every human being has inherited, this too must be earned, it is perhaps the hardest work." Kafka then adds an astronomical—or at least Archimedean—image to his reflections, as if he half remembered Brod's novel about Tycho's struggles to see the revolutions of the earth: "When the earth turns to the right—I'm not sure that it does—I would have to turn to the left to make up for the past" (Franz Kafka, *Letters to Milena,* ed. Willi Haas, trans. Tania and James Stern [New York: Schocken, 1965], 219).

56. Max Brod, *Arnold Beer: Das Schicksal eines Juden* (Berlin: Juncker, 1912), 175; see also Max Brod, "Der jüdische Dichter deutscher Zunge," in *Vom Judentum: ein Sammelbuch,* ed. Bar-Kochba Youth Organization (Leipzig: Wolff, 1914), 261–63, the final paragraph of which is a defense of his *Jewish Women* and *Arnold Beer* against similar accusations.

57. Brod, *Arnold Beer,* 175.

58. According to the preface of his study of Brod, Claus Bärsch was supposed to coedit these diaries, but Brod's heir, Esther Hoffe, decided ultimately against this plan; see Bärsch, *Max Brod im "Kampf und das Judentum,"* 16.

59. See Brod, *Streitbares Leben,* 160. In the fall of 1902, Brod delivered a lecture on Schopenhauer in which he accuses Nietzsche of being a "swindler" (Klaus Wagenbach corrects Brod's dating of this event; see Klaus Wagenbach, *Franz Kafka: Eine Biographie seiner Jugend, 1883–1912* [Bern: Francke, 1958], 102). After Brod's lecture, a slightly older student, who generally had remained silent, approached him with a few objections, and as the two wandered through the streets of Prague, Brod had to fend off a defense of Nietzsche against his Tychonic tirade (see Brod, *Streitbares Leben,* 234–37). Thus began the friendship between Brod and Kafka—spurred by the accusation that would later motivate a novel about another "B." and another "K." In this context, it is a little ironic that one of

the reviewers of this novel claimed that its style is reminiscent of Nietzsche, minus the latter's "empty pathos" (*Deutsche Jahrbücher* 166 [December 1916]: 304).

60. See Max Brod, *Über die Schönheit der häßlichen Bilder: Ein Vademecum für Romantiker unserer Zeit* (Leipzig: Wolff, 1913). The admonition to admire nothing appears as the motto for the work Max Brod, *Tod den Toten! Novellen des Indifferenten* (Stuttgart: Juncker, 1906), 2; and the corresponding admonition to admire everything forms the conclusion of the same collection (see 196).

61. Brod, *Schloß Nornepygge: Der Roman des Indifferenten* (Berlin: Juncker, 1908), 505, my translation.

62. Weltsch, *Max Brod and His Age,* 15.

63. See Franz Kafka, "Letter to His Father," in *The Sons,* ed. Mark Anderson (New York: Schocken, 1989), 166–67.

64. See Brod's account of his furious reaction to Hermann's review in *Streitbares Leben,* 345.

65. For an account of this incident, see Reiner Stach, *Kafka: The Decisive Years,* trans. Shelley Frisch (New York: Harcourt, 2005), 354–55.

66. See Kafka, *Diaries: 1910–1913,* 1: 59–60.

67. See Brod, *Arnold Beer,* esp. 143.

68. See Kafka, *Diaries: 1910–1913,* 1: 276: "thoughts about Freud, of course; in one passage, of *Arnold Beer.*" For a discussion of the relation between Brod's novel and Kafka's story, see Ritchie Robertson, *Franz Kafka: Judaism, Politics, Literature* (Oxford: Oxford University Press, 1985), 29–31.

69. See Brod, *Streitbares Leben,* 221. During the war, Brod also participated in a dubious educational program for displaced Jewish women, to whom he delivered lectures on Homer (see especially Max Brod, "Brief an eine Schülerin nach Galizien," *Der Jude* 1 [1916–17]: 32–36). Much has been written on Kafka's relation to Yiddish theater, which is obviously of great importance for "The Judgment"; see, for example, Evelyn Beck, *Kafka and the Yiddish Theater: Its Impact on His Work* (Madison: University of Wisconsin Press, 1971). One of Brod's distant cousins, Georg (Jirí) Langer, was drawn even further toward "the East" and become a follower of a Hasidic Rebbe. As a result of this turn, all nonsacred texts became suspect. As Kafka reports, Langer was allowed to read "Max's book," presumably the Tycho Brahe novel, only on Christmas, as long as it did not coincide with the Sabbath, and on the toilet (see Franz Kafka, *Tagebücher,* ed. Hans-Gerd Koch, Michael Müller, and Malcolm Pasley [Frankfurt am Main: Fischer, 1990], 3:116).

70. Kafka, "Letter to His Father," 146.

71. The first of these editions of Hasidic legends, *The Tales of Rabbi Nachman,* which Buber revised several times, appeared in 1906.

72. Martin Buber, *On Judaism,* ed. Nahum Glatzer, trans. Eva Jospe (New York: Schocken, 1995); 30.

73. See Gershom Scholem, *Tagebücher, nebst Aufsätzen und Entwürfen bis 1923,* 2 vol. ed. Karlfried Gründer, Herbert Kopp-Oberstebrink, and Friedrich Niewöh-

ner with the assistance of Karl E. Grözinger (Frankurt am Main: Jüdischer Verlag, 1995–2000), 1:466.

74. Max Brod, "Vom neuen Irrationalismus," *Die weißen Blätter* 8 (April 1914): 747–57.

75. Ibid., 750, my translation.

76. Ibid.

77. Unpublished letter, quoted in Pazi, *Max Brod,* 88. Pazi also quotes from a slightly earlier letter to Buber, in which he asserts that, from the beginning of his "development," a reconciliation of the rational and the irrational hovered before his eyes, and in "my Tycho" this ideal synthesis of the two is supposed to be realized (Pazi, *Max Brod,* 87). Felix Weltsch provides an interpretation of the Tycho Brahe novel that sees it as an attempt to foster a "new rationalism," the aim of which lies in preventing rationalism from falling prey to universal and "egotistical" mechanization: "Thus can we consider Tycho as a true representation of the good rationalist. For he withstands all the dangers that are bound up with rationalism" (see *Die Schaubühne* 13 [1917]: 478, my translation).

78. Christian Ehrenfels, *Cosmogony,* trans. Mildred Focht (New York: Comet Press, 1948), 180. In her introduction, Focht translates a section of the appreciation Brod wrote in honor of Ehrenfels for *Kant-Studien* (*Cosmogony,* viii–ix).

79. Hugo Bergmann, "Die Heiligung des Namens," in *Vom Judentum,* ed. Bar-Kochba Youth Organization (Leipzig: Wolff, 1914), 32–43, my translation of Bergmann's translation of the Hebrew.

80. See Hugo Bergmann, "Die Heiligung des Namens," in *Vom Judentum,* 42–43. This summary does not do justice to the complexity of Bergmann's argument, which is supported by a theory of the proper name. A detailed exposition of the essay can be avoided here only because Brod does so in his contribution to *Die weißen Blätter.*

81. It is perhaps needless to say that Brod rearranges a number of historically verified events, including the meeting between Rabbi Löwe and Rudolf II, for the purposes of his narrative. An accessible account of the actual events in question can be found in Demetz, *Prague in Black and Gold,* 171–236.

82. For a recent translation of this enormously successful novel about "mystical Prague," see Gustav Meyrink, *The Golem,* trans. Mike Mitchell (Riverside, Calif.: Ariadne, 1995).

83. See Brod, *Streitbares Leben,* 237.

84. Franz Rosenzweig, *Briefe* (Berlin: Schocken, 1935), letter 35 (29 September 1916); see also letter 186 (1 October 1917): "It is almost certain that, under the mask of Tycho, Brod consciously wanted to portray the Jew." This "almost" is worth noting. Both of these quotations can be found in Pazi, *Max Brod,* 155.

85. In Freud's case of *The Rat Man* (1917), he expounds on the problem of what is often translated as "deferred action." For a brief discussion, see Jean Laplanche and Jean-Bertrand Pontalis, "Vocabulaire de la psychanalyse," trans. Jeffrey

Mehlman and Peter Kussell, *Yale French Studies* 48 (1972): 182–86.

86. In his autobiography, Brod indicates that both he and Kafka became interested in Kierkegaard several years after Kafka had made his literary "breakthrough" in "The Judgment," which took place around the time Brod was beginning to work on the Tycho Brahe novel (see *Streitbares Leben,* 237). Nevertheless, as he also notes, his first publisher, Axel Juncker, was Danish, and he published a translation of Kierkegaard's "Diary of the Seducer" (from the first volume of *Either/Or*), which contains *in nuce* a theory of indirect communication.

87. The most famous exposition of this formula can be found in a treatise that Carl Schmitt wrote a few years after Brod's novel, namely, *Political Theology* (1922).

88. See Brod, *Streitbares Leben,* 100; an illuminating discussion of these remarks can be found in Bärsch, *Max Brod im "Kampf um das Judentum,"* 50–64.

89. Brod, *Streitbares Leben,* 81–82.

90. Ibid., 82.

91. Ibid., 119.

92. Einstein to Brod, 4 July 1949, quoted in Seeling, *Albert Einstein,* 209–10.

93. See Walter Benjamin, *Illuminations,* ed. Hannah Arendt, trans. Harry Zohn (New York: Schocken, 1968), 141–45.

94. Benjamin, "Letter to Gershom Scholem," in *Selected Writings,* 3:327.

95. See Benjamin, *Selected Writings,* 3:325–27. Benjamin quotes a long passage from Sir Arthur Stanley Eddington's *Nature of the Physical World* (1928; German translation, 1931). It is a mistake to say of this work that it is simply a popularization of Einstein's theories. Eddington tried to make sense of these theories, as it were, by developing the metaphysical structure that underlies their validity. He thus treats Einstein in the same manner as Kant treated Newton.

96. It should be emphasized, however, that Brod was on Benjamin's mind—and not only in conjunction with Kafka. In January 1930, Benjamin wrote a letter to Brod, thanking him for a book; but there is no indication of the book to which he is referring (see Benjamin, *Gesammelte Briefe,* 3:498–99). It might have been *Tycho Brahe's Path to God.* More likely, it was Brod's *Über die Schönheit häßlicher Bilder* (*On the Beauty of Ugly Images,* 1913). About this collection of essays, Benjamin writes the following to Scholem in 1928, as he begins to contemplate a major work on the Paris Arcades: "It is remarkable how, fifteen years ago, [Brod] self-complacently fingered something on a keyboard for which I am now endeavoring to write a fugue" (Benjamin, *Gesammelte Briefe,* 3:410, my translation). And this relation can be seen in Convolute Q of the *Arcades Project,* which begins with a quote from Brod's book: "Does anyone still want to go with me into a panorama?" (Benjamin, *Arcades Project,* trans. Howard Eiland and Kevin McLaughlin [Cambridge, Mass.: Harvard University Press, 1999], 527).

97. In his review of the novel, Otto Pick sees something similar but unfortunately reverses the names, declaring that Kepler is the "pure fool" (*Die neue Rundschau* 27 [1916]: 864, my translation).

98. The text of the *Apologia* did not appear until the nineteenth century (see Dreyer, *Tycho Brahe,* 304–5). A translation and discussion of Kepler's treatise can be found in Nicholas Jardine, *The Birth of the History and Philosophy of Science: Kepler's "Defense of Tycho against Ursus," with Essays on its Provenance and Significance* (Cambridge: Cambridge University Press, 1984).

99. Kafka, *Letters to Felice,* 459.

INTRODUCTION

I T   W O U L D   B E   a tempting task to draw the portaits of all
those poets whose power has gradually developed from frail
beginnings; for the error still seems widely current that for
every artist, youth is a period of violent activity, of high
spirits that overflow into arrogance, of self-confidence in full
flower insolently demanding attention, the Bakkalaureus in
Faust. But in actual fact, among poets is not that other species
of youth far more frequent, that species which begins with a
wondrous awe of life, with a tender melancholy, with a sweet
and much embarrassed terror at the manifold tasks awaiting
it, with a mistrust of its own as yet untried art? Perhaps
in poetic natures thus labouring under repression, the power
is already as fully present as among those who adopt a noisy
and boisterous demeanour. Only their spirit is not yet ripe
to face life and to confront it with a proudly erect head. So
it was at the outset with Rainer Maria Rilke: faint-heartedness
at first, a boundless submissiveness and self-abasement to a
role of insignificance, an acquiescence in the humility which

marks every beginning. In the same way his compatriot Max Brod, born at Prague in 1884, started upon his steeply ascending path ten years later in the shadow of the same houses, under the shadow of the same humility. I still remember him as I beheld him for the first time, a twenty-year-old youth, small, slim, and of boundless modesty. I see him in the full tide of his joy at being able to show Prague, the beloved and bewitching city, for the first time to a foreigner and to tell of all his overflowing love for this heroic world of the past. His small, girlish hands strayed gently over the keys of a piano. He spoke of music, of the Czech composers, of Smetana and Yanacek, whom he discovered for the world, but always of others, never of himself and of the songs and sonatas that he has composed. When asked about his own work, for an answer he spoke in glowing terms of the entirely unknown Franz Kafka as the real master of modern prose and psychology. If one mentioned his poetry, he would answer deprecatingly that at school there was a boy named Franz Werfel, and that he is one of the greatest poets of our time. Thus he then was, this young poet entirely devoted to everything which seemed great to him, to the strange, to the sublime, to the wonderful in every shape and form, alike in the past and in the uncertain outlines of that which was rising into being.

About him there lay an ancient city, filled with story and mystery, the giant pile of the Hradschin, where once an emperor had given laws to Europe. The young man looked timidly up to the mighty form. How could one venture to

master this past, contend with one's own few powers against
something so vast and so sublime? No, it was too great. So
for his first task the beginner took himself to the minute.
With that wonderful tenderness peculiar to him he first depicted as with a touche-pen only minute sections of the world
about him: the life of a Czech maidservant, the seamstresses
at a small tailor's establishment, a corner of landscape where
he had stayed, a few verses pronounced in hushed tones in a
quiet room, any altogether personal utterance, pure with the
purity alike of tone and of the heart. Through each one even
then ran a perfect sense for art; in all there appeared intimate
and delicate images of strangely new, indeed already expressionist originality of form. The only thing that was
lacking was a resolute leap which should carry him past
details to the generally significant, from everyday life to the
heroic, from the gentle calm of avowal to the passion of
demand for the moral postulate. No, the one thing to be
avoided was a too active participation, for that would carry
one away with it, and moreover one has no right to it. This
"indifferentism," this resistance to the forces that were violently sweeping him along, characterized his first great novel,
Schloss Nornepygge, which is full of enchanting impressions,
the first German example of pointillism in psychology. In
the world of emotion, too, he sought at first to prove his
merit on the small scale by means of details in subjects that
did not carry him too far, and so for many years we all
regarded Max Brod as one of the most exquisite miniature
painters in the German language. And all his essays—like

his stories, his poems, in the same way as his music—are no less marked by limpidity of spirit than by emotional restraint. By the very fact of this novel emphasis and by their spiritual frankness they have all influenced his generation, in particular Werfel; and much that has subsequently been ascribed to the expressionists as a discovery, as prototype, existed here in embryo and in nobly expanding blossoms. Courage is already here, but it avows its presence to itself alone; it does not yet raise its voice to the world with resolute self-assurance.

Such were the beginnings of this poet; tenderness, modesty, as with ever bowed head. His eyes were still blinded by this excessively powerful light and he lowered them timidly. So for a long time it remained impossible to look into the depths of his soul. One thing was lacking in his many-sided capacity —the noblest fault of a youth of this calibre: courage for decision, courage for vehemence in the face of the world. But suddenly this too was given him, for the war burst with all its force upon his generation, thrusting itself into the midst of our lives and stirring in us something that had not yet reached consciousness, the feeling of responsibility. An empire that had existed for a thousand years was overthrown. History suddenly drew near with the beat of rushing wings. Every hour was filled to overflowing with mighty happenings. And at once one felt that in the face of these tremendous events all playing with little things was cynical, was inexcusable. Here at last were problems, problems which could not be overlooked, problems before which a man must take up his position at the call of his own blood and at the direction

of his own spirit. Any kind of indifference, as hitherto practised, Max Brod felt immediately would now be moral cow-
ardice; and in a spirit of definite resolution he boldly confronted the present face to face, looking with unfaltering
eye at every strand of the past. The great store of goodness
which always existed in him, but which to a certain degree
had expressed itself only in acts of private benevolence, now
for the first time streamed forth in full tide into his work,
only to gush back again into him. His genius now turned
with assured powers towards the sublime. The years before
the war had already strengthened the manly impulses in him.
Now they found expression in intellectual conflict. Now to
the city where he had hitherto walked timidly, lacking courage to interpret it or to seize it with the grasp of an artist,
he raised a monument in his already finished *Tycho Brahes
Weg zu Gott* (*The Redemption of Tycho Brahe*) and in *Rëubeni, Fürst der Juden* (*Rëubeni, Prince of Jews*). The Middle Ages, that cloud of the past resting upon the smaller
present, he now dissipated, darting through it a shaft of creative lightning. The problem of his own race was sublimely
depicted in his novel *Rëubeni*. A love-affair provided the
material for the romance of a really passionate love in the
novel *Leben mit einer Göttin* (*Life with a Goddess*); and
his whole attitude towards the world and the epoch found
expression in the two-volume philosophical work *Christen-
tum, Judentum, und Heidentum* (*Christianity, Jewry, and Hea-
thendom*). Everywhere from indolent, delicate contemplation,
there sprang passionate avowal. Mere adjacency developed into

creative participation. At a single blow the miniature-painter became the artist on a grand scale, and he who as a timid, awe-struck boy had confronted the marvellous as something lying for ever beyond his reach, now beheld magic everywhere and in everything, in the very midst of life as well as in the past. He envisaged it as the miracle, lying on this side of the river ready to surrender itself to any of the faithful and to grow in strength at the touch of any hand, the willing prey of any passion, a faithful, courageously testifying witness to his own outpouring emotions.

These strong, far-flung, powerful outlines, this soaring fling at a distant aim, these were really only acquired by Brod since the war. But because of that the artist in him did not forget what it had learned before, the delicate links in the chain of the spirit, the love for creative and illuminating detail, the point lace of tender and animating fancies. Thus his novels are at once wide in their scope and replete with detail. They depict the inner and outer life, the life of the period and of the eternal light; they all derive their being from that spiritual contrast between individuals which cast gigantic shadows over the historical and the heroic. Tycho Brahe, the Emperor, the Pope, Kepler, Aretino, the Rabbi Löwe, Rëubeni, and the martyr Molcho are not merely fortuitous figures, but symbols, each representing an outlook upon the world, permeated with the cosmic spirit and by their destiny bound to the metaphysical. Nothing in these novels is a mere conceit, a decorative detail gleaned from chance reading of books that allure by their wealth of colour; but impelled by the need of expression and avowal, the poet presents his figures to the world in order to interpret himself in them, and by them to interpret the world to himself. Only in this sense do historical novels now have any spiritual value for us, when figures from the distant past become symbols for emotions that know naught of time and when their problems join the ocean of things possessing permanent value. For us few works have so fully interpreted the spirit and emotions of the Middle Ages as *Tycho Brahe* and *Rëubeni.* Secret places of emotion and of thought are lighted up by them, figures are summoned in their corporeal presence from the shadows; and yet their spiritual contrasts belong as much as any living thing to our inner life. For however rich it may be in fancy, no imagination may have any active part in anything which does not become *nostra res,* our affair in the most intimate sense. Thus it would be unjust to confine such novels as these of Max Brod to the category of the historical, for they are as much portraits of a religious and moral present as of a distant culture. Their subject matter may be laid in epochs of stronger colour and of more powerful appeal to the senses than our own appears to us; but the spirit that infuses them with their secular breath is one and the same and, as always, the only fruitful spirit; copious, sympathetic love for the small as for the great, faith without rigidity of form, yet living in every form. That time only portrays something fugitive, that it is an outward garment which does not affect anything essential, is clear from the duality of his representation, in which everything temporal is but a pretext for discovering the eternal and the august that dwells within. No one who has penetrated so far along this path and so near to the heart of all passion can stop in his course. And so it is only with a sense of the most profound confidence that the feeling of gratitude, already stirred in a remarkable degree, can accompany such a poet, who for years has repeatedly satisfied his own measure and advances grandly to an ever higher pitch of intensity.

Stefan Zweig.

Salzburg, 1927

Tycho Brahe's Path to God

A N D *there wrestled a man with him until the breaking of the day. . . . And he said, Let me go, for the day breaketh. And he said,* I will not let thee go, except thou bless me.

And he said unto him, What is thy name? And he said, Jacob.

And he said, Thy name shall be called no more Jacob, but Israel: *for as a prince hast thou power with God and with men, and hast prevailed.*

And Jacob asked him, and said, Tell me, I pray thee, thy name. And he said, Wherefore is it that thou dost ask after my name? And he blessed him there.

And Jacob called the name of the place Peniel: for I have seen God face to face, and my life is preserved.

GENESIS XXXII. 24, 26–30

CHAPTER I

HIS OWN POSITION at the Court of Emperor Rudolf II at Prague once assured, the illustrious Tycho Brahe addressed ever warmer letters of invitation to the young astronomer Johann Kepler. The correspondence had been going on for some years. Indeed, banished, persecuted, and ageing as he was, Tycho had felt himself powerfully attracted towards this new inquirer almost as soon as the name of Kepler had made its appearance in the scientific world in company with his first cosmographical work, the modestly entitled *Prodromus*. He saw that in future this was to be his sole court of appeal; he knew that he must look for approval or disapproval to this fresh intelligence, that Kepler was to shape what of life was left to him. And so from the very outset he regarded Kepler somewhat as a weary father looks upon a growing son, with mixed sentiments of anguish and joyous expectation. Every line that came from Graz was momentous in his eyes. For although his most recent experiences, which often appeared to him as an unbroken chain of disasters, had rendered him irritable, suspicious, and violent, he treated the young scholar with an extraordinary gentleness, amounting at times to humility. He was compelled to laugh at himself and to ask whether he was blinded or bewitched, that he should show so much deference to a mere beginner, whom he had never met face to face and of whom he really knew

3

very little. Yet such moments of doubt were succeeded by others in which an inner voice proclaimed in ever stronger and clearer accents: "I have been lonely throughout my whole life; I have had parrots for my followers, blind disciples, subjects, slaves; surely I ought to rejoice if at last some friendly star is pleased to guide in my direction an equal, a helper, and an heir to my science. Surely any scruple bred of preoccupation with the customs of the scientific world and all the hindrances involved in the relation between master and apprentice must crumble to dust before the one overwhelming sensation: a friend! At last a worthy comrade and a brother!" As with kindling imagination he soared aloft from a world dominated by hierarchic obstructions, the cause of so much vexation to him, into a realm where the mind alone held sway, he felt that Kepler had penetrated his very being, that he and Kepler were almost one. The mere existence of the mighty cosmos surrounding himself and his friend filled him with such fiery rapture that the enthusiastic letters in which he praised Kepler's keen and eloquent dialectic, his learning, his ingenious speculations, and his rounded style, necessarily appeared to him a mere lifeless imprint of his devotion. After so many unedifying associations marked by insincerity and having no aim beyond expediency he was determined to be absolutely sincere in this newly-developing relationship and to permit neither falseness nor prudence to enter. Accordingly he made no secret of his regret for the words of praise bestowed by Kepler upon the Copernican system, adding that he hoped some day to win him over to his own cosmic views, the Tychonic constellation. In his very first letter he wrote in this sense, betraying not the slightest compunction at communicating the most confidential matters. "Only come," ran another letter, using the familiar "thou" permissible in the collegial Latin. "Do come. You will find

4

a friend in me who in any emergency will not fail you with help and counsel. But I would not have you driven to seek refuge with me by stress of circumstance; I want you to come at the bidding of your own free judgment and of your love and enthusiasm for the science we both serve."

At that time Kepler really was in a difficult situation. His position as university professor, and "Mathematician to the Province of Styria," was in danger. His very presence in the country was attended by danger, for Kepler was a Protestant, and the Archduke Ferdinand had recently, when on a pilgrimage, vowed to root out all heretics from his territories and was taking serious steps to give effect to this promise by decrees of banishment and by imprisonment. Kepler was forced to leave his young wife in Graz and to take refuge in Hungary. His recall was effected by certain Jesuits, who followed his scientific labours with interest and hoped eventually to make him a Catholic. Yet hardly had he set foot in the town when persecution broke out anew. His efforts to secure an appointment in his native Würtemberg were fruitless and no recourse was left him but to go to Prague. Tycho's appeals continued tirelessly in his cordial letters: "I would not have you come as a visitor. I invite you as a most welcome friend and as my dearest colleague in scanning the heavens, as far as the instruments at my disposition permit. And if you come quickly, we will certainly find you a post in which better provision than you have had hitherto will be made for you and your family."

Kepler, therefore, wrote answering Tycho's exuberance calmly and composedly. The letter was followed by others to trusty acquaintances in Prague, to Johann Homelius, to his patrons, the Privy Councillor Baron Hoffman and other persons. As all advised him to appear in Prague and seek a permanent appointment from the Emperor Rudolf, he

5

ventured upon the great journey. His wife and stepdaughter he left behind in Graz.

Tycho was no longer to be found in Prague. The Emperor's favour had assigned him the castle of Benatky on the Iser for his residence and for the construction of an observatory. The Emperor himself had left for Pilsen, an unusual occurrence, susceptible of several doubtful interpretations. Kepler, accordingly, informed Tycho of his presence in Prague; and the latter at once sent his Westphalian assistant, the young squire Franz Tengnagel, with a stout and ample travelling-carriage to meet him.

On a dull February morning in the year 1600 this carriage was standing ready to start before the inn "Beim goldenen Greif," on the Hradschin, where Kepler lodged, when a thin, elderly man appeared hastening towards them from the castle. It was the court physician, Thaddäus Hagecius, Hajek in the local dialect, who made eager signs to the two as they stood just on the point of setting out. They in their turn recognized him and gave him a friendly greeting, and upon his announcing his intention to travel with them to Benatky they gladly invited him to get in at once. Tengnagel in particular was glad to have secured such a merry chatterer for the six hours' journey, for it was difficult to extract much from the taciturn Kepler, whom Tengnagel, scenting in the new pupil a very dangerous rival for Tycho's favour, had found intolerable from the very outset.

The flood of talk broke loose at once. "I must see," babbled Hagecius, "how the country air affects the old gentleman's infernal bladder troubles. I wouldn't venture into *aula Cæsaris* at Pilsen, unaccompanied by the latest reports of Tycho's state of health, this celebrated man stands so high in our master's *favor*. You may be sure of the truth of my words, for His Majesty desires nothing so much as that every-

6

thing should be ready at hand for Tycho, appointed as well as may be for the exercise of the *studium* and *ars astronomica*.

While this conversation was in progress, the carriage descended the steep main street of the Kleinseite, rolled across the long Steinerne Brücke, and then passed into the old town. Its houses, differing entirely from those in the neighbourhood of the castle on the Hradschin and of the Kleinseite, were constructed exclusively of wood and mud. Many of the walls seemed to consist of tree-trunks only recently felled and hastily put together, the bark still adhering to them. The narrow, dirty streets were filled with a horrible stench, and fortunately the walls of the fortification were soon reached. At first the guards at the gate refused to let them pass and Hagecius had to protrude his familiar head from the window before the coach was permitted to proceed.

"The guards have received strict *rescriptum* to let nobody through without *testimonium*," explained Hagecius as soon as they were upon the open road. "The fact is, the court astrologers have predicted that a terrible pestilence will overtake the city of Prague. Why, there are even many who go so far as to assert on the strength of their *spectationes cœli* that this ghastly visitation is already spreading throughout the city. That is why the Emperor has already left for Pilsen and why I am bound for the same destination. But in order to prevent a greater perturbation, nothing *publice* is to be said." Although the wrinkled eyelids of his merry countenance drooped as he said these words, he could not repress the smile which lurked at the corners of his mouth. "His Imperial Majesty would not willingly have submitted to this interruption of his habits," he continued, "if he had not believed that his own heart was the goal of the shafts from this pestilence, for that, moreover, was foretold by the horoscope."

7

"It was my own teacher, Tycho, who prepared that horoscope," observed Tengnagel, breaking in portentously upon the doctor's sceptical utterance. "He predicted that Rudolfus Secundus should not perish from any malady, but should be murdered by a monk, just as happened to Henry III of France. Events will demonstrate the truth of this."

"What are your views upon the art of reading the stars, professor?" inquired Hagecius, at this moment turning, with a start, towards Kepler, who had all the while been sitting silently, wrapped in his grey cloak. In saying this he gave utterance to a question which at that time stirred to their very depths the spirits alike of laymen and of men of science.

Kepler was silent for a space, and it seemed as if he had not heard the question at all; but as the carriage gave a sharp jerk in traversing a bend in the road, the words came from the corner which he occupied: "Pure lies and humbug. It's a pity to disturb the atmosphere with such talk and waste time in such a way. I regard astrology as no better than an *epidemia*, which has laid hold, not merely upon individuals, but upon the greater part of humanity. With their *triangula* and houses and positions of the *firmamentum*, with their *qualitates* and *dignitates* of the stars—warmth, moisture, and cold, and their influence upon war, famine, and drought—with all this our trashy little soothsayers have only succceeded in uttering one truthful prediction: that vast quantities of their worthless, fantastic pamphlets would find a sale. In that they've been right every time." He laughed harshly and flung his shoulders back against the seat, continuing for many minutes to tug angrily at his moustache.

Tengnagel gazed at him in amazement and hostility. Never in his life had he heard such a decisive utterance upon a topic of scientific controversy, for it was unusual for Tycho to express himself in very definite language, and in questions

8

directly affecting contemporary feeling he was particularly cautious. And even the facetious doctor obviously found such plain speaking inopportune, for he was one of those troubled spirits who like to doubt everything, but who relish definite denial as little as rigid dogma, and find their one pleasure in perpetual derision and frivolous indifference. Accordingly he at once addressed himself to the task of diluting Kepler's simple words into a swamp of intricacy. It was really unjust to treat all *opera* of astrology as being on a level with such mountebanks' tricks. One must distinguish between the paltry professors of the alembic, raisers of tempests, practitioners of the hermetic arts, and wandering adepts, such as Rudolf's court unfortunately harboured in far too large numbers, and those seers of the prime who in the earliest days had inscribed upon the *tabula smaragdina* their undoubtedly profound lore. Thus Tycho Brahe himself had on one occasion correctly predicted the death of the great Sultan Suleiman.

Kepler shook his head.

"But I tell you, it is so," Tengnagel thundered at him, now frantic with rage, his hand involuntarily moving toward his sword-belt.

At this, Hagecius felt that he must once more incline to the party of Kepler in order to hold the balance. Accordingly, laying a soothing hand upon Tengnagel's shoulder, he reminded him of the two English knaves, Dee and Kelly, who had caused such a furore at court, the one with his sacred stone of crystal, the other with his drinkable gold and elixir of life, each being acclaimed as a new Hermes Trismegistus. Yet, when finally they were proved false in the *laboratio*, both came to lamentable ends.

The ironical old gentleman was now in his true element, narrating court gossip in mordant phrases, giving himself, moreover, no quarter for having worked in all good faith in

9

the alchemist's laboratory and having even published a *Prager Zeitschrift der Magier*. His remarks were addressed to Kepler in particular, for he held it to be his pleasant duty to enlighten the stranger about the conditions amid which he would now have to move. Sooner or later he would certainly be received in audience by the Emperor. The Emperor, the Emperor! . . . This ejaculation was accompanied by an ambiguous smile, and the doctor's countenance, which contracted portentously at the very least excuse, now assumed an expression of profound mystery, shrivelling up like an old parchment. The Emperor! Ah, there was a difficult *capitulum*. Some believed him to be of unsound mind, *"insania captum"* the phrase ran. But that view must be ascribed to the propaganda of the Spanish and Catholic party, which was directing its efforts towards supplying the childless man while he was still alive—he had, it was true, six illegitimate children— with a *successor* and *coadjutor* of papal leanings. None the less the loyal subject might find it strange in his master —and at these words the grey cheeks were once more invaded by a smile, whether of ceremonious respect or malice was not clear—that the Emperor should live in such uninterrupted repose and retirement. He actually caused covered walks to be constructed in his garden, merely in order that he might not be observed on the rare occasions when he took his walks abroad. Months had passed in which he had been entreated to undertake a journey to receive the homage of the Estates of Moravia. Lately, indeed, he hardly left the castle at all. He did not ride or play at ball. Sometimes he had the magnificent Spanish and Italian horses, given him by the King of Spain, led under his windows and found pleasure in watching their graceful evolutions; but that was really all. But in *res politica* he was particularly negligent, attending the meetings of his Privy Council very irregularly and

10

against his will; that was why the troubles with the Turks and the Transylvanians, and indeed his dispute with his own brother Mathias, went on interminably. . . . "Well," he concluded, regarding Kepler with the utmost content, "you'll have plenty of opportunities for experiencing all these anomalies in your own person."

"At any rate, we children of the Muses have no ground for complaint," answered the young squire. "It's not without cause that for us this is termed the Golden Age. His Imperial Majesty is graciously pleased to grant us all that our scientific operations need. You'll stare, Master Hagecius, when you see the way we have already positively bullied the hunting-box of Benatky into an Academy of Urania, a second Uranienburg. Observations are already being carried on, and we have set up a *sextans* of great power." Hagecius joined in eagerly, immediately putting questions which made it clear that he had been impelled to undertake this journey as much out of curiosity to see Tycho's new instruments and inventions as by anxiety about his health. The junker replied in tones of gusto, his descriptions growing more and more grandiose. After celebrating Tycho's renown, his understanding, and his unimaginable powers of labour, he did not forget to show himself in the most glaringly favourable light, finally intimating that, as everyone knew, Tycho had always given evidence of considerable shrewdness in mundane affairs, a shrewdness which had led him to choose a first-rate son-in-law, Mr. Franz Tengnagel.

"What! what! Excellent!" cried Hagecius, and as he bounced from his seat and fell back again with the motion of the carriage, he congratulated the young squire, who complacently gave utterance to the obvious, oft-repeated jest that he had lately taken a holiday from his speculations upon Mars and Jupiter and was giving most of his attention to his earthly

11

Venus, Elizabeth Brahe de Knudstrup. Thereupon he proceeded with his boastful description, words failing him as he strove to portray the splendour and power of Tycho's family, in which, of course, he already included himself. His fat face red and swollen, he sat stiffly in his place, his hand propped upon the hilt of his sword, which he held between his knees. It is, however, no rare thing that men of such limited intelligence end by proving the very opposite of what they set out to show. Tengnagel, as if carried aloft by the sense of importance and power generated in him by his narrative, set to abusing one Kaspar von Mühlstein, Hauptmann of the district of Brandeis and administrator of the castle of Benatky. Notwithstanding a letter from the Privy Secretary, Barvitius, this beast of a Bohemian had taken it upon himself to withold from Tycho the monthly stipend promised by the Emperor, on the ground that he had received no instruction from the Emperor or the Estates. Every alteration in the structure of a room, every stove, every wagon-load of wood was the occasion of the most embittered chaffering with this man. Only the other day he had flung into Tycho's teeth the statement that the treasury was empty, adding that even if it were full, he would sooner spend the money on the improvement of dikes and the purchase of horses and cows.

"There's your Golden Age," interjected Hagecius slyly; "an empty treasury and the whole of Europe arming against us. Isn't it true that Henry of France, just turned Catholic, has entered into *bellicosus contractus* against us with the German evangelical princes? Lutherans and Romans hate us alike, and Prague itself is kept in a condition bordering upon overt war by the insurgent Estates, the Calvinists, the Moravian Brethren, the Utraquists, the Old Hussites, and malcontents of all *genera*. No wonder that a loyal officer of the

12

Emperor looks askance at an interloping professor, however great he may be."

Hagecius addressed the junker as if his intent were conciliatory. But it was evident that he had no genuine desire to act as mediator. On the contrary, his real aim was to throw a totally different light upon Tycho, lately the subject of Tengnagel's eulogies, as he had previously in his portrait of the Emperor. He termed him a sick, feeble, weary, lamentable pilgrim, a troublesome sort of man who wandered round Europe with his family of six, his attendant students, domestics, and household familiars, his immense and costly instruments and collections, which could never be properly installed, his library, and even his own printing-press. Nowhere could he find repose. He made enemies on every hand, and his inborn tendency to claim a princely and magnificent mode of living merely gave endless opportunities to anyone who desired to torment him, opportunities which were, moreover, still further increased by his choleric disposition, his quarrelsomeness and impatience.

Tengnagel denied these charges with angry bluster, his vanity forbidding the existence of the least defect even in the remotest region of his universe; but the sceptical doctor proceeded with his destructive onslaught, and for a long time they wrangled thus. But if the whole conversation was actually designed, not to elucidate the issue between the two men, but to interest Kepler, it failed in the most singular degree to achieve its purpose; for Kepler, whom they imagined to be awaiting his future in a state of tense excitement, had no difficulty in maintaining his dignified repose between the braggart and the wiseacre. From the very outset his future existence was not in doubt. This gaunt man with the little features, as diminutive as if they were immature and undeveloped, was buoyed up by a steadfastness all his own. His intellectual faculties were keyed to the utmost tension in pursuit of a single aim, which completely shut him off from the world without, rendering him inviolable and at the same time utterly unreceptive to everything which did not directly concern his science. His whole genius and, in harmony therewith, his whole emotional force were directed toward a single aim, the scientific conquest of the world; and his attention was so exclusively concentrated upon the next step in this process, the measurement of the magnitude of the stars, that it was possible for a friend to observe that if from any given moment onwards stars ceased to exist, the existence of Johannes Kepler would also cease.

Nothing indeed could turn him away from the sole aim of his being, in the service of which was accumulated all the immortal fire within his nature, all that was great and vital in his spirit. It could flare out on the slightest occasion, as his outburst against astrology had already proved to his travelling-companions. But for all the other activities of life only meagre clinkers and dull remnants had to suffice, so that in ordinary intercourse he could often appear cold and prosaic, pedantic, prudent in a small-minded way, quarrelsome, and even quite insignificant. Other men of genius might grope their way through ordinary life with a naïveté and childishness which excited affection. Such demeanour called for a measure of vivacity and freshness. Kepler, however, expended his whole personality, heart and head alike, upon his scientific labours. Nothing was left over for human intercourse but a peevish, insignificant little shadow of himself. At the same time the unnaturalness of the situation was almost entirely removed by the fact that he himself seemed unable to support his own presence in such inappropriate surroundings; and, indeed, he never remained within the

14

realms of ordinary life a moment longer than was necessary. The satisfaction of only the most pressing necessities marked the utmost limit of his concern; otherwise life held nothing for him but work, white-hot, liberating, up-striving work. Then he would surrender himself with an almost unconscious confidence to the voice within, which guided him past the sharp places of life with the certainty of a sleep-walker, without effort or perturbation, so that all his nervous strength remained intact for his mighty task. Then all that he elsewhere seemed to lack came to him during his divine labour, fire, freshness, the spirit of a child, wit, intuition, and warm-heartedness, mighty impetus, care-free devotion. It was this devotion that led him now to Tycho, but the Tycho he sought was not the dark, fate-tossed spirit; it was the original and astonishingly exact observer of the comets, of the new star, and of the movement of Mars. What had he to do with the man's weary frame, with his dubious economic position, with his family? What did he care about Bohemia and the Emperor? He quite genuinely did not attach the least importance to his own external circumstances. Why should he trouble himself about other men's difficulties? One disposed of matters of that kind as speedily as possible. They could never be the subjects of real concern. In all confidence he was now on the way, not to that perplexed mortal Tycho, but to a lucid teacher and a place where he might work; and therefore he listened to practically nothing of what his companions said. Viewed from without, such repose might seem almost a kind of thoughtless indifference, even frivolity. It had nothing of that glad serenity which exists apart from earthly affairs; it had nothing overwhelming or astonishing in it; but it was neither more nor less than his natural condition; it betokened that his feet were now once more set upon the right track, and that work was going forward within him, let others think what they pleased.

Satisfied that they had finally brought him to a sufficient pitch of excitement, Hagecius with his critical apprehension, Tengnagel with his gasconading, the two were silent for a space. Kepler thereupon raised his voice, with its clear, rather high tones, but only to inquire how far they were from Benatky.

His fellow travellers answered with some astonishment and then rather irritably resumed their conversation, bestowing no further attention upon him. Kepler was thus enabled, unobserved, to seek a more comfortable position and soon after, still weary from the exertions lately endured in his long journey to Prague, to fall fast asleep. In slumber his small face, the lips slightly parted, became quite childlike in its serenity and repose. His breathing was clear and regular and he seemed quite immune from the assaults of evil dreams. In his balsamic calm he received the full reward for the ample, unremitting, and orderly toil of his waking hours. And just as his features were peaceful and open, revealing all that lay behind, so now the lovely plain of the Elbe extended on all sides about the travellers. No one remarked the kinship between the kindly aspect of the bushes hard by, of the low hills amid which the coach threaded its way, of the distant forest masses in their blue and leaden-grey attire, tinged with white mist along the bank of the stream, between all this freshness and repose and the happy, tranquil posture of the slender, reclining figure. No one felt how the healthy slumber seemed to shape these objects as if from the substance of its own dreams, to spread them out to the very horizon at every turn in the road and then to reabsorb them into itself. Thus, unnoticed by the travellers, these two expressions of beauty, the beauty of slumber and the beauty of the landscape, had their being

16

for one another alone, each mirrored in the dumb form which the other held up, each existing only for itself and holding no warrant from any man.

The carriage had reached the Elbe and was placed together with the horses upon a large ferry and rowed across the running stream, over which there blew a keen damp wind. Having reached the opposite bank, the carriage was about to resume its journey when a woman appeared on the high-road, suddenly stepping from behind one of the first fruit-trees. She had obviously been waiting there and now ran towards the travellers and jumped to a place by their side in the already moving carriage. She at once flung herself upon Tengnagel, kissed him with passion, and cried out like one demented, pressing his hand and arm and displaying her joy at seeing him again by every kind of extravagance and by talking rapidly and in excessively loud tones.

"This is my betrothed," panted Tengnagel from amid the embraces. And stretching out his arms in a ludicrous manner, as if he were drawing aside a curtain, he for the first time invited his companions' attention to the girl.

Elizabeth started, released her hold upon her dear one, seeming only now to notice that they were not alone. There was something noble in the natural movement with which she lowered her head. She coloured a deep red, amid which her amber-hued hair and very light eyebrows assumed a kind of incandescent aspect.

Hagecius at once and without the least embarrassment began the usual congratulations, plunging into a jovial flood of conversation. Tengnagel, too, smiled complacently, and, now that order appeared to be restored, himself turned towards the girl and saluted her as if he had not already done so. She, however, still beside herself, turned from Tengnagel to Hagecius and from Hagecius to Tengnagel, addressing them in tones of gentle complaint, as if she did not understand their indifferent conversation: "I really thought he would never come back to me."

"What are you saying?" Tengnagel turned upon her.

She laughed at his angry expression and made as if she would again fling her arms about him without any regard for the circumstances. But he frowned and met every display of tenderness with a rebuff. He went so far as to turn with quite unaffected indifference towards Hagecius, just as if the girl were not present, and continued a story which the episode had interrupted.

"You don't take the least notice of me," she exclaimed after a brief interval, her pretty, rosy face assuming a tearful expression. But the gleam of vivacity which kept constantly darting forth softened the look of pain on the young features. And the unrestrained and quite spontaneous openness with which she spoke harmonized wondrously with her April-tide countenance.

"Yes, indeed," affirmed Hagecius with dry gallantry, "beautiful young women always want attention."

"You don't ask at all how things have been going with me during your absence."

"Well, how have they been going?" was all Tengnagel could find to reply, in bearish tones.

"Badly, very badly," sighed Elizabeth. "I always thought about you. And you?"

"Yes, yes. I thought about you," said Tengnagel, and he looked at her for a moment with real expression in his great, faithful doglike eyes, before pushing her away. He had obviously had enough of this conversation; such matters did not appear to him to be so important. But Elizabeth continued: "I was so troubled about you. I really thought you meant to leave me."

18

"A little pre-matrimonial tiff?" inquired Hagecius.

"I'm sorry to say that we quarrel very often," sighed Elizabeth, with her light-blue eyes looking wistfully at her betrothed. Her lips too, full and red, seemed to gaze upon him with the same expression of yearning that appeared in the eyes.

"But we must know what the word 'quarrel' means when used by such a sensitive little hussy. If it is nothing more than a tiff—" But the tyrannical look which he now bestowed upon her seemed to belie his words.

"This marriage question is certainly a difficult one," the doctor avowed, addressing himself to both parties. He then began to chant a general refrain upon marriage, couched in the same ambiguous, mordant terms of assumed impartiality in which he had previously referred to the Emperor and Tycho, so that it was impossible to know whether he meant to praise the institution or to find fault with it.

As he was an old bachelor, he had reflected much on the subject and had a rich store of anecdotes and examples. Several times Tengnagel laughed harshly and joined in the conversation, flinging about coarse expressions. Elizabeth contradicted him with impatience. She thought of marriage as undying love, without which she would not and could not live. She would gladly have expressed herself at greater length on the subject . . . but as often as she opened her mouth, Tengnagel bestowed upon her a look of strange anxiety and displeasure, a tyrannical look, as if he feared he would hear something that would surpass his powers of comprehension, something inimical, something disgraceful to him. Several times she joined quite jubilantly in the conversation; but on each occasion he commanded silence by one of those dark glances or whispered words such as many men are accustomed to use when they appear with their wives in society. The ridiculous element lay in the fact that Elizabeth said nothing that was not full of devotion and gentleness. But he seemed to feel every independent utterance upon her lips as an offence, as something that involved danger, at least as a disagreeable disturbance of his repose, as something which he was under no compulsion to answer. Elizabeth's entire personality irritated him, and somehow or other the annoyance must be stopped. Like a man who would put out a fire with his own body and all his clothing, he seemed to fling himself with his clumsy threats and menaces upon the hot-blooded, lively girl and to wish to extinguish the soul of fire that darted within her. And as if the flame had now laid hold upon him, his features assumed a painful expression of passionate fury, the expression of a man suddenly assailed and insulted.

The coach was now passing through dense forests of pine-trees. The snow-covered soil and the chilly green of the needles glowed with a dull frosty lustre in the midday sun.

"Who is the third gentleman here?" suddenly asked Elizabeth, who had devoted the enforced period of silence to surveying the wide, dark interior of the coach. Kepler slept on, crouched in his corner so that he looked quite small.

"Nobody," shouted Tengnagel, once more annoyed.

"What, are you jealous?" asked the doctor in jest.

The girl at once turned, quite radiant, in his direction. "Do you really think it is jealousy? If only I could believe that Franz was jealous! I often feel quite sure that he is already tired of me. . . ."

"Jealous, no, no," rapped out the junker, taking his head between his hands. "Jealousy is the one thing wanting. You'd like that."

"I think he is jealous, Fräulein."

"Well, tell me who the gentleman is. He is a very good-looking handsome man, and I am sure he is clever," teased Elizabeth, joyously perceiving her advantage.

20

"Quiet, keep quiet!"

Hagecius leant towards her ear, but so that Tengnagel could hear his words. "And if I were to add that he is also a famous man, the great astronomer Johannes Kepler?"

"He! He is now to live with us in Benatky. For a long time, isn't he? Oh, I am glad!"

The slow-witted Tengnagel looked at them in utter perplexity. They seemed to have come to some understanding over his head. He clenched his fist as if Elizabeth were in it, like a little bird that sought to fly from him. His fingers contracted ever closer, while his features were twisted in despair. He had known from the very beginning that this interloper Kepler would bring him anxiety and misfortune. And now, when Elizabeth bent far forward, to obtain a close view of the sleeping stranger, and in doing so assumed a humorously amorous expression, the junker lost all self-control and shouted a brief sentence in Danish at her. She became deadly pale and sank back upon the cushion. Great tears gathered in her eyes and she spoke no more. Tengnagel, too, sat in morose silence, and the doctor's adroitness seemed exhausted. Elizabeth did not at first appear to feel the full force of the words which had been flung at her. At length, after a pause, she began to sob, but leaned her face against the side of the carriage so that she could not be seen. She trembled throughout the whole of her frame.

Happily the castle was soon reached. They passed a number of farms belonging to the domain, then through vineyards ascended a hill, taking their way between two long walls, and at last entered the huge gateway of the courtyard. The coach came to a halt. Dazed with sleep, Kepler rolled out of his seat. Although they had already awakened him as soon as the castle came in sight, he had continued peacefully to doze without any sign of curiosity. The consequence was that in

21

getting out he nearly stumbled over Tengnagel, who was standing before him and caught him by the shoulder. Tengnagel, however, naturally quarrelsome and now thoroughly roused by the dispute with his betrothed, was not inclined to give ear to the excuses of the clumsy scholar, who was still only half awake. He shook him off, uttered a roar of fury, and flung himself with menacing fists on Kepler. He would at once have administered a thrashing if at the same moment a sturdy young fellow, attracted by the sound of carriage-wheels, had not run out of the house and instantly caught the object of these threats in his arms. It was Tycho's elder son. He greeted the two guests in a friendly manner and invited them to accompany him. Upon Tengnagel he merely bestowed a few contemptuous words, uttered in a low voice, and left him standing in the courtyard, where a swarm of women, showing every sign of terror, collected about him and the weeping Elizabeth.

CHAPTER II

W HETHER IT WAS this unlooked-for scene at the very
moment of his arrival or the expectation of meeting the great
Tycho that stirred him, Kepler trembled somewhat as he
mounted the great wooden staircase, with its ancient steps. In
accordance with local custom the staircase ascended the outer
wall of the castle uncovered, and terminated as a spacious
platform, roofed over after the manner of a veranda, in the
upper part of the single story. Having climbed thus far, the
guests proceeded through several rooms, in which men were
hard at work upon carpentry. The hum of turning-lathes and
the sharp sound of planes could be heard; the odour of newly-
hewn wood, such as one inhales in sunny forest clearings,
pervaded the whole house; and a thick carpet of curly, white
shavings lay everywhere over the bare, half-finished rooms.
They next entered a laboratory, one-half of which was occupied by an oven-builder, who had spread his implements and
tiles about on the floor preparatory to the construction of an
alchemical furnace. At the wall occupied by the window, a
young man seemed to be already at work over a temporary
open fire and as profoundly absorbed in his glass tubes as if
everything about him were in perfect order. Tycho's son led
them farther through an ample but entirely empty hall,
after knocking, opened the door of the nearest room, and then
stepped aside. Hagecius entered, followed by Kepler, while
the youth withdrew.

23

The room was somewhat obscured by curtains. Towering above battlements constructed of piles of books and papers, there appeared a head, shaven to the scalp, and beneath it a broad face with prominent cheek-bones and frontal protuberances. It was covered from the moustache downwards with a growth of grizzled, fair hair. This was Tycho. At once he sprang briskly to his feet and greeted the court physician.

"This is—" began Hagecius, indicating Kepler with a wave of the hand, but Tycho straightway interrupted him:

"No one need tell me that. He is the young Hipparchus, my Benjamin, for whom I have waited long enough." And without giving the astonished Kepler a chance to utter a syllable Tycho flung himself with the full weight of his sturdy old frame upon his far smaller guest, thrice encircled him with his arms, thrice clasped him to his bosom, kissing him each time upon the lips and ejaculating: "Oh happy, happy hour!"

"With all reverence I salute the phœnix of astronomy," answered Kepler, deferentially stepping back.

"You may well call me phœnix, Kepler," cried Tycho, "for they have burned and destroyed me and all that is mine. Whether I shall ever rise again from amid my ashes, as the poets sing of that wondrous bird, the year that has just dawned will show, and it is true that it opens with a quite unprecedented conjunction of two bright stars." With these words he again took Kepler's hand and pressed it to his heart. "Ah no, today is not the first occasion of our being near one another, my dear friend! As I once wrote to my good comrade Pratensis: 'Our eyes, which cannot see one another upon earth, met in the bright heavens.'" Tycho's eyes grew bright, and in reverberating tones he began to quote some Latin distichs which, years before, he had dedicated to that friend: "When my eyes behold the same star as that upon which your gaze is concentrated, the vault of the heaven unites us whose

24

bodily union the earth will not suffer." In the very act of declamation, as he beat time with mighty sweeps of his left hand, he stopped and with the right pushed a chair towards Kepler. Then he kept silence for a space and gazed rapturously upon the new-comer's countenance, as if only now he beheld it aright. Taking his cap from his hand, he laid it carefully upon a pile of books and stationed himself again so as to face Kepler, stamping his feet upon the ground as if he could not contain his joy. "This is the first happy moment I have known for months, I might say for many years," he cried, and turned to Hagecius, upon whose arm he leaned heavily. Thus leaning backwards, he viewed Kepler from a distance. The latter sat not without embarrassment in the place assigned to him, while Tycho's expression, his strange, his, as it were, ardent silence, the twitching of his eyelids, and his almost coquettish smile seemed to say: "Now isn't he a treasure, my Benjamin?"

The spell cast by Tycho's singular, vivacious behaviour, which filled the whole room, held not only Kepler, but even the otherwise experienced Hagecius. The latter, indeed, seemed somewhat disappointed; for he had hoped that the graceful salutation, with allusions to Hipparchus and the phœnix, would be followed by some neat mythological remarks, according to the custom prevailing among the learned. Instead of this, Tycho, whose natural emotionalism broke out, entirely neglected the Latin interpolations so indispensable among people of cultivation. His speech came bubbling forth, forceful and unadorned, like that of a labourer, with a purity (and simplicity that the courtier found barbaric. Tycho, however, observed nothing of the astonishment which he spread about him. With a downright childish arrogance, one leg thrown forward, the mighty belly thrust out, the face flung upwards, and both hands tugging at the thick moustache, the ragged ends of which he twisted still farther down, he seemed to defy the whole world with his huge frame, mingling now with his words contemptuous insults for his enemies, in particular the Scot Craig and the court mathematician Raymarus Ursus, whom he termed a dirty Ditmarsh beast. "Let them all come now. With my Kepler at my side I am invincible."

Someone knocked at the door.

"What is it?" cried Tycho furiously.

A tall, fair woman entered; it was Tycho's wife, Christine. "I am only bringing something for your guests, Tyge."

Although she pointed clearly enough to a maid who followed her, bearing a large tray with a cold collation and bottles of wine, Tycho seemed unable or unwilling to understand the connexion. He barred the way to the advancing women and harassed them with continual repetitions of: "What is it? What is it? What is it?" so that they withdrew again to the door. The maid cried out; the glasses rattled. When his wife rejoined, it was with an obstinate, unamiable expression. "What is it?" he replied, cowed. "Is it bad news?" His imposing demeanour shrank to nothing. Now it was noticeable that the fiery words and gestures of a few moments ago sprang from no constant source of energy, but from a short-lived intoxication, which from fear of reality he would gladly have prolonged. "Here are my friends. Here is my temple of the Muses. Why am I disturbed?" he demanded of his wife, who took no great pains to soothe him, but placed the tray upon a pile of books and departed at once. Her care-worn features made it obvious that she was utterly weary of these eccentricities. "Even Phœbus must put up with the clouds," observed Tycho, and then turned to his guests and bade them fall to. Yet it was amazing how the formerly vivacious countenance had shrunk into an empty shell, almost cunningly harsh in its lifelessness; all the furrows carved by enthusiasm seemed

26

to have disappeared behind the smooth, stony, and now some-what pallid surface of his face. It was altogether another man that stood before them, a shrewd, calculating personality, no longer one that wantoned in the abundance of his emotions. And now his voice was lowered and he spoke quite differently, although somewhat sharply, of other matters, more immediate and trivial. Thus he observed the fresh bruise upon Kepler's brow, dealt him by Tengnagel, and jestingly inquired whether he had come by it in the course of his love-affairs and warned him, indicating his own nose: "A reminiscence of my student days at Rostock. My friend Parsbjerg and I quarrelled about a lady. We fought our duel in the dark and he cut away half my nose. Do look at it. I now wear a plate of gold and silver. It is well and strongly made." In response to his desire the guests were forced not only to examine, but also to touch the artificial part of the nose. He attached great importance to it, he urged, as they seemed unwilling to proceed to this in-timacy. Their reluctance was caused by their having at this moment observed that the peculiar rigidity of Tycho's coun-tenance seemed to originate in this very plate, and so the region made a somewhat uncanny impression. He attached great importance to it, he continued, since his pampleteer-enemies, such as the aforesaid Ursus, were in their coarseness not ashamed to write jestingly of him that he carried out his astronomical observations through his nose, which he used as a sight-vane. Moreover, he was at that very moment employed in dealing a master-stroke to that sorry wraith. Professor Magini of Bologna had last year promised to compose a eulogy upon him; of this promise he would remind him on the occasion of sending him his new work, in order that the childish detractor might once and for all be silenced by the voice of a foreign witness of great repute, one free from bias.

Speaking in this wise, Tycho had approached his writing-table, to which Kepler, too, now drew near, keenly expectant. The work alluded to—Tycho's catalogue of stars—lay in a number of fresh copies, all ready for dispatch to the most eminent of scholars and patrons. Tycho pointed to the carefully contrived accompanying letters, which he had written that day; to the Emperor, to the Archduke Mathias, to the Vice-Chancellor Corraducius, to Wolfgang Theodor, Archbishop of Salzburg, to the Bishop of Lübeck, to Professor Brucäus in Rostock, to Heigel in Augsburg, to the Duke of Kassel, to the Prince of Orange, and to Sçaliger in Leyden. Kepler was astonished at this stupendous correspondence; Tycho, however, added an observation to the effect that this was only a small portion of that which was dispatched almost every week from Benatky. Every passing trader brought questions from learned colleagues, requests for an opinion and for a design for the construction of instruments; quite often, too, requests bearing upon purely mundane topics, such as, perhaps, for Tycho's good word with some great lord. All this must be conscientiously dealt with and, if possible, answered by the next postal opportunity that presented itself. Despite all industry, of course, such labour occasionally overwhelmed one—Tycho pointed with a laugh to the shelves ranged along the wall, wherein piles of letters, neatly bound together, lay in readiness on every side. The floor, too, was covered with files of pamphlets and papers of every sort, ranged in rows. Everywhere one saw the marks of a strong inclination to orderly arrangement, albeit it was no less obvious that this surging mass of trivialities in its formlessness made light of all control by man. With an air of satisfied pride Tycho displayed a list of all the scholars with whom he maintained correspondence. "The man of science," he observed, "is cosmopolitan. He must, if possible, be in all countries at the same time and teach everywhere; he must grudge

28

no labour where it is a question of making straight the paths for a truth which he has discovered." Then, however, he began to lament the difficulties of this task. No one would believe what obstacles one had to contend with in the most matter-of-course affairs! He produced a bundle of documents relating to transporting his instruments from the island of Hveen to Benatky. The simple removal of scientific apparatus had grown to the stature of a veritable political question, since the Senates of Hamburg and Magdeburg, hostile to the Austrian Government since the Schmalkald War, had dealt with the matter with intentional dilatoriness and the Emperor himself had intervened by letter.

"Such misfortunes I meet with in everything," sighed Tycho, "but what matter? *Tu ne cede malis!* One must do one's duty and despise chance." A picture of sober worth and industry, he laid his hand now on one bundle, now on another, as if to appease them, and gloated over Kepler's amazement when finally he opened yet another drawer, in which copies of all letters which had been dispatched were laid out in orderly rows.

"That I could never imitate," admitted Kepler in unfeigned contrition. "Now I see for the first time how slovenly I am. I have not even the energy to answer the most important letters. They lie about and get lost, how I don't know. Years after, I come upon scraps of urgent letters still unanswered. I am a terribly negligent, slothful man."

"I can confirm that, as far as our correspondence is concerned," laughed Tycho. "Anyone but myself would assuredly have felt bitterly offended at such irregular replies. But I am tolerant and prefer to let everyone manage his affairs in his own way. But, as regards myself, I will admit in strict confidence that I find that every species of disorder in human intercourse, including, therefore, correspondence, is a

29

convenience that one permits oneself at others' expense. Either out of sheer light-mindedness one does not reflect, or one lacks the power to imagine how seriously one injures and obstructs the other and robs him of energy, by letting him wait God knows how long for an answer which he is entitled to expect. I find it inconsiderate, I find it unfriendly. Granted that the task of writing entails a serious digression from the more important labour in the service of Urania; we are upon earth not only for our own sakes and for the sake of our work, but also for the sake of our neighbour, with whose just demands our own desires must come to terms." And with a laugh he added that he begged Kepler, even if he should no longer require instruction in the mighty sphere of starry lore, to be his pupil at least in those matters.

These words were uttered jokingly, but his flashing eyes proclaimed that with this relationship between pupil and teacher was bound up, and far more completely than he avowed, his inmost desire, a desire of which perhaps he was himself not fully conscious. With the evident joy of the teacher he added that he had in general observed even in Kepler's letters to other people which had chanced to come to his notice, how lightly he took the titles of the various recipients. Nor did he bestow due care upon the orthography of the names, although he must know that everybody found in the spectacle of his own name being spelt with consistent inaccuracy a most offensive form of negligence.

"You must free yourself of that habit," he said in gentle tones, bending confidentially towards Kepler. That now, after the ardour of his first remarks had flagged, he should retain a familiar form of address for the uses of a more tranquil conversation proved how profound was the sympathy which he felt for the young scholar.

"I am so slack in these matters," sighed Kepler, who seemed

30

to find no difficulty, but even a certain pleasure in depreciating himself.

"Slow lead has its own strength no less than lively mercury"; Hagecius bestowed his compliments upon both sides. "Let us hope that this new amalgam of the two may result in giving us the philosophers' stone."

The remark was only aimed at the obvious difference existing between the two temperaments; it went, however, far deeper than he himself realized. For two fundamentally different mentalities met in Tycho and Kepler, the simple, uncalculating Kepler plunging forward upon his own path, defying all obstacles and almost unconscious of his course, and the discordantly fashioned Tycho, whose soul lay irrevocably sundered between the wildest emotion and the shrewdest powers of judgment and self-criticism. Everything in Kepler, in spite of his youth, was well adjusted and without difficulty set in train for the loftiest achievements; whereas Tycho, almost breaking down under the burden of the manifold contradictions of his nature, seemed to exert all his energies in striving after unity. Perhaps there was in this unity for which Tycho strove something higher than that characterized by Kepler's innate equanimity; perhaps the decisive factor lay in the first instance simply in Tycho's more impetuous and many-sided humanity or merely in his age and experience. Whatever the cause, he was for the moment quite secure in his role of guide and instructor, and neither he nor Kepler had the slightest presentiment that the relations were soon to be reversed with demonic force. Tycho spoke with enthusiasm of his "Herculean task," the combination of the duties of life with those of scientific inquiry, Kepler listening devotedly the while; and when Tycho now opened the doors of the next room, which was equipped as a temporary observatory, the young man felt that he had reached the goal of his dreams.

By breaking down some of the walls a large room, which on two sides led to roofed balconies, had been formed in the corner of the building. Here, too, as everywhere in the castle, there was an odour of fresh woodwork and damp mortar. The wall which faced one on entering was completely dominated by Tycho's great wall-quadrant, one of his most famous instruments, absolutely indispensable to him, the only large piece that he had brought with him from Hveen. It consisted of a brightly shining bow of brass, with a radius of nearly six feet, clamped to the wall by strong steel screws.

Kepler immediately hastened towards it, not knowing what to admire first, the peculiar sight-vanes, invented by Tycho himself, the improved graduation, the new clock-work, of a kind which he had never yet beheld, or the ingenious apparatus for adjusting errors in calculation.—Suddenly the habitually taciturn man burst into a flood of adoring ejaculations, ran to and fro along the wall covered by the apparatus, and finally seized Tycho's hand and imprinted a long kiss upon it, upon the wizard hand which had summoned all these marvels into existence.

Greatly touched, Tycho stroked Kepler's hair. It gratified him to receive recognition from one who could appreciate as no one else the full significance of the work which he had accomplished. And indeed it was his principal merit to have realized for the first time the value of careful measurements and systematically conducted observations, and to have stated that view with insistent emphasis. For, strange as it may sound, it had never occurred to his predecessors, not even to the great Copernicus, to verify the astral positions handed down from antiquity. They had contented themselves with incidental observations, satisfied if their systems harmonized in a general way with the exigencies of philosophy and mathematics.

On a small table standing before the great quadrant lay
32

manuscripts whereon were traced the paths of Mars and other planets, which Tycho had for decades plotted out day by day. "A jewel fit to be set amid the regalia of princes!" exclaimed Kepler in a transport of joy, at once beginning to glance through the pages, from which he would only too gladly never have severed himself.

Tycho, however, forced him to bear him company, not letting him dally by the other magic inmates of the room, the powerful armillæ, the Jacob's staffs, and the globes which automatically recorded the movements of the sun and the phases of the moon. For the memory of his observatory in the island of Hveen brought with it a stab of pain, that incomparable building which he had caused to be erected entirely in harmony with his own taste, with such royal magnificence and elegance that it had become a romantic wonder of the world of his day. Twenty precious, fruitful years he had passed there, and then, three years before the moment of which we are speaking, he had been driven away. What now awakened wonder in his guests was for him a mere paltry fragment of the days of his grandeur. He much preferred, therefore, to exhibit his new labours, which if less imposing in appearance were in his eyes many times more valuable, as proofs of a yet unbroken strength.

Accordingly he did not pause in the next room, where almost the whole space was taken up by a celestial globe upon which for the last five and twenty years he had registered the stars in harmony with his own observations. Kepler would have preferred to show his appreciation for this almost fabulous achievement by putting a few expert questions. But Tycho pulled a cord, and a silken covering floated down from the ceiling, ingeniously shrouding the huge sphere on all sides.

Only in the next room, which contained his library, did he

permit himself solace. He exhibited some rare books, pointing with particular pride to an original manuscript of Copernicus, the unprinted *Commentariolus*, which had been distributed in a few copies to contemporaries, friends of the scholar, and had reached Tycho through the good offices of Hagecius. (The doctor, to whom the two had been paying less and less heed, now enjoyed a brief spell of importance.) Kepler caught at it. Without letting the manuscript go, Tycho gazed at him with a momentous expression. "Now you see," he said, "what an injustice is done me when I am represented as an enemy of this great man. No one can hold him and his works in greater honour than I." With these words he restored the sheets to their place and drew his guests' attention to an armilla, the first and only one which he had hitherto had prepared in Benatky. He lingered by it with particular affection and explained the numerous little carved figures with which the tastefully gilded tripod was adorned. At every corner of this tripod sat enthroned one of the monarchs who had most notably advanced the cause of astronomy: Alfonso of Spain, Charles V, Rudolf II, and Frederick II of Denmark, the two last of significance as patrons of Tycho. Beneath the kings the great astronomers themselves were portrayed, looking up towards the rulers: Ptolemy and Albattani, Copernicus and Apianus. Tycho himself was among them. Latin epigrams were inscribed upon metal plaques. Tycho read them out, and it seemed almost as if these poetic works of his were as important in his eyes as his scientific achievements.

Kepler stood strangely affected and shook his head as with great seriousness Tycho now began to pass from one to another of the remaining marvels with which the room was equipped. Every free space on the wall was covered with devices and symbols. There were rampant lions, whose tails, raised high above their backs, ended in hissing serpents, which

34

in like manner reared themselves against a shield. Then came Tycho's armorial bearing, with the device: "Nor power, nor wealth, only the sceptre of the spirit shall prevail." A column bore the inscription: "I stand firm and am secure. Let the winds howl and the waves beat." A distich over the door contained an encomium upon Benatky, termed on account of its beauty, not because of its frequent floodings, the Bohemian Venice, and expressed a joy that here a place of repose was found.

Hagecius found such verses and heraldic allusions greatly to his taste. Kepler, however, stood first on one foot, then on the other, quite openly bored. Both, it is true, the dried-up courtier no less than the energetic young scientist, found something incomprehensible in Tycho's propensity towards this environment, with its wealth of allusions. Assuredly one must oneself have been a storm-tossed soul, the object of much hostility, sympathetically to appreciate so profound a seclusion of the spirit within itself, the building up of such ramparts, in which lay the hunted, wounded hero's whole craving for repose, such a profound longing in that bosom, habituated to woe, to hearten itself ever anew by means of mottoes, secret signs, recollections of youth, as if by magic formulæ of exorcism, to exhort and comfort itself, to treat itself with a portentous seriousness upon every issue and in defiance of the world, and to hold fast with every fibre to each happy minute as a gift of an otherwise niggardly destiny, in order to drink from it new draughts of energy for action.

Oh, there was no trifling, but the direct need for protection and comfort, implicit in these verses and designs, which Tycho himself conceived. Here he made light of his banishment from home: "Everywhere heaven is above me, earth beneath my feet." There he poured contempt upon his comrades of the estate of nobles who had rejected his learning as an unworthy occupation; a tree was depicted, the branches on the right fruitful, those on the left barren, with the device: "We live by the spirit; all else perishes." Beneath the half that was in bloom sat a youth with a laurel wreath about his brow, a celestial globe and a book in his hands; under the withered portion a skeleton stood by a table, on which lay a sceptre, a crown, cards, and dice.

Tycho pointed to this relief with a fervour that was positively religious, and then to a little board with threadbare ribbons hanging from it. It was the small edition of the Ptolemaic almagest, the first astronomical book which, at the price of two Joachimsthaler, hoarded with difficulty, he had bought surreptitiously as a young student in Copenhagen, when he should have been studying jurisprudence.

"Truly these are things of good omen," said Hagecius with forced gentleness and respect.

"One must surround oneself exclusively with things of good omen," answered Tycho excitedly. "Life is so evil that it at once combines with everything evil near us and becomes overwhelming. The best thing of all, therefore, is to inhabit an island which one has prepared and cleansed in accordance with one's own wishes. With sea all about and walls too, no entrance . . . I am not referring to my own island of Hveen," he hastened to add in horror, as if caught by surprise; "I mean every island in general, a separate kingdom . . . See, my friends, how a man must cut off from himself that which is evil. If it can't be flung into the sea, let it at least be enclosed in a stout leather pouch." He indicated with a laugh the little box in which he kept concealed Christian's ungracious letter of banishment. It must not, as it were, infect the other things in the room. He came forward with the box jestingly, yet his action revealed the superstitious gravity of the man who, so often and so unexpectedly assailed

36

by fate, expected every minute new and mysterious calamities.

Kepler had not been listening to Tycho's last remarks; he stood by the bookcase and inquired whether he might borrow certain works. Tycho handed him the desired volumes with alacrity. But when Kepler further demanded the *Commentariolus,* he started. It seemed to displease him that Kepler should show so much interest in the discoverer of the rival system of the universe and he made no attempt to conceal it. "The work is out of date," he said, and, producing a register in which with his accustomed care he entered the books just borrowed, he continued murmuring that that was quite enough for the present.

CHAPTER III

Hour after hour, the afternoon was passed in conversation of the kind described. At last Hagecius remembered that the real motive of his visit was a medical examination. The kidney disease which he had recently discovered in Tycho's system would assuredly call for careful treatment.

But with an ardent glance at Kepler, Tycho rebuked him: "Not you, doctor; this is the man to bring me new youth and health." And he refused to be interrupted in his exposition. Darkness had fallen long before and only the flickering fall of snow, which continued to descend outside, spread a pale glimmer throughout the library. There was a knock at the door and two of Tycho's pupils entered. "Do you bring bad news?" he flung at them, and involuntarily advanced a few steps, as if to expel them, a recently acquired habit of his.

No, they had only come to bid him to their common repast.

"Is it really as late as that?" laughed Tycho, extending his hands in invitation to his guests. "This is Kepler. These two are only Longomontanus and Johannes Müller of Brandenburg," he introduced them in jest. Kepler bowed, confused and a little offended at Tycho's offhand manner. His astonishment increased when he observed that the two assistants who had been accorded such abrupt treatment, who, moreover, had already made a name for themselves in the scientific

38

world, were the same men whom he had come upon in one of the first rooms busied with carpentry.

They descended to the ground-floor, where in the great hall a noisy company already sat, ranged about oaken tables. Tycho took his place with dignity by his wife's side at the upper board. "Like Zeus beside Hera," whispered Hagecius. And indeed the scholar sat enthroned a veritable ruler of the gods, as overlord of so many men who derived their significance and dignity from him; for according to the patriarchal custom the pupils and the assistants of lesser degree, the older family servants, and also the serving-men and women of the domain were present together with the guests at the repast, so that from the upper to the lower end of the table all who supported the family by their labour were now united by the bond of common enjoyment. Tycho would have it thus, and it was with pleasure that he surveyed a numerous assemblage of his own folk, even if this very exuberance of young life, which often rose with its intractable designs in revolt against his domination, at times occasioned anxiety and discord. A considerable part of his energies indeed went to the fulfilment of this administrative task, and yet he did not abandon it. As a symbol of his patriarchal power he had all the plates duly ranged in pillars before him, and likewise the mighty spoon from which, after saying grace, he dealt out to every one his portion of soup, which was then passed from hand to hand to the appointed person. Only the following courses were carried round by the servants; the solemn opening of the meal had, in accordance with an old custom of the house, to proceed from the master himself.

"Why is Elizabeth absent?" inquired Tycho, turning to his wife. His glance was stern, like that of a prince who discovers that his court lacks its full complement.

39

"She is unwell; she doesn't want to eat," answered Christine.

"What is the matter with her?"

"Well, she had a quarrel with Tengnagel," his wife replied in a low tone, yet with a harsh note in her voice. Only now did Tycho remark that his wife's expression, like that of the elder children, was moody, as if some disaster threatened everyone. Tengnagel, on the other hand, sat there expansive and cheerful between the two younger sisters, who were still children, entertaining them with his sallies.

"Once more I repeat," whispered Tycho in low tones to his wife, "this betrothal has never been to my liking. The junker is a rough man without culture, without love for learning, and, what is more, without love for the girl. He wishes to marry a woman of high rank, a Brahe de Knudstrup; that is the sum of his emotions. This betrothal, I am sure, is less the result of Elizabeth's wishes than of your scheming."

"Do I ever interfere with your affairs?" his wife answered sharply. "Then keep your hands off mine; you don't understand them. You are quite blind where your children are concerned. Your enterprises have almost brought us to starvation; there must be an end of that. This marriage will be my work, that is quite true; and what is more, it must and will come about. Yet instead of advancing it, you are such a clever man that you send the betrothed, when finally we've got him here, to Prague, so that in the end he may run about the world just as he pleases and never come back again."

"I really don't understand you," observed Tycho unwarily. "I could easily have got over the loss of the junker."

At this Christine lost all patience. "So you mean to act with Elizabeth as you did with Magdalena?" Tycho turned pale.

Belonging to a distant past and usually never alluded to, the matter was one that still gave him pain. Years before,

40

Magdalena, the eldest daughter, had been betrothed to one of his pupils, Gellius Sascerides; but a quarrel between teacher and pupil, which was fought out in public and had actually reached the jurisdiction of the senate of the university, had severed the tie. Since that date the already delicate Magdalena had withered; she would speak with no strange man, and her silent presence in the ever bustling house constituted a perpetual reproach to Tycho, who, in addition to much trouble coming from without, had now to bear this calamity originating in his own family. He did not consider himself responsible for the unhappy issue of the affair, yet in secret it weighed upon him and he now felt it as something malignant that his wife should unexpectedly remind him of it. He sat silent and drank with Kepler alone, each in turn emptying a bumper.

In the mean time Hagecius was once more making himself prominent with his court gossip. Tengnagel and Tycho's sons were always at hand with questions, that his flow of talk might not run dry.

Above them Tycho sat with bowed head, staring before him at the table and emptying his bumper again and again. When after a long pause he began to speak, his countenance, looming above the stiff white ruff, had become a deep purple. As before, he spoke only to Kepler, but his voice soon expanded to its natural strength and it was impossible not to hear him, although the room resounded with the incessant din of the other talkers. The wine had loosened his tongue, had dissipated his reserve and regard for his entourage into a gentle misty twilight full of a sweet weariness, and now permitted him to speak without disguise of that which was at once his pride and his greatest grief, of the island of Hveen, from which the young Danish King, crediting the slanders of malevolent tongues, had so ignominiously driven him. In

41

exuberant and yet solemn language, now hardly addressed to any audience, as if intoxicated by his own deep sorrow, he seemed to be chanting a lament at the loss of this prized possession: "There I had everything that was dear to me, everything that I needed for the practice of my art. And I had built everything for myself, drawing it forth from the bare white reef, with the aid of God and of the good King who is no more. Of course he understood as little of my art as his son, may God amend him, in this respect—in no other respect will I say anything against him, nor cavil at him—let all hear me—or find any fault whatever—but the father, who, as I said, understood astronomy no better, that royal father loved and trusted me, and so in his wisdom lent his aid to a work which will give his name with mine to eternity. It was my work; everything was set up in accordance with my estimates and calculations, according to my wishes and needs, a real stronghold of my Muse Urania, the like of which before me no scholar of the stars has possessed. Oh, what a mighty achievement, a labour without parallel! A castle reared itself upon the island, built in our tasteful modern style, richly adorned, in all respects after my heart. It had a great number of pointed roofs, which could be removed when we examined the stars. The whole castle, with the exception of the living-rooms, was filled with my magnificent apparatus. Every single instrument was placed just as I needed it, so that I could use it to the best advantage. Every pupil, and pupils swarmed into the castle, had his task, his appointed time, and his chamber. What a divine order reigned there! Every day some profitable discovery was made in the service of science. Our harvest was expanding and soon, as sheaf was quietly heaped upon sheaf, we should have grasped the key to the seven spheres of the firmament! And above this sublime and assiduous labour our token, a golden weather-vane in the form

42

of Pegasus, gleamed across the sound towards Helsingör. O my Hveen, isle of Venus, as I rightly named you, scarlet-hued island, star of the northern seas, how I loved you!

"I have not yet told you anything about a second building designed purely for our scientific purposes, which was constructed on the southern side of the island. It was called Stellæburgum, the citadel of the stars, and was situated entirely underground; only the cupolas projected like hillocks above the ground. This was my new method of protecting the instruments against the wind. I also composed an inscription wherein I represented the Muse as expressing her astonishment at this cellar and promising to point the way to the stars from this very spot, from the depths of the earth. No less prodigious, I must admit, was the astonishment of the King's treasurer when the architects presented their accounts for our crypt. Notwithstanding, every account was at once paid with the utmost generosity; the good King even gave me a benefice over and above, when he discovered that I had expended my private fortune on these buildings for the glory of the land. But our achievements justified the extraordinary outlay; that everyone saw. We were at our instruments day and night; there was work for twenty students and more. Sovereigns of all lands came to investigate these activities, which seemed so strange to them; kings and Grand Duchesses were my guests. Poets and artists came in haste to celebrate these new wonders of the universe. Oh, there was plenty to look at on my island. I laid out fish-ponds; there was hawking and shooting; provision was made for recreation after work, and we even had our paper-mills to produce paper for my books and those of my friends. I spent more than half my revenues on laying out the park, for I thought that I should end my life there and hand down all this beauty to my children. And now they have let me grow old there and then suddenly taken everything from me. No one will be able to carry on what I so gloriously began. Alas, the work of construction and of cunningly directed, healthful creating is followed by the work of hatred, of demolition, of senselessness, of injustice. Oh, injustice that knew no bounds! Why am I chastised so unjustly, so harshly, so senselessly? The sanctuaries of my art were made a desert, the hills of the Sternenburg, those breasts of the Muses, were torn open and laid waste by peasants' ploughshares. And there is no one, no one there to turn aside this destruction from a work for which I have given the best strength of my youth, myself without reserve. . . ." Tycho ceased speaking; he sang and sobbed, quite unconscious of the unseemliness of an outburst in this place. Only Kepler, to whom his words were immediately addressed and at whom he stared fixedly during his declamation, listened to him. All the others, quite unconcerned, exchanged noisy conversations across the table, shouted him down, and laughed undisguisedly.

Suddenly Tycho broke off abruptly and, turning towards the whole company, stood up in his place and cried: "Listen, I give you a poem, an elegy to the ungrateful fatherland."

For a space silence reigned. The crackling of the great fire in the chimney and the guttering of the torches upon the wall could be heard.

In expressing his feelings in language which he had shaped some time previously, with a special view to publicity, Tycho was undoubtedly trying to come back into the circle of the meal-time gathering; yet it argued not a little blindness that he should not feel that he was making an exhibition of himself before these half-drunken, full-fed men, readier for grossness than for enthusiasm. Some did not understand his Latin; others, as members of his family, found pleasure in a singular attitude of ridicule and disrespect towards him. While

44

in peremptory hexameters he now declaimed his indictment of Denmark, the uproar speedily broke loose again, and finally nothing but the rhythm of his booming phrases could be heard. At last he realized his forlorn situation, came to a hasty conclusion, and resumed his seat, to seize Kepler's hand in an ebullition of the most profound and affectionate yearning. "Now you tell us something. You speak. Tell us all about your life."

But Kepler, who entirely lacked the aptitude and the desire to play such a role, whose cool, accurate glance, moreover, had completely taken in the unseemliness of the situation, refused. Thereupon Tycho exhorted him all the more passionately, the more so as he was vaguely conscious that in his previous exuberance he had behaved foolishly. "Give us at least a toast; say a few words!"

All at once Tengnagel intervened: "Yes, why doesn't he speak, the supercilious fellow? I knew very well what wind was carrying him along to bring him here in the end."

The ever gentle Kepler answered that he had unfortunately caught cold and was hoarse, and in order to substantiate this he raised his voice to a higher pitch than before. He did not, however, get very far. Hardly had he uttered two complete sentences, which Tengnagel again boisterously interrupted, so that an altercation seemed inevitable, when he was stricken dumb with amazement at a horrible apparition which suddenly reared itself above the table. A creature, half-man, half-dog, rose up by Tycho's chair, at the foot of which it had previously lain, a dwarf, with tawny countenance overgrown with hair, wearing cap and bells and a red jacket, which closely spanned his pointed hump. This was Jeppe, Tycho's fool, who from time to time under the table received morsels of food from his master's hand; more fitly to be termed a faithful, harmless animal than a man. It was rare for any sound to emerge from this monster. But when he did speak, he was listened to with some attention, for it was already a matter of experience that Jeppe's dark utterances came to fulfilment. He was accordingly credited with the gift of second sight.

The dwarf now rose to his feet, emitting a sound like the blast of a trumpet, while the wrinkles of his swarthy countenance trembled in convulsions, until from the rigid, protruding lips the words burst forth, as in poignant anguish: "On guard! Guard the master!"

All looked at him in astonishment, for Tycho sat at ease in his elbow-chair before his wine and food, still beyond the reach of any strife, while immediate danger seemed rather to threaten Kepler and Tengnagel. "Guard him? Against whom, then?" inquired some derisively.

"Against that man there!" stormed Jeppe, brandishing about with trembling hands, until the bells on his cap tinkled.

"Against that man there! Against the new scholar! Against Kepler!" cried Tengnagel, availing himself of the dwarf's onslaught and seizing his quivering hand as if it were a divining-rod to turn it in Kepler's direction. "Yes, that I will!" And already he was standing between Tycho and Kepler, as though he would thrust Kepler away and so at the same time reconquer the place of honour at Tycho's side, which until this evening had been his.

But with a rough blow Tycho flung Jeppe's head back under the table. For a minute this strange figure had really seemed to fit in admirably with Tycho's mysterious visions; it had simply appeared like a symbol from the library come to life. But already Tycho had assumed his other mien, that of cool, deliberate forcefulness, and commanded tranquillity about him. All would have ended satisfactorily if Tengnagel, undoubtedly somewhat bemused with wine, had not flung further

46

opprobrium at Kepler and finally cried out: "I won't put up with it. One of us must give way, Kepler or I!"

"Then it will be you." Tycho now raised his voice to the pitch of thunder and sprang to his feet, so that the plates rattled.

The junker hesitated, taken aback, but the next moment his sword had left its scabbard.

Then, without the least warning, Elizabeth, his betrothed, seized his arm. Hearing from the next room her father's noisy utterances about the island of Hveen, she had slipped in and, hiding behind the back of the nurse, had taken her place unobserved at the lowest end of the table, where, almost alone of the company, she had heard every word of what Tycho said and had carefully taken it all in. Soon she had broken forth into low, bitter sobbing, as if she felt within her own breast a like fate of lost beauty, of shame and misfortune, as if every tone of grief uttered by her father found an echo and an intensification in her. When Tengnagel began flinging forth his challenges, she had crept nearer and now stood by him on the right. "What do you want, Franz?" she cried to her betrothed; and then, turning a tear-stained countenance, white as death, towards her father, she implored him: "Don't send him away, father; spare him and spare me!"

"Just tell your father all that you told me today," burst out her enraged mother, now also in tears. "Tell him that he may at last understand. He won't listen; he sees nothing." But Elizabeth no longer knew how to repel this attack on three fronts; she sank weeping at her parents' feet, at the same time raising her hands in entreaty to the storming junker. Tycho's wife seemed to have lost all her self-control and behaved like one beside herself, her eldest son with difficulty restraining her.

But Tycho maintained his iron demeanour, although shaken

to the depths of his being by this unexpected and to him utterly incomprehensible scene. With his arm outstretched towards Tengnagel, "Leave the room immediately," he cried, "you damned mischief-maker."

"Then I shall go too," cried Christine. "And Elizabeth will go, we shall all go. For that can't be." And in very truth the children rose from their places, all united against Tycho.

The latter, as if unconscious of it all, stood fast amid the tumult; he could hardly discern any longer what was going forward about him, but merely continued to make a helpless movement of the hand in the direction of Hagecius and Kepler, as if begging them to excuse him. "I must conclude the meal," he muttered, utterly exhausted, and stumbled towards the door; from there, once more thundering out with full strength, "Go to bed, all of you," he cried, and repeated it to his guests in gentler tones in the form of an invitation, making a final effort to uphold his dignity. But no one listened to him any longer. The members of his family contended for or against Elizabeth, who hid her face in her hands, and the servants, who at the spectacle of such dissensions considered themselves also entitled to a certain degree of insubordination, remained seated at the table, even when the pupils repeated the master's command. The men drummed with their fists on the table, banged their mugs together, making a sound like the breaking of stones, and began a chorus which with its horrible glee drowned the wild clamour of strife. All the order seemed to be at an end. At the door Christine held her husband back, speaking abusively to him in words which he seemed not to understand. He turned wildly upon her and asked what she meant. But thereupon his eldest son flung himself forward to protect his mother, standing like a solid block in his father's way, and spoke in low tones to the shattered man, who gave him no heed. In the mean time Jörgen, the second son, struggled in the corner with Tengnagel and dragged the sword from his hands. Magdalena, with her frozen calm, who had beheld everything with wide-open, terrified eyes, was the first to recover herself. She passed Tycho in silence and left the hall. Now, moreover, the two guests awoke as from a state of torpor, bade a servant conduct them to their rooms, and soon left behind them the uproar, with which the shrill outcries of the fool were once more mingled.

CHAPTER IV

"THERE IS NO doubt about this being an enchanted castle," said Kepler, as he stood in the cold, dark corridor, taking leave of Hagecius before the door of his room.

"Didn't I tell you so?" replied the old man, exultantly; "but you will experience very different kinds of *tumultus* here."

At this moment a frantic outcry was heard mingled with the barking of dogs and reports like blows struck with the flat of a sword.—The two hurried to the lattice-window at the end of the passage, just in time to see Tycho's sons driving the still resisting Tengnagel out of doors into the dark park, where the noise died away.

"It must be difficult to study the stars here," observed Kepler reflectively, after a long pause.

They went once more to the doors of their rooms. Hagecius continued to snigger, as if Kepler had said something very amusing in his last remark. When, however, he extended his hand to bid him good-night and in the light of the candle beheld Kepler's countenance, deeply moved and full of compassion, the doctor's derision was succeeded by a hypocritical gravity. "One really must admire old Tycho for the manner in which he retains his passion for his exalted *opera*, notwithstanding all *dissensiones familiœ*, and again and again astounds

50

the scientific community by the fertility of his *ingenium*."

Kepler merely nodded a brief good-night and disappeared into his room.

Even when he was alone in his room, Hagecius continued to indulge himself with a little philosophical laugh. He was soon in bed and fell quickly asleep, in a state of gentle but by no means disagreeable agitation. Perhaps the term "excitement" would be more appropriate to describe that comfortable condition produced by his vacillating habit of thought, which never hardened to a tangible consistency, when he reflected upon the mighty and stirring destinies of other men.

MEANWHILE in a distant part of the park Elizabeth Brahe and Tengnagel walked to and fro, the whole night through to and fro. What they had to say to one another seemed as if it would never end.

Hardly had all the lights been extinguished in the castle when the ardent girl had slipped out into the darkness to seek for Tengnagel. The brothers and their dogs had failed to get on his tracks. But Elizabeth ran, as if attracted by some mysterious force, straight down the Weinberg. to the wall parallel with the road. There indeed she found her beloved, huddled into a recess by the gate. He was in a sorry state, half frozen, bleeding from little scratches on the forehead and hands, his face expressive of apprehension and dread as he heard the approaching footsteps. He had clearly intended to await day-break in this place and then, as soon as the porter had opened the gate, to make good his escape.

He recognized the girl. "You, you," he groaned, beside himself with fury. Straightway, however, he regained his self-control, and, turning imperiously upon her, cried: "What do you want here? What more do you want from me?"

"Here are your cloak and hat, Franz; you mustn't take

cold." Elizabeth was strangely excited, but by no means so overwrought and grief-stricken as before. On the contrary, she seemed positively merry; she giggled and laughed outright. Her voice was clear and her tone was frivolous.

He regarded her, gnashing his teeth. Was she laughing at him?

But no, she laid the cloak carefully upon his shoulders, to do which she was forced to stand on tiptoe, and at the same time she skipped and danced about as if it were quite impossible for her to be quiet. She placed the barret on his head. As she handed him the sword-belt which she had picked up from the floor of the dining-hall, his anger partly yielded to astonishment. "What has come over you? You are in very good spirits today."

"Oh no, Franz, no, indeed." And already she began to sob, the tears running down her cheeks. Yet in the very act she felt happier in her heart than she had at any time of late. She felt relieved, though why she could not say. She merely continued to stroke her lover repeatedly, to embrace him amid tears and laughter, and to bestow endearing names upon him. She had brought fine linen with her, with which she bound up his wounds, and he—he put up with it. For it had come to this situation: Tengnagel stood in need of help. He was cast down from his position in the family where his greatness and power had been treated as accepted facts, he was now thrown back upon Elizabeth. Assuredly he had never ceased to love her. But since she had given herself to him, she was in a certain sense conquered, as far as he was concerned, and an accomplished fact. For like all men of simple nature, who after the attainment of one end think solely of the next in their path, he had from that moment onwards posed as the master and, whatever his true inclinations might have been, had displayed but little tenderness. But now, be the situation
52

what it might, whether good or ill awaited them, their love would regain its fire and vitality. This the girl had felt, quite unconsciously, at the very first glance, when she beheld her lordly betrothed crouching in the snow-clad recess of the wall. Only for a brief space was this clear in her mind; then it was straightway obscured and drowned in a thrill of rapture. And at this moment, moreover, the idea entered her mind to say something to her beloved that she had not previously had the courage to utter. Oh, what bliss to be able to say it to him at last! . . . But first she must comfort him and care for him, and that, too, was very sweet; it established a new tie with the almost alienated spirit of the loved one and she knew not whether to regret or to exult over the unfortunate episode at table. Her fear and her ecstasy found a single vent: long kisses upon the hands and cheeks of him she loved.

It was not, however, so easy to calm Tengnagel. "Your father does me an injustice," he cried, again and again, "a grave injustice." And standing against the wall, he laid his face upon his arm and began, great grim man though he was, to weep like a child.

Elizabeth trembled. She was frightened at the sight of the giant's weakness, yet at the same time it filled her with pleasure. Oh, how she loved him, this obstinate, this proper man who made no secret of his feelings, but in the most natural manner revealed in clamour and tears everything that took place in him! Much could be said against him, but false and hypocritical he was not, nor capable of any dissimulation.

"Haven't I always been loyal to Tycho?" he now wailed, beating desperately on the walls with his fists. "Elizabeth, tell me, openly and from your heart, tell everyone, haven't I been loyal?"

"Yes, you have always been loyal," she said from her heart,

and secretly included even herself within the scope of her reply.

"Tycho is unjust to me. He hurts and insults me. Just for the sake of this intruder he injures me, me, the friend of proved loyalty, the comrade of his wanderings. But this Kepler, I say it to you and to all, will bring him no good fortune; he won't take my place. He has laid a viper in his bosom, your father, and the viper will sting him. And he has driven me away. Haven't I . . . Elizabeth . . . always and in all respects haven't I been loyal?"

She was compelled to reply again and again to this one question. If she strove to speak to him of something else, he would not let her utter a word. All she could do was to keep repeating: "Yes," and "Loyal, very loyal." These words alone seemed to do him good; others were of no avail. His childish discomfiture at length struck her as being downright comic, and although she could not for an instant forget how serious it all was and how matters of the utmost moment to her were involved, she finally, when he paused for a brief space in his lamentation, could not help bursting out, a roguish expression on her face: "Now my father will have heard how shamefully you spoke to me in the carriage this morning. And he loves me dearly, very dearly. He won't allow anyone to speak like that to his Elsa."

"Nonsense! How should he have heard it?"

"Oh, that is very easy. Anything so very extraordinary can't remain hidden, especially when it happens before witnesses." Her face twitched with insidious whimsicality, while she said in a low voice and apparently with great earnestness: "Wench —to call me wench! Is that how one speaks to one's betrothed? Is that loyalty? To a betrothed who is herself so loyal, more than loyal, foolishly and credulously enamoured and in her loyalty forgetful of her honour—to use such un-

54

becoming words to her! Say, aren't you ashamed of yourself? And shall that go unpunished? Don't you think it quite right that such ruffianly insults should be punished?"

Her assurance made him hesitate; he believed her to be in earnest, and roared angrily: "For this, too, there is only that Kepler to blame. If you hadn't looked so languishingly at him, I shouldn't have so far forgotten myself. This vagabond has brought confusion upon everything!" Suddenly, however, it seemed to dawn upon him that Elizabeth was jesting. Her eyes shone so strangely! He snatched his hand from hers and regarded her with that same puzzled look that he had worn in the carriage, that he always wore when she said things that passed his powers of comprehension. "You are laughing at me. Oh! I am betrayed by all of you. I'll go, go away from here, to a new life, to Germans! You Danes are all ungrateful and deceitful!"

She actually felt flattered at being treated with a little brutality. Without this she would really not have recognized her Tengnagel. And his great, brown, paw-like hand, which he had drawn away from her, oh, how she longed to feel this brave, simple hand once more in her own, how she already regretted her wanton jest! . . . Now he once more wept, standing against the wall and refusing to be moved from the spot in spite of her frenzied tugging at his garments. It was just this senseless weakness in him, mingled with brutal directness and rough explosions of wilfulness, that so enchanted her; self-control and complete presence of mind, all passion notwithstanding, of these she could taste to the full in her own Tycho's blood. . . . Deeply moved and abandoning herself to him, she laid her little head against his heaving shoulders and begged him to collect himself and to tell her what he really wanted and what must be done to appease him. . . .

They began to walk up and down a narrow path running between vines. A row of trees screened them from the moon. The hard snow would have crackled beneath their feet, and so, notwithstanding their great distance from the castle, they walked with circumspection, as near as possible to the vines, where there were spaces free from snow. . . . When in later life Elizabeth recalled these hours, the impression of frost and chilling blasts was always accompanied by this feeling of creeping along on tiptoe and of a state of painful and tense joy within. It was a joy that she had caught by ambush and surprise and that she now for a short time held convulsively in her hands, in the semblance of a twitching, bleeding, wildly beating heart.

"What must be done? Your father must dismiss Kepler at once. Instantly. Or I go, if he prefers my enemy and his to me."

"I don't understand how he can be your enemy. And my father's enemy. Why?"

Tengnagel at first did not follow her; her words did not penetrate his understanding. Kepler not his enemy? A man whom he had known but for a single day and who from the beginning had obstructed him in everything, who sought to expel him from his privileged place at Tycho's side, who obviously concealed the most dangerous plans in his taciturnity, and who in any case was manœuvring to exploit Tycho?

"But is it not at least thinkable and possible that he is as well disposed towards my father—as you yourself?"

"Do you mean by that that I have robbed your father?" cried Tengnagel, turning upon the startled girl. And although it was hardly possible for anything displeasing to her to occur if Tengnagel was the agent, the tyrannical senselessness of his remark lent a special potency to the spell whereby he held her. With her subtler mentality she could laugh at much of

56

his extravagance and injustice, but the unshakable firmness of his conviction carried her away, when he now began in a long tirade to recount what good services he had rendered Tycho's family in recent years, ever since he had joined company with them, how everywhere he had uncomplainingly assumed the heaviest tasks as *maréchal de logis*, had found quarters, had chastised evil tongues with the sword, and had strengthened Tycho's party against slanderers, intriguers, and riff-raff of all kinds. "Tycho has enemies enough; he is simply surrounded by enemies, and sick and weary, a mere shadow of his former greatness, a lamentable pilgrim, as Hagecius called him today. He needs an honest and undaunted man at his side who will lay his lance in rest against everyone for his honour and renown. And I have done that, I have always held by him and by you. I have defended you, I alone, you who are like orphans, unprotected and abandoned and in need of a guardian. Yes, I have been the master of your disorderly household and have put it straight when your father was more concerned in the service of the heavenly regions than in that of the earthly. . . ."

"You loyal creature, you guileless one!" Elizabeth rapturously interrupted him, again flinging her arms about him and showering kisses upon him.

"Isn't it true, then?" grumbled Tengnagel.

She faltered, perplexed and submissive, her joyful expression clouding over in an instant. It was indeed all true, all that he said; true it must be throughout all eternity, unassailable, because she loved him and because in the depths of her soul she found in him alone a support for her volatile character, with its combination of weakness and vivacity. It must be true, say though she might to herself a thousand times over that her father was by no means so much in need of help and so decrepit as Tengnagel for his own purposes represented him. It must be true even though she might have a vague intuition that Tengnagel had emphatically not ordered the administration of certain domestic interests at the request of a willing family, but had on the contrary violently possessed himself of it, in defiance of the views of the two sons, who had wished to have some say in the matter. But that was of no consequence; Tengnagel was unquestionably right. And more than that, it would have been a shame and a lie—and she said as much to him forthwith—to cast doubts upon his love and self-sacrifice, upon the services which he had rendered to the importunate train of the Brahe family.

He, however, still felt himself to be inadequately appreciated, even by her. He reminded her of a certain episode in Wandsbeck. He had helped even with money. And in Wittenberg, when it had been a question of restraining the students who had been stirred up to riot! She had to recount to him everything in detail; he literally examined her as if she were a schoolgirl, upon all the good deeds which he had done.

"Now, this is at least a man who is not prodigal of himself or of those who are dear to him," said Elizabeth to herself. For during the recital all had culminated in praise for her betrothed. "No, he cares for them, and such a man is the right man for me." This idea, too, either because or in spite of the fact that it ran directly counter to her fantastic and inconstant mentality, she felt to be a source of peculiar joy, to be something which in her woman's frailty she could lean on and cling to. More even, she actually contrived to bring this thought into a wondrous association with her secret, which burned upon her tongue and which brought her such bliss, with that secret which, ere the night passed, she would have confided to her dear one.

And if he still continued to thunder away and to lay bare his mind in good earnest, raising his arms towards the clouds

58

that chased one another across the night sky, if he called upon Tycho to recognize the good that had been shown him and the merit entailed and to reward like with like, friendship with friendship, loyalty with loyalty, and, on the other hand, self-seeking with self-seeking—here he referred to Kepler— the poor, shrewd, yet utterly faint-hearted girl felt herself literally penetrated by the thunder of these outbursts. She drank them in greedily and yet suspected with a kind of delicious horror that Tengnagel's fidelity stood exceedingly close to his love of domination and to self-interest; above all, she felt that it clamoured far too loudly for vengeance, but that he would never see or admit that, and therefore— But the present was not the time to think about such things, and, notwithstanding all her superiority, Elizabeth certainly had not time for it now, when she was thinking exclusively of her pressing secret.

Well, at all events, he was a splendid fellow, whether for that or for other reasons was a matter of indifference, a splendid fellow, intractable, unbreakable, a protector forged of steel; and where she felt, perhaps from afar, the presence of something inferior, or, rather, of something entirely alien to her in him, just at that spot she felt herself chained to him by the incomprehensible magic of this strange, this unfathomable force.

At last he had roared himself to a finish. Like a child that weeps for a long spell because its desires are not gratified, he suddenly grew calm of himself. Elizabeth had waited for this moment to represent to him that she was indeed entirely on his side and would do everything to sever Kepler from her father; but that it could by no means be effected by a mere turn of the hand, but must be gradually prepared some days in advance.

New outbursts of wrath on the part of Tengnagel. He asked

59

the girl what he was to do in the interval; whatever ideas she might have, there was no staying in the house for him as long as Kepler was not dismissed, before whom he had today been so greatly humiliated.

And suddenly it struck him how far all this was driving him from his special aim. For in everything that he did Teng-nagel followed a particular aim; it was his ambition to become a diplomat. At that time, indeed, everyone who found the opportunity for it busied himself with the destinies of peoples and creeds. Moreover, there was no question that Tengnagel had a certain aptitude for the energetic game of politics. This he had displayed on the occasion of some minor commissions, wherein he had made amends for his lack of subtlety by his obstinacy, ruthlessness, and unflinching bearing. In practical matters, where action was called for, he even showed a very nice touch, a keener instinct at least than he showed in astronomy. He had always considered his intercourse with the renowned Tycho and marriage with Elizabeth as preliminary steps to his introduction at court; indeed, he had made no secret of those plans of his. In his simple, almost primitive mind this community of interests, as he termed it—he supported or protected Tycho, who in return had to advance his interest—perfectly harmonized with his species of genuine loyalty and adherence. And all that destroyed, or at least postponed! What was he to do—and with no money, too? he asked, finally becoming utterly dejected. "I will ride to Prague tonight; that is best."

Once again Elizabeth gloated a little over his helpless rage. Then, giving him out of sheer wantonness a little fillip—she could never refrain from playing with the danger of his wrath—she said: "No, I'll hide you here."

"Here in the castle?"

60

"No, in the castle church. In the tower. There are rooms there completely hidden, used only for mass-vestments and lumber; no one will look for you there.—And in the mean time I shall have won over my father and expelled the evil spirit."

"And in the mean time I shall have starved to death."

"No, my dear," answered Elizabeth caressingly, "I will look after you and bring you food; you shall have the best from the kitchen. Oh, it will be great fun."

"Fun! Thank you.—No. I will leave for Prague. You can write to me when Tycho has come to his senses. That is safer. Besides, if your brothers should find me in the church tower! And your mother will soon come to know of it."

"My brothers will look for you in Prague rather than up there among the bells. And my mother," cried the girl exultantly, "—oh, I shall tell her myself where you are, the good soul. She will be ever so glad when she knows that I have kept you there. She will make them cook dishes for you and bring wines from the cellar, the kind that only a beloved son-in-law can desire. . . . For, do you know, today, as you were so long in returning from Prague, I confessed to her . . . She knows more than you, my love. . . . " Elizabeth faltered, but she could no longer keep silent, although now while she spoke, she was suddenly seized with a terrible dread. "I told her that you are the father of a child that I shall soon have."

Tengnagel stared at her. Then he caught her in his arms and raised her aloft. "My wife!" he cried. His countenance grew radiant, a mighty sense of unfeigned rapture had suddenly filled his sullen spirit to the brim. He drew Elizabeth to him, so that she at last experienced her supreme moment, for which she had fought so gallantly and ardently: for the first time in many days he kissed her; he felt himself genuinely drawn to her, and kissed her in the boyish, clumsy, almost shy manner which she so loved.

Now, too, he had no longer anything to say against being locked up by her, as he called it. He entrusted himself unreservedly to her, let her lead him on bypaths to the courtyard of the castle, in the immediate proximity of which stood the church. And what did it matter if he said quite openly that he was happy, not only on account of the child, but also because the entire situation would thereby be considerably altered in his favour? "Now your father must certainly hold by me, whether he will or no, and as for you, my dear wife, it must now be of the utmost importance to win him over to me. Yes, I have now no difficulty in believing that you will do everything in your power." He gave her a hearty buffet upon the neck and laughed, as if he had executed a stroke of genius.

She showed no resentment, she understood him; motives that in any other man would have been irreconcilably opposed, pure love and this delight at one's own advantage, dwelt together in his simple heart honourably and peacefully, without hampering one another. Of conscientious scruples of such sort he happily knew nothing. Pampered souls might busy themselves with such matters.

THE earliest cock-crows were resounding when Elizabeth awakened her mother and rapidly reported her conversation with Tengnagel. The doors of the sacristy were flung open and the winding stairway ascended. Magdalena, too, lent willing aid in preparing a warm nest for her sister's treasure; the bitterness of her spirit had not degenerated into envy. The three women had soon kindled a large fire on the hearth and had prepared a preliminary couch from the accumulation of

62

unneeded altar-cloths. They brought light, fruit and pastry, and some books.

Tengnagel in the mean time sat quietly in the chimney-corner, letting them wait upon him, without uttering a single kind word. His sullenness had returned; he merely muttered from time to time: they would all find themselves in a nice mess; they would soon see that they could not get on without him; Tycho above all would not endure it. . . . Suddenly he cried aloud; they had no right to ask him to sit day after day, or perhaps week after week, in the tower and await what the others out of the kindness of their hearts would do for him. He intended to act for himself. He thereupon demanded that his servant should be summoned, at the same time letting fall something about a wonderful, secret plan that he had devised against Kepler and that would overshadow everything that the three women might be able to do for him.

Then he wrote letters, gave them to the servant, and sent him off with vehement exhortations to make haste.

Outside, Elizabeth coaxed the servant into showing her the letters. They were addressed to Tengnagel's brother and several friends in Vienna. Without depicting his situation in any detail—he felt it himself to be really rather ridiculous—he urgently bade them send him money, as much as they could raise, each letter concluding with the words: "The issue is to set me free and destroy a dangerous enemy."

Aghast, Elizabeth restored the papers to the servant, who at once took his departure. It subsequently occurred to her that it would perhaps have been better entirely to have prevented the dispatch of the letters. But this she dared not do. She feared Tengnagel.—But, at all events, it was clear to her that she must set to work at once and with all urgency entreat her father to banish the disturber of her happiness, Kepler.

63

To crown all, at the very moment when she sought to enter her room, to sleep for a brief space, her brothers burst out of their chambers. "There she is. She knows quite well where he is hiding."

"No, no, I know nothing," she cried in alarm, hastening past them as quickly as her feet could carry her.

This situation was certainly unbearable; she must act at once.

CHAPTER V

As soon as day dawned, Elizabeth sought her father. For years it had been his regular habit to rise very early with the servants and to employ the first hours of the morning in supervising their labours. He often directed them in person and joined in their work. Sometimes he came straight into the field or poultry-yard after a night spent with his apparatus in contemplation of the stars, only in the forenoon allowing himself a little sleep. But even on misty or cloudy nights, when no observations could be taken, he suffered from sleeplessness, and particularly of late. Therefore he was glad, as soon as it was light, to hasten into the open and labour.

Elizabeth took the path into the nursery garden. She was perfectly acquainted with her father's habits and with his manner of occupying every moment of the day; indeed she was the only member of the family whom he occasionally trusted, not, it is true, in matters which were sources of personal anxiety to him, for upon such topics Elizabeth was too modest and too timid to touch. He did, however, give her his confidence in many questions, often those of some importance, especially those which arose from his general meditations upon the course of events and the misfortunes attending human existence. Every morning Elizabeth rose at the same time as her father and met him at the appointed place, where work or some important alteration was being carried on. Alterations, indeed, were always among Tycho's activities; he had a special inclination for them. He invariably had some new, gigantic idea under consideration; he felt himself continually urged to remedy some imperfection in his surroundings by this or that ingeniously imagined expedient. It was as if his mighty technical gifts were unconsciously always seeking for some new opportunity for activity. At one time he had invented machines for draining marshes; at another, and particularly of late, he busied himself with the cultivation of trees. During these earliest hours of the day, which he devoted to the administration of his property, Elizabeth was always at his side. She listened to his discussions with his agents and occasionally came in for a remark herself. True, her father had not much time to bestow upon her, but the girl felt even this taciturn confidence to be an overwhelming honour; her admiration for Tycho was absolutely unbounded, and her infinite love for him, which often, on the occasion of some trifling word in conversation or of a mere glance, completely overpowered her, she could express only by means of silent, hidden tears. Often, too, she passed the whole night in weeping when she saw his features darkened by some care which passed her comprehension. In order to understand more of the great man's honoured personality she had, on one occasion, devoted some months to learning the elements of astronomy with a pupil, the good-natured Longomontanus, and thereafter Tycho, whom she astonished one day with a telling technical observation, prepared long in advance, had himself taken charge of her education, which proceeded with unusual rapidity. But this intellectual endowment and the participation in his work, greatly as all this pleased him, did not alone make Elizabeth admittedly his favourite child; a far more deeply seated community of feeling drew the old man to this tender creature,

66

for he understood in her a devotion and readiness to serve him such as no one else had ever shown. It is true that he never alluded to this in conversation with her. On the contrary, he often treated her with an unwonted roughness and brusquerie which he deemed a necessary educational measure to avoid disturbing still further his daughter's already delicate disposition. She must become harder, more self-assured; he would even have her somewhat more defiant. He did not suspect that it was only in her subjection to him that she was so completely lacking in self-reliance, so immoderately submissive, and above all so serious and adoring; with others she could hold her own little part very well, and with her swift sallies, wanton, bizarre conceits, lies, and artifices could prove a very dangerous opponent. Of other aspects of her life he knew little or nothing, being always too much engrossed in his own affairs; otherwise he would assuredly have observed more keenly what occasionally presented itself to him as a very distant, fleeting presentiment, that Elizabeth possessed almost the same merits and the same weaknesses as himself, that with her alloy of unreflecting passion and a consciousness almost satirical in its lucidity she was a species of Tycho metamorphosed into female shape. Had this become clear to him at the right time, he would assuredly have judged her more aright in many respects, and perhaps much of the grievous mischief that subsequently occurred would have been avoided.

In the mean time Tycho was very far from subjecting his daughter's mentality to a serious examination. The very self-evident character of her veneration and love for him and of his love for her, the facility of their mutual relationship, which never called for many words or explanations, revived the tormented man, accustomed to obstacles of every species. It was his very occasional habit to say to Elizabeth—the only remark by which he displayed his attachment—"When you are near me, Elsa, I feel so tranquil." Had he, it is true, realized what a tempest of exuberant rapture he called forth in the young spirit by means of this one strange observation, he would assuredly have expressed himself with even greater economy and prudence. Elizabeth literally dreamed about such sentences; their notes were heard in all the sweet melodies that she knew; angels' voices chanted them to her from on high. Nay, her whole life was for a space entirely dominated by these words of her father, and all that she did, however quietly, however much apart, was secretly directed to the sole end of once more conjuring them from the beloved lips.

The nursery garden was situated in the highest region of the park, in a spot where it bordered upon neighbouring hills, with their woods. Elizabeth had to make her way, several times ascending and descending the hill-side. At length she climbed the last eminence. A chilly wind, seemingly only half awake, blew upwards from the Iser, upon which the morning mists were beginning to disperse before the slanting rays of the sun. The sharp angle of the half-frozen stream, still carried onward by its powerful fall, gleamed brightly between fields of snow and lustre-lacking shrubs, covered with hoar-frost. The sky was clear and bluish white in colour, almost as in spring. Directing her steps toward a group of old lime-trees, Elizabeth caught sight of the knot of workmen. High above them towered her father, his blond beard gleaming in the full rays of the morning sun on the open plain. For a moment Elizabeth stood still. Did he not look like one of the blond warriors of the North, her father, one of the unconquerable heroes, one of the old gods?

Good, then, she would pray to him as to a god and he would not reject her prayers; such great, powerful, godlike men are certainly more ready to do one a kind action than the sick and discontented. Her heart beat with joy; already she believed her cause to be won; already she beheld the sorry Kepler strapping on his wallet and sadly riding away, perhaps on some little thin, bony donkey. She burst out laughing at these imaginings and ran with outstretched arms up the last steep stretch of her way towards her father. Aware of her presence, he looked up with pleasure. . . . Although at closer quarters his fresh, godlike Donar-mask disappeared beneath a network of wrinkles on the forehead and furrows on the cheeks, although the giant form literally shrivelled together before her eyes, or rather retained a strangely forced and weary uprightness, which drew its support exclusively from within, yet her courage did not fail her and she sought to begin with her request immediately. Tycho, however, came towards her with his usual greeting: "Do you bring bad news?"

Mechanically she shook her head.

"Well, I am very glad you don't," he cried, and drew a deep breath of relief. Out here in the open his voice resounded more harmoniously, more firmly, than in the house, like a hunting-horn. His whole being was free and healthy, as if he had entirely forgotten the untoward excitement of the previous night or had easily got over it. Without delay he turned joyously to his labours, swinging the hammer in his right hand and zealously nailing a board to the wooden panel which he had recently caused to be erected as a wind-screen for the nursery garden. While doing so, he spoke without intermission, emitting words between the hammer blows in single volleys, addressed to Elizabeth and the bailiff, who was standing at her side: "One must really supervise everything—nothing goes of itself, nothing prospers by itself—the master must always look to it if anything is to be accomplished—last night the wind again tore down twelve of my

69

little trees.—Naturally, if holes the breadth of a hand are left in the screen!—I am not one of the lucky ones—if only the wind would not begin to blow before the screen is ready! —No, misfortune pursues me; I ought to know it.—The big storms always visit me in advance, just a day or a night too soon.—I must be on my guard, must be able to rely on my people.—Yes, yes, yes, but what I don't do myself is never done at all—I should have known that already: chance is never on my side." These words of reproof were not, however, the fruit of ill temper; they resounded rather as an explosion of his own spontaneous humour, and he laughed outright and unrestrainedly as he let fall his hammer. "Isn't it comic? I have to instruct the world in everything, I and nobody else. Not only in star-gazing. They can't even set up a wooden paling without me. Heigh-ho! Old Tycho has to show them the way in everything."

The bailiff was then dispatched with a number of commissions. Elizabeth now felt that the proper moment had arrived for her request. She wished to go far back, to depict the very beginning of her love for Tengnagel and to keep back nothing, not even the latest happenings, the consequence of her surrender, although she feared that in his pride Tycho would take a much graver view of it than her practically minded mother. Tycho, however, was not inclined to give ear to her that day; he seemed entirely in the grip of some strangely heavy and dreamlike mood, and as he lifted a new unplaned plank, he whispered very quietly and mysteriously to his daughter, drawing her shoulders towards him: "Just smell what a perfume! Oh, how I love this smell of wood! How I love trees, forests altogether! It makes one healthy, this smell, it makes one strong, it lays hold upon my heart like a powerful spell! It smells like the trees in Hveen, like my room in the Uranienborg. Could you believe that it stands in some

70

connexion with my creative labour? How comes it so? Perhaps only because always when I labour so happily, new apparatus with their smell of fresh wood, new implements, new floorings, and all possible kinds of work rise into existence about me. It is the excellent savour of work that comes forth from these wooden beams. Nay, there must be a deeper relationship between me and this fragrant resin in the tree-trunks. I myself must be a kind of tree, I feel myself impelled by such fraternal emotions towards them. Just look at the woods there on the Iser!" With outstretched hand he pointed far out into the plain, where amid perfectly white fields little clumps of Scotch firs stood out everywhere like bluish-grey, blue, or black cushions. "Aren't these forests quite black with the thick, overflowing sap of life, with the green sap which moves sluggishly in them like a dark blood, awaiting the coming of spring, to burst forth again and pour itself out over the white meadows, to bestow upon these dead fields the colour of life? In these forests life is stored up to supply the whole of nature. And so I often think when I feel exceedingly downcast and wintry: in myself, too, dwells life, waiting upon spring."

"Father!" cried Elizabeth anxiously. Suddenly she detected the underlying note of distress resounding with terrible clearness in all that Tycho had said in apparent joyousness.

"Yes, yes, this scene last evening," without any warning Tycho actually continued, in a different, gloomier and harsher tone; "that showed me once more very clearly that God's blessing does not rest upon me. I fight and fight, but to what purpose? Not a day passes without misfortune, no longer is there a single quiet, undisturbed day for me in the gifts of God. Not a day without ill luck. I often wait hoping till the evening and say aloud: 'Today's misfortune is still due, Lord God!' But He does not let me wait in vain, never. Either I

71

hear of some serious loss of money, as lately when the Duke of Mecklenburg failed to repay me ten thousand thalers I lent him; or if I still have for a time that which just suffices to maintain my children and me, I am taken ill, or a pupil deserts me and covers me with calumnies, or someone else in whose eyes my presumed renown is an offence begins bickering with me, or someone in the family falls sick. It's too much, too much! The blows of misfortune give me no time to breathe; they follow one another without any interval. . . . It was just the same yesterday. After so many years there finally came once more a day when something that I longed for intensely happened just as I should wish it to happen. That day began with the fairest augury and might have ended happily, without a cloud, a veritable festival of the spirit. And how it ended!"

"Something that you longed for intensely? What was it, then?" asked Elizabeth, suddenly seized with evil forebodings.

"Why, Kepler came! Don't you understand that? Don't even you understand? You used not at other times to stare at me with such empty eyes as now. . . ."

"Is Kepler—so precious to you?" stammered Elizabeth in terror, almost weeping, while she flung her arms about her father.

"Kepler! Is Kepler . . ." Tycho cried aloud, and angrily thrust the girl from him. "Yes, don't you know who Kepler is? Are you still asleep? Are all of you around me asleep and have your hearts no part in what I long for, strive for in my labour?—Now, now, be calm. You must not cry. For that is how the world runs; of that I have had full experience. Everyone has his eyes open only for his own path. But that you may know it now and bear it in mind for ever: Kepler is, in one word, the most important man for me in the world. A man of altogether revolutionary, independent, almost pro-

72

phetic habit of thought. And now he wishes to place himself in my charge, ally himself to me, learn from me—could any greater good fortune ever befall me? He is the only one upon whom I once more bestow all my hopes, my researches and powers, to whom I turn my heart. The last stay of my life. He is my fellow worker, no mere pupil; my saviour, and no mere friend. From the moment of his coming a new, joyous, and rich life of labour might have begun for me. But the demon does not rest; he straightway stirs up your mother and the others and brings me shame, vexation, grief, until I could stifle. And yet, notwithstanding, I tell you, Elizabeth, and I tell all, notwithstanding, with Kepler's appearance a new life really will begin for me, a spring, which all of you will not be able to check."

Tycho had advanced upon his way storming. Elizabeth heard him giving instructions to the labourers near by. She did not see him, for the garden path rose before her eyes like a brown sail, inflated by the wind, and struck her painfully in the face. She continued for a while bewildered. Her first thought was to run to Tengnagel, set him free, and fly together with him to the wide world without. In her parents' home there was no more room for her and for her beloved; her cruel father drove them out.

Yet even as she bestowed the word "cruel" upon her father, she already thought with grief that from that day onwards he also would never again feel tranquil in her proximity, that those happy times were ended for him and for her too. She felt that her youth was gone at a single blow and that this moment marked the beginning of something evil, unknown. . . .

But Tycho was soon back and laid his hand on her head. He did not know, he said very gently, as if he had already completely overcome his violent agitation—he really did not know why he had said all that to her. She must not take it ill that his storm of reproaches and that the exasperation of his spirit provoked to the utmost by great hopes and disappointments should have burst upon her, who of all about him was the most innocent.

He ceased speaking and reflected. "It just strikes me," he continued, "that I was not the only one who fought yesterday before all the servants and the guests. You fought with me, in your own way. Moreover, that gross fellow, the Westphalian junker, insulted you. Me also, perhaps even more deeply. Now you never tell me anything about your affairs. I must divine everything, I shall only reach the final act of the tragedy when concealment has ceased to be possible. . . ."

"Now, now," cried a voice within Elizabeth, "now you must throw yourself at his feet and tell him everything, as he himself has begun to speak of it."

But she lacked the courage. Tycho continued in impressive tones: "I don't mean to reproach you for withholding from me all that has happened between you two. I know that you don't do it from ill will or defiance. I understand you; you say nothing to me because you are afraid of adding a new anxiety to my many vexations. It is so, is it not? You turn red? Again those tears? Elsa, you little fool, if only you were more constant, more stubborn—I should have less anxiety on your account. For although I know that you mean well in maintaining this secrecy, I must reproach you with grossly undervaluing me in doing so. Look at me! Don't I endure whatever comes? It is true that I have more than my share of misfortune. But perhaps it is only because I have a stout back and because Misfortune knows: 'I can lay all my weight with impunity upon old Tycho; he knows something about weights; he won't collapse under me like a tree out of which the worms must creep almost before they have de-

74

voured it. Heigh-ho! old Tycho!'—Yes, child, take note of this: there must be misfortune. Adversity is the most wholesome broth. . . . But you are far too yielding, you are much too fastidious with me—with yourself, too, Elsa. One must torment oneself, harden oneself; that is the whole secret of life. One must credit oneself, and sometimes even others, with a power of endurance like that of an oak-tree, if it is necessary. Don't out of pure consideration leave your father to grope about in the dark. . . ."

"Can I tell him after he has spoken like this?" Elizabeth asked herself. She was conscious of the underlying demand that she should speak, a demand that came straight from the heart. But at the same time she felt the impossibility of speaking—for utter shame that she had been on the very brink of withholding altogether that consideration with which her good, kind father had credited her and the use of which he now forbade for himself.

"Hear one thing further: every misfortune can be countered. It is for this that our cunning is given us. We must parry every blow, above all must seek for the right course ourselves, must be behind everything. I have long lost confidence in mere nature, in things' taking a happy course. It is we who must bring things to reason, we, only we. What we don't do ourselves does not happen. I said so today to the lads yonder, when I was scolding them; but I say it to you in all seriousness. Everything rests with us and—everything succeeds if we will it. I do will it, and therefore I will still settle accounts with all my enemies. And you, too, must be hard, apt, courageous. This Tengnagel—today I mention his name for the last time—must have given you enough trouble. You didn't say as much to me, so I could do nothing to hinder it. But now I will endure it no longer. As for you, be glad that his hateful conduct yesterday evening has set you free from him for ever; for I will no longer tolerate him in the house—"

"But I—father—" stammered Elizabeth, interrupting him. She sought to say that she really loved him, this despised, trampled Tengnagel, and that she would give her life for him, as also for her father. But the words refused to emerge from behind her chattering teeth. In bidding her take heart Tycho merely rendered her less courageous, caused her to feel even smaller and more insignificant in his presence. For she heard or divined very clearly in the brave-sounding words the full force of the obstacles that he had to overcome with so terrific an exertion; she realized from his effort the tremendous nature of the destiny with which he grappled. How trifling did her own sufferings appear, how almost alien to her by the side of this which laid hold upon her with an utterly overwhelming force. Moreover, she was struck by the fact that her father had not for a long time expressed himself in such confident tones, with so much of the fire of battle, indeed with so much pride on the subject of his misfortunes; and she now realized that the reason for his new joy in life was this very Kepler against whom she had intended to speak. . . . No, she could no longer even think how she could have had such a design. How could she have taken it upon herself to act thus towards this great, tempestuous man, whose song of triumph—that she clearly divined—would have been turned to despair at the slightest attack upon his new bond of friendship?

They were once more in motion and had reached the edge of a hill, from which the wind saluted them with buffets of loose snow. "No, I don't like this wind," Tycho shouted, and laughed in his exuberant way; and as he had in the mean time continued speaking at some length, she did not at once grasp the significance of this last remark. "If I had created

76

the world, I should not have called winter into being; in fact, I should have ordered many things better, you may be sure of that. Now I have to play the creator of the universe in microcosm and myself take a hand everywhere and hold frail things together; otherwise things don't go well. But what does it amount to? I play many a trick upon the Almighty! For example, I mean to erect hothouses—not only for flowers, but quite new kinds of hothouses—for green trees. Green trees, too, must endure the winter, if it is our pleasure. Is it not so, Jeppe?"

The dwarf had observed them from afar as they approached and had come tumbling towards them. He kissed the hem of Tycho's garment, while the latter did not shrink from stroking him upon his pustule-covered forehead, as he asked: "Have you made good progress?"

With a burst of joy the dwarf exhibited his sickle-shaped implement, a tree-scraper. He immediately left at a run in order to exhibit his skill.

"Do you see?" continued Tycho; "him too I have placed in a kind of hothouse. And doesn't he blossom nicely now, the little monster? It is only a question of setting everyone in his proper place; then all can render some service. As I have already said, everything is possible. On the day when I snatched the luckless creature from the hands of his tormentors, no one would have given me a penny for his life. Unpaid English *Landsknechts*, in their passage through our district, burned a gipsy encampment. I have told you the story often enough, with the exception of a single detail, which I understand aright for the first time today. We came upon the place where the fire had been and there found this little scrub, half roasted over the hearth and tied up by his feet to a gallows. Probably he had betrayed the whereabouts of treasure. In any case he had already lost consciousness and has never since regained his powers of understanding. It thereupon occurred to me to rescue this creature so ill-used both by Nature and by men and bring him up in defiance of all the powers of evil. Hardly had I loosened his garments and given him refreshment when close by me from a heap of rubbish there resounded the voice of an old woman, who died soon after—it may have been his mother—"Take Jeppe for yourself, for if he dies, you won't have long to live." At the time I laughed and bade the superstition avaunt. But now I find a meaning in the old wife's words: as long as I have the strength to protect this weakly creature, I shall have strength enough for myself as well. For we two, Jeppe and I, are in like case: from the very beginning no good was designed for us, we must wrest our salvation from heaven." As he uttered these words, with a glance that suddenly darkened Tycho lifted his hammer menacingly. There he stood, his legs wide apart, as if he had grown out of the earth. And now to Elizabeth he really bore the aspect of some heathen nature-deity, like the god Donar with his hammer, and this spectacle filled her with horror. It terrified her, too, that her father had spoken of his death. In tones of entreaty she cried: "Father, if only you would remain a Christian and not strive against God Himself with such deeds and utterances!"

"Against God?" said Tycho, in tones from which all levity had departed. "That is the great and final question of my art, whether I shall succeed in discovering the law of God in all this waste of earthly misery and in uniting myself with that law. I don't think that I do fight against God. Sometimes that thought surprises me in hours of sadness, but then again it seems as if it were the Devil, against whom I defend God's law. For don't imagine that I'm only concerned with discovering the harmony of the starry spheres. That would never be

78

anything but piece-work. The harmony above is but a reflection of that beneath; God has established a connexion of deep import between my happiness and the laws of heaven and I must hold in the hollow of my hand the law of these two, the law that governs the world, as well as the law that governs heaven. Otherwise I have lived in vain. With anything less I will never be content—and here comes one who will understand and sympathize with me in these feelings of discord."

Kepler had turned the road of the park. Tycho hastened joyously towards him.

The brief time during which Elizabeth remained alone, sufficed for her to come to a decision which had been gradually maturing during the whole course of the conversation; she must take upon herself the entire weight of the responsibility for her action, in its full implication and unrestrictedly alike for her father and for her beloved. She could no longer hope to lift the burden from herself on to the shoulders of either; that would be a cowardly evasion. Above all she must undertake nothing against Kepler; on the contrary, in her dealings with her father she must think only of her father and of his well-being, as if there were no Tengnagel, and towards Tengnagel as if there were no Tycho.

Her slender frame braced itself gallantly as these thoughts passed through her mind. As yet she saw no way out, could not for a moment imagine it possible for the matter to have a happy issue. And yet, in spite of all, she was conscious of a vague hope welling up within her. She was taking upon herself lightly and with no special deliberation laborious, conflicting tasks, to accompish which she must summon to her aid the whole force of her acuteness. She was conscious of a secret and profound belief in the omnipotence of the will of the heart, existing in a veritable opposition to the cleverness which lay upon the surface. She was herself hardly aware of this force, but she felt with a devout intensity that it was the essence of her own being as it was the essence of all things. She believed herself to be setting out upon a new, undreamed-of pathway of her life. And it was just in these reflections that she showed herself to be the true daughter of her father.

KEPLER began with an apology, which he uttered with so much sincerity and simplicity that even Elizabeth, the most nearly affected, heard his words with pleasure. He deplored the fact that his arrival in the house had been the undesigned cause of painful incidents, the full results of which, alas, could not yet be calculated. For, so he reported, Tengnagel's room had been found empty in the morning and his servant had been seen riding away while it was still night.

"All the better," cried Tycho, and dismissed the whole episode with a wave of the hand. Then he looked more keenly at Kepler, his countenance wearing an expression of boundless amazement. "You really acted entirely right in refusing to give a toast to that horde of Philistines yesterday evening. It passes me to think how I could have spoken in their presence of the Holy of holies, of Hveen. I was quite blinded." Suddenly he was seized with terror, as if it were only now that he realized how low he had allowed himself to sink the day before. And if he clapped Kepler approvingly on the shoulder in a magisterial manner, Tycho only now became aware of that indefinable superiority and simple "rightness" that proceeded from Kepler. For the first time he began to divine that this apparently harmless, perfectly open man spoke and acted at the dictates of some unconscious, of some very profound wisdom which was closed to the more prudent. "You acted quite rightly," Tycho re-

80

peated, shaking his head. Then with a stamp of the foot he banished the disquieting impression.

Elizabeth, too, was in a state of uneasiness, not so much at what had been said as at the difference in tone between the two men. Kepler spoke so lightly and his words came so much as a matter of course; Tycho enunciated every word with emphasis and readily repeated individual phrases, as if he could not believe that words let fall by him would quietly bear fruit, as if in harmony with his own axiom he must "himself take a hand" here too and transmit the meaning of his words to his auditor, since in every direction he had lost confidence in mere nature.—Elizabeth could not represent this distinction clearly to herself, but she listened tensely to the conversation, always hoping that the next phrase would throw light upon it.

The three took breakfast in a greenhouse which could be heated. It was built in accordance with a design of Tycho's upon a spot in the garden commanding one of the fairest prospects. Here Tycho could once more point proudly and unconstrainedly into the distance, repeat the names of the villages belonging to the domain, speak of improvements which he projected in the cultivation of vegetables and in the castle, which lay just below the hothouse. With a motion of his finger he erected new buildings and observatories. Somewhat strangely, this seemed of little interest to Kepler; his thoughts were manifestly directed upon other things, and he answered only in monosyllables.

Thereupon Tycho, always obliging and courteously anxious to entertain his guest, recollected that he had something with him which could not fail to attract his attention more closely. A letter had come for Kepler the day before, actually prior to his arrival, brought by a passing merchant from Graz; in the heat of the first conversation Tycho had forgotten to deliver it. With a few humorous remarks about his senile forgetfulness he now drew the letter forth. While Kepler opened and read the letter, he continued speaking: "Alas, nothing more agreeable has been prepared for you here. I don't readily hand over letters; they always contain something unpleasant. But that we may trace solely to the fact that we mortals are simply born to suffer misfortune."

Kepler had read the letter through, and put it indifferently in his pocket.

"Well, what was it?" asked Tycho, not without curiosity.

"A matter of no importance, which I don't fully understand," replied Kepler. "My wife writes that she has been able to carry through the sale of the property on very advantageous terms."

"Well, surely that is very important and wonderful; don't you understand? Why, there was a danger that it might be simply confiscated." Tycho shook his hand with violence. Kepler, however, muttered that he did not occupy himself with such matters and did not even understand them.

"Well, then," continued Tycho, "in these things, too, I will be your instructor. But for the moment we will go to our labours." He gripped Kepler's arm and nodded to Elizabeth.

The latter, however, quite terrified, seized him by the cloak and whispered in tones audible only to him: "Father, so there are men who are born to happiness. Kepler is one of them."

"Then may happiness enter my house with Kepler," cried Tycho, addressing her and his friend at the same time aloud and joyously. Then he led the latter down the winding path towards the castle.

Elizabeth stood appalled. For a long time she continued looking after the pair, unable to turn her eyes from Kepler's

82

slim back. Some supernatural, uncanny power must have accumulated in this being. Who was this man who had travelled to Benatky in a sweet, care-free inactivity, but who notwithstanding found everything made ready for him here: good news from home, which he rated as naught, and Tycho's powerful protection, which he accepted as his due without a word of thanks? Who was this enchanter who had driven her beloved from the field without striking a blow, who won over all hearts as by magic, constraining even her own? For she could not seriously deal evilly with him who assuredly had within himself nothing hostile or dangerous, however much harm he might do her. Moreover, by one of those strange, inexplicable coincidences which seemed to work on Kepler's behalf, she found herself amid circumstances in which she could not do anything against him.—Her father, on the other hand, so afflicted and yet so confident, she beheld striding, full of belief in his own fortune, towards the castle, in the church tower of which Tengnagel lay concealed—like fuel awaiting the slow-match. She glanced anxiously down at herself; her time had not yet come, but there, too, misfortune lay in wait for her father and would soon become ruthlessly evident. . . . At that moment the doctor, Hagecius, with, so Elizabeth thought, a keenly observant, malevolent expression, stepped forth from the castle and approached Tycho. . . . "Is there no help?" cried a voice within the girl. She took a few steps down the hill-side, remained standing. . . . "Yet I must be on my guard against this Kepler," flashed through her mind, "not for Tengnagel's, but for my father's sake. I must warn my father if it becomes necessary. Oh, God, it will not be impossible to repress all evil thoughts which out of regard for my beloved I nourish against Kepler, to avoid all extravagances which creep into my mind, to see through all deceitful images, which, under the pretence of a child's solicitude, only minister to my passion, and yet, so far as the case calls for it, to keep this terrible guest away from my father. . . . No, it will not be impossible! For I take it upon myself and it must be."

CHAPTER VI

Kepler had started upon his morning walk in an
ill humour. This Benatky, to which he had fled from the
storms and dangers of Graz as to a peaceful haven of labour, disappointed him with the excitement, the tension, and
the passion which he found.

In a letter to his wife, composed immediately on waking,
he gave unreserved expression to his displeasure. He had
the impression, he wrote, of having fallen among utter luna-
tics, not of having entered the seemly, peaceful household
of a scholar. Then he found sharp terms for Tycho's senseless feasting and carousing, for his waste of time and energy.
Nor had he imagined the man to be nearly so old. Moreover,
he harboured a feeling, which would perhaps pass, that Tycho
was unwilling to speak upon his own subject, that he was
niggardly with his learning and preferred to fob off empty
phrases upon his pupils, actually fearing that they might be
able to penetrate his designs. Further, he did not forget
to note the fact that Tycho treated his assistants with scant
respect, making them perform menial duties. In short, his
first impression was a thoroughly unfavourable one, so that
he could not help having justifiable doubts whether there
was any possibility at all of doing worthy work with Tycho.
His instruments, it is true, were beyond all praise; the
methods he applied, in spite of a number of whims and the

falseness of his system, were original and deserving of admiration; his stock of manuscripts, containing the records of observations, were a truly inexhaustible mine of research. The only question was whether Tycho would consent to proper use being made of these materials. In any case, the letter concluded, it would only be later that he could decide whether his wife and daughter should follow him to his present abode.

In the very act of writing, his resolution stood out clearly before him: today he would go straight to the main point and summon Tycho immediately to a definite pronouncement upon the tasks to be undertaken and upon their relations, rights, and duties towards one another. For this situation based upon pointless enthusiasm by no means pleased him; although he was compelled to marvel at Tycho's flight of thought as something great, he found it disadvantageous. On the other hand, he had had more than enough of idleness, thanks to the disturbances at Graz and the wearisome journey to Prague, and yesterday's vision of the apparatus had secretly excited in him positive lust for labour, an almost painful presentiment of new results. It was to this, indeed, that his ill humour was very largely due.

Kepler realized this himself on closer reflection and put aside the letter, with its unduly gloomy tones and biting language, determining for the time being not to send it. Nay, he even felt ashamed, on reading it through a second time, that his bitterness should have led him to so manifestly paltry a judgment of the eminent man.

But the natural result of Tycho's cordiality in the garden, his extravagant manner of speech, and his humour was to strengthen Kepler in his feeling of dislike instead of pacifying him. Sullenly silent, he followed the master into the castle.

86

The latter, however, now really led him into the great instrument-hall and remained standing by the little table containing the manuscripts. "If it is agreeable to you," he said, "we will now proceed to the agenda and begin with what is before us." Thus Kepler saw his wish gratified without having as yet really uttered a single word to effect it. He did not, however, give any further thought to the matter, for he was already entirely absorbed in the study of the volume lying open before him, which contained the record of the last observations made at the Uranienborg. Figure followed figure, row after row, with a bare word of explanation here and there. Tycho picked out some particularly remarkable figures, recording measurements of Mars, which did not correspond with any of his theories of movements and yet were indubitably correct. Kepler recited the figures of his own corresponding observations; he knew them by heart. "Now," cried Tycho, "doesn't it grieve you too? We can't get at this refractory planet, the defiant war-god.—I spoke just now with my daughter about my ill fortune, recounted to her all the blows that fate had dealt me since my expulsion from Hveen. But these were mere trifles; I didn't really allude 'to the chief calamity, for the girl would not have understood such a thing anyway. To you, however, I may unfold it. My principal woe lies in my science, which utterly refuses to admit of good, harmonious conclusions. Everywhere there is some cavity which I can't bridge over; it is as full of contradictions as a capricious woman . . . But we must not treat it in such a superficial spirit. No, there is a manifest connexion between the two phenomena. On the one hand we have the feverish flickering of stars, which never appear just where our calculations predict; we have this confused and apparently quite lawless stammering in the heavens, upon which we vainly expend our energies. On the other hand, we behold the inexplicable divergences, discords, base and criminal actions of our fellow-creatures, of all creatures, indeed, and the blind, foolish wishes of our own hearts, our sufferings and failures. Yes, there is a connexion between the two: both heavenly and earthly discords alike come from a single source. And that is assuredly God. Now I have revealed to you my extreme, final calamity: I do not understand God. Nay, more, I do not feel Him anywhere—however much I wrestle with Him. I do not find Him, the all-wise, all-righteous, the all-law-giving Ruler of the universe. And that is just the reason why my most zealously undertaken labours, my purest aims, miscarry. Doesn't it seem so to you too, my dear Kepler? Haven't you suffered in a like way?"

Kepler admitted frankly that he had never really reflected upon the subject of these harmonies on a higher plane. In his curt, self-depreciating way, which differed so profoundly from Tycho's perpetual efforts to justify himself and to raise himself above the reach of any kind of attack, he avowed that hitherto he had devoted himself exclusively to calculations in the most Philistine manner, and that, as a beginner, the mere delight which he experienced in observing the stars and in approaching the laws governing their movements had held him back from indulging in such profound philosophical contemplations. And as regards God, he believed in Him in accordance with the teachings of religion.

"God does not answer me when I consult Him," cried Tycho with an expression of despair. Then he approached the window and gazed up towards the clouds. "A great book, these heavens. Every evening its leaves are turned over, bearing letters radiant with light; but I can't read it, or what is worse still, I read in it senseless, fantastic phrases, full of evil. . . . Assuredly I am not so modest as Copernicus. He once said that he would deem himself happy if the real course of the stars

88

did not differ from his calendar by more than ten minutes measured upon his arc. That seems to me to be altogether too unexacting."

He was silent, awaiting an answer; as ever when he spoke of Copernicus, he seemed to demand a declaration from Kepler that now he realized the errors in the opposing system of the universe. But Kepler was already again occupied with the writings; naught but figures came from his lips.

"I hope we shall find that your records tally closely with these figures here," Tycho at last interrupted him. . . . But then it appeared—Kepler avowed it in tones of contrition—that he possessed no properly kept records and that he lacked the energy to keep his manuscripts together. They got lost, just like the letters.

Tycho gave vent to his astonishment. It was indeed strange that this spirit, which could not possibly dispense with the fever of labour, seemed to attach such little importance to the actual fruits of its toil. . . . Tycho, on the other hand, showed the greatest solicitude in collecting the smallest scrap of paper, the most trifling contributions towards his theory.

For Kepler astronomical labour signified something entirely different from what it did for Tycho. For Kepler it was a kind of intoxication, whereof he drank his fill, from which he desired never to emerge; it dominated his whole existence, his whole imagination. In his brain the process of work seemed in a state of continual flux, as if it were undergoing a perpetual series of transformations; it consumed and digested itself, in the complete darkness of the unconscious gradually shaping itself to its final form. Thus amid the accumulating material he lived as in his natural element, and accordingly very rarely felt the need to unburden himself of his thoughts by writing them down. On the contrary, his remarkable memory upheld him by its feat of always retaining the essential and rejecting everything else or perfecting it, and, with never-failing patience, holding all in readiness for the one mysterious moment, in which from near and far his "laws" should rise up before his eyes. Until then —and that moment was still decades away in the future—he accepted everything as purely provisional, one might almost say unreal, assertions. He had given his allegiance to no theory, trembled for nothing, and longed for nothing; he readily rejected his own earlier convictions, for any new discovery might overturn all previous results. Labour supplied his mind with a perfect equilibrium, and it was perhaps due to this very equilibrium that his mind was in a state of constant turmoil and that it was free and without bias in the truest sense of the term, ready and resolute for any unexpected act.

Quite otherwise Tycho. For him every detail was of importance. For many years he tormented himself with efforts to bring these details into harmony with one another and with his system of the universe. He saw—and in doing so he was fully justified—that his principal advance upon his predecessors consisted in his exactness. It was thus with the consciousness of the most manifest superiority that he now chucked the quite enraptured Kepler under the chin and rebuked him in a friendly manner for his carelessness.

And Kepler readily permitted himself to be rebuked. It did him good. For, strangely enough, this man, who outwardly presented the picture of a purposeful, ever expanding, happily progressing existence, was inwardly profoundly discontented with himself. Nay, if one took his complaints seriously, he was in all respects the laziest, stupidest, most incompetent, and most unfortunate of all the children of men. It is true that he rarely went the length of complaining, since it was not often that he thought of himself at all. As long

90

as he was buried in some piece of work, he was utterly un-conscious of himself and lived in the most perfect tranquillity. His unhappiness began only when he was forced to reflect upon his work and upon himself. And in any case a large part of this unhappiness and discontent was traceable to the fact that introspection was an altogether unwonted occupation for him. But it was equally true that the other part of his unhap-piness took its rise in much deeper, darker sources of his genius, sources which he himself could not probe, and was in-deed as much a state of demonic possession as a mysterious and instinctive gift for certain scientific problems.

There was something peculiarly winning and moving in Kepler's manner of openly avowing his helplessness and freely admitting his distress and dissatisfaction with himself when subjected to such assaults in his most secret places. In-deed, it bordered upon the comic. Often after such outbursts he would sit with open mouth, protruding eyes, and fingers all splayed out—an utterly forsaken, impotent man, to whom even the most pitiless were constrained to speak a word of comfort. . . . When one left Tycho, who assuredly lamented his misfortunes with far greater frequency and violence and with far more eloquence and effective argument, one always had the impression that this man had strong, powerful defen-sive forces with which to confront the most poignant distress. It was a magnificent and dramatic spectacle to behold him suffering, cursing, playing the berserker, but at the same time subduing and forcefully calming himself, and in the end one felt certain that he needed no one, that he would settle conclusions with everything by himself. On such occasions there was an inclination to over-estimate his powers of re-sistance or to take no account of the fact that in these victories over himself he might end by exhausting himself, eventually to collapse under the stress of his own triumph. Never did people feel disposed to render any special measure of help to Tycho. They realized that he would look after himself and would ask for what he needed—and for that very reason he was often refused the barest necessities; for to the majority of men the presence of such strength and self-command in others is an eyesore, and instead of feeling grateful to him who burdens them the least and prefers to settle everything by himself, they find it more convenient to ascribe to him a "bright and happy nature" and with these words of praise on their lips to leave him entirely in the lurch.

If the haughty Tycho stirred people to such conduct as this, Kepler gave them no excuse for it. When he was helpless, he avowed his plight. There was a not quite accountable state of stress passing all bounds, with not a trace of counter-energy. No one would have had the heart to leave him to his own devices.

Tycho, too, was at once filled with compassion. Hardly had he observed Kepler's expression of hopeless abandonment, when he changed his tone, and in order to encourage him he turned the conversation into those fair first-fruits of his labours, the *Prodromus*, which was, however, a model of discipline and good order. But Kepler was no longer to be lifted out of his mood of depression. "Yes," he wailed in pitiful accents, "but no merit whatever is due to me. If it had rested with me, the book would never have appeared at all. Perhaps that would have been better; for, if I may say so, the book is a collection of refuse, a *charta cacata*. Friends put it together for me out of papers scattered all over the place and sent it to the printer; I myself had nothing to do with it. And, moreover, I am not at all grateful to them for their short-sighted exigency. No good whatever came out of it, then or subsequently. It would have been quite soon enough if we had waited a few years." He continued to speak, now

92

catching the spirit, giving vent to his astonishment that a man like Tycho, a man of such learning and strength of will, could ever go the length of speaking even a few words with anyone like himself. Without the least intention of flattering he broke into exaggerated laudations of Tycho. He praised him as an intrepid investigator, in spite of which he remained a man of the world. He pronounced him happy in his stormy eventful life. He declared that in the most perfect contrast with his own narrow outlook he continued receptive to the whole range of variety which life had to offer, and in all that he did he wrought on the grand scale. As for himself, he was for every possible reason a dolt and a clown.

"That is the first and last of your views that I must oppose tooth and nail," laughed Tycho, taking his hand in a friendly fashion.

They were interrupted by Hagecius, who wished to take leave. Before doing so he insisted on submitting Tycho to an examination.

Tycho went with him to the door, treating him in an altogether more friendly manner than on the previous day; he evidently feared that yesterday's scene at table might through the doctor's talkativeness become public property. The examination, too, caused him anxiety, but he now saw that he must let the doctor have his way, in order not to provoke his hostility. He treated him with almost servile courtesy. Hagecius at once perceived his advantage, and with some words of gloomy reproach directed at the colour of Tycho's complexion he took command of the conversation. He felt his pulse. That too seemed to him to portend nothing good. "Be more sparing of yourself, if I may ask as much. Live in a more reasonable manner. Limit your work," were the words that fell from his lips. A closer examination was to follow immediately in the adjoining room, the prospects of which seemed to be of the gloomiest. A disagreeable, malicious smile appeared with increasing distinctness upon the doctor's face, without his making any effort to contend against it.

Tycho prayed him to possess himself in patience for a while longer. It was painful for him to be forced to break off after the very first words of a conversation that had opened in so promising a manner. Besides, Kepler had still to be comforted. Full of sympathy, he turned again towards him.

Kepler, however, no longer stood in need of comfort. Once again he was swimming in his ocean of figures and had cast away all the garments of earthly cares. . . . It would be unjust to blame Tycho for entirely failing then and for a long time after to understand Kepler's mentality, judging it in accordance with his own joys and desires. In actual fact he had all the will in the world to take a hand and help. But Kepler's state of lacerated emotion ceased with as little apparent reason and as suddenly as it had begun. The great difficulty in helping him to emerge from these crises lay in the fact that in general they were not provoked by any outside cause. The greater, more important part of his existence was enacted upon the stage of the unconscious and was in the truest sense of the term inaccessible to others, as to himself, to friendly as to hostile influences. . . . When, therefore, Tycho remarked with a kindly nod that if he did not show a readiness to speak more favourably of himself, he too would be submitted to a medical examination, by way of punishment, Kepler merely replied: "Yes," absent-mindedly. Without any transition he at once turned the conversation to the only topic which was important to him in this place, and upon which, unknown to Tycho, he had made his further stay dependent. "Will you have the kindness to lend me all these records, that I may go through them thoroughly in the quiet of my own room?"

94

Tycho frowned. Did not Kepler at all realize that his remarks upon his careless handling of his own papers had not been productive of much confidence?

"Must it be at once?" Tycho inquired in ill humour.

But Kepler perceived nothing at all. He was endowed with a happy blindness for everything which diverted him from his scientific aims.

"Yes, I should like to take the first volume with me at once," he answered quite innocently.

Tycho reflected. Then, instead of replying, he urged him to beware of all friends and pupils. He took up Kepler's story about the first edition of his book and continued: "I was actually disposed to take your part. But then I was not at all pleased at what you just told me, that your friends can rummage at will in your records." And he recounted the unpleasant experiences which had fallen to his own lot. One ought not to trust anyone, for in the final analysis all are disguised plagiarists. So it had been with his pupil Wittich, who had behaved with the most extraordinary friendliness and had even called himself Tycho's fidus Achates. Yet despite all, when in Kassel, he had given it out that the master's improved instruments were his own inventions. And so with Heliæus Roeslinus, and even with the Bear, that Ursus, who was now his avowed enemy, who insinuated himself into the Uranienborg as a common servant and stole Tycho's system of the universe. He had simply carried it off and published it as his own discovery.

Kepler grew indignant at such dishonest actions, but found them in no way connected with his own request, to which he returned, nothing daunted.

Hagecius, however, cried out sharply: "It is to be hoped that you are not so mistrustful as to think that all your guests rob you of problems." And raising both arms aloft, he proceeded to revolve in a circle, as if to show that no secret pockets bulged out of his spindling frame.

Aghast, Tycho beheld himself threatened from both sides. "Now," thought he, "it can no longer be put off," and after an attempt to appease the doctor with a few words, he invited him to enter the adjoining room. Then he asked Kepler to have patience for a brief space and followed the doctor.

The examination lasted a long time. Restlessly Kepler paced up and down. He turned over some leaves of the manuscript, but could not collect himself. "It will always be like this," he thought, "new excitements and new obstructions every day. And as for leaving me alone with the papers . . . Tycho will never consent to that. This was how I imagined it this morning. All work will be impossible, utterly impossible. Ambition and feelings of bitterness, they are ill comrades for labour. . . ." He talked himself into an even fiercer rage; he was firmly determined to leave that very day.

Suddenly the doors were flung open. Hagecius was the first to appear, his countenance literally iridescent with wrinkles of every size. Tycho staggered after, his cheeks grey and without a trace of colour, his eyes wide open and staring. . . . The two men seemed already to have taken leave of one another; Tycho stood there speechless, not moving a limb. With solemn gesture Hagecius extended his hand to Kepler. Then he turned once more to Tycho. "Perhaps I have exaggerated a little. *Mala* that have been completely neglected have been known to take a turn for the better with good nursing. I shall come again soon to see whether you have duly introduced my *mixturæ* into your system. Good-bye, professor." Tycho still did not move; only his heavy eyelids fluttered downwards. Hagecius accordingly bowed and left.

Hardly had he closed the door behind him when Tycho,

like one set free from some terrible spell, flung himself upon the table holding the manuscripts, sank into a chair, and letting his head fall into his hands, sobbed aloud. . . . In great alarm Kepler leaped to his side and threw his arms about his shoulders. Tycho looked up and beheld Kepler's eyes radiant with a light of genuine sympathy—at that instant all selfish thoughts about Tycho's manuscripts were really banished from them—beheld them directed upon himself with an indescribable gentleness and a devotion entirely free from calculation.

"My Benjamin," he cried, and began to turn the papers about, "here, take everything; everything must be yours; do what you like with it. One thing alone: carry out my work; don't let this tremendous labour utterly perish. . . ." Suddenly he arose to his full height; a shudder ran throughout the whole of his frame; his cries swelled into a roar: "No, I will not die yet, no, no, no! But I must hasten, hasten, ay, hasten tirelessly, or it will be too late. You must help me, my John, my Benjamin. I have no time to lose. Everything shall be as you wish. Take everything, share with me, help me— only don't abandon me, never, never abandon me!" And weeping, he pressed him to his bosom, with fierce caresses such as no lover in his passion ever expended on his betrothed.

CHAPTER VII

THIS PROVED TO be Tycho's last outburst of suffering for a considerable time. It was succeeded by some weeks of salutary composure and quiet labour for him in co-operation with Kepler, just as he had represented it to himself.

The two great investigators, indeed, supplemented one another admirably, both by their special gifts and by their methods of work. Tycho's principal strength lay in his at once daring but entirely reliable method of observation; Kepler, on the other hand, by reason of his feeble sight could achieve little in that direction. At that time, prior to the discovery of the telescope, the nicest data of the night sky had to be deciphered by means of the naked eye, aided by nothing but sight-vanes. Kepler, for his part, displayed an astonishing mathematical genius and an energy in calculation which nothing could weary. His groups and combinations were reached by careful processes, and the majority of them proved perfectly correct, as if given by inspiration. Tycho, too, had shown considerable capacity for theoretical work, and in particular his investigations regarding the course of the moon, which he was at that time bringing to a close as the fruit of years of laborious, meticulous labour, were destined to become a permanent possession of learning. In general, however, he found some difficulty in making the transition from his original collections of striking details to generalizations.

When he attempted to do so, he often fell into excessive generalizations, into the fantastic and the emotional; it was as if that same fissure which divided his character into two such widely separated parts, into cold intellectual calculation and passionate, overflowing emotion, reappeared in the structure of his scientific equipment. For there, too, there seemed to be a certain deficiency in the power of discovering the connecting link in a chain of argument.

During that period, however, through Kepler's co-operation, everything was adjusted on the best possible basis. In Kepler, Tycho's enthusiastic inclination and his understanding found a kind of common focus; here at last, so he believed, his interest and his carefully weighed advantages no longer stood in the way of the free outpouring of his heart. On the contrary, both pointed in the same direction—to Kepler, whom he might love with impunity, nay, to the salvation of his art; there, accordingly, after so many years of constraint the old man could allow his strength to burst forth in full tide, without exercising that perpetual prudence and foresight which embittered his life, without feeling anxiety at the prospect of small-minded spite and trifling obstacles.

The results at once showed themselves, indeed in the very next days. Tycho regained his health; entirely of their own accord, without the aid of any doctor's prescriptions his evil symptoms disappeared, creeping fever and sleeplessness; his cheeks filled out and his hands ceased to tremble; the work went impetuously forward; the eyes became clear and keen, peering with the freshness of youth into the abyss of the night sky; and whatsoever offered itself to the eye was held fast in the records of the untiring pen. Amid the onslaught of new stimulative influences Tycho determined to resume his favourite plan of a great comprehensive work, for which since his departure from Hveen he had lost courage. Like everything

99

that he conceived, this plan was on a vast scale. All the facts relating to the starry universe, which, in accordance with his principle of accepting from his predecessors nothing untested, he had established anew, were to be assembled therein and expanded to the proportions of an irrefutable system. Of this work in many volumes, entitled *Astronomiæ Instauratæ Progymnasmata,* only the second volume, dealing with the comet of the year 1577, was at the moment of which we are speaking finished, having been published some years previously. Everything else was present in outline or in the form of key phrases, and these were now zealously sought out and set in order.

Tycho also encouraged Kepler to work upon a new volume and gave him certain indications regarding the direction to be followed. Kepler expressed his gratitude, promised to follow Tycho's suggestions—but in answer to inquiries made some weeks later, had nothing to show, not a single page or memorandum. With much head-shaking Tycho pondered upon this weakness on the part of his assistant, who with all his dazzling capacity seemed to lack the final degree of resolution necessary for undertaking a work; already he reproached himself silently for possibly misusing for his own ends this inexperienced man, who was so deficient in energy. He was genuinely doubtful whether he was justified in letting Kepler continue to work for him; for his subtle observations, thrown out in conversational form, could never receive honour in any book of his own, but would have to be woven into some work of Tycho's. And having on this point a very delicate conscience, he at the same time vowed to give Kepler due recognition in this new work, and to protect him not only against the wicked world, but also against himself, who was so much the stronger.

This feeling, indeed, developed into a positive yearning to

100

give Kepler his support, to take up his cause, to render him famous as soon as possible. In none of the letters that he wrote at that time did he omit to ask the recipient whether he had yet read Kepler's important *Prodromus,* or rather whether he had studied it and estimated it at its real value; it was that Kepler's who was now a source of unending joy in his house, to whose wise utterances he listened as to those of a new Hipparchus, and with whom henceforth he desired for ever to co-operate in extending the frontiers of truth.

As Tycho wrote of Kepler, so, too, he spoke of him and to him. It was an unceasing banquet of admiration, understanding, and friendship. Kepler could not utter a single word without Tycho's breaking forth into enraptured laudations.

It was the very fact of this excessive confidence that caused Elizabeth anxiety. She was frequently present during the conversation between the two men, and the impression which she had received at the very beginning perpetually renewed itself: that in this relationship there was at work something hidden which she could not penetrate, while none the less suspecting its danger for her father.

She made little timid efforts to discover the tracks of the evil thing. Whenever she caught Kepler alone, she submitted him to a cross-examination, beginning with some such question as to how he liked Benatky. Then she would touch upon Tycho and inquire what Kepler really thought of him. Kepler's answers were always open, manifestly honourably intended, but, alas, so devoid of content that the girl could derive no comfort from them. At times she really received the impression that outside his own sphere of scientific interests Kepler knew but a few well-established phrases of courtesy, so scanty were the words which sufficed for his purposes. Accordingly she advanced still closer to him and embarked upon particular topics. She asked him whether he had already

101

remarked that Tycho was drawn towards him in an unusual way, and whether he, for his part, felt anything like genuine love or gratitude towards him. Then she felt amazement at the continual failure of the Kepler family to arrive. Her keen woman's intelligence found in this very circumstance, to which Tycho paid no attention at all, something suspicious.

The really remarkable point was that Kepler was not in the least embarrassed by such questions, although he was obviously not prepared for them; that he never sought to avoid them, although he did not encourage them with anything like enthusiasm. He answered simply and clearly, and one felt that he held back nothing that was in his mind; yet a closer scrutiny revealed his statement to be devoid of any solid content. The sincerity and the sympathetic cadence of his words were all that distinguished them from an entirely ordinary, impersonal utterance.

It was inevitable that such conversations should gradually give rise to a species of confidential relationship between Elizabeth and Kepler. At every encounter it now gave signs of its existence by a friendly exchange of observations, by smiles and nods. One day, indeed, Elizabeth was forced to admit that she found Kepler really very lovable and agreeable, that in any case she was far removed from any desire to contend against him, that, on the contrary, his quiet, even-tempered, and yet in no way obtrusive bearing might soon be no less indispensable to her than to her father. She could not help laughing when she reflected that an entirely senseless piece of jealousy of Kepler on the part of her betrothed had been the cause of the ensuing dissensions. But supposing that this jealousy had really contained a grain of truth, a just presentiment of coming events! . . . Poor Tengnagel! Now he sat imprisoned in his narrow chamber, never suspecting that his betrothed was conversing in the utmost cheerful-

102

ness with his rival. Now he was completely impotent, the great, bellowing child. . . . Elizabeth found genuine pleasure in playing with such ideas; and as these whimsical, dangerous imaginings were her sole consolation in her pitiful plight, her only alleviation amid the many trials which she had daily to endure, her behaviour with Kepler was even more insinuating and more bantering than her mood prescribed.

This conduct filled her mother with boundless amazement. The simple woman was utterly at a loss to understand why Elizabeth did not bring her whole influence to bear upon Tycho to injure Kepler, why she maintained such friendly relations with the enemy. She constantly scolded her on that account. But on those occasions Elizabeth always reverted to a plan which, in spite of all, she secretly pursued, and when she revealed it in part to her mother, the latter grew really tranquil. But only for a short time. When subsequently nothing ever happened and matters merely continued in their former manner, the mother, who had conceived a deep, honest hatred for Kepler as the disturber of her daughter's matrimonial happiness, resolved to take matters into her own hands. This she did after her own fashion. Since she did not venture to reveal the real state of affairs to her husband, she began with little gossipy remarks, such as, for instance, that Kepler, a thorough star-gazer, had trampled one of her chicks to death; that his presence was a nuisance everywhere; that she needed his room for storing kitchen utensils. As this had no effect, the worthy woman became more insistent. She deplored the heavy expense which the new comrade entailed upon the household; the necessaries of life were exorbitantly dear; in short, she could not cook for him without payment. Tycho gave her money and sent her away. She returned with a new idea: had Tycho observed that the dwarf would by no means accustom himself to the guest? Whenever he saw him, he disappeared with a piteous howl; he manifestly scented some misfortune. . . .

"Misfortune, yes; fools always scent misfortune when a wise man makes his appearance among them," laughed Tycho. He gave his wife a hearty kiss and disappeared through the other door.

"ARE we alone today?" were the words with which Teng-nagel was accustomed to greet his betrothed when she entered the room in the tower.

"Of course, quite alone," replied Elizabeth in coaxing tones, and laid her arm about his neck.

But a few minutes later invariably Magdalena or the mother would appear, only for a short time, just to see if all was well. But then they would return and establish themselves with their needlework in the little room, which was quite a charming living-place for a brief period; in short, precautions were taken that the lovers should never be left by themselves for any length of time. The greatest regard was shown for polite etiquette and moral considerations. Tengnagel felt this to be a particularly burdensome piece of malice. Before, when he was at liberty, he had naturally been able to enjoy entirely undisturbed encounters with the girl, whenever he wished. Now that it was too late, they were subjected to a rigorous supervision! He was robbed of his rights of possession! He laughed bitterly; what a comedy! Still this is what it had come to. For the time being he must give way to feminine caprice, awaiting a better future.

"Just wait till my servant is back," he would often say to Elizabeth, "till I have money and can move! Then you'll soon see what I'll do."

"Well, what will you do? I am not afraid of you." Yet she trembled at his words.

104

"I am not going to tell you. I have my plan; it is my secret."

"You'll leave us, won't you?"

"Leave Tycho, my friend, my father and my friend! What can you think of me?" he stormed in grief-filled tones. During this period of solitude the relationship between him and Tycho had assumed in his imagination an even more ideal shape. It was now quite genuinely his heart which attached him to the famous man in whose house he had lived for years and with whom he had shared weal and woe; he had entirely forgotten the words of insult. What is more, it was his daily expectation that Tycho would remember him; nay, that, overcome by an irresistible longing for him, he would send to seek him out. "No, no, in any case I will stay near him; I shan't go far. The hour will come when he will need me. And then Tengnagel will be at hand."

"What would they say in Prague if it were suddenly rumoured that you were no longer with us?" Elizabeth asked, with a sanctimonious expression. It brought her no slight pleasure to cause a little embarrassment to her beloved. She knew well that Tengnagel attached the greatest possible importance to his breach with Tycho not becoming public property and to his continuing to be numbered by the world at large as one of those whom he trusted; in his eyes this was an indispensable condition to his further advancement. As long as he continued in his retreat, it did not occur to anyone to feel his absence in any particular degree, and a subsequent reconciliation would lead everyone entirely to forget this inglorious interval. Far otherwise if he had left Benatky and openly shown himself elsewhere. In those circumstances it would not have been possible to keep the quarrel hidden any longer.

"Why, then, do you really need so much money, if you are going to stay here?"

105

But he only answered phlegmatically: "You'll know all in good time."

Thus Elizabeth could not free herself from a certain feeling of alarm, especially now that Tengnagel's servant had recently arrived at the castle of Benatky. He had carried out his commission to his master's relatives most successfully, and returned with heavy bags of money. Elizabeth lost no time in hiding him in a room in the fore-house, out of sight of the tower, and forbade him under pain of death to show himself in the court.

"Now," she said anxiously to herself, "I have two powder-chambers in the house."

However, nothing daunted, she continued to reflect upon the execution of her plan, which appeared to be her sole escape from trouble. She wished to be married in secret to Tengnagel, that her father might at least be spared the worst, the disgrace of a child born out of wedlock. The endurance of Tycho's wrath, his subsequent reconciliation with the already accomplished fact, and his reconciliation with herself and with Tengnagel—all this she wished to take upon herself; she felt that in bearing this humiliation she was expiating her offence. Yet she had imposed a far worse humiliation upon herself at the hands of Tengnagel: she, Tycho's proud daughter, had actually to entreat him to marry her, that too, in this strange and not very honourable form. Tengnagel would certainly not approve of it offhand, attaching as he did so much importance to a union with the family of Brahe in such circumstances that all might behold it. Accordingly she must now represent to him that the union would be made public, that it would be her duty, immediately after the marriage had been concluded, to bring about a public peace between Tycho, Kepler, and her husband. This was unspeakably degrading: she must invent and communicate excuses and arguments in a matter which for

106

her had hitherto been love's free devotion, a joyous resolve of the heart. Yet no other solution offered itself if she was, as far as possible, to spare the two others who were involved, her father and Tengnagel, and concentrate all the bitterness upon her own heart.

But while the presence within her of this heroic resolution was by no means incompatible with occasional outbursts of girlish caprice and with a peculiar, sharp sensation of pleasure at the adventurous character of the whole situation, she did not in practice advance directly towards her aim. Her comprehending anxiety at the prospect of the distressing conversation with her betrothed always drove her, whenever she sought to speak the decisive words, to turn aside in the direction of some sort of insinuation. A hundred times she registered a vow that today she would discuss nothing with him but this question of capital importance. Yet hardly had she opened the doors leading to the room in the tower when her imagination conceived some extraordinary species of prank which she could play upon him, some little piece of malice, some cunning joke. Without doubt she derived pleasure from tormenting him and putting his patience to the test. His defencelessness excited her and made her want to profit to the utmost by the superior strength of her position. Was it not really a wonderful, an almost magic position? All she needed was to ascend a winding staircase, to turn an old key in a rusty lock, and there, at her will, stood her beloved entirely at her disposal; he had no power to flee to the adjoining room if she annoyed him too much with her tales of the high esteem in which Kepler was held in the house; he was forced to listen with the meekness of a lamb and, moreover, as long as she wished. If he, however, uttered a single word which was not agreeable to her, she could go away immediately, free as she had come, and with a turn of the key leave the poor caged animal to himself. And she made a fairly extensive use of these rights of hers. Without being herself conscious of it, she surrendered herself to feelings of sweet revenge in the infliction of this bantering persecution; at the same time she avenged herself in advance for the abrupt rejection of her plan which she feared from Tengnagel. Moreover, an even deeper note may have been struck by the secret wish to render her beloved perhaps more compliant and humbler by means of the policy of little pin-pricks. Yet this was at the same time something before which she stood aghast. No, never did she wish to see her Franz humiliated; in God's name, let that never happen. Thus every torment which she inflicted upon him with a view to bending his pride she felt to be a source of torture, a peril to which she herself was exposed. She desired to revive his spirits; yet once more upon her tongue her words of comfort were transformed into jest. She truly pitied Tengnagel. At this moment she loved him more than ever, loved him for his courage and for the stubbornness with which he endured his embarrassing position. In actual fact this imprisonment brought his best qualities into prominence, his unbroken will to life, his earnest, simple confidence in the future, the steady, inflexible bias of his spirit, which had nothing in it of the trivial. These were genuine qualities, which Elizabeth profoundly admired in him and which she herself did not possess. Never did he admit himself to be in fault; never did he abandon hope. Yet to many the sojourn in the narrow little room in the tower, reeking of incense and mouldy linen, would have been absolutely intolerable. What terrible ennui it entailed to hold out! His visitors could only slip into his room for half an hour during the day; more would have been discovered. And in the evening, at the very moment when one felt oneself most hopelessly abandoned, he could not even kindle a light; that would have be-

108

trayed him. Already at six o'clock the long, winter night must begin for him.

Several times he begged her to procure him a key, behind her mother's back. She hesitated. What if he should one day open the doors, inspired by the desire to go down the stairs? Or quite unexpectedly appear in the castle? The brothers were always on the look-out for him, searching in the neighbourhood. . . . "No, I will not enter the castle until my friend Tycho summons me. I promise you that," he assured her.

"What is the key for, then?"

In reply he expressed himself in mysterious language, hinting that it had some connexion with his far-reaching schemes. In Elizabeth's mind this scheme was something projected into a remote future; she knew that Tengnagel would not precipitate anything. Moreover, she had long wished to see her lover at least symbolically free. She felt an intense resentment that he should be imprisoned in so paltry a style. And on one occasion, when after covering him with ridicule she had roused him to fury, she slipped the key into his hand by way of reconciliation. He flung it back. He had in the mean time converted his sword into a jimmy, to which he pointed with pride.

The relations between the two were marked by an increasingly open hostility; there was conflict in every word and in every action. So Elizabeth beheld herself thrust ever farther from her goal. Yet she could not keep back those wanton utterances which roused Tengnagel to transports of fury. If as a result she felt herself utterly hateful in his eyes, her love for him blazed up amid her pain, deriving twofold zest from his rage. . . . In order to help him pass the time she had brought with her a set of chess-men. They played often, but it was no idle, indifferent pastime; they really struggled with one another for victory, and the game, in which they measured their strength, became serious. Tengnagel loved an obstinate

109

defence, a solid gambit; Elizabeth bewildered him by strange sacrifices of pieces and unexpected knight's moves. If, however, despite all she could not attain her purpose, she had recourse to what was assuredly an even more astounding expedient: she simply caught up with her nimble, dainty hand that particular piece of her opponent which stood in her way and threw it out of the window. "Go down and fetch it," she would cry; "you've got your thief's jimmy."

Once when Tengnagel, his face distorted with rage, looked out after one of the pieces, whom should he behold passing beneath the window but his servant?

Elizabeth blanched.

He turned upon her. "Why—why didn't you tell me this long ago?"

"It is—today—only today—that he arrived."

As she said these words, he scanned her with so terrible a look that she saw that this time he was really in earnest. He collected the pieces and without another word sat down in the corner, apparently only waiting for her to go. Her exhortations and tears were all in vain. Suddenly she was seized with a feeling of terror and hastened away—she longed to go to her father; in her sharp distress she could think of no other aid.

ON THIS very day the unbroken happiness that Tycho had enjoyed for a considerable time received its first alloy of trouble; the news came that his arch-enemy, the imperial court mathematician, Raymarus Ursus, had returned to Prague. On Tycho's arrival in Prague he had fled to Silesia; now, knowing Tycho to be at Benatky, he ventured to return. And, so the tidings ran, he had recently in a public lecture bestowed the most outrageous insults upon Tycho. On that occasion, it is true, Hagecius had courageously taken Tycho's

110

part and refuted the mathematician's arguments in a learned speech in opposition. Further, Ursus had published a pamphlet against Tycho, which was now provoking a great sensation in Prague. Tycho had accordingly lost no time in writing to Hagecius to procure him a copy of this compilation. But even that did not suffice to calm him. He feared that the attack might injure him at court and rob him of the Emperor's favour; he saw his position, his sources of livelihood threatened. He therefore gave himself up to conjectures as to what could be urged against him, and defended himself with all his might against the still invisible enemy.

Elizabeth appeared at the very moment at which Tycho, in a state of the utmost excitement, was recounting the matter to Kepler: "It is certainly true that I myself began this feud. In the name of truth I felt bound to take upon myself the task of punishing this old thief and swine-herd who had forced himself into the world of decent scientific investigators with the robbery of my system. As if I had not a hundred more essential duties towards humanity! Now, however, it has happened. I've written violent letters against him and then had them published. He answered in his way, that of a foul-mouthed slanderer. Insults instead of arguments. In his first pamphlet he constantly alluded to my old friend Rothmann in Kassel as Rotzmann; that's the kind of weapon he employs. But even with this reply he couldn't rest content. Year after year he must continue his attacks upon me. He has, of course, nothing better to do; for him insult is the most agreeable occupation and undoubtedly the one best suited to his capacities. But he keeps me from my more important work; my time is too valuable for this senseless brawling. In the end there'll be nothing for it but to employ the law as a means of getting peace. . . ."

Elizabeth could not pay attention to Tycho's angry

111

discourse. She was too much occupied with herself and feared too much for the next moment. She therefore ran out again, intending to return later, when Tycho should be alone. She went into the courtyard and from all sides looked up at the church tower. There it stood quietly, upon the old spot; nothing stirred. That calmed her somewhat. She wandered about in the garden, looked back again, and beheld the summit of the tower, with its bells and dormer-windows, looking out very good-humouredly, with an air of positive kinship, over the trees. No, perhaps nothing evil would happen. She mounted once more to Tengnagel and found him uncommunicative, but not unfriendly. She sought to appease him altogether and at last believed that she had succeeded.

Towards evening in the best of spirits, she came to her father.

She found him in the library, having his hair cut. He sat in a comfortable arm-chair. A book lay open on his knees; with jerks of his hand he flicked away fragments of fair hair which had fallen here and there upon the pages. On a second chair, behind him, stood Jeppe, the dwarf, like a lackey behind a state coach; he was zealously at work with the scissors upon Tycho's skull. Whenever he did not apply them sufficiently close, Tycho exhorted him: "Closer, closer!" It was a weakness of the great man always to insist on being shaved to the scalp, in order that, as he imagined, his increasing baldness might not be noticed.

For an instant this comic spectacle made Elizabeth forget all her cares. With a laugh she clapped her hands above her head. "But, father," she cried, "how often must I tell you that I can't bear you in that style. I'm vain on your account. I want to have a handsome father."

Tycho regarded her almost mournfully; his smile was but a partial assent to her clear laughter. "I may perhaps have

112

to go to Prague during the next few days. Whatever happens, I'll see to it that you . . ."

"To Prague?" she replied swiftly. "Why don't you send Kepler?"

"Kepler?"

"Why, yes. What is he going to do for you in this matter? Has he said nothing?"

"No, he has said nothing." Tycho reflected. In actual fact Kepler would have been the most suitable person to put Ursus in his proper place once and for all. Far fitter than the gallant Hagecius, who pursued scientific studies merely as an amateur. Kepler's thorough methods, on the other hand, would have torn up an opponent's weak counter-arguments by the roots and swept them away.

This had not hitherto occurred to Tycho. His daughter's remark, however, at once unfolded before him a hundred possibilities of overcoming Ursus through the agency of Kepler.

"But he must have given some answer to your complaints," pursued Elizabeth. "I was standing by while you were in full swing. You didn't see me. But you spoke with so much emphasis and were so forcible in the statement of your case that no one could have resisted you."

"Now, what did he answer?" Tycho reflected in vain. Then he said gloomily: "I haven't asked him to do anything for me."

"And does he ever have to implore you to do anything for him?" Elizabeth went on with growing passion, suddenly seized with a more profound insight into the relationship between the two men. "No, you do it without any entreaties from him, willingly and of your own accord, following the dictates of your own magnanimous heart. You do it without his even thinking of it; you invite him here as if he were your

113

own child and share with him everything which you have, material things equally with the treasures of your spirit. He had no need to open his mouth; you divined his needs and met his wishes as far as you possibly could. And if you have become so far merged in one another, if you are his friend, what need is there of entreaties? Has he no ears? Hasn't he heard the voice of your despair? Wouldn't anyone in his place have seized the opportunity and have stormed out to fight for Tycho and his right, for his friend, his benefactor, for this good and great man? Would you have delayed an instant if he had been the one attacked and had complained so bitterly in your presence?"

Tycho's face grew ever darker. Elizabeth, whose painful agitation illumined so many things like a flash of lightning, touched upon matters which had already for a long time been a source of suffering; hitherto he had not felt any need for troubling himself with them. . . . Suddenly he cried frantically to the dwarf: "Shorter, Jeppe, quite close, quite close!" Then he sank again into his broodings.

Elizabeth continued passionately with her exhortations. As she spoke, she could not help thinking of her Tengnagel; in his narrow way he felt a thousand times more deeply towards Tycho than the more learned but coldblooded Kepler. Yet his goodness of heart had been rewarded by incarceration in the keep. "No, no, your friend Kepler doesn't behave well towards you," she cried; "you go on concealing it from yourself, you refuse to observe it, and yet you know it. He may be a genius, but he is no real man. And so you must be on your guard against him, or he will do you mischief. For he is an evil man, with all his alienation from the world and absence of self an evil man."

"You speak just like your mother," broke out Tycho at
114

last, brought back to himself by the obvious exaggeration of Elizabeth's last words. "This is a regular conspiracy, just women's tricks and nothing else! You, your mother, and Jeppe, too, you have taken into your pay; his hands twitch on the scissors when the name 'Kepler' is mentioned. Yes, Kepler— Kepler—you little abortion, I'll scream it in your ears until it deafens you and you cease your silly convulsions!—Let me see how you've done it." He caused a mirror to be held before him and expressed himself satisfied. He did not seem distressed at the prominence given to the stunted nose and overstrained red eyes, which stood out with almost horrible ugliness upon the shorn countenance—so long as the bald patches were not immediately visible. He stood up and began to move about the room, still excited, but already gaining control of his agitation. "Do you see?" he asked Elizabeth, pointing to his head; "it is by such violent means that one succeeds in getting round nature; nothing else avails. I stick to it; everything is possible; stubborn perseverance will win everything. Only not everyone is the man for it. Not everyone has the hard, inventive head of old Tycho. Kepler himself is a different sort of man from me. What do you want of him? He has capacity of a sort different from mine, while for other tasks again he is altogether useless. But lay no hand upon my Benjamin! Kepler an evil man! Elsa, Elsa, if you can say that—who knows? Perhaps Ursus really was right when he called me a cheat and a scoundrel."

THAT night Tycho worked as usual with Kepler. He made no further allusion to the feud with Ursus.

Next morning, however, Kepler burst in upon Tycho in a state of the greatest indignation. His room had been broken into while he was with Tycho. He had only noticed it on waking up; the drawers of the writing-table and the chests had been violently broken open and the floor was covered with papers.

"My annals!" cried Tycho, and at once hastened to the disordered room. It was clear that the records which Kepler had borrowed from Tycho remained untouched in their covers. Kepler's own papers, on the other hand, had obviously been ransacked and lay strewn about in the greatest disorder. "Isn't it, after all, only your usual state of disorder? You said yourself that you couldn't keep your manuscripts together," laughed Tycho, whose countenance had immediately lighted up.

Conjecture suggested a recently dismissed servant, who had perhaps wished to avenge himself in this way. In reply to questions as to what he had lost, Kepler could only give vague answers. Neither money nor clothes were lacking. Tycho, accordingly, paid no further attention to the matter. . . . Then he was overtaken by a rumour, which had already disseminated itself throughout the whole castle—Elizabeth had suddenly fallen to the ground dead.

With a wild cry Tycho burst into the women's apartments. Elizabeth lay upon a couch—she was alive and had just recovered from a deep faint. Magdalena and her mother were attending to her. Tycho wished to draw near to her, but his wife looked at him with hostility. All he need do, she said, was to go; everything was his fault. Elizabeth uttered a loud sob; she could not answer him. Then in half-intelligible words she asked that she might be allowed to stand up at once; something irreplaceable would be lost if she could not at once take a part in the search. She was speaking of the burglary upon Kepler; she obviously knew more about it than she could say and her swooning was evidently in some way connected with it.

Next her brothers entered the room and asked her whom
116

in particular she wished to search for, upon whom her suspicions rested. They laid angry hands upon their swords, swearing that at length they would restore order to that house. Suddenly the name was uttered: Tengnagel. Elizabeth pressed her head down in the cushions; a spasm ran through her frame. "Why do you torment her, you two? You all torment her," cried her mother. She wished to thrust her sons and Tycho from the room. Suddenly she seemed herself to be overpowered by the agitation; she staggered. Servants supported her and led her to her bedroom.

Tycho followed her, shut the doors behind him, and refused admittance to everyone. He placed his wife on the bed, gave her water, and pressed her hand and forehead, until she had somewhat recovered. Then he said sternly: "Now I must know what really is happening in my house. What is the meaning of these mysterious proceedings?"

She half sat up in bed. "Well, Tyge," she said, "you have destroyed your child's happiness."

"I? What do you mean?"

"No one else but you and Kepler!"

"Christine," replied Tycho in grief-stricken tones, "if it is in your power, speak more calmly to me. . . . We haven't had a good life together. Whose fault is it? I have succeeded in unlearning defiance. When will you give it up? Perhaps we could find some way. I have the best will in the world to bring about a lasting peace. Only you must speak openly to me, in a straightforward way. Have confidence in me for once, conceal nothing from me. How are things going with Elizabeth? What am I to do for her?"

"There is only one thing you can do for her."

"And what is that?"

"Send Kepler away at once."

Tycho's rage flared up again. "You are all against him.

What has he done to you? Why do you want to take him from me? What connexion can he have with Elizabeth's sufferings?"

"It is just that that I can't tell you, until you have sent him away."

"The eternal caprice," thought Tycho. He looked sadly at his wife; seating himself on the edge of the bed, he spoke long and earnestly, but Christine's wrinkles of anger remained, darting across her face like little tongues of blue flame upon an unquiet hearth. . . . These wrinkles had once been the cause of Tycho's love for her. She was at that time an ordinary peasant girl upon his property at Knudstrup. Tycho had credited himself with the capacity of overcoming the inequalities of education and mental gifts solely by means of the power of love. He wished to master all difficulties and to teach his beloved to share in everything that was great, to share in his work. She was to become his friend, consciously assisting him from the depths of the primitive strength of her strong spirit, her wrath, and her clean passion. Ah! what fair dreams! . . . He stroked her thick, iron-grey hair with two fingers, which sank deep into it. He still loved her. It was not without emotion that he felt through the coverlet the warmth of the powerful body, with which he had so often been united.

"What good is this fellow Kepler to you?" she asked, now attempting to win him over. "What does he do for you? You have quite enough pupils to serve your purpose. But you have gone mad about one of them and are ready to sacrifice your family, yourself, and everything to him. I must say, all I see is how you live and work for him. But I don't see what you gain. What has he done for you to pay you back, say?"

"Am I a tradesman that I must always seek my own advantage in everything? Is it only myself and my compensa-

118

tion that matter? What of the spirit that dwells above us all and the furthering of our eternal art, which is of greater importance than these transitory shadows, Tycho or Kepler?" He paused, observing that this was not the right way to work upon Christine's simple disposition. "And supposing I am seeking solely for my own advantage in everything that I do in regard to Kepler. Kepler has great gifts; he is a light for future times. He would have found his way without me, even in my despite. Such a genius can't remain hidden. Isn't it, therefore, wiser if I make myself from the very beginning of some use to him and thereby bind him to me, laying him under a perpetual obligation? . . ." Tycho gave utterance to these words with a cunning laugh, quite alien to his habits; for a space he did not know whether these thoughts, which had never before been present in his mind, were invented for the occasion or whether, in the final analysis, they did express the secret motives of his fondness for Kepler. Then he shuddered as if he had looked upon Medusa's head. He beheld all that was most noble and beautiful in his soul profaned and dragged through the dust. He became uncertain, began to falter, and actually blushed. A feeling of pain such as he had never before experienced prevented him from speaking. "For even the just man sins seven times a day," he continued after a long pause, while the smile froze upon his grey cheeks.

"Yes, you do well to look within yourself, once in a while," said his wife in a chiding tone, misinterpreting his sudden rigidity; "it would be a very good thing to tell you the truth; that would open your eyes. But we are all afraid of you. You want nothing near you but just toadies. God knows how that Kepler flatters you; that's why you cling so closely to him. If you could endure the truth, we should still be all at home and not compelled to wander about the world like vagabonds.

119

But you didn't get enough flattery at home; that is why we had to go away."

Tycho got up and left the room.

He felt that these family quarrels stained the purest that was in him. They were already entangling him in the brakes of wild despair and in torments of conscience; they were beginning to devour his natural, deeply seated feeling for Kepler; they belittled him and had already brought him to the point of quite groundlessly suspecting himself of low-minded calculations. . . . No it must not go as far as that; he would strive no longer. He pitied his wife; the poor creature could not forget her Denmark, she was suffering from homesickness. But it simply did not lie in his power to help her. And what was he to do for Elizabeth? Some transitory fright which he did not understand might have brought her to this state. No, to preserve the purity of his spirit he must shut himself off, he must withdraw from this perverse family. After his conversation with his wife this was clearer to him than before. He must simply work, and not consume his energies in introspection and idle subtleties about profit and compensation; they only had a shattering and pernicious effect upon him and led to no result. And finally he must never again utter a single unbecoming word about Kepler. The relationship between the two men must gradually come to be understood by all as something quite natural, like the beating of the heart or breathing. "It is, indeed, heart-beat and breath of life to me," said Tycho to himself.

TOWARDS noon Elizabeth succeeded in escaping unnoticed from her room.

Her first act was to proceed to Tengnagel's tower. Her conjecture was correct. The door was open and the room empty.

120

Although she had not anticipated anything else, she turned giddy with terror. Then, however, she told herself that she must keep cool. Without further consideration she ran through the vineyard, the shortest way down to the main road. There she took the direction leading to Lissa. That was the nearest town of any size and she reckoned that Tengnagel would not have got any farther. At first she was full of confidence, believing that she must meet her beloved on the high-road. Arrived in the town itself, she grew more anxious, asked more and more frequently, and described the object of her quest in closer detail. Despair overcame her. What if, heedless of his reputation, he really had ridden to Prague? It was already growing dark when she started on the return journey. Out of breath and panting, she still forced herself to hasten. Her absence must not be observed in Benatky, or she would not be able to pursue her inquiries on the following day. The uncertain light of the earliest stars illumined her path. At the edge of every wood she beheld her betrothed, his image was reflected in every little brook, he leaned his back upon each of the hills that gradually disappeared in the distance. The huge purple archway of the evening sky was filled with his breath. Her boundless yearning took its course throughout the silent landscape. Elizabeth paused in her running; she heard her last footfall echoing in the wilderness, the only sound in a wide radius around her. But now, as she felt a silence about her, profound as that of the grave, she could not restrain a wild shriek; it was as if her last hope fled from her with this strange outcry. Then she dropped into a weary trot; her powers of resistance, during the last week strained to the utmost, were broken. And thus in the dark she came upon the turning leading round the first huts of Benatky, along the Iser. . . . Suddenly she heard her name called.

It was Tengnagel. He was standing by a group of peasants,

apparently occupied with some kind of agricultural labour.

All her muscles at once grew tense. He came towards her and without a word of salutation led her into the hut before which he had been standing. . . . As soon as they were alone, she screamed at him with all the fury accumulated from the despair of the afternoon: "You are the thief. You robbed Kepler's room. I know it."

He laughed roughly, gripping her so firmly that she could make no resistance. Then he kissed her. "Now," he cried, "I have you once more. At last we are together again and free from your mother's protection."

"You thief," she cried, and tried to free herself from his arms, "you thief, I despise you."

"You have been looking for me, darling, and now you have me just as I am."

She spat over her shoulder into the middle of the dark room: "Bah, thief, robber. Oh! how I hate you! Now deny it; say you didn't do it, this common thief's action. Let me go, I tell you; let me go, liar!"

The more she struggled, the closer he held her to him. "You call it stealing. I call it politics. . . . Just look here." He indicated the table with a jerk of his chin. "Important papers. A chaste little letter from Mr. Kepler, who is a traitor and an enemy to Tycho, as I had suspected." He led her to the table, releasing her from his embrace, only holding her hand with an iron grasp. The first thing that he handed her was the draft of the unpleasant letter which Kepler had written on the very morning after his arrival, but had not dispatched. Then he showed Tycho's first letter to Kepler, which Kepler had undoubtedly adorned with some exceedingly sarcastic marginal comments. Thus to the passage in which Tycho expressed his expectation that Kepler would soon pass from the Copernican system of the universe to the Tychonic was

122

added the comment: "Everyone is in love with himself."

"And you wish to show that to my father?" Elizabeth started wildly up. "You wish to break his heart? That is just like you."

"No, darling, I'm not going to do that. There are more important things to do first. I have found other documents; it is high treason and conspiracy that we are concerned with. I've already composed a letter to the Chancellor. Kepler is corresponding with the Evangelical Free Cities. I am on the track of a whole conspiracy. Now, you know nothing about it. I shall sit here and study these fragments of paper. . . . Just wait, one of these days the tipstaff will come for that fellow. But I shall be there then and shall not hurt my friend Tycho with these letters; no, they will enable me to comfort and tranquillize him."

"If he doesn't first have you put on the wheel for a common house-thief."

"Oh no, I have provided for that. My friend Tycho is very irascible. When we were at Hveen, we all experienced the sternness with which he treated his dependants and the recalcitrant members of his household. That is why I have constructed a stronghold for myself here."

"A stronghold?"

He led her to the window. "I can certainly call it that. The wall about this house will be finished in the course of this night. And with the sturdy lads whom I have recruited as garrison, I shall at least hold out until the Emperor learns of my well-founded representations. . . . Anyway Tycho won't look for me here. He thinks of me as long ago over the mountains, far away; your brothers think the same. But I have promised you to stay near him until a decision is reached. I have exchanged my tower for freer quarters. But I keep my word, Elizabeth; a liar I am not."

123

It was quite unnecessary for him to have mentioned the tower in so triumphant a tone. Elizabeth felt that her power over him was at an end. This, together with the horror inspired by the warlike preparations which she beheld directed against her father, paralysed her thought and flung her into utter disarray. All she could still feel was a dull, impotent aversion towards Tengnagel, mingled with a secret rapture at his strength, his escape, and his courage. This sensation increased as he once more threw his arms about her and pressed his cheeks upon her burning face. She felt herself on the verge of suffocation. "No one will tell him where I am," he whispered in her ear, "unless you betray me. Will you betray me, dearest?"

"Yes, yes, I shall betray you," she cried in ever feebler accents. She felt herself to be falling over a precipice; she felt that everything was lost. Now events must take their course; she had done all in her power. Suddenly it was as if she had been deprived of all sense of responsibility; an altogether new, strange repose overtook her in the midst of the uproar of her senses.

"Really, you'll betray me?" His voice was now nothing more than a snigger, a malignant hiss. She heard it resounding sweet and warm in her mouth; it travelled into the depths of her throat.

"Yes, I will," she moaned, and kissed him.

Thereat he struck her in the face with his fist. They strove together as in their conversations in the tower, but this time body against body. Soon both fell to the floor. . . . A love which knew no bounds filled Elizabeth's heart. The beloved now washed the stain of imprisonment from himself and she felt herself set free together with him. She bit him hard on the ear and on the lips. "I will, I will betray you," she kept panting. . . .

124

THAT afternoon vouchsafed no peace to Tycho. His two sons, Tyge and Jörgen, appeared in the observatory and wished with Kepler's assistance to open an inquiry into the burglary. Since Tengnagel's disappearance they had arrogated to themselves a kind of police power in the castle. Tengnagel had tyrannized over them and had lost no opportunity of making them feel that they were immature boys; in consequence their hatred for him knew no bounds. They now suspected that Tengnagel had had a hand in the burglary. For that reason they were unwilling to let the matter rest. Their energetic conduct was, however, also directed against Kepler; they disliked his growing consideration in the eyes of their father and feared that he might prove a second usurper of the paternal rights. They accordingly represented to their father that since Kepler's entry into the house there had been no end to the vexatious incidents, that he did not fit into the family, and that, moreover, they themselves would help their father so zealously in his scientific labour that he could quite conveniently let Kepler go. . . .

Tycho stared at them and then dismissed them with a wave of the hand.

He strode angrily up and down. "And if I must be at war with everyone, Kepler and I are inseparable!"

During the evening he sat with Longomontanus and Müller at his apparatus—Kepler had excused himself on the score of agitation and indisposition and had retired early to bed. It was already very late when a messenger on horseback was announced.

He came from Hagecius and brought the new book of Raymarus Ursus, as requested, with a humorous letter from the doctor. In it he interpreted the title of the compilation, *Chronotheatrum*, to mean that it was as trivial as a stage-play and as malevolent as a chronic disease.

"Now, that shows good friends still exist!" cried Tycho, delighted at the speedy execution of his commission. Then he impatiently hurried into the next room to look through the polemic undisturbed.

It was just what he had expected. The old lies were repeated, and while shamelessly bringing forward against Tycho without investigation the most outrageous charges that he had ever heard, the author added mysterious insinuations, designed to give the impression that good breeding compelled him to withhold far more damaging facts that were in his possession. Not only was Tycho assigned the lowest place as a scientific inquirer on the score of ignorance and incapacity; he was further styled a criminal, a hypocrite, an intriguer, a thoroughly abandoned character. With no small display of wit and acuteness brief passages were violently extracted from some clumsy and arrogant writings of Tycho's youth and juxtaposed in a context which they had never possessed, in proof of the blasphemous character of his opinions. These sentences, in no less arbitrary manner, were confronted with quotations from Tycho's later books, and contradictions discovered in places which actually gave evidence of a process of gradual evolution. And if he really had been guilty of some trifling error, some piece of inadvertence here and there, he might rest assured that it would be underlined a hundred times over as a show-piece on the enemy's parade ground.

Tycho felt the blood rising to his head, the veins in his temples beginning to throb with a twofold speed, and a sudden flow of warmth spreading over his face, descending to his nose, then to his mouth. . . . He was used to attacks and unfavourable criticism; at times he even regarded them as profitable, and never had he deluded himself into believing that it could be otherwise, that the honourable character of his intentions would be understood by men. What, however,

126

threw him ever anew into a violent state of agitation was this evil miasma of hatred and malevolence which beat upon him in token of gratitude for his services, in place of love and affection. Now came this circumstantial, cunningly thought-out hatred on the part of Ursus! So a man had sat down reading his works throughout weeks and months, nay, studying them, but not for one instant with the intention of drawing improvement and instruction from them—always in the spirit of the hunter on the track of his prey, vigilant and hostile. This idea confused and oppressed Tycho. "So that is what I have worked for!" He could not help grinding his teeth. Then suddenly he found his courage anew: "No, I will not give way! I will be stronger than my enemy." And for a while he was actually conscious of an increased joy in living and of a defiant desire for work. But how well he knew this stage of transition! How often had he experienced it, too often, and for that very reason how it tortured him, that forced, artificial comfort! For future creative work it was equilibrium that he needed, not such abnormal excitement, such unnatural antidotes. . . .

He read on further, as if a zealous search must result in discovering some note of friendliness in the pamphlet. As he did so, he leaned upon one of his great celestial globes, caressingly stroking with his left hand the wooden circles, which he himself had made. Suddenly his eyes quivered; his expression grew troubled. . . . Kepler was mentioned in the writing. . . . He did not at once understand the sense of these lines. Yes, Kepler was spoken of with praise; his achievements were celebrated in the most dulcet language. . . . "How can it be?" thought Tycho. "His system must seem to Ursus in particular far more absurd than my own. . . ." And yet there was no possibility of doubt; Kepler was applauded and recognition was bestowed upon him in most judicious terms. And

127

further—but what did it mean? Kepler was compared with Tycho, rated above Tycho, played off against him, lauded as his enemy, as Tycho's conqueror. . . . "What, then, is this Ursus become insane merely from hatred?" Tycho asked himself. "He would bring my Benjamin, my Hipparchus, into enmity with me; he would alienate my dearest, nay, my only friend, whom this very day I have recognized as the true pole of my heaven, for whom I sacrifice my wife and children; for he is my son in a truer sense, not according to flesh and blood, but according to the spirit; he is my hope, my future, my labour, and my art. . . ."

He turned over the pages with greater violence. Where did the explanation lie? Then just behind the frontispiece he found the name of Kepler again. This time printed in particularly noticeable type. . . . "To the most renowned mathematician Raymarus Ursus!" . . . It was a letter from Kepler. A forgery! No, Ursus was not to be credited with such clumsy audacity. . . . It was an original letter of Kepler's. With his signature. And what a letter! Honour, admiration, mastery . . . fulsome praise in every line . . . Tycho sought to cry aloud. His tongue had grown quite thick; it refused to stir. His heart beat so speedily and abruptly that in his breast it already seemed to have hammered out an empty space. . . . Kepler, then, was one of Tycho's bitterest foes; that was the explanation.

"Treachery . . ." stammered Tycho in low tones.

His daughter's objections against Kepler began to rattle like stones through his head. Black stones, heavy as lead, beating from within upon the walls of his brain, like something living, bending his whole body, now upon one side, now upon the other. . . . Treachery, treachery, Kepler a scoundrel. . . . Now he must regain his voice, now his chest expanded, now he desired to cry aloud. Then the stones began

128

to roll into his mouth, down his windpipe. He lost his breath. . . .

The pupils in the adjoining room started up in terror. A dull thud was heard, and the sound of something cracking into pieces. They rushed into the room. Tycho lay unconscious on the floor, his left hand still convulsively clasping the gaping tubes and circular network of his globe, which he had dragged down and broken in his fall.

CHAPTER VIII

THE NEXT DAY at the accustomed time Kepler appeared in
Tycho's presence to continue their common work on the *Progymnasmata*.

Tycho trembled so much that he could hardly stand. Nor
could he look Kepler in the eyes. This disillusionment was one
of excessive bitterness. He almost felt ashamed of it; therefore
he looked past Kepler at the bare wall. He felt ill and exhausted, but there was nothing of violence in his grief; there
was even something of sweetness. Since the previous evening
sonorous Latin verses had been passing through his head,
verses for an inscription upon a tomb; an enchanting note of
melancholy pervaded them in the constantly recurring line:
"Do you ask who has overthrown me? Not my many enemies,
the ingratitude of a friend, of the only . . ."

In clear, modest tones Kepler began to read his report
upon the conclusions to which he believed his examination of
Tycho's manuscripts was leading him.

"Can this voice, so full of loyalty and steadfastness, utter
lies?" thought Tycho.

He had determined to say nothing at all to Kepler about
this matter of the traitorous letter. He wished still to retain
him for a few days and then to send him away upon some
pretext which would not hurt his feelings; thereafter he would
hold no further communication with him. In such a way he

130

would best succeed in retaining a pure memory of this, the most sympathetic relationship of his life.

With great difficulty he mastered his emotions; he did not utter a single word. But soon he could no longer contain himself; he interrupted Kepler with the words: "Ursus's libel arrived yesterday evening."

Kepler paused, nodded, and proceeded with his exposition, in which he was entirely absorbed.

Tycho was forced to leave his seat. He strode up and down. Suddenly he held the book under Kepler's nose. "There," he cried.

"So small!" laughed Kepler, and turned the pages of the thin volume, readily pushing away his own writings. He read on, the corners of his mouth curling contemptuously. "Well, now, he'll smash you and your theory with this just as a snail might destroy the earth."

"No, he won't, he won't," moaned Tycho, taking the book in his hand. He turned to Kepler's letter. "There is also a letter from you to him printed here. In it you express yourself in different terms about him. Was it really written by you?"

Kepler read the whole page carefully, from top to bottom. "Yes," he answered.

Tycho stood as one turned to stone. Not a word of excuse, not a syllable of contrition escaped Kepler's lips. So, after all, it was quite in order to calumniate one's teacher behind his back, and he was alone in regarding it as a scoundrel's act, in this as in all things differing in his opinions from everyone else. He was utterly bewildered. He bent down once more to have a near view of this Kepler with brow at once brazen and gentle, the man of the insidious laudatory epistles; he even wished to enjoy this strange apparition to the full.

Then his eyes fell quite by chance upon the date of the letter. The date was 1596. "You sent this letter to Ursus," he said gently and utterly overwhelmed, "in the year 1596, Kepler?"

"Yes, at the same time as my *Prodromus*," answered Kepler, who in the innocence of his heart still did not understand what Tycho was really aiming at.

"At a time, therefore, when you still didn't know me, when we had no personal relations with one another?"

Kepler was forced to reflect. "No. You wrote to me for the first time on the occasion of my *Prodromus*. And this Ursus?" Kepler burst out laughing, and to Tycho it seemed that it was the first time that he had heard him laugh. "Coming from him it is a piece of utter roguery." Anger seized upon him. . . .

He was about to continue. But Tycho convulsively gripped his arm. He did not wish to hear any more. He yearned for a profound repose about him, a repose that by reaction would bring healing from that brawling chaos. Greatly moved, he stared up at the ceiling, with moist eyes. . . . "God be praised for this!" he burst out with sudden violence. "Kepler," he cried, and held out both his hands to him, "friend, how I suffered last night owing to this letter!" Then, after a long pause, he continued more calmly: "Now I understand. You wrote this letter to Ursus at that time just as you must have sent a hundred other copies of dedications." He forced his still trembling lips into a painful smile. "Naturally the young scholar, without appointment, addresses himself to the imperial court mathematician, and in such circumstances phrases of admiration are quite in place! You were probably advised to have recourse to him."

"My friends wrote all these letters for me. I never contributed anything but the signature. I am idle in such matters."

"Your friends? And to me too? But no, no, I understand. I am not so paltry. All that is a matter of indifference to me. One dedication or another, I know how they are contrived.

132

They are things that come into existence when one is half asleep; there is no real or great love there. But then came our friendship, and that was and is genuine, O my Benjamin, isn't it? I know it. I understand everything now. Do we want to trouble about it any longer? Assuredly not. It is all over and you are unsullied, my friend, even as I am unsullied. Oh, my joy, my holy joy, that you are pure and great, and that your heart is noble, my dear Kepler! But this Ursus, of whom I will never, never, speak again, he sought at a well-calculated moment to play off against me as his trump-card your harmless, long-forgotten letter; that is the meaning of it. It was to seem as if you, whom I was proclaiming before the world as my friend and as sharing in my opinions, had attacked me from behind and passed over to my mortal enemies. Four years ago, ha ha, four years ago! That date was to be overlooked. It was successful with me, too. I was blinded, completely blinded. But do read this ordurous book through and you will see if this *perfidia* might not really rob one of understanding. These lies! You stare at me? Don't you understand me? You don't realize how such attacks can stir one? Oh, you have certainly never experienced them. You have always been either praised or passed over in silence. Yes, that is the best, to remain unknown, unspotted, virginal, to work only for oneself and for science. With longing I think of those days when as yet that coxcomb could not whet his bill upon me. I often think, if only I had never published anything . . . But this Ursus bestows the most tremendous praise upon you. Won't you read it?"

Kepler thrust the book away with a motion of the hand.

"Be honest about it, Kepler. You don't really understand my fury at these iniquitous, cunning critics, do you?"

"No."

"And why not? Won't you tell me?"

Kepler looked upward somewhat anxiously, like a school-boy faced with a difficult task. He reflected as though in duty bound. At last he said slowly and simply: "It can never be of any importance what criticisms one's works encounter on the part of others as long as we truly believe in ourselves."

Tycho laughed good-naturedly. "Now that is at least as clear as twice two. That is an obvious piece of wisdom. . . . But these matters are not quite so simple. Admitted that outward failure does not deprive one of one's inner confidence in oneself, it certainly takes away tranquillity, freedom from prejudice, or, though doubtless a grossly material consideration, one's portion of acclaim in the world and the money necessary to be able to lead an undisturbed life of creation. Will you say that external matters are never of importance?" As Kepler made no reply, Tycho pointed to his escutcheon hanging upon the wall. "You have yourself only given utterance to that which constitutes my device. Here it is: 'Nor power, nor wealth; only the sceptre of the spirit shall prevail.' But how if one needs power, not for its own sake, but to be able to raise aloft the sceptre of the spirit? If upon our earth each is involved with the other, the external with the internal?— No, no, it is more complicated than you imagine. If my impotence does not injure my pride, I don't trouble myself at all about it. But who is to carry my intellectual labour to completion if I become impotent? It is out of consideration for that that I must defend myself. I must come back to the knave Ursus, although I wanted to forget him. . . . His wife is a common strumpet," he suddenly burst out. "I know it from reliable sources. And he takes the wages of her shame to deck his own concubines. That is the kind of worthy he is. Oh, he shall leave Prague and go back to his herds of swine in Ditmarsh, whence he came. And you, Kepler, you'll help me. For his treachery has involved you,

134

too, in this sorry business, and you must be a man and hew a path out of it for both of us." He seized Kepler's hand passionately. "You must defend me! Will you? Promise me!"

"Yes, I'll do it readily," said Kepler with some hesitation. "Only I don't quite understand how."

"Are you really so unskilful? My dear friend, it is quite a simple matter. You yourself would not willingly acquiesce in Ursus's treating your letter as a permanent and enduring token of assent to his infamous activities? That would surely not be agreeable to you? Now, it is for you to say quite openly what you think about it, in the eyes of the world to set Ursus's insolence in its place. I don't ask you to write anything that doesn't in all respects proceed from your own convictions. But do read the book through; that alone, with all its mistakes on points of fact, and its personal nastiness, will stir you to answer."

"Yes, I'll read it," said Kepler calmly, and he took the book. He did not, however, open it, but placed it under his manuscripts. He seemed pleased that for the time being a way out had in this way been discovered and a conclusion reached. Or did he view the matter as settled, leaving him nothing to add to his promise? In any case, Tycho found no further occasion for reverting to the subject. . . . From that moment the two discussed Tycho's *Ephemerides,* just as on other days. . . . "At least when he goes away, he may feel a desire to tranquillize me by repeating his promise," thought Tycho. But no, Kepler took his leave at midday as if absolutely nothing had happened. Tycho observed with some annoyance that Ursus's pamphlet had already slipped in among his other papers. As he went out, it lay in Kepler's arms completely covered and invisible, as if forgotten.

Thus there still remained a sting in Tycho's breast. Although the agitation of the night had proved to be without

135

foundation, its traces still made themselves felt through the torturing mistrust which gained an ever stronger hold upon him. He was filled with doubt. Had Kepler promised anything at all? Read, yes, of course he would read the pasquinade. Did not that sound like an evasion, like a cunning reservation? What, indeed, had been achieved if Kepler just read the book and refused to let his peace be further disturbed? . . .

Unable to await their next meeting, he sent for him during the afternoon. Kepler entered, with his slim, elegant form, his open countenance, and his characteristic movement of the hands, which Tycho so much loved—he sometimes appeared with two fingers pressed upon his forehead, as if to startle himself out of a state of oblivion. At once all Tycho's suspicion disappeared and it was with his whole heart that he greeted his friend. He felt an oppressive darkness lifted from his spirit as soon as Kepler's gentle black eyes rested upon him. "I am a second King Saul," he said in some confusion, "who must always send for his David with his harp to assuage his melancholy. Do you think that one day I shall cast the spear at you? Now, 'Saul hath slain his thousands, but David his ten thousands,' they are already crying aloud in the streets, or even worse . . . but I don't wish to speak of it. I wanted to ask you when you intend to begin the reply to Ursus."

"At once," replied Kepler, in astonishment, with a vague nod of the head.

Tycho pressed his hand delightedly. "Ah! that's right. You give me a feeling of real satisfaction. Moreover, it is genuinely necessary that it should be done at once. Blow must answer blow. During the following week we shall publish the *Apologia Tychonis contra Ursum*, shan't we? You see, I have already found a title for the work. I have taken that labour off your shoulders, and in other directions I shan't give you unneces-

136

sary trouble. Only say what is absolutely necessary; two sheets of print would be enough. . . ." He had talked himself into a state of excitement and took his burning cheeks between his hands. Then he uttered a sigh. "There is something not very graceful in constraining you in this way; I realize it. And yet, and yet . . . There is a secret hidden from the world, which the old Tycho with all his fifty years doesn't know how to handle." He stared before him, deep in thought, and only after a considerable silence repeated: "It's not very graceful to constrain you in this way. There is no denying it. And yet, however much I reflect upon it, I can't make out what it really is that is so ungraceful. What is it? And the strange thing is that quite often I come to a point where my feelings tell me: 'No further,' and where, none the less, my heart urges me on; for with the best will in the world my understanding fails to descry what it is that should be forbidden.— Is there anything, after all, more natural in the world than that friends should stand by one another, come to one another's help in all the honesty of their conviction? Well, then. Do I ask anything different or anything more from you? No. And is there anything great and difficult involved in what I ask of you? No, again. You'll sit down, take the book, and read it through in less than an hour; then you'll take paper and ink and have it all done in less than two hours." In the excitement of what he was saying Tycho had actually opened a book before him and spread out paper and ink; he even indicated a few letters, just like an actor, as if it were necessary for him to show Kepler how to do everything, down to the smallest detail. Then, with a satisfied smile, he shut the volume. For an instant at least Kepler's reply was actually finished in his imagination. "Now you see," he said joyously, "how easy everything is in the world. As I am always ready to say, everything is possible. Men

137

make purely superfluous difficulties for one another and stand in each other's way out of mere incapacity for understanding. So someone with a clear head must come along and remove these purely imaginary difficulties without any timidity, just sweep them away.— It is even as I say: it would have been more agreeable if you had offered to write this answer of your own free will and I had not been forced to ask you, to constrain you. But you didn't do it. And, after all, what does it amount to? Is it an irreparable misfortune? No, I know quite well that it isn't your way to put yourself forward. That is why I have constrained you. And now the whole matter is in order. Or would it perhaps have been better if you had said nothing and I had said nothing, if I had got thoroughly out of humour and again said nothing to you, not telling you why? You would naturally not have asked me about it—I already know you to that extent—and would in your turn have grown displeased, and in the end our love for one another would have gone to pieces out of sheer fine feeling and a desire to appear distinguished. Is it not so, my Kepler?— Ah! one simply mustn't leave Nature in undisputed control; one must take the reins from her, and from time to time set God's rule to rights in small matters. That's all. But enough of these unpleasant interruptions of our labour. To work!"

Work, however, was of brief duration. Hardly had Kepler raised his voice to ask a mere question of detail when Tycho, as if excited by the very sound, at once turned away from astronomy and reverted to Ursus, although he had sworn not to speak of him again. "That is another thing that this bestial hound casts up against me, that I want to put God's rule to rights. In the recklessness of my youth I really did write something of the sort. From that he deduces that I believe in no God. Besides, I am too shrewd, too cunning. That

138

is his favourite charge against me. In his opinion I take too active a part in worldly affairs; I cunningly court the favour of the mighty, calculate my demeanour; out of prudence I am anxious to find nothing in the stars that doesn't chime in with the wishes of kings. Thus he casts doubt upon the freedom of my spirit, upon my investigations, and upon everything noble in me, everything that springs from intuition. I am a mere hair-splitter and blasphemer. . . . Ah! the shameless wretch! If he had only an inkling of the terms upon which I am with my God! How I do not blaspheme Him, nay, but pray to Him, day and night, for a single token! . . . Yet what right could an enemy have to pass judgment upon this secret of mine? An enemy, too, who misinterprets even those elements in me which are most obvious. A man who doesn't realize that I have never asked those in authority for anything—take note of this, Kepler; you must include it in what you write—excepting the means of carrying on my scientific labours. It is only for the sake of these labours that I have grown prudent. I will gladly forgo everything else; indeed, I already have. 'Nor power, nor wealth . . .' You know. And I am always learning to renounce; the circle of my desires grows ever narrower. Dear Kepler, now I speak confidentially to you; I owe this to you. I learn from you, yes, I learn from you, and gladly I admit it, to forgo, to become one-sided, to think only of the higher arts and of nothing else. Formerly I thought, for instance, a great deal about my children or my wife. It had been my intention to look at the riddles of the heavens in co-operation with her, to work with her. Now I see that it cannot be. I must come before God all alone and in my nakedness. I must surrender that which is dearest to me in order to reach Him. And I do it. Since yesterday I have hardened my heart against my family; yesterday saw the decision.—You, too, have a child and wife at home, my Kepler.

139

How do you arrange it that they don't disturb you and distract your attention from the heavens? I should like to know."

As Tycho asked for full details, Kepler recounted how he had married a widow, who kept house excellently for him and with whom he lived on tranquil terms. She had brought him a handsome fortune at marriage. He had not yet any children of his own, only a stepdaughter, of whom he was very fond, named Regina, "Rögel."

Tycho groaned. All at once he felt that a worthy, seemly mode of life was possible only on the basis adopted by Kepler.

Without waiting to be asked he told Kepler that he had certainly not chosen his own wife so wisely. He did not, of course, regret his choice. He had seduced the fifteen-year-old servant-girl, but had thenceforth remained faithful to her. This had, of course caused dissension in his family, of such noble, ancient Danish stock. "What a struggle I was forced to carry on for the legitimacy of my children! Even now they are not reckoned as my equals in all respects; otherwise such humble squireens as Gellius or Tengnagel would never have dared to come forward as my daughters' suitors. And when, after struggles lasting for years, I was driven away from Hveen, the old calumnies of the courtiers were revived; they said I lived with a concubine and that I ignored the obligations imposed by religion. . . . Ah, if you could record all that, Kepler, all the wrong that has been done me! It would be a book worthy to rank with Plato's apology for Socrates. How much wrong has been done me, ay, and still is done me! Now they say once more that I am too shrewd and self-seeking. Amazing shrewdness and calculation, forsooth, to make such a marriage! Now, am I too unthinking, as some say, or too shrewd, as others say? I don't know myself. I feel only that I have to carry a world of woes, like Atlas. Perhaps I am at once too shrewd and too heedless.
140

Perhaps I suffer so much at the hands of my critics just because they are all in the right against me, because I really am the most ill-conditioned, abandoned, unfortunate creature that God ever made."

"Master," said Kepler in gentle tones, "you occupy yourself too much with those wretched scribblers; you bestow too much honour upon them."

"Do you think so?—Oh no, I really feel as if something evil that will not dissolve lies in the depths of my soul. And it is just that point that those who censure me always strike. Perhaps they don't realize it; perhaps they really only find fault with me upon issues where in reality they are wrong. But, none the less, I always shudder when I feel that they would have been right if only they had gone deeper. . . . I am boundlessly vain, writes Ursus. No, that is a lie; vain I am not. But he really is right when he says that in my house there are portraits of me on every wall. Look about you! How I grin down at you from every wall, from every medallion in the instruments! *'Quid si sic?'* I cry boastfully yonder and point complacently to an exposition of my system. The painters always do it in that way, and the instrument-maker thinks his work incomplete if he does not print a portrait of me somewhere on the armilla. Am I to blame? Can I attend to all these matters? Yes, if I really were as shrewd as my enemies allege, then perhaps I should attend to such childish trifles. I am well aware that they search for my defects with Argus eyes, finding fault with everything in me. Oh, it is insupportable, an insupportable situation. . . . Come with me, Kepler. I'll show you a portrait after my own heart, which no one has yet seen. I painted it myself once, when in a state of rapturous excitement. It is my holy relic. Then you will be able to say from your own judgment whether I am self-seeking."

141

They passed through the library, with its allegories and apophthegms, its portraits and votive tablets. Tycho lifted a bolt which was hidden behind a picture frame. A secret door opened, giving access to a little chamber resembling a chapel. Its windows were darkened by heavy curtains; the walls were bare; in the middle of the room there stood upon an easel a single picture, painted in faint colours and uncertain outlines. Without uttering a word Tycho pointed to the inscription, which could only with difficulty be read: "Give not the honour to Tycho, but to the Tychonid, to the heir of his art— master of all masters." It now really did become possible to detect a mysterious figure, in the greenish, uncertain light striding forward towards the future.

"You painted that yourself?"

"Yes, to console myself. Years ago. In order to raise myself above all earthly contingencies. And quite genuinely, it was as if some spirit-hand guided the brush for me; I had never touched a brush before, nor have I since. This picture seemed to me to be a painted oracle and I have faith in it; I believe that in far, far-away days there will come one who will understand me more perfectly than at present I myself can survey the perplexity of my own spirit. And he will look like that; in that shape he has revealed himself to me in advance. . . . But look, my Kepler, isn't he like you, the Tychonid?"

Kepler cried out, so violently had Tycho caught hold of him, to pull him immediately opposite the picture, all the while apostrophizing him in ever more confused language. Now Tycho was speaking of astrological symbols which had appeared in clear conjunction at his birth and at that of Kepler, of the harmony of the universe, and of the great scholars of all centuries, whose souls dwelt as models upon the planets. He wandered off into a realm of lofty fantasy, filled with

142

the same atmosphere of spectral and confused devotion as the room itself, with its wild image, its bare walls, and the keen, damp air which seemed to float in through invisible slits. . . . Kepler shrank in horror before Tycho's violence. And now he imagined that he beheld in a corner a vague, cowering form; yet Tycho, although Kepler drew his attention to it, refused to interrupt his bombast, but continued rhapsodizing, dragging at his arm like one demented. The figure seemed to assume ever larger proportions and to be issuing forth from its corner. The horror of the situation was too much for Kepler; he tore himself away from Tycho, leaped to the window, and with a jerk flung back the curtain.

The uncanny spell of the place vanished in an instant. A small, unfurnished room, containing an easel, struck icily cold in the prosaic light of the day. Tycho stared straight before him, blinded by the invading sun. Kepler stood at the window. Before the two stood—Elizabeth.

"You here?—In my adytum?" Tycho turned furiously upon her. "Who told you—how did you come here? And why?"

Elizabeth bowed her head in mortal distress, remaining silent.

"Once more, Elsa, you won't speak? This time, too? Won't you speak to your father?"

There was a long pause.

"Come, Kepler," cried Tycho suddenly. "What are we standing here for? My shrine has been profaned! Come!" His features expressed horror and profound aversion. "Let us leave the undutiful child."

Not until he was alone with Kepler in the room containing the instruments did he continue: "I won't trouble myself any further about Elizabeth. Nor about my family. They shall see how they will get on without me, in a foreign country, obstinate as they are. What are they without me but a nameless, helpless horde? I have known uneasiness on their account times without number; I have toiled for them; I have been 'too shrewd' in their interests, and all in vain. Each is determined to go his own way; no one obeys me.—So be it; I will let them fall upon their own ruin, for I can't hold them back, not when I strain every nerve. But I will follow you, Kepler. You are now my model, my teacher; I am the pupil. I will be free as you are free, not shrewd, but blind, without self-consciousness, living only for our art and for nothing else in the world."

ON THE previous evening Elizabeth had returned home very early, without attracting any attention. She sank into a deep and dreamless sleep. She had remained without sleep throughout all the weeks during which she had fought for Tengnagel and for her honour. She had still continued to hope. Now she had nothing more to hope for. Her fate was decided and the decision was as bad as it could possibly have been. She was overtaken by a dull, heavy slumber, more unrefreshing than any degree of sleeplessness, a slumber which seemed utterly to stupefy her.

On the next morning she awoke with but one wish and thought: to see Tengnagel again. All her good resolutions were forgotten; of dignity and decency she no longer took count. There was but one emotion that filled her, the purely animal fidelity of the woman for the man to whom she has once given herself, and whom she follows unhesitatingly, even though he might subsequently have proved himself a wretched, unworthy creature. Elizabeth had struggled courageously enough against this emotion, which had for a long time dominated her; she had enlisted in the struggle all the cunning and malice of her girlish intelligence, her deep love for her

144

father, her consciousness of her moral duties. . . . But since yesterday, since Tengnagel's escape had run counter to the plan which she had devised so craftily, she looked upon herself as conquered; she felt her powers of resistance shattered to fragments. And so she surrendered herself to fate, with a full realization of her abandoned condition and of her misfortune. She felt more distinctly than ever that Tengnagel, whose strong points fascinated her, was fundamentally unsuited to her; she saw that it had been the greatest act of folly in her life to chain herself to this uncultivated brute. But the louder the warning voices sounded, the more fiercely flamed within her the agonizing love for Tengnagel, a love which no kind of reasoning could gainsay. Something was carrying her away against her better judgment; she no longer resisted.

She knew every corner of the old castle. Even Tycho's secret cabinet she had long ago discovered. This was situated in a corner of the building, jutting out from the wall. It was quite easy to get into the open from the window. . . . Accordingly Elizabeth had made her way to this chamber quite easily, to seek for an opportunity, and was unpleasantly surprised by Tycho, who almost never entered the room. She had listened to his conversation with Kepler and had detected her father's terrible distress in the wild enthusiasm of his words; but even that, much as it pained her, could no longer stay her upon her course. . . . There now remained only one way leading to Tengnagel; it led through Kepler's room, which was situated directly under the secret chamber, in the same salient, and was, moreover, level with the ground and therefore much more convenient. But her dread of Kepler, who had already brought her so much misfortune, had at first resulted in Elizabeth's choosing the cabinet, situated higher up. Now she disregarded even these scruples. On the very night on which Kepler was sitting with Tycho above in the observatory, she opened his room and ventured to climb through the window by means of a rope. She then scrambled down the rough wall of rock sloping from here directly to the main road. Still glowing with warmth from these efforts, she flung herself into Tengnagel's arms. He was sitting in his hut wide awake, in full expectation that she would find just such a desperate way of reaching him.

And so it continued night after night. A strange absence of restraint had come over her. During the day she lay in a state of paralysed torpor in her room or on a sunny bench in the garden. She spoke to nobody. She did not even think any more; she merely dreamed and slumbered. Only at night did all her senses awake to warn her of the danger of her reckless course. And when she was with her beloved, she again grew languid; she let everything take its course, inquired about nothing, noticed nothing. Something had perished in her. Tengnagel wondered what process of transformation had taken place in the lively, keen-tongued little creature. She told no more stories; she never laughed; her countenance was pale and indifferent. Only when he chanced to speak of Tycho did she burst into tears and entreat him to make no further allusion to her father. Thereupon he in his turn became sad, for he loved her sincerely. So they often sat together, hour after hour, reproaching one another and weeping.

Once, on a clear moonlit night, as she was making her way down the steep descent, her glance perpetually wandering anxiously in every direction, she observed two figures approaching above her on the edge of the wall of rock. She recognized her brothers, saw, too, that they were looking down upon her and had already noticed her. . . . Her first thought was to escape into the shadows of a vast block of stone that stood near and from there to continue upon her way with

146

all speed. That, however, would only have brought her pursuers upon her traces and have led them to Tengnagel. In an instant another device occurred to her. She continued swiftly on her way, keeping to the middle of the wall, hopping and springing over gaps, where there was not even a bridle-track, putting into every step her tense will not to stumble. In this manner she advanced as far as a bright green and white strip of moonlight which poured down from the opening between two trees, slanting right across the declivity like a broad, shining band. Following the direction of this straight upwards, she scrambled along, soon proceeding with an increasingly gliding motion. Her eyes were half closed, like one walking in her sleep. But even while her thoughts were exclusively occupied with disguise, she felt how the cold light of the moon, playing about her countenance from all sides like water, penetrated her being and filled her head with a confused surge of folly and madness; she became conscious of her head only as of a transparent vessel upon her shoulders. Suddenly she realized this to be the true condition of her immeasurably tortured spirit; suddenly she ceased to play a part and was in real earnest borne aloft by the force of her suffering as by an enchantment. Her pale lips emitted a gentle singing note; her arms were raised on high like those of a prophetess. In such guise she drew near to her brothers and sought to drift past them. . . . Rude fists detained her. "Where are you going? It's time to go to bed."

"Ah, don't wake me," moaned the girl. "Don't wake my poor heart. Leave Elizabeth's ghost in peace." Slowly she passed the startled youths, moving in the direction of the castle. . . .

Next morning, however, Jörgen observed to Magdalena in Elizabeth's presence: "Do you know what we have discovered? Tengnagel is here in the village of Benatky. He has a stronghold with a wall and trenches, aha, a stronghold as impregnable as a mole-hill. Ramparts made of boards and rubbish. During the next few days we intend to go there with a few lads and have the fellow out. Then he'll kick his heels at the gallows, the old moss-trooper!" He looked at Elizabeth as he said these words. She did not betray herself in any way; in a friendly voice she turned the conversation to indifferent topics.

That night, wild with anxiety, she told her beloved all that had happened. "I'm not afraid," said Tengnagel. "I can easily beat off an assault on a small scale. And just look at this letter. It comes from the Privy Secretary, Barvitius himself. He has read my information against Kepler and admits its value. In a few days the Imperial Commissioner will come to the castle of Benatky to investigate the matter. And what is more, they have selected a very cunning fox, who will conduct the inquiry with great skill. He is a friend of mine, besides."

"But what will father say to it?"

"Tycho will suspect nothing at all. The Commissioner will come as his guest; everything will take its course without stir, with as much consideration as possible."

"Behind his back?"

"Of course."

Elizabeth in despair beat her hands together above her head. "And who is this—excellent guest who merits all the rights of hospitality?"

"I can tell you. You won't betray me, darling. It is Doctor Hagecius."

"My father's friend!" murmured Elizabeth in a dull tone of bitterness. She had no tears left. But when she thought of the immediate future, horror forced out the drops of perspiration. So her father was surrounded by hypocrites and false friends,

148

and no one was loyal to him! She herself, his daughter, had sold him; she had failed to warn him when, shrouded in fatal darkness, he had in all the goodness of his heart trusted himself to the hands of traitors. He strode upon his way like Œdipus, blinded and abandoned, but she, who should have been his Antigone, turned aside with no trace of compassion!

S PRING had begun. Now there was much to be done in field and park; the alterations in the castle, too, were pushed forward with greater energy, much to the annoyance of the Brandeis Hauptmann, who resumed his niggardly practices in questions of money. Thus the long nights devoted to astronomy and the brief, dim days of winter given up to rest were succeeded by new distractions and cares for Tycho. As soon as the roads improved, visitors arrived once more from Prague, men of learning and courtiers, who marvelled at the growing wonders of a second Uranienborg. The guest-chambers were no longer empty. Tycho became immersed in his duties as master of the house, and these brought him once more into contact with his family, with whom he now associated on unpleasantly formal terms. . . . How distant all this was from the hermit's existence to which he believed destiny had called him! Although he daily renewed his resolve to follow his destiny, he saw no means of carrying it into effect.

To these perturbations from without, inner disquiet was soon added.

At that time the spring-tide was in a far greater measure than today the means of making known what had been thought and written in scholars' retreats during the winter. During the winter, news from snow-bound towns and from all centres of literary life travelled backwards and forwards only with difficulty and in a fragmentary manner. With the improved weather, communications became brisk and regular. The old feuds, which had been dormant for some months, soon flamed up anew; from the pens of a hundred scholars, in correspondence with one another, there speedily arose a public opinion of specialists regarding what had recently appeared. Tycho, too, was naturally at once overwhelmed with daily reports. In all he was soon able to detect the theme that resounded with astonishing unanimity, that Johannes Kepler had suddenly, as if overnight, become famous throughout the world.

It suddenly appeared that all men of any importance had long previously read the *Prodromus* of Kepler, which had been shelved years before, and had been convinced of his genius from the very beginning. . . . Tycho laughed cunningly. He knew that nothing had attracted the general attention to Kepler so much as the circumstance that he was Tycho's assistant at Benatky and that for some time Tycho had never dispatched a letter without alluding to Kepler with all the enthusiasm of a devotee. "Such are the methods by which scientific opinion is formed," he said to himself, and the contempt which he had always entertained for literary advertisement now reached its zenith. How completely he penetrated all these men of learning, even the best, even the disinterested and independent! But for Kepler's sake he was pleased at the rapid turn of events. For the thing for which he had so ardently yearned had happened: the friend was recognized and accepted. Now there remained but one more thing to do, to find a permanent appointment for Kepler, to hold him fast in Bohemia. Tycho promised himself results without end from several years of collaboration with Kepler; science would in consequence make more rapid progress than during whole centuries. He wrote, moreover, to this effect to the Imperial Privy Secretary, Barvitius, recommending Kepler for a post of distinction with a special reference to his achievements

150

and to the unanimous opinion of the learned world. The secretary's answer was obscure, almost unintelligible; he referred to certain inquiries still in progress, reserving his final decision.

"Now you see," said Tycho sullenly to Kepler, "I never have any luck; no one ought to have anything to do with me, not even the most fortunate. I spread the contagion of my ill luck over everything. Something isn't granted merely because it is I that asks for it. If it were only you that was concerned, then everything would certainly be all right. But because my interest is also at stake, it at least remains undecided. We two are travelling in different directions; well, we shall see which is the stronger, you with your good fortune, or I with my ill!"

During the last few days Tycho had had reason enough for gloomy reflections. The spring campaign in the learned world had opened very unfortunately for him. Opponents raised their heads on every side; every newly-published book contained attacks upon Tycho's opinions. The wild polemic of Ursus seemed to have inspired a rabble of the same species with courage to fall upon Tycho. . . . Could it always be solely ascribed to chance that Kepler's name was so often mentioned in connexion with that of Tycho and on every occasion in sharp opposition to him? Kepler himself had in his *Prodromus* appealed to Tycho. Now the young man's modesty was applauded and the discovery was made that in reality he stood in no real relation with his alleged teacher; his methods were pronounced to be totally different from and far superior to those of Tycho. Only one critic found Tycho and Kepler pursuing a common direction, and he, unfortunately, was the only one who entirely rejected Kepler's conclusions.

It is quite comprehensible that these constantly repeated assertions began to produce some effect upon Tycho's

151

disinterested attitude towards Kepler. He now began during their conversations to assert with some anxiety that he really did agree with him on questions of fundamental importance. It was truly moving to hear him continually emphasize this: "We really are of the same opinion, aren't we?" Anyone else would have been struck by the caution, amounting almost to bashfulness, which Tycho now displayed in his intercourse with Kepler; Kepler himself was alone in not observing it. At this decisive moment his indifference towards all personal emotions asserted itself; he had no feeling for anything but the fire of knowledge. He did not attach the slightest importance to the testimonies of homage which had recently poured in upon him from literary men. On the contrary, they were a source of mirth for him; he laughed at them in moments when he was impressed by the trifling character of his previous work, gazing in joyous wonder at the immensity of the task that lay before him. Indeed, he often thought in all seriousness that it was some sycophant who wished to insult him! In general, however, he paid no attention to the new relationships which forced themselves upon him. Letters and brochures lay unread; the old disorder showed itself increased, not removed as the demands grew. . . . Tycho contemplated Kepler's conduct in this matter with speechless astonishment. The point was now reached at which his destiny began to assert itself. It was not the vast weight of misfortune which Tycho had throughout his life endured, hardily and like a man; it was Kepler's good fortune at his very side and the way in which he heedlessly accepted this good fortune that shattered the very foundations of his outlook upon the world.

Tycho had never really believed that the good and the upright find recognition in this life. It would have run counter to his principle that nothing happens of itself and that everything follows its course only when driven. Moreover, his own life was in too great a degree evidence to the contrary, and in consequence the opinion that the majority alike of scientific inquirers and of the patrons of science were either imbeciles or rogues had become increasingly confirmed in his mind. In his view, truth had to force a passage for herself in the face of a world of misunderstanding and malevolence, and for that reason, unfortunately, she could not be fastidious in her choice of methods. Tycho fought everyone with his own weapons. Before princes proud of their lineage he displayed his escutcheon, on which otherwise he prided himself but little. He showed to members of his own profession, who were accustomed to appreciate books only out of regard for the laudations which they hoped to receive in return, the usual courtesies, in so doing, of course, taking care not to commend anything lacking in value. For this was his constant care, to hold the balance between what was profitable in life and his own fair will to truth. Upon this last he would never inflict the least hurt; but if only one were really versatile and vigilant enough, could it not be combined with many incidental activities pursued upon an entirely different plane, which would not occur to a less diligent mind, but which were, as far as truth was concerned, to say the very least, indifferent, while at the same time they were beneficial to one's life and to one's reputation? Undoubtedly this course involved the risk of contamination and peril; it called for an unrelenting vigilance in distinguishing between profit and matters of essential importance. Sometimes, however, when he felt himself to be in full possession of his strength, Tycho regarded this never-ending game as an occupation particularly worthy of a courageous and energetic man. This ever wakeful consciousness, this increasing interplay between his two interests, in worldly gain and in pure science, actually seemed to him

153

to guard like lines of fire the inviolable frontier of the noble core. Beyond it there lay something which could never be smirched; unessentials might be surrendered. In all his relations with the world both elements appeared, the compliance and the quiet, inviolable reserve. As the world permitted itself to be deluded by large, round figures, he had brought the number of stars recorded in his catalogue as observed to a "millenium," thus surpassing the ancients; and in order to make up the number he had finally included some not altogether reliable observations of Longomontanus, describing them, it is true, as fragments. Science had remained pure, but here as elsewhere his soul had become increasingly entangled in a net of compromises, false associations, and disingenuous half-measures, which he himself styled sordid and oppressive, but nevertheless viewed as a sacrifice necessary in the interests of truth. He had almost succeeded in reconciling himself with this imperfect ordering of his life before coming to know Kepler, satisfied if only he could keep some inmost corner of his soul untouched by the commonplace dirt of mundane "relations." . . . And now, when he seemed to have finally completed the structure formed by such reflections, Kepler appeared and shattered it to fragments. For this man, Tycho saw quite clearly, had not only anxiously concealed his being in some inmost nook, but lived with the whole, pure, spotless surface of his soul, which he brandished before the world unswervingly, unhesitatingly, nay, with a certain rigour and ruthlessness. And what was strangest of all, the world recognized this purity; it did obeisance before it, preparing for it a general, lasting success, which Tycho, so it seemed to him, had never in his life attained with all his little tactics, his vexatious and self-denying abasement. So perhaps everything that Tycho had hitherto practised was wrong? Was the whole tormenting process of his dissimula-

154

tions actually superfluous and fruitless? Must he with all his experience in his old age begin anew like a little child? . . .

At that time a soldier paid a brief visit to the castle of Benatky. It was Colonel Albrecht Wenzel von Waldstein, despite his youth an uncommonly serious man, even majestic in appearance. Besides knowing the craft of war he was a zealous student of alchemy and celestial lore. He only bestowed a rapid glance upon Tycho's apparatus and then put a few unambiguous questions regarding the "nativities" of certain of the most important princes and military commanders of Europe. Kepler was, however, the chief object of his interest, and of him he made detailed inquiries about conditions in Graz; he was actually on his way there from his Moravian property to offer his services to the Duke Ferdinand. Although Tycho penetrated the political calculations of the young adventurer and saw in them the explanation of his long conversation with Kepler, with its numerous questions, he could not help feeling distressed at being eclipsed by his pupil. This was the first time in his life he had played a secondary role in the presence of a visitor. Painfully affected, he withdrew, and when Waldstein wished to take leave, made an excuse for not receiving him again. . . . The results soon appeared; "for," so Tycho had afterwards to admit to himself with bitterness, "I am not like Kepler, who can despise the great lords and is for that very reason courted by all of them. If I neglect a single opportunity, I suffer for it keenly and at once." And indeed a few days later a messenger brought a letter to Kepler from Waldstein inviting him to enter his service as an astrologer. The letter did not contain a single word of reference to Tycho. The remuneration offered by the rich Waldstein was naturally high and tempting, and so Tycho could not help fearing that he would lose Kepler, for whom he had not even been able to secure a scanty allowance from

155

the Emperor. "If I had shown myself more of a courtier in my dealings with my powerful guest," he reflected, "he would assuredly not have thought of coming forward with suggestions so ill-disposed to me." However, in the end Tycho got over the matter, the more so as Kepler, according to his wont, laid the letter aside and, for the time being at least, seemed to have no intention of accepting Waldstein's offer. But all the ramparts of reflection and all goodwill could not withstand the circumstances that the same messenger brought a little packet for Tycho, entrusted to him by an unknown person in Prague—a packet containing a box of snuff. This was a malicious joke which constantly occurred; Tycho's enemies allowed themselves to play it several times a year. In consequence of the artificial plate set in his nose it was impossible for him to take snuff. On any other occasion he would have submitted to the trick with appropriate humour. On this occasion, however, this vexation in conjunction with the favour bestowed upon Kepler operated to render him fully conscious of all that was displeasing and distressful in his position among his fellow-creatures. That his life had ever been violent, sultry, and lowering like a stormy night, to that he had already accustomed himself; but the bitterness of it all lay in the fact that in this night of tempest a glimmer of kindness and of human goodwill broke like a stream of moonlight through the clouds. And this streak, which fell not upon him, but upon someone very near him, upon Kepler, revealed the terrible wilderness in which Tycho wandered unprotected, and which hitherto had remained veiled in kindly darkness. Its sudden manifestation brought with it an overwhelming sense of horror.

T H U S the storm raged in Tycho's spirit. He took the greatest pains to keep his feelings for Kepler free from alloy.

156

Whatever might come between them, he was filled with undiminished tenderness for his friend. In actual fact he really did not envy Kepler his success. At the very most, the self-evident and in all respects becoming and worthy manner in which Kepler had achieved renown sometimes excited in him an emotion bordering upon envy. But in general Kepler now inspired him with a feeling of awe. The tranquillity with which he applied himself to his labours and entirely ignored the warblings of flatterers was to Tycho almost superhuman. There was something incomprehensible in its absence of emotion, like a breath from a distant region of ice. . . . And at times, during moments of depression, when Tycho beheld his life unrolling before him and nothing, nothing whatsoever, able to stand before his conscience, his arraignment of himself turned abruptly into an arraignment of Kepler. He recalled that popular ballad in which a *Landsknecht* had sold his heart to the Devil and had received in exchange a bullet-proof coat of mail. Of such sort was Kepler. He had no heart and therefore had nothing to fear from the world. He was not capable of emotion or of love. And for that reason he was naturally also secure against the aberrations of feeling. "But I must love and err," groaned Tycho. "I must be flung hither and thither in this hell, beholding him floating above, pure and happy, upon cool clouds of limpid blue. A spotless angel! But is he really? Is he not rather atrocious in his lack of sympathy? A word from him could protect me from all uncertainty, could beat like a refreshing shower upon my dried-up heart, could sweep away everything ignoble, everything in me that is contrary to nature. But one word—that he will not speak, no, not at any price. That would be too much for him, too great an effort—ha ha—for my Benjamin."

When Tycho reflected more calmly, he did not himself

know what word of redemption he awaited from Kepler. Or did he know, but would not admit it to himself?

One thing at least was certain: Kepler seemed to avoid all discussions of principle respecting the most fundamental questions of the system of the universe. Nor had he ever yet openly expressed his assent to Tycho's system. Was that due to prudent calculation or to pure chance? Everything depended upon the answer to this question, which Tycho propounded to himself often enough, already with a certain bitterness. He had in particular expected that Kepler would declare himself in his promised pamphlet against Ursus. And that was not the least reason why he so ardently wished to see the pamphlet finished. Kepler, however, was obviously in no hurry. He made no further allusion to the pamphlet; he had very likely entirely forgotten it. Was this the final outcome of it all, that Kepler's silence upon this all-important point expressed the fact that he did not really agree with Tycho? And if so, would it have not been more friendly to avow this openly, to inform his friend? Tycho, who had almost reached the point at which he must regard the whole of his life up to the present as one vast mistake, would willingly have submitted to his teaching. Only Kepler must speak, speak out openly. Truth must conquer in the end. Truth was the only matter of the moment; neither Tycho nor Kepler counted a whit. . . . Thus did Tycho once more assemble his strength to the full stature of his mighty spirit. He was ready to abandon his system if Kepler would teach him a better one; he was most ready to begin his life's work anew and as the pupil of his pupil. Only the position must be clear; there must not be this agonizing silence touching the fundamental opposition between them, a silence which, as he now saw in retrospect, had disturbed their relations from the very beginning. With a kind of guilty reserve, they had hith-

158

erto touched upon nothing but the subsidiary problems of their science. Henceforth Tycho wished to attack the main question, which indeed did not present itself in nearly so unambiguous a form as he would have gladly believed.

In his first book Kepler had, it was true, declared his hostility to the theory of Claudius Ptolemæus, dominant since the age of Alexander. In accordance with that theory the earth stood immovable in the centre of the universe, and the planets, including the sun and moon, together with the fixed stars, attached to eight crystal spheres, circled about it. But Tycho, who so readily affirmed his agreement with Kepler, could assert that he too did not adhere to Ptolemy; on the contrary, like Kepler himself he regarded with suspicion the fact that it was necessary to have recourse to utterly artificial constructions such as epicycles in order to bring the observed course of the planets into harmony with this theory.

Fifty years previously Copernicus had put forward the view that the sun occupied the central position, the earth and planets circling about it. But this theory also, and that must have been known to Kepler as well as to Tycho, could not dispense with a similar if not so highly elaborated complement derived from the epicycles and in fine did not altogether correspond with reality.

Undoubtedly Tycho's ingenious system supplied the best explanation of the body of phenomena hitherto observed. This theory, however, was attended by a strange fate. . . . It is a very common occurrence that those very men who aim at dominating their life by means of their understanding betray an inexplicable distaste, quite impenetrable to reason, for any severance from something already acquired, above all from something that they have at some time experienced. They lack perhaps instinctive self-confidence, which is a confidence in change, in the actual present, and in danger, and

159

for that reason, wherever they go, they always drag along with them memories and past relationships. To abandon something which was once in their hands—however worthless it may be—that is too much for their strength. . . . So, without accounting for it to himself, Tycho was conscious of a secret adhesion to the Ptolemaic system in which he had grown up, and probably with all his extraordinary delicacy of fine moral feeling he would have felt it to be a piece of gross ingratitude if he had sought the truth otherwise than by a further development of Alexandrian fundamentals. His own system of the universe had arisen as a curious compound derived from this barely conscious motive. It was, moreover, in all respects harmonious with Tycho's peculiar manner; in his efforts to steer a course between unfettered ecstasy and absorption in earthly matters he always stood in need of a patchwork of concessions and counter-concessions elaborated to the most remote detail. The earth, it is true, occupied the centre of the universe, as with Ptolemy, and about it moved the moon and the sun, but not the planets, which, as with Copernicus, moved round the sun.

But now came the question, did Kepler accept this view or was he unreserved in his adhesion to Copernicus? Tycho availed himself of the next opportunity to confront Kepler quite frankly with this question, which had hitherto been the subject of strange evasions.

It was night and they sat in the great instrument-room at a table piled high with papers. On the floor beside them, too, there lay pages covered with writing and figures. Amid these records, all ready for use, the dwarf Jeppe squatted at their feet. He was examining the geometrical figures with a grave, thoughtful expression, much as a child turns over the pages of a picture-book; sometimes, too, just like a child, he ran his index finger over the lines of writing and nodded as if

160

he could read and understand them. But at the same time he glanced at very frequent intervals towards Tycho in order, at the slightest motion of his hand, at once to pick the desired paper from the floor and spread it before him on the table. If Tycho indicated that he should lay the paper before Kepler, the dwarf obeyed slowly and reluctantly, always keeping himself at the greatest possible distance from Kepler; he placed the sheet before him on the table, touching it only with the tips of his fingers, and distorted his miserable little body just as if Kepler emitted stinging rays which could hurt him. And the glance which he bestowed upon Tycho after rendering such an obviously very painful act of service was more than usually devoted and enthusiastic; it was positively the look of an animal which after sufferings endured, enjoys refreshment and cleansing. . . .

"Well, now, what is the position in regard to your own system of the universe?" inquired Tycho once more, as Kepler had not immediately answered. "What is your decision as between Copernicus and me?"

"A difficult question, which doesn't admit of any straightforward answer," replied Kepler, with an imperceptible smile.

"Of course, of course," Tycho hastened to interject; "it can't be expressed in a few words. I myself, as you know, am no enemy to Copernicus. It is only the foolish who say that of me. . . . Oh, I admire the genius of Copernicus, I revere that proud, independent spirit! Look at these three frail, worm-eaten wooden staves." He pointed to a corner of the room. Jeppe was swiftly at hand limping towards them with the curious primitive instrument. "Here, lay hold upon them, feel them devoutly. What do you suppose you hold in your hands? It is nothing other than the genuine *parallacticum* with which our immortal Copernicus gazed upon the stars! Yes, *his levibus baculis!* I composed an ode upon these holy

161

relics, I'll read the verses to you when the opportunity arises. Ah! it was one of my fairest days, the day on which this instrument arrived at Hveen, a gift to me from the chapter-house of Frauenburg. *O tanti monumenta viri!* On that occasion we all decked our heads with garlands, my pupils and I; the ship was adorned with flags and we all waited on the shore. The instrument was brought with great honour into the Sternenburg. My stupid peasants stood in long lines, not comprehending why I and all my company kept kissing and kissing the wood. Oh, it was a radiant day, a day of my youth! And the peasants, they knew henceforth for certain what they had before whispered to one another, that I was an accursed sorcerer and worshipped the full moon with my wooden apparatus. So you must laugh, my Kepler, laugh! But, after all, should one laugh at the peasants when Luther himself seeks to refute Copernicus with the objection that, according to Holy Writ, Joshua bade the sun and not the earth stand still? Ah, these adversaries! These men!

"Now, I at least do not put forward objections against Copernicus of such a trifling character. You must admit that my arguments are weightier. Ha ha! That, of course, was only spoken in jest. Now tell me seriously how you regard the matter. I have spoken enough. It won't do for me always to speak. You, too, must have your say, my Kepler." He laid a hand on his shoulder and looked in friendly wise into his eyes.

"I have little to say," replied Kepler. At these words Tycho's friendly smile spread over his countenance and streamed forth with such a radiance of gentle confidence and limpidity that Kepler himself seemed to feel this wonderful peaceful glow and to drink it in. For a while he sat completely self-absorbed, wrapped in bliss.

"Well," said Tycho in encouraging tones.

162

"I am still undecided. I can't come to a decision. Besides, I don't think that our technical resources and experience are yet sufficiently advanced to enable us to give a definite answer to this question."

Tycho waited for a considerable time to see whether Kepler would add anything. He did not. Accordingly Tycho resumed: "You said before that I should receive no straightforward answer to my question. But that was assuredly a very straightforward answer."

"Strictly speaking, no answer at all," corrected Kepler, always with his idyllic smile.

"You are right. If one takes it in that way, strictly speaking, no answer," said Tycho, already somewhat exasperated.

There was a pause, which Tycho again had to break. "And does this satisfy you, Kepler, this state of affairs? I mean this uncertainty regarding the most essential points of our art. Doesn't the lack of decision sometimes take your breath away? Doesn't impatience deprive you of all your happiness?"

"I am not happy," Kepler answered simply. "I have never been happy."

"You—not happy?" Tycho stared at him with wide-open eyes. "You—not—what do you lack, then? What more do you want? What would you have in addition to that already bestowed upon you?—Oh, fie, how immodest you must be if you don't reckon yourself happy, you who are the happiest of all men! Yes, must I, then, tell it you for the first time? Don't you feel that you—now I will put it in one word, that you are on the right way, on the only right way?—Oh, what would I have done, what hymns of praise would I have lifted up to God, how would I have extolled my destiny, if once in my life—no, now I don't mean the outward success, the applause surrounding you, which has been accorded you. But inwardly, inwardly, my Kepler—must I really say it to you?—inwardly, in the heart of our science, you are on the right path, the path blessed by God; and that is the noblest, happiest fate that a mortal can encounter."

"No, I am not happy and I have never been happy," Kepler repeated, with a dull obstinacy. Then he added quite gently: "And I don't even wish to be happy."

Tycho was at his wits' ends; he sank into a brooding reverie from which there seemed no issue. He had put a definite question on a point of fact to Kepler, with the deliberate intention of leaving their personal relations on one side. And yet he had at the very outset plunged into the midst of "personalities," wherein one was prevented from advancing by feelings of bashfulness and delicacy, wherein every step entailed obstacles. It seemed just as if Kepler had intentionally slipped away from him into this region in order to avoid giving a clear answer to his question. But even while he laboured to represent Kepler to himself as a cunning, calculating man, an intriguer, it was fully clear to him that this in no way tallied with the facts, that Kepler was the very opposite of an intriguer; he never pursued a definite aim and in fact transacted all affairs lying outside the bounds of his science in a sort of dream. Why, he did not even realize that he was happy. So far did his mental confusion go that he did not even observe that. He was in the strictest sense of the term *incapable of calculation;* he was not responsible for anything that he did. Or neglected to do. . . . Neglected, yes, yes, for that, too, not responsible. And suddenly Tycho saw quite clearly, as if a veil had been drawn aside, saw that Kepler would never write that refutation of Ursus which he had asked of him. Never throughout all the future. Nay, that Kepler had actually never seriously contemplated carrying out the work, not even at the moment when he had given his promise. His intuition carried him even further; he saw that Kepler really stood out-

164

side all the laws applying to mankind, that one had not even the right to require him to keep his promise. Inasmuch as he was irresponsible, he himself, Tycho, would actually have incurred a grave responsibility if he had condemned Kepler's conduct, viewing it as treachery or ingratitude, an attitude of mind towards which every consideration impelled him. No, Kepler was without guilt—that was the great fact revealed to Tycho for the first time at this moment. With all his happiness, which another man would have had to purchase at the expense of unending suffering on the part of his conscience, Kepler was pure and without guilt; and this absence of guilt was the crown of his happiness; and this happiness—thus the circle closed—did not for a moment weigh upon him, for he was not even conscious of it. . . . He really had no inkling of his good fortune. There he sat at the table opposite Tycho, and while Tycho was tossed hither and thither by his thoughts, he sat with upright, somewhat rigid torso, in the attitude of one whose gaze is fixed upon the distance, sat in complete calm and composure, observing nothing of Tycho's disquiet and— as usual continued calculating.

This spectacle was unendurable to Tycho. He suddenly felt his whole responsibility for their relations as a terrific burden weighing upon his shoulders alone, whereas from the very out- set Kepler had been assured of complete immunity. He could not yet grasp this oppressive thought in its entirety; it was too much to envisage at once. . . . An insane fury had seized upon him; he could find no issue from it. He wished to have a man before him, not this "*Landsknecht* without heart, with the bullet-proof cuirass," ha ha, this cunning, prudent—no, not cunning, imprudent, happy, unhappy—Turk, this Turk, this monster Kepler, devil take him, yes indeed, devil take him—a man whom one could seize and chastise. . . . Then his glance fell upon the dwarf, who was still playing upon

165

the floor. "What are you up to there, you little abortion, among my manuscripts?" Never before had Tycho assailed the little creature. Now, demented with rage, he seized the staves of Copernicus and with violent curses showered blows upon the face of the dwarf, who in terror sprang to his feet. His clamour filled the room. "Yes, I'll flog you, I'll strangle you!" roared Tycho, springing after him. In an instant Jeppe had taken refuge behind a great astrolabe. Tycho pursued him and lifted up a folio volume in both hands, intending to hurl it down upon the dwarf. Kepler was at his side. "Master!" he cried. . . . A twofold howl of lamentation arose. The dwarf fled wailing, while Tycho leaned against the wall, as if beside himself with distress, thundering after him the most frenzied vituperations.

ON RETURNING to his room towards midnight Kepler was astonished to find Elizabeth standing at the window. She was on the point of winding about her waist a rope, which was fixed to the cross-bars of the window. He remained standing at the doorway.

"Please shut the door," cried the girl, taking a few rapid steps towards him.

He obeyed. Then he stood still, even more disconcerted.

It was weeks since she had spoken with him. Since Teng-nagel's flight she had abandoned her efforts to investigate his personality in her father's interest. Since then she had troubled herself about nothing. Painfully the thought of this now occurred to her. She had indeed long foreseen that Kepler would at some time surprise her in his room, which she had used every night. She had prepared herself for this eventuality and knew what she must say. But a general sensation of weakness hindered her from beginning aright. Another idea invaded her, and although she felt that it merely added to the con-

166

fusion of a situation that was already strange enough, she could not repress it. "Well," she said, "you certainly think now that it was I who stole your papers?"

"No, no, not at all," he assured her with an absent-minded courtesy. The stiff, conventional manner with which he at the same time raised his hand in deprecation had something peculiarly comic in it.

"Why not?" Elizabeth pursued. "Don't you credit me with the capacity for such an act? Do you think I am too cowardly for it? Or too bad? Or too good? And who could the thief have been but myself? Isn't this the second time that you've caught me in the house? First in my father's secret chamber and now here? That must arouse suspicion, mustn't it?"

Kepler had seated himself at the table, his chin sunk in his hand. He looked tranquilly at Elizabeth and it seemed as if he was thinking of entirely different things. Suddenly, however, he said, with an unexpected keenness of observation: "I see no ground for suspicion."

"How not?" she replied violently.

"Because you, Fräulein Brahe, have quite empty hands and because you were not trying to enter the room when I came in. . . ." He broke off somewhat indignantly, as if it were not worth while to pursue the subject. "Besides, absolutely nothing has been stolen from me."

"Indeed?"

"I miss nothing, absolutely nothing. The maid had cleaned out my room and thrown everything into confusion; my agitation at the time was without foundation. I hope the ladies of the house will pardon me for having sounded the alarm." He bowed in a formal manner, which was perhaps intended to be humorous, but merely produced an impression of melancholy. "It was a mistake."

"Is all agitation in your opinion unfounded and mistaken?"

167

Elizabeth seemed indignant. "So unfounded that, granted your fish-cold blood, it is quite comprehensible and the most ordinary thing in the world to find me here in your room at night. It is apparently quite enough that I didn't want to enter by the window. Is that really what you think? Whether I wanted to get out of the window and why I wanted to is obviously no concern of yours, it doesn't in any way affect you. All that remains is to shut the window, which I now do —so, and wish you a good, peaceful night. Then everything, as far as it concerns you, is settled, isn't it?"

He looked in astonishment at her angry countenance; he did not understand her. Then he said, as if acting on impulse, but at the same time in that state of unsuspecting naïveté in which children sometimes stammer the truth: "You reckon me a barbarian, don't you?"

This observation seemed to fling Elizabeth abruptly out of the path upon which she had undesignedly entered. He at once surprised and terrified her. In any case either she still could not collect her thoughts or she did not wish to. At first she was silent; then she observed in apparent indifference: "I had a betrothed."

"Yes," he assented, "the junker Tengnagel."

"The same who fetched you from Prague and brought you to Benatky. Do you remember him?"

He nodded.

"Where is he?" she asked, still in a tone of indifference, in the tone of one asking a serious question. "Where is he?" She became more insistent. "Haven't you thought at all where he may have disposed himself? Did it never occur to you that his presence might perhaps be missed here, that I might miss him? Have you ever thought anything at all about other people's affairs?"

"Do you mean by that—"

168

"I mean by that," she interrupted sternly, "have you your-self ever missed my betrothed? You yourself? That is the point. Yes or no. Have you ever missed Herr Tengnagel or have you not?"

"I don't know why or with what right such questions are addressed to me. I come into my room and I want—"

"Want to go to sleep, just as I really always am asleep and even during the day bother about nothing but a good thick, soft pillow about my ears. Now, now, what else do you wish to observe?"

For a space it seemed as if Kepler was disposed to feel in-sulted by the girl's harsh words. His face grew dark. Now, however, he laid two fingers upon his forehead, and the countenance which appeared beneath this accustomed move-ment of the hand betrayed an entirely unwonted expression of kindness and sympathy. The shrill note of distress in Eliza-beth's remarks had opened his heart. Suddenly he seemed to grasp and to understand everything; he said: "You were actually on your way to your betrothed?"

She let her head fall, abashed. Immediately, however, she flashed forth suddenly: "Yes, through the window," and it sounded as if she laid all the blame upon him.

Perhaps he, too, felt this, for he repeated several times, shaking his head: "Through the window." As he said these words, his expression was one of such helplessness, such genuine despair and embarrassment, as to bring her com-pletely to her senses. Indeed, she now felt almost compassion for him; at least she saw the impropriety of allowing herself to be pitied by him. It was manifestly he that was the more astonished and in all respects the weaker. As she beheld him before her with his brilliant, dark eyes set beneath the arched brows, which were clearly designed for quite other ends than self-torment over the lamentable events of that night, he

169

seemed to the unhappy woman who stood on the edge of complete moral ruin to have issued forth from a better, grander world, and a strange feeling of satisfaction, which she had already felt when in his presence, once more made its way to her bosom. Why had she just on this occasion assailed him with such harshness? She no longer understood it. Had the violent occurrences of these latter days so far brutalized her? How could she have so far forgotten herself in the presence of this gentle, kindly-natured man?

Now the sense of guilt which she had already half loaded upon Kepler returned upon her own shoulders and extorted from her the words of entreaty: "You won't say anything to my father about what you have seen?"

"That would really be my duty," he replied with deliberation.

This reply filled her with a secret gladness. She felt, indeed, that it involved a refusal; but that very fact did not impress her disagreeably; it presented itself rather as a proof of Kepler's solicitude for her and as an invitation for further conversation. Accordingly she seated herself at the table and said gently: "Thank you."

He made a gesture of deprecation and addressed her in kindly terms. Sooner or later it must be noticed that she played such tricks, which were quite unworthy of a Brahe.

"You don't understand, Master Kepler," she objected, now speaking quite as gently as himself. "We Brahes are just the people for such escapades. We are the real gipsies in the land."

"Gipsies?"

"Yes, what are we really but a family of necromancers on tour? Driven from home, we wander from country to country doing turns with sorcery and queer tricks, here today, there tomorrow. Nobody likes us much; we are just tolerated, and,

170

to tell the truth, we ourselves know quite well that we are a nuisance. Where shall we fit in eventually? I really don't know." She flung her head back; the aspect of her lips was haughty, yet they seemed sullied as by some unseemly jest. Upon them was imprinted her whole sorrowful disarray, and this now became particularly noticeable, for she seemed with her somehow importunate glance to enlist Kepler as a partner in her fate. "And you, master, what are you but just such another necromancer?"

He withstood her glance in perfect tranquillity and then inquired as if in genuine curiosity: "Necromancer—gipsy—that you really must explain to me."

As if it was now the time for lengthy explanations, she reflected. Yet even this thought did not jar upon her. On the contrary, she could not help laughing, and even in all the keenness of her tension she was conscious of agreeable feelings, so much so that she crossed one leg over the other and gently beat upon her knee with the cord, the end of which she held in her hand. "If Tengnagel were to see me here, chattering comfortably!" she thought, and broke into a roguish giggle. She felt at that moment powerfully urged towards confidential relations with Kepler. "You really are a gipsy. I can't help you," she said laughing.

He looked at her with boundless astonishment.

His simplicity afflicted her. She caught his hands. They were quite cold. A shudder ran through her. Immediately the conviction seized her that she was not fit to lay hands upon the veil of so precious, immaculate a soul, and she let him go. As she did so, she said swiftly, as if the words burned her tongue: "No, Kepler, no one can call you a gipsy; you are too upright. Too orderly, and too composed. There you sit like a model pupil in your clean, good clothes." For the first time it now struck her that with her fair hair all tousled for the night, with the old, dark cloak flung over her night-dress, she manifestly presented a very different figure from himself. Yet at the same time, and herein she resembled her father, at the bottom of her disordered heart, stripped of its verdure, she felt a powerful attraction towards the blossom-like, reticent Kepler, towards his seemly and decent mode of life. She felt a genuine impulse to shed tears. "Why," she thought, "can't I stay sitting here, in a warm, elegant chamber? This man would be better suited to me than that coarse lout; he would comfort and calm me, weak, unstable woman that I am. . . ." And she stared out into the clear, spring night, which was so stormy that a brief abatement in the roaring of the wind filled one with dread. In all good conscience, why must she go forth into the storm, into the realms of folly? . . . But even while her thoughts pursued this course, she realized in the depths of her being that she was chained to that other man without by a passionate constraint, to the man who awaited her; and during these very minutes which she passed tranquilly with Kepler, she was conscious of all her instability, her dreamlike abandonment.

"What could one possibly do in such a situation?" thought Kepler, and took the matter so greatly to heart that he involuntarily caught hold of the rope which she held in her hand.

His friendliness reacted favourably upon her. Once more she was seized by the feeling that with this man she would be in good hands and have nothing to fear. "I would know what could be done," she said sadly, "but that is so far off that one can't even speak of it."

Not even at this moment did she represent it to herself as a possibility that Kepler might at the very next instant spring up, lay hold upon her, and carry her off, far from here, to a land where there was no distress and no con-

172

straint, where life might be begun anew in complete innocence. But, although she did not believe in it, it hovered before her eyes as something uncommonly sweet and soothing. Yes, this very idea, to which all this time she was clinging with all her might, was a source of comfort to her. But while still filled with these strange thoughts, she, in whose power it lay to alter everything at a single blow, was forced to summon all her arts of persuasion to make it clear that nothing could be altered, that the only possible and the only right thing was the thing that actually happened, that no yielding could ever be hoped for from Tengnagel's obstinacy, while, on the other hand, it was useless to look for any insight in her father; everything that she did was desperate, and she could not and would not resist the destiny that bound her to this man whom she had chosen. She loved him, although he inspired her with horror; and he, in his turn, loved her, although he mistreated her. She would be unhappy without him, yet today and in this place she was unspeakably unhappy. And this unhappiness, she entreated, as she reached the end of her lengthy utterance, must on no account be intensified by giving information to her father.

"Do you think, then, that it would be a happy marriage between you and Junker Tengnagel?" Kepler slowly took up her words in order to elucidate the matter according to his honest habit.

She sighed and looked mournfully at him. It was already too explicit and somewhat disconcerting that she had spoken of her own and of Tengnagel's "love." And now it was sought to wring from her lips a prophecy about a "happy marriage." "This Kepler is really very stupid," she thought; "if possible, even more stupid than my Tengnagel." At this moment, too, she was struck by the thought, which until then she had inexplicably forgotten, or at least had not reflected upon in the

173

present connexion—the thought that, according to the papers that Tengnagel had shown her, Kepler was a traitor to Tycho. It was true that there appeared some element of impossibility, at least of improbability, therein. Perhaps Tengnagel was mistaken and had imagined the things which suited his purpose.

Anyway she found no issue from all this confusion but suddenly to begin to cry and then to fix her glances, inflamed with weeping, once more upon Kepler's countenance, alluring and expectant. He, however, stood firm, intact and unmarred, quite as inaccessible to every onset of Elizabeth as to her father's outbursts of passion. He resembled a pure stream gushing from a woodland rock, which continues unaffected by the most sultry heat of a summer's day. . . .

Elizabeth had let the rope drop to the ground. He handed it to her and, with a certain emotion in his tones, said that he would betray nothing to her father, that she must not be afraid and, above all, must not weep.

When, still sobbing bitterly, she glided through the window, he aided her with quiet friendliness, holding the rope as it stretched taut.

174

CHAPTER IX

T HE RECENT PAINFUL shocks brought back Tycho's old malady. He became bedridden and shut himself up in his room. No one was admitted. Only the faithful dwarf attended upon him. For a space it had been his intention to make an exception of Kepler and to invite him as his only visitor. Subsequently, however, he abandoned this idea. He inscribed one of his devices, *"Tandem bona causa triumphat,"* in large letters on a sheet of parchment and bade Jeppe affix it to the door, at the same time instructing him to refuse admittance to every visitor.

There began a period of tormenting solitude. In feverish dreams Tycho bickered, sometimes with his wife and children, whose loveless self-will affected him as an insult, sometimes with Kepler, whose innocence he actually reproached as a particularly cunning piece of knavery.

"This innocence of Kepler's," he once cried out, "is simply the counterpart of my goodness and penetration. I see through everything, I understand everything. And it is just for that reason that I am always being swindled. My integrity disarms me every time." It seemed to relieve him to be able to cry aloud his most secret, most painful thoughts before Jeppe and the bare walls. For after each of these stormy attacks, which came like spasms of the soul, he felt somewhat more tranquil. Often, however, it happened that he was seized with a

175

convulsion of rage at the very moment when his wife or Elizabeth stood before the door. For, like the other members of the family, they were naturally caused the most grievous alarm by Tycho's strange behaviour and by his illness. As they could not now gain access to him—to do so would have entailed breaking down the bolted door and doing away with the vigilant dwarf—they frequently stood for hours before the door and listened to every sound that issued forth. Often they would be suddenly shaken by Tycho's powerful voice, and a hideous din would arise when they answered him with voices raised equally loud and he in turn cursed them and the entire world, threatening to set the house on fire if they should attempt to penetrate to him or to summon a doctor. Sometimes these deafening conversations lasted a very long time. Only words pronounced in the loudest tone were heard, often nothing at all when both parties shouted at the same time. At length the family realized that they only infuriated Tycho with their exhortations. He never ceased until the voices without were completely silent and had for long been so. The women accordingly resumed their taciturnity and squatted anxiously on the wooden steps before the door, having first coaxed the two sons into going away. There they would sit as if benumbed. Only when the dwarf came out for a few moments did they fling themselves upon him with whispered inquiries.

Tycho repeatedly asked the dwarf whether Kepler had come to inquire after his health.

He learned that Kepler had certainly called on the first day, but had then taken the rebuff and the prohibition inscribed on the door so literally that for the time being he had not repeated his visit. "Good, at last I am alone, as I have always wished," said Tycho to himself. "I have put away everything superfluous and can at length bethink me of myself, ever the

176

most pressing need." But strangely enough he did not feel exalted at this thought; rather, he was deeply injured. Nay, in all his life he did not recall having ever been so unhappy. On the other hand, he was filled with a kind of wild joy, closely resembling gratified malice, that Kepler still did not appear before him on the following day. For now at last he had caught him in a piece of undeniable disloyalty and ingratitude. And although he fully realized that this apparent absence of feeling resembled that vagueness in Kepler's mentality with which he was already familiar, he hardened himself with a painful stubbornness into calling it ingratitude and nothing but ingratitude.

"Ah, how differently the fellow behaved towards me when he still needed me, when it was a question of enticing me to part with my manuscripts. Why was he not then—vague! He styled me phœnix, a dauntless inquirer, a man of the world. He was fair-spoken and yet had full knowledge of his aim. The hypocrite wondered how I could ever bring myself to exchange even two words with him. This feigned humility—now he can't bring himself to exchange two words with me. I am no longer necessary to him. He can easily find a hundred better protectors if he will. That Waldstein and the rest. They simply press round him, everyone wants to do something for him. By the bait of his helplessness, his lack of counsel, he catches everyone. That I was the first to fall into the trap—is that a reason for special gratitude? No, no, no, I understand you, my Kepler, I can quite appreciate your feelings. Why trouble about me any more? I have done my duty. Now one can marvel in coy modesty at the next on the list, how he can bring himself to exchange but two words, ah, but two, but two little words with young innocence! It always draws, it is a brilliant idea!" . . . In the depth of his soul Tycho was conscious of the falsity of these charges, ever raked

177

up anew, deliberately exaggerated, lasting for hours. But he really wanted to lie, he wanted to torment himself and to lower himself, he wanted to flee from truth, even at the price of the most ignoble martyrdom. For martyrdom at the hands of truth he feared even more than the martyrdom of lies. Yet sometimes he recognized the hopelessness and ignominy of the proceeding, and then this mad contest with his better self would melt away in a helpless outcry: "Justice! The earth refuses to support me any longer! I feel it trembling beneath my feet! Justice for me! The earth seeks to shake me off."

"Justice," replied the voice of Jörgen on one of these occasions from behind the door. "We, too, demand justice."

". . . Who is it that dares . . ."

"Everyone dares everything now. If the master of the house abandons his post and neglects to punish, we'll inflict punishment."

"I don't want to know anything about it. Let everything go to rack and ruin. I want to know nothing." Tycho continually interrupted in frenzied tones, shouting down his son, who was speaking about Tengnagel. Now, he said, they knew for certain what they had not been able to discover from their own spies or from Elizabeth: that the rebellious junker was living in a secret stronghold on the edge of the village of Benatky, brewing mischief. For now Hagecius had arrived. . . .

Tycho caught the name and listened.

For now Hagecius had come, Jörgen continued in more confident tones, and declared that he had recently received tidings from Tengnagel in Benatky. Nay, more, Hagecius had expected to find Tengnagel in the castle. It was evidently something of importance, for he had already held a discussion with Kepler, lasting for hours.

"With Kepler? Why was he not brought to me?—It hasn't
178

yet got as far as that with me!" Tycho had leapt from his bed and flung the door open. His eyes blazing with anger, he looked down upon his son, who did not comprehend his violence. On the contrary, he entered the room and asked for leave to proceed against Tengnagel with a company of mounted men. . . .

"Don't bother me with silly war-games. If you want to see blood flow, go and slaughter fowls."

"Then we'll do it without your permission. I warn you, father!"

"And I laugh at you.—What, don't you realize that the decisive hour is at hand? What is Tengnagel to us? Kepler must be put to the question. Friend or foe? Let him speak! It is well that Hagecius is here—the only man who has espoused my cause against Ursus—my only friend. He will be the impartial judge. . . . But what impudence to intercept my visitors, to prevent them from gaining access to me. Does Kepler mean to alienate my partisans from me and to continue stirring up feeling against me? Does he think that he can do this with impunity? . . . Am I ill? Am I to be entirely ignored? The guest is to decide on his own authority. . . . Servants, call my servants, ho! I want to be dressed, I won't lie in bed."

"You don't listen to me, father. You yourself are responsible for everything that is now happening." With a resolute movement he turned his back to go.

But Tycho continued talking wildly. He dragged him back. "Boy, fetch my boots!"

Then he staggered and the dwarf was able to put him back to bed.

But now he began with all his strength to struggle against himself. It was as if his spiritual fever had reached its zenith and was now abating. He reflected, he gradually beheld

179

everything in a much calmer light. Kepler was not a cunning scoundrel, but only one favoured by good fortune and natural dispositions. One could look him calmly in the eyes. All that was needed was a single open discussion with him about everything, a demand for an explanation regarding their differences in astronomical and personal matters. And it must take place in the presence of Hagecius. He had arrived at a fitting moment. At last for once fortune was favourable.

Towards evening Tycho caused himself to be arranged in his ample indoor cloak and to be carried, together with his bed, into the great instrument-room.

There he found Kepler still in conversation with Hagecius. Longomontanus and Müller were also present. The greeting was hearty. As soon as Tycho beheld Kepler before him, he utterly failed to understand how he could have entertained such evil imaginings about him. How falsifying had been the effect of the long separation! What apprehensions and what vileness did it not breed? . . . On the other hand it surprised him that Hagecius, contrary to his usual practice, remained exceedingly cool and reserved; he inquired only in a cursory manner about the effect of his purges and potions and merely made a brief examination. So it was not at all as a doctor and sympathetic friend that he had come? Was he, too, caught by the contagious enthusiasm for Kepler? In actual fact he always kept near Kepler and had before him a little book, in which from time to time he noted down observations, without paying any attention to Tycho. How strange that in reality everything seemed disposed in such a way as to influence Tycho's jealousy against Kepler!

But the old man was by no means inclined to allow the whim bred of his recovery to be thwarted. As happens with powerful natures of his breed, recovery had come of itself after many weeks of agitation and filled him with a frivolous,

180

groundless exultation. But not for one minute did he forget his plan to bring the issue between himself and Kepler to a final decision today. To that end he took up an unimportant point raised by Longomontanus, to proceed at once to discuss the vital questions of the theory of the universe. At once all laid aside their diagrams and apparatus and took up positions near Tycho's bed. The arc of the great wall-quadrant, lit up by moonlight, climbed obliquely over their heads like a Jacob's ladder, its lustre streaming over the globes of the lamps set upon the work-tables, and Tycho fixed his gaze upon this great light, while in gentle tones he began his discourse. He set it forth that in his opinion motion was nobler than rest; for that reason it must be regarded as natural that the world of ether should circle about, while the heavier lower earth remained immovable. The inert earth could assuredly not move, whereas the planets, sylph-like forms created out of light and some other rare substance, were designed by Nature for flight and, together with the fixed stars, were assuredly not set upon the immovable Ptolemaic spheres. On the contrary, by the very riot of their unchecked revolutions they bore witness to the wisdom and omnipotence of God. Thus the view of Copernicus, which, moreover, had already been put forward in antiquity by Aristarchus of Samos and could not, therefore, have been unknown to Ptolemy, ran counter, not, indeed, to mathematical, but so much the more to physical laws. . . .

"But it still remains to be proved that the planets are composed of ethereal substance," replied Kepler with a certain note of sternness, while the others almost ceased to breathe. Tycho started in alarm. His first thought was a hideous one: that quite recently Kepler had not thought of any objections, but that now, because Hagecius was present, he opposed him in order to cause trouble. But he speedily rejected this fancy.

181

Kepler was assuredly innocent; once and for all he must accustom himself to this established fact. Yet he could not help suffering acutely at seeing Hagecius's attention exclusively fixed upon Kepler. The doctor, whose entry into the field against Ursus Tycho prized so highly as the sole proof of friendship shown him for a long time, listened with an inexplicable tenseness to every word uttered by Kepler. His notes, too, seemed to relate solely to Kepler. Tycho turned his gaze away—towards the stars, he gently told himself. Then he began a passionate defence of his position. But Kepler, too, was this time really more eloquent than usual, perhaps because scientific details were under discussion instead of undemonstrable fundamental theories. Arguments were now weighed, one against another. The tremendous idea that the earth itself was nothing but a planet, like those distant little stars Mercury and Venus, stood opposed to the arbitrarily conceived theory of auxiliary spheres, assailed by Kepler. . . . The two pupils listened entranced and sought to note everything; never had they listened to so powerfully conducted a controversy. Tycho's bosom, from which the metallic voice continued to issue its clear notes, contracted ever more closely. He began to despair, finding no sign of decision on either side. Kepler, on the other hand, seemed to drink in a copious draught of pleasure and strength from this very uncertainty. The more obscure and the more difficult the decision, the more did he find himself in the humour for jesting, this man who was ordinarily so dry. When confronted by "Nature," this riddle of the Sphinx, his whole being expanded, he seized without difficulty upon the object, jovially assailing it upon every side, as it were, and firmly rooted himself in it. His voice even took on an unfamiliar, joyously consequential bass-note when he cried in reply to a caustic remark of Tycho's: "Well, perhaps the laws of nature agree only fortuitously."

Longomontanus burst out laughing and Müller remarked that in that case bad mathematicians, himself for example, had the best prospect of being right. So the conversation escaped Tycho's guidance and, notwithstanding his displeasure, sank for a brief space almost to the level of a beerhouse discussion.

Tycho raised himself, breathing heavily. "Now at least the system of Copernicus remains unproved, and as it runs counter to the Bible and as I may not needlessly affront the Catholic Majesty of my Emperor, I have no reason for espousing it."

"That is going too far," observed Kepler, still smiling. "Catholic or not, the hypothesis alone is being considered here, not the Emperor's favour."

"Catholic or not . . . splendid! What was that? Pray, say it again." Hagecius rolled his eyes with an expression of fulsome approval towards Kepler, who, however, paid no attention to him, but seemed completely absorbed in his subject.

Tycho answered hotly, feeling that a fundamental principle of his life was being assailed: "But without the favour of princes and of the rich we could construct no expensive apparatus, and truth would remain uninvestigated. Am I the first to perceive it? What would Regiomontanus, our great prototype, have been without Walter of Nuremberg. Purbach without Cardinal Bessarion, Rothmann without the Landgrave of Kassel? And how much benefit have I myself derived from the burgher Hainzel, from King Frederick, and from all the exalted personages who visited Hveen!" Tycho lost himself once more in the description of his days of splendour. Suddenly his expression darkened. "Assuredly all princes are not equally distinguished. Duke Julius of Brunswick was once my guest and was so pleased with a beautiful automatically movable statue of Mercury that he took it away with him,

183

promising to send me a copy. Often enough I have reminded him. Make a note, Longomontanus; tomorrow you must write to him more urgently." His countenance became hard and covetous and seemed to inventory every fragment of his possessions. But immediately afterwards he collected his thoughts, as if with a powerful effort, turning them back to speech, his eyes gleaming with keen logic: "Thus the princes help us and the truth; so it is for us in our turn to respect them and to defer to their pleasure."

"It is just this that I contest," cried Kepler excitedly; "we must defer to truth alone and to no one else."

"Excellent. To no one else," nodded Hagecius in great content.

"Why to no one else?" Tycho addressed himself to the pair, who seemed to have entered into a secret compact. "When I have already put it before you that one can serve the truth only if one serves princes. It is quite true that it is more comfortable and simpler to follow your practice, my dear Kepler. You pay regard to nothing in going your own holy way, turning neither to right nor to left. But does it seem less holy to you to belie oneself for truth's sake? 'Be cunning as serpents and harmless as doves'; so did our Lord Jesus Himself speak to His disciples. You are no serpent, you never belie or constrain yourself. Thus you really serve, not truth, but only yourself; that is to say, your own purity and inviolateness. But I see not only myself, I see also my relations with these among whom I must live in the determination to serve truth with the aid of adroitness and every shrewd device. And isn't our whole science comprised in a knowledge of relations, of what binds the cosmos, what unites humanity with the stars?"

"You speak of astrology," interjected Kepler.

184

A terrible pause ensued. "Isn't astrology also a science?" The question came from Longomontanus, who looked from Tycho to Kepler and back again, hoping in this sphere, too, to acquire valuable information.

Tycho trembled throughout his whole body. "Call it astrology or anything else you please. Most certainly we wish to carry our inquiries into the most exalted places that are set above all things. And yet, if one strives after something so tremendous, can one remain shut up within the original affections of one's ego? Will God not bestow the favour of knowledge only upon the best, upon the most unselfish, or do you think that every self-seeker and every scoundrel is entitled to stare at the stars? It is reported from Asia that mighty peoples pay worship to a king's son who, although he had attained to the highest bliss in solitude, yet afterwards went about among men to live with them and to instruct them. And this they style his greatest deed, that he did not continue alone, although he could have drunk his fill of the most exalted wisdom, but that he gave up his divine purity for the lot of humanity, with all the uncleanness and tortuousness of strife. . . . And Christ, the Son of God, how was it with Him? He redeemed us by ceasing to be a deity free from desire, pure, and becoming a toiling, laborious teacher among men. . . . And I think it is a better imitation of Christ to work among men, even though subject to the protection of princely favour, than merely to dream away one's life in ecstasy and thus to forget all labour and vexations." In fiery agitation Tycho pressed his hands despairingly upon his brow, stirred to the depth of his being. He fully realized that he was not altogether in the right, that all that he had said was but half true. Suddenly everything that he had uttered seemed fruitless to him; he was seized by acute anguish, and words that no one

185

had expected were forced from his lips: "You are pitiless, Kepler. God has sent you to ·chastise me." With these words he sank back upon the pillows.

All gathered anxiously round him. Hagecius felt his pulse. "Aren't you well, master?" asked Kepler.

"Everyone is as well as he deserves," replied Tycho, casting a bitter glance at Kepler, whose cheeks had been rounded and coloured by the country air at the castle of Benatky and who beside the declining Tycho showed up like a fresh rose-tree against a decayed giant oak. "But we want to reach a conclusion." The old man stubbornly pulled himself together. "If the debate is once set going, it must not come to an end without attaining some result."

More out of a desire to oblige than from any more profound motive, Kepler said reflectingly: "But really I don't see how regard for our Emperor Rudolph can prejudice the cause of Copernicus."

"You have never seen the Emperor." This was Tycho's only remark; after it he fell silent. For now he himself beheld the fine, melancholy countenance of the Emperor before him, just as it had appeared to him in the only audience hitherto accorded him. In what friendly terms on that occasion the sovereign had encouraged him. And now he was to wound him by a premature, still undemonstrated attack upon Ptolemy; for with Ptolemy stood and fell the whole fabric of astrology, the Emperor's last refuge. No, that would have been inconsiderate and ill done on his part, an act of ingratitude. Tycho desired to strain every nerve in investigation and to discover the truth, and only then to appear before the Emperor with the fully assured truth, with the whole truth, whether it spoke in favourable or unfavourable terms. He wished to act honourably, but not by frivolous haste disturb His Majesty, who, as it was, had every day so much folly

186

and malice to reflect upon and to adjudge in his Empire. No, Tycho was not ungrateful, even if all about him, wife and friend and children, should abound in ingratitude; Tycho loved his imperial master; he would never forget his kindly reception; he would fall down upon his knees and cover the hem of his mantle with kisses. . . . While Tycho thus became entirely absorbed in this image of a grateful man and of the recipient of his thanks, there suddenly shot up within his heart a warm feeling, a feeling of which he had never yet been aware, which had floated but dimly before him while he was speaking of Buddha and Christ, half disguised under the masks of duty and subsidiary interests. Now it seemed present in streams of liberating, hopeful abundance; a perfect happiness, a joy in himself, in his own sensitive, thankful heart. Suddenly he felt himself set at liberty. A joyous agitation seized him as he felt that here lay the seed for a new, a better life. All at once there arose within him a yearning to sacrifice himself, to devote himself to humanity. What was it to him that they did not merit his sacrifice, that they treated him abominably? *He loved them notwithstanding.* That was it; that was the fundamental emotion from which he could not escape, on account of which he had felt shamed throughout the whole of his life, the feeling that had involved him in a thousand embarrassments and ambiguities. Today for the first time he willingly surrendered himself to this emotion; he literally felt how it grew within him, how it menaced him with its sweeping volume of energy, how it constituted a certain danger, but now he no longer felt fear of it, of this perilous love of humanity. What did it all mean, then? He was positively mad, quite mad from pure love for humanity; he wanted to be absorbed in it. This love had become his nature; nothing could alter it. Thus he was compounded, thus and in no other manner, hot-blooded to the pitch of madness,

187

full of understanding, mindful of everything that occurred, and always ready to help. And now he desired to help, even if jeering grimaces were made behind his back, even if he were laughed at and his goodness were rewarded with ingratitude and indifference, as it was by Kepler. . . . He flung a glance at that Kepler, and immediately in his new-born enthusiasm discovered his true relation towards him, for which he had throughout weeks struggled so desperately. It had even been disingenuous always to seek for some point between the two from which he would have had to pass judgment upon both, unaffected by prejudice. "I have not the right to be without prejudice," thought Tycho exultantly, "I have nothing else to do but to pursue my own path of love to the end, just as Kepler goes on his way to the end. I am indeed a man, a real man, standing upon my own feet. And even as he may perhaps be in the right with his lack of feeling, so I, too, have my right. In my course there is only one thing to avoid, being misled. I have the right to love him with all my strength, in all despite, to love him quite blindly, as my emotions demand, to abandon myself to my friendship and to that which seems to be the only proper course, the only thing that gives value to life—enthroned high above all right and gratitude."

For a space he lay with eyes closed, his lips muttering inaudible words. Now he looked about him and wished to answer Kepler, but no longer in the spirit of acrimonious debate, only in a friendly manner and in ample detail. Then he observed that Kepler was no longer looking at him, but had half turned towards the window. The others, too, bestowed no more attention upon him, but looked anxious, whispered, and made signs to one another. Involuntarily Tycho followed the direction of their gaze. All were excitedly contemplating the night sky, the lower edge of which had taken on a singular hue of brilliant red; it even streamed over the moon and

188

threw blood-coloured reflections upon the glistening metal surface of the quadrant. Uncanny sounds were heard from the distance, women's cries in the courtyard, and farther still a sound resembling the dull roll of drums. Suddenly the alarm bells on the castle church began to peal with a shrill clamour.

"Fire! Fire!" cried Müller, who stood nearest the window.

"Down on the Iser! The wood is on fire!" yelled Hagecius.

Kepler had flung open the window and was shouting to those below. A wild clamour was raised in reply, voices which had never before been heard in that place. And suddenly the whole castle seemed densely crowded with men; footsteps clattered and cries resounded from every passage.

In an instant Tycho had thrown off the quilt and stood upright, clad in his indoor robe. "Saddle my horse! I wish to be on the spot without any further delay!"

"But you are ill!" they cried in horror, and sought to force him back into bed.

"I—ill? Come on if you want to measure your strength against mine." He paced up and down the chamber with great strides, barefoot, dragging behind him his bellying cloak, which beat upon his hips. "I *was* ill. . . . Bring my boots, spurs, sword, jerkin. . . . Now I am well. Now I feel my strength again in the right place. I will help you and those down there. Once more I know my duty. I must take a hand everywhere, plague myself about everything, fill my skull with cares, bearing it all patiently; that is my path. . . . Here, you fellow, bring my hat, my hat, you lazy dog! . . . I was ill and weak; that is true. But now I must protect my peasants' property and I can. . . . Bring the horse. I need no one's arm to support me. Make way; I am going alone! My way, my own appointed way. Nothing shall turn me

189

from it . . . least of all you, Master Hagecius." Like one demented, Tycho shook off the doctor, who had laid his hand upon his pulse and in that posture was walking with him up and down the room, while the servants ran hither and thither at their master's bidding and brought his clothes. "Least of all you, with your poor, pitiful arts. Yes, let mysterious wrinkles gather on your brow. You don't frighten me any longer. Nothing frightens me any longer. Even you, Kepler, from whom I had expected better physic than ever Hagecius can concoct, even you no longer frighten me. . . . But hurry, hurry! I mean to be my own doctor. To work! And you there —out of my path."

He was already dressed and storming down the steps. His horse was brought and he galloped off to the scene of the conflagration. Two trusted retainers had at the same time risen with all speed and now bore him company. . . . The calvacade passed through the park and down the steep road from the castle into the unlit village. In the mean time the red glow of the fire had become purplish, its dusky, flickering light disclosing strange figures amid the huts, who were hurrying in the same direction as Tycho. He overtook them, without bestowing any attention upon them. Already the cracking of smouldering tree-trunks and the fall of the branches could be heard. Was not that really the roll of drums that broke through the other sounds? . . . Tycho's servants hastened in alarm to his side, in their anxiety to warn him: "There are brigands there!" In the darkness a heavy piece of artillery with full team clattered by. But Tycho saw only the reddened sky before him. "They are certainly soldiers," he replied to the anxious servants, and again rode a few paces ahead of them. He had already reached the end of the village, at the spot where the road dropped downwards towards the Iser; he was looking down upon the open

190

country and the burning wood before him when suddenly a pair of strapping fellows barred his path with crossed halberds. The next moment he was dragged down from his horse, seized, and conducted to a watch-fire that was burning near by.

Tycho at once realized that he had not to do with regular troops, such as the Emperor maintained, but with men from the free bands which were raised to fight against the Turks, and who, as soon as pay became seriously overdue, were accustomed to desert from the colours and to plunder the country far and wide. In an instant he drew himself up to his full height. In reply to a man who, sitting in a swaggering position before the fire, seemed to be their leader and who had inquired with an insolent stare: "What is your business?" he thundered: "It is for me to ask you that question, footpads and marauders that you are; I am master here." As he said these words, with a mere turn of his frame, still powerful in spite of illness and malformation, he flung to the ground the two who beset him and almost overturned the commander. "Lead me to your captain, you swine," he bade them. Even these unruly spirits could not altogether escape the influence of his mighty glance. They did not so much conduct him as follow him along the edge of the forest to the next group. There was, as Tycho saw during his progress, a whole circle of watch-fires, which ran along the bordering hills and, circling the burning wood, which lay beneath, joined in the angle of the Iser. No efforts were made to extinguish the fire in the wood; on the contrary, white-hot fire-balls fell from the hills, discharged from covered positions in the upper forests. The wood beneath had evidently been set alight by musketry fire. The shots were answered by volleys from the river. A small, low-pitched building in the wood beneath seemed to form the centre of the warlike clamour which filled the whole country-side. It was undoubtedly the intention to lay siege to this fortified hut. Already a dense stream of thick, white smoke issued forth from its roof, but the salvoes continued unremittingly to thunder forth from the loop-holes, mingled with other sounds from the valley and the mountains around, shrill trumpet-calls and whistles, curt words of command, and the hideous yells of the terrified dogs in the village. . . .

In a clearing stood a group of chiefs and soldiers assembled about a great fire, as if for a council of war. Wild with anger at the impious assault upon his property in a time of peace and already suspecting behind it some new trick on the part of his detractors, Tycho strode in among them. To his bitter amazement he found himself confronting—his own sons, Tyge and Jörgen, among the leaders.

"We've dug out the fox's earth," were the words with which Jörgen, the more valiant of the two, greeted him, playing idly with his sword-belt.

"What fox's earth?" replied Tycho, who feared that he was going mad.

"What but Tengnagel's? He's already roasting down there."

"Speak up. What is going on here? Or it is your last hour." He drew his sword and advanced threateningly upon his children.

Straightway, under the full force of their father's wrath, their hearts failed them. The elder of the two began an apologetic speech: "But only today Jörgen pronounced sentence . . ."

"Pronouncement! A fine pronouncement, you brigands, you dirty tramps, you tups! Who dares give judgment here without me, behind my back? What has happened to Tengnagel? Where is he? What has he done to you?"

"We wanted to conceal the worst from you, father," cried Jörgen defiantly. "But as you force us at the sword's point, so be it."

192

"Down on your knees, boy! What worse can there be than this devastation and breaking up of all laws?" Tycho was stirred to the very depths. He found it quite impossible to listen quietly to Jörgen. The reports of the firing continually interrupted his authoritative utterances, for even as they stood and conversed, men were being slain and fires kindled. Yet Jörgen actually announced it as an action of considerable merit, that he and his brother, without causing their father needless agitation, had profited by his sickness and solitary condition to hire a company of volunteers and to capture Tengnagel's barricaded mouse-hole by a *coup de main*. In this, it was true, they had not succeeded, for Tengnagel was on the watch and had a stout little garrison about him. But he could not hold out till morning; that very night his blood should expiate the shame inflicted upon the house of Brahe. . . . Tycho only heard scattered sentences from Jörgen's arrogant, almost jovial utterance. His gaze rested as if spellbound upon the prospect before him, dismally lighted by the glow of the fire. This appalling night, with its altogether unexpected eruption of entrenchments springing up from nowhere, from behind which men fired upon one another, with its clamour and its stinking tongues of smoky flame, borne upwards by the wind, with this senseless discussion between father and sons, with all the desolation, the hideousness, and the licence, suddenly seemed to him to be nothing but the embodiment of all the hateful thoughts over which he had brooded upon his bed of sickness. It was like a dream made flesh to punish him, a dream that one could no longer shake off; and now, to crown all, the inevitable name "Kepler" resounded over this desolate landscape with a spectral distinctness, even as it did amid the landscape of his fantasy. It resounded with the same incomprehensible note as in his thoughts, compounded of guilt and innocence!

193

"The next on the list is Kepler," Jörgen boasted. "He is really much more mischievous than Tengnagel and we have far more serious evidence against him. It was on Kepler's account that Tengnagel had to leave the castle, and as Elizabeth could not keep her betrothed in honour, she was forced to do so in dishonour. You can't be surprised that she has become a whore!"

"Do you speak of my daughter?" Tycho had thrown away his sword and hurled himself with the howl of a wild animal upon Jörgen, striving to seize his throat between his two hands.

With a swift turning movement, however, the youth slipped away. "Of no one else. Night after night she steals out of the castle like a wanton little nun."

"I myself have seen her creeping to Tengnagel." It was the graver Tyge who was now speaking. "We have been keeping watch and ward while you, father, kept your eyes fast closed, simply out of love for Kepler."

Tycho turned towards his first-born, whose measured, matter-of-fact tones somewhat calmed him amid all the horror that surrounded him; yet already Jörgen intervened once more, a kind of involuntary scorn always mingling with his words: "And Kepler was the scamp of a door-keeper in league with her! With my own eyes I saw how he gallantly held the rope on which our sister let herself down to go forth to her pastime of love. Truly, a charming spectacle! Thus the loyal pupil repays you for your instruction."

"Is this true?" cried Tycho, once more turning towards the elder son. He trembled throughout his whole frame.

"Of course it is. For weeks Elizabeth has slipped out from Kepler's room to join Tengnagel every night. And that is why you find us here, ready to take vengeance upon our sister's seducer."

194

Tycho had lost command over himself. While still in his own room, it had been his wish to exert all his energies in acquiring a more conciliatory outlook upon this to him entirely hostile dispensation; and straightway everything was hurled into annihilation by a test too rigorous, too sudden. Overwhelmed by his grief, he fell upon his knees, wringing his hands and invoking his unseen destiny. "So is this one hour to destroy me altogether? My daughter shamed! My sons incendiaries and gallows-birds! And Kepler not a rod of chastisement for my good, but an enemy!" He felt his heart ceasing to beat; he felt death draw near. "If only I have not lived in vain! If only I have not lived in vain!" he stammered in his agony like a last litany.

At that moment a soldier approached his sons and reported that Tengnagel's men were already forced to leave the house for water to extinguish the fire, and would therefore be excellent targets. The sound of strange, rough voices awakened Tycho from his mumbling. He rose to his feet. "Put out the fire at once," he stormed at his sons. "Send your bands of Huns about their business without delay, and see that the forest fire spreads no farther, or I will hand you yourselves over to imperial justice for breach of the peace." He made a sign to his servants and pointed to Jörgen. "Bind his hands, bind this thief's hands! The little pasteboard hero!"

Jörgen shrank back disconcerted. But Tycho himself seized his hands in an iron grip and bound them with a leather girdle which he had snatched from the lad's waist. "I'm in earnest, in deadly earnest. Now put him on a horse and take him back to the castle.—Tyge, I hold your brother as hostage that the night passes quietly and that at sunrise you send a flag of truce to Tengnagel. He is to go free. And as to your horde, pay them their due; after that send them whence they came. Do you understand?"

195

He leaped swiftly upon his horse and turned back to the castle, while the servants carried out his behest.

All the windows of the castle were brightly lighted, an unwonted spectacle, which violated the purity of the night. Tycho entered the courtyard. The servants were running terror-stricken hither and thither. His awe-inspiring mien restored their courage. The screaming women became silent at the sight of his grim countenance. "Where is your mistress?" he inquired. For answer they pointed to the long entrance hall, situated on the ground-floor. There, however, he did not find his wife; a new surprise awaited him: ten or fifteen wounded soldiers were lying there upon benches and chairs, the first victims of the wild shooting. Some rose awkwardly to their feet as he entered, others groaned hoarsely. They were terrible fellows in stout leather jerkins and high boots. Some of them still wore wide-brimmed hats decked with cocks' feathers of many hues, and convulsively clutched heavy muskets and rests; there they sat dully, just as they had been brought from the engagement, their newly-inflicted wounds clumsily bound up and still dripping with blood amid innumerable brown scars, the trophies of earlier days. All wore their hair long, flowing down to the shoulders. The one who now bowed before Tycho, apparently a leader, had even snow-white hair; it was stained with mud and drops of blood and hung uncombed about his defiant features like a faded ensign.

At the sight of these savage old warriors Tycho's tears, against which he had hitherto manfully contended, burst forth. "Welcome, in God's name, old war-dogs," he cried in frantic tones, and then at once sharply repressed his emotion. "It's true I haven't invited you, but none the less as unbidden guests I will have you properly housed and cared for. You are just like old comrades to me, although it is the first time I see you here. God's blood, I, too, have grown old in the

196

game of war; I've flayed the country-side and grabbed at the last mite like you. Let us shake hands, my friends, give me your hands."

And he went from one to another, looked to their bandages with an experienced eye, and bade the servants make haste to procure them better linen. He dispatched the dwarf, Jeppe, to the cellar for wine. "You must drink in proper fashion to my health and to your own, lads o' my heart. If, after all, you've not been able to rob, vex, and torment as you had wished, the wine shall console you."

The *Landsknechts,* who had not looked for such a good reception, applauded him tumultuously. But their white-haired commander, the most impudent of all, already began to grumble. "Send us a better wine-porter, Herr de Brahe. Your hunchback is stingy, he wouldn't even show us the treasure-chamber. . . ."

"I keep a gallows ready for thieves down in the village, comrade," Tycho laughed and laid a hand on his shoulder. "But no one who is my guest shall lack anything. Take note of that, my gallant Trojans."

From the neighbouring room Christine's cry of pain forced itself upon their ears. Tycho threw open the doors. Immediately his wife flung herself at his feet. "Mercy, only for her. Forbear! She is a mother."

"What do you mean?"

"Elizabeth is with child by Tengnagel. Oh, if only I had told you before—"

"So that was it." Tycho beat with his palms upon his brow. "Oh, that I could have been so blind! That I should not have understood your words!"

"I wished to force things through by my own efforts and bring them to a happy conclusion," wailed the luckless woman. "But today this misbegotten gang have ruined all."

197

"The earth casts me off," groaned Tycho dully. But straightway he burst out into a wild cry: "Elizabeth? Where is she? Bring me to her. . . . No, no, let me be. I want to be alone."

"What will you do, Tyge? You mean to kill her?"

For a space he had forgotten that his wife was on her knees before him, feeling himself already quite alone, far from this crazy, vulgar world. Now he started with terror and, with a sharp onset of shame and sympathy, raised Christine from the ground. "Only leave me alone, let me think all this over. It is too much at once. Do leave me!" He freed himself from the anxious grasp of her hands. "You need have no fear. Nor need Elizabeth have any fear of me. . . . I am too old. . . . Let me be. Is there anyone at all who can feel any fear of me? Everyone can spit on me." His voice, which had been intended to carry words of comfort, was taking on a hideous note of menace. . . . "If I were to kill her, I should at least do it in a seemly way, as becomes a father. But you kill me and spit on me into the bargain." At the door he once more turned, his eyes blood-shot, his beard disordered, and his face convulsed in a grimace. He clapped his hands and cried aloud with hideously clear, almost joyous tones: "And Jeppe shall bring me wine, our best wine!"

Slowly, as if labouring under some heavy burden, he dragged himself down the steps into the room in which he had passed the sad days of his illness. As the bed had previously been moved out, it seemed more spacious and more empty than before. Only a rough table with a few chairs stood in the corner. Robbed of all his strength, Tycho let himself slip down. Feeling the downfall of his family as an epitome of the whole course of his ill success, he hid his head and softly, vacantly, repeated his new slogan again and again: "If only I have not lived in vain!"

Presently Jeppe came trotting in with tankard and glass.

198

Tycho snatched thirstily at the wine and emptied the glass in great gulps, as often as the dwarf filled it. The warmth which mounted to his cheeks mingled with the flush of shame that had spread over his features at the sight of his wife on her knees and had remained. Shame, scalding shame, formed the mid-point of his grief. "How is it possible that such things happen in the world?" he kept asking himself. "How shameful to live in the midst of such atrocious happenings, with no power to avert them!" And as he thus reflected, he no longer thought solely of himself, taken all unawares by this new blow of misfortune; he felt shame also on behalf of his wife, who had for so long been struggling helplessly amid all these abominations, and above all he felt compassion for Elizabeth herself. What must have happened before this good, merry creature, whose proximity had always seemed to him to bring peace, could have so entirely abandoned the path of right? He strove to picture it to himself: Elizabeth slipping treacherously through the night, to fling herself all dishonoured into a seducer's arms, a common strumpet, shamed, betrayed— that same Elizabeth, just as he had always beheld her, a rosy, beloved girl, eager for knowledge, full of interest, even versed in science, and learned like Sophie Brahe, Tycho's gifted sister, whom she declared she would willingly emulate. Tycho could not reconcile these two pictures. And other images came crowding upon him. He saw his favourite daughter as a little child, heard her first utterances, rendered almost defiant by her exertions; he remembered how in the evening he had often stood by her railed cot, marvelling at her blissful slumber. Oh, how long must it be since she had ceased to sleep so peacefully! Who troubled about it now? In those days of her childhood they had counted every breath that she drew and brought immediate remedies for every little pain, for every cough. Yet now the selfsame creature, the product of a long,

199

painstaking education, went to ruin just like a mangy cat. So this was the meaning of Elizabeth's life, tonight's work; in this it was to reach its highest point, if her blood was to be shed by his hand. What a glorious dispensation! Oh, how vulgar it all was, trangression and punishment, sinful woman and avenger, both so vulgar! The further he penetrated this idea, the deeper was his own sense of shame; it was as if he himself in some way shared the responsibility for all these happenings and for the course of the world. In all this misery he was overtaken by an entirely new emotion; from the depth of his shame there arose a mysterious humility, which his proud heart had hitherto never experienced. Yes, Tycho was conscious of a profound remorse, without really knowing wherein his offence lay. But the consciousness of guilt was nevertheless there, and it grew. The presentiment of his own utter inadequacy and base-mindedness, just as it had stolen upon him as in a dream while he gazed upon the desolate scene of conflagration, soon laid so powerful a hold on him that he felt that he understood, albeit somewhat vaguely, why it was himself and his house that must bear such an excessive burden of suffering. And now that he perceived this remarkable, barely comprehensible connexion, he was conscious of something that seemed to assuage, to tranquillize. Assuredly it held no agreeable element, no touch of gentleness, but rather the stability of a good, final resolve. It was clear to him that he must root out the whole of this misery, himself and his house, to bring about repose. As he already many times vaguely imagined, he would kindle a fire, he would set the castle alight at its four corners, and not only Elizabeth should perish in the flames, but also the old, impotent, despairing Tycho and all, all with him. . . .

When, after a long interval, he looked up, Elizabeth was standing before him, weeping, silently biting her lips. Tycho's

200

first impulse was to fly into a rage; then, however, holding his hand before his eyes, he regarded his daughter, but did not let her observe him. He felt ashamed of himself. It was as if he now beheld her for the first time. Finding this body standing erect before him, tall and free, the body which he had himself begotten, but which had cast itself adrift from him long before, he was seized with a sudden feeling of anxiety. Abashed, he let his hand fall and gazed upon her broken and helpless. She too in her turn gave way to her dismay and said in a high, gentle voice, which threatened to break as easily as a thin thread: "Father—I no longer know what I should do."

"And now you come to me?" he asked with a malevolent harshness, which he himself did not understand.

But she seemed not to fear him at all. On the contrary, amid these terrible events, a childish confidence in him had returned to her. "Yes, to you," she said, once more in slumbrous, chanting tones; "you can assuredly still help. But I know no more what to do."

He stood towering over her. "And you know what you have done?"

As she inclined her head in reply, some muscle or shadow upon her countenance warned him with all the force of certainty that Elizabeth had received her hot young blood from no one but himself. Nay, more, she behaved with her betrothed in exactly the same way as he himself had earlier with her mother. And with what was she now confronted, with what tortures springing from indiscretion, desire and ill fortune! All that was behind him was still before her! For the first time he felt his own soul beginning its course anew in this other body, writhing and toiling. Thereupon all plans of revenge and annihilation faltered; he felt nothing but sympathy for this being who innocently suffered for his offence. He alone was guilty and responsible; he must atone. With piteous look Elizabeth entreated his forgiveness; her superficial composure vanished, and enervating death-dealing words stood already upon her lips. Then he bent forward and laid his cheek upon her deeply bowed head. So for a long time they both remained standing, both with bowed heads. Their hands, with which, on account of some secret fear, they dared not touch one another's bodies, remained unjoined. Both stood in this loose, vacant pose, shedding no tear and uttering no word, conscious of their own common helplessness, neither aiding nor cumbering one another.

The feeling that passed through their minds was perhaps the most sorrowful that humanity can ever know, the feeling that two are together, understanding one another, knowing all of one another, and yet unable to deliver one another. . . .

"You love Tengnagel?" Tycho asked at length. He sat down once more; his knees trembled too violently for him to stand.

"Yes."

"And have you considered whether you are suited to one another?" "As Christine and I suit one another," was the thought that flashed through his mind even as he put the question, and he laughed so grimly that Elizabeth began to weep aloud. Henceforth this laugh pursued him; throughout that night it kept bursting forth. He raised Elizabeth's head, not gently, but with a rapid grasp, just as before he had repelled with his rebuke the ruffianly bands of *Landsknechts*. Then he caught her by the shoulders and pressed her down into a chair. "There, sit by me, drink with me. What does it matter whether you and Tengnagel suit one another? What does anything really matter, life or death, happiness or misfortune, anything?" With outstretched right arm he described a gigan-

202

tic half-circle in the air, as if gathering the whole world for good and all into a bundle to thrust it away from him. As he did so, he laughed so loudly that his powerful body rocked hither and thither; but the laughter did not resound clear and distinct—it was as if it were striking backwards into the body, as if it were stifled by the mighty waves of suffering, which with all its strength it strove to burst.

Elizabeth no longer understood her father. She had often seen him storming and violent, but never in this uncanny mood. "Father," she cried, summoning for a moment all her spiritual energy to an enforced composure. "Father, have pity; they are firing upon my betrothed, they are killing him."

Instead of answering he leaped wildly to his feet and flung the window open.

"Father, father," she wailed, and her sunken, bloodless face flushed deep red in this moment of extreme agitation. It seemed, indeed, as if the blood were mounting right to her fair hair and whitish eyebrows. Now they gleamed with a strange unnatural brilliance amid the warm air streaming in from the summer night.

"Stupid child," he flung at her, and again there resounded his prolonged, stifled laughter. "Don't you notice anything? They have already ceased firing. I have intervened. The armistice holds until dawn; then we'll send someone to treat with your—betrothed. We'll court him, court him, I say, just as if he were a little bride. We'll entreat him most urgently to take Fräulein de Brahe. Jörgen is locked up and Tyge obeys. Oh, I have a powerful fist; I am wise, I am an ancient buck with a keen scent. But what good is it? What good? There, drink with me, I say." He pushed the glass towards her and, seizing the tankard, poured a deep draft. "Shame, humiliation, dirt, strife, folly, withering, fading, madness, darkness, ruin—

203

such has been my life, and so I see it still before me. Am I wise or not? It is all the same! Everything that is mine must perish.—Do you love Tengnagel? I ask you for the second time."

"Father, yes," breathed Elizabeth, folding her hands.

"Then you shall have him. Then you shall go to ruin with him. . . . And who can tell me whether it was well that I restrained my sons from the most atrocious crime? Perhaps it would have been better if they had left their heads dripping with blood upon the palisades, and everything had been burned, you and I and they and Christine and Tengnagel, all at once and all the forest about us. Look there. Do you see? The fire is smoldering only a very little. They will still save the wood that lies nearest, my trees that I so dearly love, whose scent refreshes me when I saw them down to construct new apparatus. But of this too I say: what profits it? Even with new apparatus I shall not come to know the divine law in this sorry world of woe. Everything is fruitless! But in the final issue everything is without importance, too."

"Father, father," moaned Elizabeth. Still gentler moans came from something in the corner by the door. Tycho precipitated himself in the direction of the sound and dragged forward his elder daughter, Magdalena, who had hidden herself there. She had come in with Elizabeth.

"Ha! So you have brought your little sister with you, Elsa," cried Tycho in genuine amusement and scorn. "She was to be your protector, or no, she was to have instructed me in the uses of chastity. One is wrecked on the rocks of chastity; the other perishes by her unchastity. Isn't it so? Wasn't that your aim? It really doesn't matter; ruin on this side and on that, whatever I do. The one flower withers away, the other is devoured. I am a happy father and have happy daughters. . . . Wine, Jeppe, more wine."

204

The dwarf came hasting from the antechamber and changed the tankards.

"If only I understood the meaning of it all!" Tycho curved his back and sprang up again. "The meaning, my Lord and my God, the meaning." He reflected. "Or must it mean this, that in the midst of these unworthy happenings I felt myself to be the most unworthy of all, that I divined how all evil proceeds from me; yes, that nothing of ill can happen in the whole world without my being involved in it or sharing the responsibility for it? . . . You see, my dear daughters, that I am a scoundrel. One accursed. A vile, base soul. Haven't you been aware of it? Have you never remarked it? Now that would be something new, that you know it from today onwards. . . ."

"But, father, you are so good!" moaned Elizabeth. And Magdalena kissed his hands.

"Good? Yes, I myself believed that. Until today I believed it. And that was, indeed, my most deadly sin. I was self-righteous, I was impenitent, I believed that old Tycho, old Tycho—" His grief prevented his speaking further. He drank several glasses, one after another. "A little while ago I still thought within myself: 'Go on your way of love to the very end and let Kepler go his way. What a swine's thought it was, what vain imagination, what self-satisfaction! Fie upon me, I am disgusted at myself. I could deliver a lengthy discourse, but it must be to a larger audience. I would confess all my sins, openly acknowledging them. All must see what a wretch I am! No, no, no, in me there is nothing but spleen, passion, arrogance, naught of good! . . . The way of love! And quite apart from all criminal vanity, how false, how deceitful it is! Was that the way of love, that I troubled myself in no way about you, my Elsa, that I suddenly resolved to ape Kepler—presumptuous, ridiculous fool that I was!—

205

to imitate him quite wrongly and very unwisely as regards myself, casting myself off from my family and abandoning you to your fate? Well, herein is quite clearly written my guilt, my crime, my lack of love. Assuredly it was my duty to watch over you, Elsa; yet out of baseness it was just at your expense that I husbanded my resources."

"But you have so often inquired about my trouble! I was obdurate and wouldn't speak."

"And why didn't I ask you thirty thousand times? Why didn't I ask you until my tongue was blue and swollen?— My children!" He drew them close to him on either side. "Yes, now we can again venture to touch one another, to kiss one another, to weep together. For a sudden light has been shed upon everything. When you came in as suppliants, there was a falseness and reserve between us. But now come to me, quite close to me; for now it is revealed to me: it is I who have wronged you and who must crave your pardon. Will you forgive your father?"

He drew his daughters to him, although they struggled and sought to kneel before him. With strong arms he held them close. But now Elizabeth, stirred by the most intense agitation, gave way to a not unnatural bewilderment. She could not interpret the strange conduct of her father save on the supposition that, nothwithstanding his protestations, Tycho had already caused Tengnagel to be destroyed. "He is dead! He is dead!" she cried, and, tearing herself away, hurried, wringing her hands, to the window.

Tycho rose. His voice had changed; it had become almost cold, and again one heard in it that cutting, astounding mirth which like a tempest seemed to sweep circling round the earth in a single moment. "I'm not a liar, Elsa. Tengnagel is alive. But you are right, I ought not to make such a clamour with my repentance and regeneration. That, too, is without importance; it is of no concern. That is my chief fault, it is true. But I think I have already in the course of this hour spoken of a number of cardinal sins; that, too, is only due to the fact that I ascribe too much importance to myself. Every sin is a cardinal sin. Every man is a soul of cardinal importance. Without more ado, away with this sin-laden me, this useless, disordered Tycho. If I am remorseful now—what is the significance of it? Every man knows remorse. Shall I be able to accustom myself to the thought that I am just a man, quite without importance for myself and everyone else? Whether I entreat your pardon or not is a matter of no importance. I do it, it is my duty, by no means could I neglect it. But if I only do my duty—isn't it entirely without importance, because it is something to be taken for granted? That is perhaps the last word that I can utter: one must do one's duty, but it is not a matter of importance. It should not render one proud nor even bring relief or satisfaction, for the whole world is still there and it is an evil world and you have to take trouble about it. And even if you have fulfilled a thousand duties, you have still neglected the thousand and first. . . ."

The last sentences, which he uttered with an entirely matter-of-fact, simple solemnity, were no longer directed to his two daughters alone, but also to Kepler and Hagecius, who had entered with Longomontanus and Müller. The four men had waited for a reasonable time after the suddenly interrupted conversation and had then sought for him everywhere in the castle and village. At last they had been directed hither. But Tycho did not allow himself to be disturbed by their arrival; he did not even recognize them, but continued speaking just as before, as if addressing an assembly.

His glance was troubled, directed towards the infinite. Alarmed at his agitated appearance, the four sat down in

207

silence. Tycho paced up and down, now speaking like a preacher, now bursting into angry explosions of laughter, now standing at the table and drinking. He called Jeppe to bring glasses and in tones of fury bade all pledge him. Suddenly he bestowed a keener glance upon Kepler. "There you are, Kepler, my beloved ferule. You, too, good man, I must ask for pardon, as well as my daughters." And turning to the latter, who wished to rise and take leave, "Do but stay," he cried, "we'll pass the last hours of the night together. I shall betray nothing; you will have no need to blush. But isn't it better if we are all together? Nothing can be attempted before the dawn; until then we have time to discuss everything. Then our fates will be decided. It is a pity that Christine isn't here too. Call my wife.—No, don't call her. Just remain sitting quietly, all of you. You wouldn't come back if you once got outside. I trust nobody. I know that today it is not very agreeable to be near me. That is why I command and do not request; that is why I command, I say, everyone to stay here. Until sunrise. At sunrise accounts will be settled, as I have already said."

Kepler, whom Tycho had been holding tightly by the wrist the whole time, sought to free himself. Tycho now turned abruptly towards him. "And the settlement will begin with you, my ferule. Today you must drink my health, not as on that evening when you refused to toast me. It was your first evening in my house—yes, that was the evening when we drove away the junker Tengnagel, and that was how all these disorders began. Now I realize it. What matter? That, too, is of no importance. I mean to be quite brief. I know, Kepler, my rod of correction, whom God has sent me, I know that you are innocent of all. And even if I did want to ask you what you have done to my daughter and myself, what happened every night with a rope at a certain window, innocent you would remain. Nay, stay, Elizabeth. I shall say nothing

208

more on that subject; it would be quite futile. Kepler would always retain that unblemished, childish brow, and all the guilt would remain, as is only right, accumulated within me. It is for Kepler to guard my honour? And even if he held the rope himself, he is free from guilt. Innocent Kepler, give ear, then, and do but drink with me—for all that is without importance. One can drink quietly notwithstanding. Hear me. You are guiltless, but you consume me, as the innocent acid eats away the metal that it touches. We can't live together; that is the simple, unemotional, and unimportant conclusion. And there again it is only I who am to blame, for it was I assuredly who summoned you, and you only came as one who innocently obeys. But my sin lay in this, that I expected help from you, that I saw you on the path to truth and bliss, and that I wished to hold you by me and to be led by you. But no one can be led to truth; everyone must go his own way alone.—It is unimportant, it is obvious.—Now you see. Possibly your way is the better, but notwithstanding, it is only upon my inferior way, but my own way, that I can advance. And that is why the worst misfortune could come only from the very source from which I expected the most valuable aid. Without wishing it, you were compelled to chastise and consume me. From that evening onward when your insight was so great that you would not call a toast. I was aware of it and I was very angry, and this anger was also a sin, which you must pardon me. But after that, you and all your innocence must make ready to depart and never set eyes on me again."

"It was my intention, anyway, to ask leave," stammered Kepler, in confusion, "to attend to some business at Graz."

But suddenly Hagecius intervened, crying: "That won't do, it can't be hurried in this way."

Tycho rolled towards him. In an instant he would have

flung himself upon him like a rock falling from a crag. "What can't be hurried?"

The little man began to talk aimlessly. It was not right that two *viri egregii,* who had worked so long together to the gratification of all the Muses, should part on account of a little *dissensio!* For even now the Emperor was making ready to return from Pilsen to Prague and it might be foreseen that he would pass the *arcus* of Benatky on his journey and feast his eyes upon the labours of the two friends. . . .

"So you propose to deliver a dissertation upon friendship," cried Tycho, roaring with laughter and throwing himself into a chair. "I will gladly listen, the subject is worthy of a new Plato and interests me mightily."

This produced a painful impression upon Kepler. "No," he said, "we will go to bed and hear no further disquisitions. And tomorrow, if you yourself approve, master, we will take leave of one another."

"Yes, my dear Kepler, we have mad times here. Fencing practice and academy discourses at night; that surely is somewhat strange. You will be glad to be free from these interruptions to your studies, won't you?"

Tycho bent forward until he was close to Kepler's face and looked keenly at him in an attitude of childish challenge.

Hagecius, however, still did not understand that the last terrific contest in the encounter between the two giant spirits was about to be decided. These two true men had stated briefly and simply to one another how matters stood. For his part, he wished to stifle everything in long, elaborate discourses, to wander round the real point at issue, and to meditate. It was impossible to conceive of anything more ludicrous than the eagerness with which the dried-up little fellow urged peace and tried to penetrate and to control the antagonism which flashed its lightnings miles above his head. In great

210

amusement Tycho listened to him for a space, then flung the words at him: "Well said, doctor. And for that very reason everything will be exactly as I have directed."

Hagecius capered, snorting, from his seat, his cheeks flaming. "Then I forbid it . . . I have a secret *rescriptum* by the imperial authority . . . Kepler can't be dismissed *sine approbatione judicis* . . . I have secret documents."

"There are no secret documents in my house," roared Tycho. "Take care, Master Professor of Friendship, no one comes to me to gain information without my prior knowledge of it. What are such things to me? I want to know nothing about your secrets. One thing, however, I do know now with terrible certainty: you, you, Hagecius, I genuinely regarded as my friend! So abandoned was I, so far had I fallen, that I raked up any kindly word out of the dirt, where anything happened to my advantage, where anyone for no matter what silly reason spoke in my favour. So easily satisfied was I out of pure self-seeking and pretentiousness. I have already warmed to you on account of your controversy with Ursus. Oh, the conceited fool that I was! Shall I now at last be able to distinguish the genuine from the imitation? I send Kepler away and would keep Hagecius as my bosom-friend? Was I really so blinded? . . . Oh, believe me, I still am blinded, even at this moment. But I have the fixed intention of being rigorous and of regarding everything concerning myself as of no importance. And for that reason I will set forth everything before you. We still have time and I am assailed by a mighty longing to continue the disquisition begun by my friend Hagecius. But you must drink as I drink, or we shall cease to understand one another."

Tycho was now standing in the alcove of the window, the floor of which was raised so as to form a kind of podium. Without wasting any more words, with a bang he set a chair

211

on this podium, drew the table towards him, close to the alcove, putting a footstool upon the top, which was now too low. In this way a kind of lectern was prepared, behind which Tycho took his stand, wearing an expression of exaggerated gravity. The spectators, who in response to Tycho's mock-serious gesture had ranged their chairs in a row at a little distance from this singular pulpit, observed with horror that the old hero's mind was becoming increasingly disordered. His proceedings might have been taken for a piece of wanton buffoonery, but the note of deep affliction which was present in each distorted word in association with this exaggerated merriment created the impression of madness. The two girls were there too, sitting pale and tense, ready every moment to spring forward and aid their father as if he were an invalid. Kepler, too, whom Tycho continued to contemplate, had long forgotten all his resentment and was a prey to the most terrible agitation; in his extremity he began to pray in a gentle, childlike voice that the night might swiftly end and Tycho's madness be cured. Longomontanus and Müller had lost their heads; they wept at the sight of their honoured teacher a prisoner of this delirium. Hagecius alone, who even in the midst of this dissolution of all order continued to yield to his propensity for ceremonial, made desperate efforts to treat Tycho's utterances as part of a regular learned discourse which had nothing unusual in it. He had not correctly appreci-ated the affronts which Tycho had laughingly flung at him. Moreover, curiosity drew him on, and soon he was the only member of the whipped-up audience who listened attentively.

"I have never had the honour," began Tycho in a tone of magnificent self-contempt, "to propound my views before a university. It is therefore with satisfaction that I now avail myself of a favourable opportunity to begin my lectures in the presence of this select public. I shall set forth the experi-

212

ences of a long and, it may assuredly be said, a laborious life. I shall make use of my most recently acquired experiences to bestow upon my course the title: 'The experiences of a life of no importance.' Of no importance—pay heed to that; it will be explained later. Originally I had intended to choose as a title: 'Ahasuerus, or the Life of the Wandering Jew,' or 'Failure and disquiet.' But I have abandoned that, just as I intend to abandon every kind of poetic comparison, every kind of elegant and precious language. . . ."

At this moment Tycho was interrupted. A troop of soldiers, drunken and angry, burst into the room. They were obviously engaged in pursuit of Jeppe, who shortly before had come with newly-filled tankards. He entered beset and breathless, but with a rigorous self-control he denied himself this time as always any sound or movement not demanded by his service. This poor dwarf was the only creature who completely subjected his will to Tycho and took the most careful pains to avoid causing him annoyance.

"Here comes a new audience for me," Tycho greeted the soldiers. "Brave sons of Mavors, you too might learn much from me, although you also wander restlessly like Ahasuerus through the land and are full of ulcers and hardships in body and soul. Do you but sit near me and listen. Bring chairs, benches. Take glasses and wine; we drink and philosophize." His pale, inflated countenance inspired them with fear; they sank down upon the ground like cowed beasts and listened to the strange bombast, which bewildered them. From this moment on, however, the disorder increased. Other soldiers, following the first, entered, began talking in loud voices, and were called to order by those who still listened. Several went away after a short time, as the room was hot and overfilled. Two were already scuffling in a corner. It appeared that some were pious and took Tycho for a monk,

213

from whom an indulgence might be purchased. As he would not cease speaking, they called out the sums of money which they offered. Last of all came the white-haired commander. He at once produced dice from his pocket and loudly called for a drum. It was brought and very soon the busy little pieces of the players were rattling upon its skin. All drank; but when a song was started, Hagecius in savage tones bade them be silent. For answer he was met with a tumult of laughter and curses.

Quite undisturbed, Tycho continued his address; he seemed to be quite unaware of the noise. He was telling how since his youth he had been pursued by misfortune; he was really speaking only for his own ears, although his voice retained its accustomed unflagging metallic clang. Then for a space he entirely lost himself in senseless tittering. Without any real reason, as far as could be seen, he began, still tittering, to imitate a professor of Rostock University whose lectures on medicine he had attended thirty-five years previously. He then offered his audience a little comedy, imitating the gait and manner of his former preceptor, Vedel, whose duty it had been to see that the little Tycho, in accordance with the wishes of his aristocratic family, studied nothing but jurisprudence. Naturally Vedel had speedily to forbid him very strictly to occupy himself with astronomy, so that his earliest recollections of that science were accompanied by painful obstructions. At that time he had bought with hardly-accumulated savings a celestial globe the size of a fist, on which the most important constellations were depicted, and at night, when Vedel was asleep, the lad would bring out this treasure, which if necessary he could conceal in his hand, and absorb the knowledge for which he craved. "So hard was the very beginning made for me," cried Tycho, "and my life continued just as difficult. I had to get everything by fighting. If I was

214

negligent for a single moment, the mischief was done. Many a man has played the bully all his life; my first and only duel brought me this." He raised his forefinger stiffly to his injured nose and paused, his eyes becoming quite empty and pale.

"Why do I say all this?" he cried suddenly, and sprang up. "Why do I say all this, Elizabeth?" He pointed at her with his finger, like a teacher who during his lecture addresses a question to one of the pupils, to make sure that all are attending. And with astounding obstinacy he continued his burlesque role, as Elizabeth did not answer, assuming the angered tone of the teacher who has surprised an inattentive pupil: "I tell all this only to show how unimportant it is. Well, then, it is my lot to trouble about everything, to get everything by fighting, or, more accurately expressed, to go under in the struggle for everything. But it is nothing but my duty, the way Nature has disposed me; anyhow it is in no way remarkable. In my earlier days I used to be proud of my power to help myself and everybody about me. And even today I know that it is right to help everyone and to consider one's own interests simply as far as it is needful if one is to give adequate help and redemption. I know that it is right to be conscious of this vast suffering in the face of the whole world in agony, of the world which awaits help and redemption. But woe to him who finds the least savour of sweetness in this suffering, who is proud of giving help, who feels it to be, not a bitter and painful necessity, but an ultimate, satisfactory state of affairs, a wantoning in grief!—You soldiers—" he now raised his voice to its full pitch, so that it pealed forth and drowned all the noise and disorder and dice-playing and all the coming and going in the narrow room—"you soldiers, are you Christian *Landsknechts,* or do you wish to be held no better than heathen?"

215

Grinning and jeering, some of them looked up at him; the business began to prove entertaining. They nudged one another with their elbows and jested in low tones. Only the captain insisted upon continuing his game with the man squatting next to him. The others urged one another to be quiet and only whispered as they circulated the tankard, so that it became a strangely peaceful carousal.

Tycho allowed his glance to wander with barely restrained anger from one to the other, and then let it rest on a cherry-cheeked boy, just like a professor at a public examination. "Now," he said, "tell me, are you a Christian or are you not?"

Thus summoned, the boy sprang up and stood at attention, as if the commander were speaking to him. "I am a Christian," he answered with a strangely discordant, shrill voice.

"Then tell me, what were the last words that Christ our Lord spoke upon the cross shortly before His physical death?"

The young soldier was speechless. As the company about him began to laugh, he sullenly sat down again upon the floor.

Another soldier came forward and said diffidently: "I thirst," whereupon the captain with devilish mockery at once held out to him the full tankard. All regarded it as a joke that had succeeded and broke into wild peals of laughter. Hagecius, too, who from his seat had half turned in the direction of the disreputable crew of worshippers, could not restrain himself from emitting a dry cough of applause. Tycho, however, seemed to refuse to realize the comic aspect of this situation; he continued to look in expectation of an answer along the line of soldiers, and there ensued a long,

216

angry pause. Some were already beginning to murmur in a very threatening manner and it was quite impossible to foresee in what way the next minute would relax the tension. Then Elizabeth and Magdalena, who sat as if paralysed with anxiety, holding each other's hands fast, simultaneously found their voices, and the foul air of the chambers vibrated with two sweet, gentle, girlish utterances: "It is finished."

Now, however, Tycho threw off all restraint. "No, no!" he cried. " *'It is not finished'; thus the text should run.* The tradition is at fault, I feel it quite clearly. . . . As the Lord felt His strength growing dim, He cried out: 'O God, My God, why hast Thou forsaken Me?' And by that He meant that He fully realized that He left behind an uncompleted task and an unredeemed world, full of evil men and misdeeds. It is just therein that one can measure the unspeakable holiness of our Lord, in that He Himself at the very moment when He was hanging upon the cross, at the very moment when He entirely yielded Himself up, still thought that He had done too little. Even when He died for mankind, when He offered Himself as a sacrifice, even then was He—dissatisfied with Himself and with His labours. And for that reason His final utterances were no hymn, such as our trashy poetasters would love to intone; they were no conclusion, those last words, no seal such as might grow cold for very satisfaction and hard in a fair contour. No, these last words, quite feeble and broken, were uttered without any pride and were full of the most profound sorrow. Yes, in bitter suffering they were breathed forth into the void. 'It is not finished, it is not finished,' wailed the Lord. 'Oh, weep with Me, for it is not finished!' What a fountain of sorrow, compassion, of discontent and inconsolable naked despair lies in these words! Oh, if I could drink them to

217

their very dregs, if I could climb down to the hideous depths of their precipices! *'My God, it is not finished; why hast thou forsaken me?'*

"Yes, from this shall you learn, from our Lord Jesus shall you learn this extreme measure of self-consciousness, the consciousness of the utter void. That is perhaps why I have always been so wise, so discreet, cunning, full of foresight, and deeply conscious, so entirely without self-oblivion, so continually vigilant in my passage through life, just to experience this present moment, this zenith of the wakeful consciousness and of prudence, wherein man communes with himself: 'Sacrifice thyself, perish, but know, even on the cross —it is never finished. No, no, no, give aid and in giving it go to destruction and know that thou hast given far too little aid. Contemplate thy failure. Behold the Devil, who triumphs, and yet, although it is senseless and vain, help and help and help again, receiving no thanks and satisfaction, with shame and the consciousness of guilt in the heart, fully aware of thy failure. Help, ever help. . . .'"

He turned swiftly to the window at his back. The first glow of the dim lustre of dawn had fallen upon the surface of the table and attracted his attention. "A new day, a new duty. And always this burning in the soul that shall never be extinguished, this cry for redemption which finds no answer. . . ."

He became silent. Outside the cocks began to crow. A cool breeze arose in the grey light, which from the distant edge of the forest climbed the dome of heaven like a delicate exhalation, as if to leap about it with gentle violence. The breeze passed in through the window. The trees in the park bowed, murmuring, and then, once more raising their heads, cast their leafy boughs, hissing and crackling, against the walls of the castle. Within the room the candles, burnt to

218

their sockets, guttered out. . . . The pallor and the flabbiness of Tycho's face now became fully visible. Drops of sweat stood on his forehead and on the bald head. His doublet and shirt, flung wide open, hung loosely about his breast, which rose several times with a prolonged sigh to meet the cool breeze. And now he spoke more gently, still didactically and still obstinately, but as if nearing the end of the masque he had forced himself to perform: "Yet the aspect of the new day also arouses new hopes. Perhaps it is just this tormenting thing in us that will never be satisfied and can, therefore, never repose, that struggles from hope to hope, from non-fulfilment to non-fulfilment, that breaks my pride and shows me my baseness in the very moment when I bring help—perhaps it is just this 'It is not finished' that is really the divine spark in us. The goad that keeps me alive. My inexhaustible source of nourishment. Whether I help or not, disaster always comes, and never is it given to me to rejoice. Never do I accomplish. And yet, and yet to help—isn't that God's business, just this—God's business? . . ." He continued murmuring these words only: "If I could believe it, oh, if only I could believe it!"

At this point Kepler rose and approached Tycho, saying in impressive tones: "Master, it is enough. You are weary." He had been carrying on a discussion in low tones with Hagecius and they had agreed that Tycho must be put to bed.

Tycho started back. "No," he cried, "until sunrise, as I have said. . . . Wine, I want wine, Jeppe, Jeppe!"

But the dwarf, who already for some time had not been seen, still failed to appear. Tycho angrily repeated his summons. Thereupon the white-haired leader rose and went out, as if to seek for Jeppe.

The red glow of dawn began to spread out in the sky.

It seemed to issue forth from the same spot on the horizon as that at which on the preceding evening the dusky gleam of the fire had appeared, but it pursued its course gently, its strong, transparent light having nothing terrifying about it. . . . Tycho received it quietly; with his arms, which lay upon the table, he indicated with infinite tenderness the gesture of an embrace. At length, after a long silence, he turned again to the men in the room, but now no longer with any strangeness in his manner. He spoke in a melting tone, as one most profoundly moved: "Ah yes, my friends, I believe it—I give ear to what is deepest within me and believe it—it is an eternity which I hear in the beatings of my pulse and in my yearning.—We are eternal; there is no end to us with our loneliness, murmuring inconsolably over our half-finished labours. In our terrible grief we are indestructible—for we can never help one another to the utmost. Say, my friends, must we not for that very reason remain together for ever? Just as we have kept watch together through this night, until sunrise, must we not sit loyally together and love one another until the spiritual sun shall rise?—O my friends, how I love you!—Hapless Elizabeth, whom I cannot help. Magdalena, irretrievably lost. I rivet you to me for all time by the power of vain desire to save you. I press my eternal wounds upon yours. And you, my Kepler, who cannot stand by me, who are for ever severed from me—and you, cunning Hagecius, with your inexhaustible reserves—for a long, long space must we continue to play together, throughout a whole eternity, before we meet as brothers—and you, my dear pupils, and you that are distant, you warriors, I feel myself so closely related to you all today, we will not abandon one another. We are all chained to one another by our participation in a tremendous destiny—in this very moment try to realize it; something is happening

220

that will unite us for ever. Don't you hear it, how eternity rushes upon us as time stands still—will you ever forget this moment?"

He had pushed back the table and now came down from his podium with arms widely outstretched. . . . The band of soldiers, among whom an uneasy whisper had for some time been passing to and fro, now split up. It was as if they were all expecting a miracle, even as Tycho's expression, at once anxious and transfigured, seemed to be conjuring up some terrible portent.

The door opened. Two soldiers entered with the dwarf. They were carrying him. He was dead; his thin little hands hung slackly down from the wide-mouthed sleeves.

The footstool which stood upon the table was turned upside down so that it pointed upwards with its legs and was now just large enough to act as a bier for the poor little manikin. There he lay, with a face as white as chalk, his arms contracted upon his high, pointed breast, in the first golden beams of the rising sun. He moved no more.

The soldiers began to murmur angrily: "Who did it?" Voices replied: "The captain. Down in the cellar. I saw it myself; he strangled him. An hour ago. And now the swine has ridden off. . . ."

"Where did you find him?" Tycho asked the bearers in a tone that showed that he was putting forward his final effort to utter what would be for some time his last words.

"Here before the step."

He approached the corpse, lifted it out of the little cradle, and took it in his arms as if it were an infant. Then he did something which he had never before done. He kissed the dwarf and remained bowed over him, with one cheek pressed against the cheek of the dead body. Then he looked about him and there was no one who under this reproachful, infinitely sorrowful glance did not feel in a positively physical sense that consciousness of guilt extending throughout the whole world of which Tycho had spoken. At this moment all had taken part in the dwarf's murder; all had feared for him; he had been murdered by all and for all.

No further words were uttered. There was no more need of speech. All understood and divined how Tycho had toiled unceasingly to bring him up and how none the less he had been unable to secure him from a sudden end. Those who knew more about the dwarf's life, Elizabeth and Magdalena, became rigid with horror at the thought that once Tycho had saved Jeppe from the hands of rude mercenaries, and yet now with his hasty action he had only secured a brief respite of fate, once more losing the child, as it were, to the same hireling hands. The uninitiated saw the dwarf falling down into the cellar, then laboriously crawling up the steps, mortally wounded, and collapsing at the door, near his beloved master, whom he could never again reach.

So in arresting proximity, the vanity of human love and human beneficence appeared before the eyes of all present, yet all felt not only the sorrow, but also the sublimity of this representation. . . . At the sight of Tycho, his head, furrowed with weary wrinkles in all directions, pillowed on the little head of the dwarf, there began to emanate a ray of that higher love surpassing earthly love.

CHAPTER X

BARELY A QUARTER of an hour later Tycho was at the advanced posts which still held Tengnagel's blockhouse within their ring.

On the edge of the forest he found his son Tycho already occupied in paying off the leaders of the bands and sending them away. In silence Tycho contemplated the operation, and then, before the eyes of all, he strode down the slope towards the besieged.

He fully realized that the circumstances called for something more than merely sending the first person he happened to encounter as mediator. He himself must go to Tengnagel as advocate of his family; he himself must humiliate himself before the young man for Elizabeth's sake, must bow the knee before him if necessary, as once Priam bowed before Achilles.

But it was strange that Tycho's thoughts were less occupied by this stern "must" than by an altogether new feeling of expansion and love, which was not in any real sense an agreeable sensation and was entirely free from that "pride of being upon the right path" which Tycho had for ever forsworn during that night of terror. Nay, this new feeling was just as palpable as if it had always been present in him, but had lain distorted and concealed under a waste of false sensations. For the very reason that it did not present itself in him as something adventitious, but as a most fundamental, natural emotion, which had at last cleansed itself from all accessories, it forbade comparison with anything else. It was, therefore, in no way burdensome to Tycho; it caused him no amazement and did not even require his attention. But as he passed down the slope, it abode, invisible and gentle, in the recesses of his spirit, and not only allowed him to reflect actively upon the coming conversation with Tengnagel, but even gave him time as well to inhale deeply the fresh morning air of the grass and the wood, strangely darkened though it assuredly was by the death of the little cripple.

Moreover, to judge from his feelings, he was in a normal, everyday mood; yet there was something quite unwonted in his condition, something that lay hidden and that expressed itself in the fact that he felt absolutely no fear, although he was directly approaching the enemy, exasperated by the encounters of the night. . . . The roof of the hut was half burnt away. A sentinel who protruded his head between the sooty timbers covered Tycho at once with his musket. Tycho took it all in, saw the black mouth of the barrel directed upon him; but he neither hastened nor delayed his steps; he proceeded calmly upon his way. Although he fully appreciated his position, he had no sensation at all of danger. He saw the span of the hills of the Iser valley lying opposite, sharply outlined against the white heaven, sink a little at each of his well-poised, easy strides, and then a vaster mass rear itself up. He felt himself protected, tranquillized, and, as it were, initiated into the landscape by this gentle undulation of the uplands, which gradually from right to left closed over his head as a pool closes over the head of a drowning man. . . . Now the shot rang out. The echo came thundering back from the mountains, drawing about him like a mantle. But he did not flinch; on the contrary, for the first time, amid the

224

din and the white smoke, he felt quite sure of himself and inviolable. . . . For a second the idea flitted through his mind that in his present feeling of security he could for the first time understand the inner workings of Kepler's soul, instead of always gazing at it in astonishment as at something uncanny. . . . But he had not time to grapple with this idea, for he had already reached the stockade. They had at last seen that he was without arms. The sentinel lowered his musket and without Tycho's uttering a single word let down the drawbridge.

Tycho entered. The defenders leaned by the loop-holes on the ramparts in a weary half-slumber, with cheeks which seemed to be wrought into the wall. Colourless and sunken were these cheeks in the chilly morning wind, like the cheeks of dead men, distorted by the terrible hours of conflict. The dying and sorely wounded had been placed against the wall of the hut or stacked up in heaps. Their torn clothes, their faces and hands, blood-stained and blackened with powder, no longer had any human characteristics; they had become useless, broken things. The poor bodies lay there just as if it were intended to use them as a mere mass, as a last wall before the hut, after the rampart had been stormed.

The most pitiful among all these pitiful figures rose from a heap of turnip-sacks in a corner, where it had lain stretched to half its length. It was Tengnagel. He staggered forward, his eyes riveted on Tycho as upon some terrible supernatural apparition.

His men, with their simple helmets and brown attire, presented not half so deplorable a spectacle as he, with his still rich apparel hanging loosely in sorry fragments and tatters, muddy, damp, and fluttering tumidly about his body. The sudden onset had not given him enough time to change his clothes. He had fought clad in thin shoes, in his velvet cap and his slashed puffed sleeves. Now in habiliments and expression of suffering he presented a picture of the direst distress.

In an instant Tycho had forgotten all the careful language which he had thought out on the way. A suffering man stood before him. It was by no means so difficult to make his apology to him as he had imagined. During the night Tycho had seen only the comfortless, desperate, dreary side of the good action. Of all this he was still conscious. Even while he was approaching Tengnagel, he was still convinced of the ultimate futility of human aid. But something which he could not have foreseen came to redeem and to relieve: the deed itself. It was just the same as the gloomy reflections of the night, with their weight of renunciation, and yet something quite different; it was in very truth palpitating with life and radiant with liberating realities, whereas those reflections had been pure negation. A feeling of courageous, brotherly cordiality streamed about it, and senseless, nay, ridiculous as it may seem, a great tide of mighty love for Tengnagel. Tycho held out his hand to him.

But Tengnagel shrank timidly back and looked aside, like a whipped dog.

Tycho pointed with a friendly gesture towards the hut, which he sought to enter with the junker to discuss everything in due order.

Tengnagel continued to gaze at him as if petrified; he did not understand. For him Tycho had always been the man of the distinguished, nay, of the mighty name, a figure of towering greatness and importance, before whom he had to bow reverently. Even through all the months of his banishment he had not ceased to revere Tycho, and in the depths of his heart he had regarded the night's bombardment as a just penalty for his insurrection against his master. Now it

226

could not but inspire with terror his spirit, robbed by the desperate conflict of all its strength, to see the avenger suddenly appearing in the very midst of his encampment. How had he arrived, without weapons, without password? Was it to fetch him in order to execute with divine authority the punishment against which he had vainly striven?

Already in his terror Tengnagel beheld a fiery sword flashing. "I am guiltless of all that has happened," he stammered.

It was only now that Tycho remarked with intense astonishment that Tengnagel was afraid of him. The knowledge of this fact caused his countenance once more to be suffused with that flush of shame which had visited him in the night. Oh, how ashamed he was of this dispensation under which men feel towards one another as cattle feel, so that they tremble at the presence even of the lowly and of the bringer of peace, because they no longer have within themselves any belief in peace or honourable friendship! "I, too, am guiltless," he wished to reply, but the words stuck in his throat. A hideous precipice gaped before him; he saw himself in all his weakness, his destitution, and his humiliation—and yet they trembled at him! What a hapless being it must be whom he could still inspire with fear! This sympathy for Tengnagel unexpectedly suggested to him the only right words which could make any impression upon the distraught creature. He said: "I have sent Kepler away. He leaves the castle today."

It was astonishing how these two sentences transformed Tengnagel's features. He at once regained confidence and enthusiastically took the right hand that was offered to him. Forthwith he unburdened himself of what was in his mind: "Yes, Kepler, Kepler, he is responsible for everything. I knew it! O my Tycho, my friend, if I can so call you again, now I understand the whole episode. Everything is clear at a stroke. Did not Hagecius arrive in Benatky yesterday?"

"Yes," answered Tycho in astonishment.

"Then it is certain; I thought I recognized his carriage, but I was not sure. Yet I at once expected mischief. . . . Now Kepler knows what reason he had for fearing the Commissioner."

"What commissioner?"

"Why, Hagecius, as I have said; I will explain everything to you later on. Later on. For the present just let me recover my breath.—So Kepler, threatened with the immediate disclosure of his proceedings, could think of nothing better to do than finally to rouse you, my friend, against me. He knew who was behind Hagecius."

"So it was you who brought Hagecius down upon me?"

Much embarrassed, Tengnagel answered Tycho's smile: "Was there any other way open to me? Forgive me for it! But do you see? Even this way was almost barred to me. Hagecius arrived in the afternoon—three hours later Kepler started bombarding me. At the last moment I was to be destroyed."

"Kepler—bombarding—" For an instant, despite the gravity of the situation, an expression of irony passed over Tycho's lips, an irony full of tenderness, insight, and forgiveness. "Why, the fellow would be responsible, then, for everything! It is gradually becoming too much of a good thing. And now the bombardment into the bargain! . . . My dear junker, believe me, Kepler is purer than either of us. His immaculate purity is the very thing that causes offence to us sinners, and so we are very glad to make him the scapegoat for our faults. But now I really think that we have overestimated the excellent Kepler. We have exaggerated him beyond all conceivable limits. Kepler is really no longer a man at all, but a phantom. As I understand things now, Kepler does not exist *outside* of us; no indeed, each of us has his

228

Kepler within him, and it is in facing him, in facing his own Kepler, that he has to endure the sharpest spiritual tests. Oh, how beautiful it is, Tengnagel, my friend; now for the first time I feel God's rugged beauty and sublimity in all that! Kepler is at once our devil and our redeemer, both at once, my Tengnagel."

A joyous fanfare of trumpets rang out in the distance like a ray of light in the wind. Tengnagel, whose expression had again grown dark at Tycho's last utterances, laid his hand upon his sword, but Tycho caught his shoulders with a grave and appeasing hand. "They are no longer sounding for the attack. They are going away. I vouch for it personally, for it's my order. And one more thing; it is not Kepler, but my sons, who ordered this outrageous assault. Will you bear your brothers-in-law resentment for long, if Elizabeth intercedes for them?"

"Elizabeth!"

With a gentle gaze Tycho looked closely at the young man, who coloured. "So far we have spoken too little of her. The spectre of Kepler has darkened our whole horizon; we are both too much occupied with him. But this must be the last time that we neglect our dear Elizabeth. Let us promise one another."

Speaking thus he led him for further discussion into the hut.

SHORTLY after, Tycho returned to the castle leading Tengnagel like a tamed lion. His betrothed flung herself upon his neck and the brothers, lately so warlike, shook his hand with the somewhat embarrassed jest that after last night's uproar the wedding would not be long delayed. Christine's simple heart found no other expression for her joy save tears. Tycho, for his part, quietly escaped from the festive turmoil which at once began. Alone in his study he might well reflect that now came his real renunciation of his family—to feel their grief and anxiety as if it were his own pain, but to leave them to their own discretion in their hour of joy. This, too, was a source of satisfaction to him, and as he now felt within himself a more definite sense of freedom than ever before, he deemed that the moment had come to break his last fetters.

He accordingly sent for Kepler and asked him to forget the wild nonsense that he had uttered throughout the night. But he would not conceal from him that today also, in all sober sense, he considered it advisable that Kepler should return to Graz and wait for the fulfilment of his hopes there; for unfortunately, as was quite evident from the replies of the Chancellor Barvitius, it would not be possible in the immediate future to procure any independent position in Bohemia. "But," he pursued, "your ability and your great intellect, my Kepler, are far too highly developed for you to continue to assist me in the capacity of a pupil. I must admit that I can teach you nothing; if in our guild there existed such things as diplomas of freedom and mastership, I should have had to hand them to you long ago."

It was not out of mere politeness, it was in expressing his most fervent convictions, that Kepler at once contradicted these words of Tycho. He could and must still learn much, he said modestly, and Tycho's experience was indispensable to him in the literal sense of the word.

"If by my experience you mean my manuscripts," replied Tycho, not without humour, "rest assured that I gladly give you all that I have lent you to take with you on the journey. You can continue to use them just as you like. But if you mean by it the Tychonic system—but no, you don't."

Kepler was silent.

Still smiling, Tycho continued: "Now you have become ac-

230

quainted with my cosmic system, in so far as there was anything to learn in it. It is not entirely incorrect, but meagre and incomplete, no doubt, like many earthly things. None the less I do not think that you will waste your time if you continue occasionally to give it your attention and address me questions and give explanations by letter regarding certain points in dispute, which have forced themselves upon us in pleasant hours." He fell once more into that warm, insinuating tone which he could not easily lay aside when speaking to Kepler. "Sometimes we were so near to one another. Do you remember? About that time when my mistake about your letter to Ursus was cleared up. . . ."

Kepler nodded, but only after so long a period of reflection as to suggest that he had, as it were, to extricate this fact from under a mountain of the past.

"Or then, when I showed you the portrait of the Tychonid, my Holy of holies?"

"I was anxious on that occasion," answered Kepler, gently but honestly.

"When was it, then, that we stood very close together, my dear friend?"

"I have always honoured you as my master, as the phœnix of astronomy." Kepler took the hand which Tycho had stretched out to him. "My feelings towards you have always been unalterably the same. To feel myself near to you, for that I certainly lacked the courage. I have always been conscious of having to look up to you. . . ."

Tycho shook his head. He was already familiar with these somewhat empty tributes; a single word endowed with a living significance would have been more to him. But this was simply Kepler's strange, reserved way. Tycho already foresaw how within Kepler's brain a coherent image of the time that he had spent at the castle of Benatky would form itself,

231

an image from which all extraordinary occurrences would be banished. In the end there would be nothing left but a few well-executed astronomical observations and a mass of logarithms. . . . It struck him as strange that Kepler had not yet inquired at all concerning the events of the night and of the present morning. "Junker Tengnagel has returned," he said, as if to test Kepler.

"I have already seen him," was Kepler's sole response.

"They are even now celebrating his betrothal with Elizabeth."

Signs of joy appeared on Kepler's face. "I congratulate you, Master Tycho," he said.

"What a gulf there is between us!" felt Tycho. "I, too, have now attained a certain security within myself, but this absolutely blind and deaf man will always surpass me in that respect. Even the bombardment in the night did not wake him up; it is really incomprehensible that he should not ask about it."

His thoughts suddenly assumed new direction: "Poor Jeppe! Now he is gone. Wasn't it strange, my Kepler, how he was always fearful of you!"

"Particularly of me? I really had not noticed it. He was so peculiar in all respects, so . . ."

"So irrational. Just say it. Irrational he was, but he was very fond of me. And of you he was always terrified. Yes, yes, it was so. They say, too, that he had second sight. Perhaps he even foresaw his death—from the moment when you entered the house." Tycho sank into silence. For the first time he was conscious of the full sadness of the loss of the loyal, taciturn servant. And, in the final analysis, was not Jeppe right in his anxiety? His death was only the last link in the chain of stormy adventures into which Kepler's arrival had thrown the house. . . . And once more Tycho regarded Kep-

232

ler's insignificant form and narrow face with that uneasy feeling which had so often assailed him. How silent the man was, how little active and unassuming! Yet all about him the atmosphere was tense. . . . Now Kepler pressed two fingers vehemently upon his forehead as if to arouse himself from his dreams. Tycho observed this habitual, characteristic movement, realizing that from now onwards he would often look back upon it with yearning. For he loved Kepler; it was as if he was under the influence of his charm. Involuntarily he imitated the movement on his forehead with his own fingers. Did he wish to practise it? It would perhaps be a comfort for the long, empty time that lay before him. . . . He smiled. Kepler, too, smiled back, an entirely harmless and yet such a powerful, such a magnetic smile. It seemed as if in this smile something inexpressible passed between the two men, a question which had never been asked, an answer which had never been given, a sigh in common, rustling gently and yet sweeping along within it whole worlds and the span of a thousand years, like the sigh uttered in unison by two lovers, the sigh in which a child is created. . . . Not a word, nothing. . . . Then Kepler rose. He evidently wished to pronounce the final words of farewell. But almost with violence Tycho dragged him back into his chair. Suddenly a thousand things occurred to him which he still had to discuss with his friend. Assuredly a farewell for ever, for all eternity, without another meeting, was what stood before them. "Will you write to me?" he asked.

"Yes."

"Long and frequent letters? I will communicate to you every inquiry that I make and all my thoughts. And you, will you answer?"

"You know me well—my terrible indolence."

Tycho fell back a step. . . . It was a decisive moment.

233

All at once it was clear to him that he was well on the way to that "exaggeration" and "over-estimation" of Kepler with which he had reproached his son-in-law an hour previously, down in the fortress. Oh, was it not possible to treat Kepler's harmlessness as something really harmless? Must one make so much out of his reserve? And out of his indolence, as he termed it; in short, out of all those unworldly characteristics which so perplexed Tycho, the man of the world? . . . Suddenly Kepler shrivelled before his glance; he became as something without importance. Nay, much more; there dawned in Tycho a feeling with which Kepler had never before inspired him, a feeling of compassion for this spirit which now appeared to him so straightened and solitary in its unawareness. Place him in such a case and he would feel as in a room without air, without a window. How empty and how dark was this inborn, never-questioned purity! How Tycho now understood for the first time Kepler's oft repeated utterance that he had always felt himself unhappy! Hitherto he had regarded it as pure affectation. Oh, how great was the distance between this innocence of Kepler's, imprisoned within itself and all unconscious, and a pure, self-sacrificing, understanding open-heartedness! Did it not now appear as if Kepler's purity was but a lower step set in Tycho's path, in the first place as a hindrance, upon which, however, he had mounted to a higher stage, inaccessible to Kepler? . . . Tycho was overwhelmed. He strode to the window and stared out into the sunlit landscape. This recent sudden reversal of his relations with Kepler was more than he could bear. The pity that he now felt for his friend's imprisoned spirit assailed him like a stab of pain, like a new feeling of shame and guilt. Ah, how weak was this mighty spirit of Kepler! How entirely hemmed within himself, within his manner of unintentional ruthlessness, of which he himself was conscious merely as of a species of indolence. Tycho almost felt that he ought to say to him the same words that had risen in his mind yesterday when he was with his daughter and today when he was with Tengnagel. They were the words which came to him when in the presence of these beings who stood before him in all the nakedness of their weakness and lack of tuition: "You still have much tribulation to endure in life. . . ."

"Well, now I shall go," said Kepler, shuffling with his feet.

Tycho embraced him warmly, "My Benjamin, what more can I do for you? What pleasure can I give you, what desire fulfil? The manuscripts, yes, take them. I am glad if they can be of any assistance to you. . . . But wait, something else!" He hurried to the library and came back with the *Commentariolus* of Copernicus, which on the very day of Kepler's arrival he had refused to him. "Take this little pamphlet as well. I will give it to you. You may perhaps find something useful in it."

Kepler expressed his delighted thanks, but seemed far from suspecting what an effort of self-restraint Tycho had sustained at that moment.

'As you see, I am no longer jealous," added Tycho, after they had shaken one another by the hand. And as Kepler even now remarked nothing of the contest in Tycho's spirit, Tycho's last thought, as Kepler already stood at the door, was that really throughout the whole time his treatment of the young scholar had been fundamentally wrong; he felt that he ought to have trained him by means of a patient course of instruction to a more clear-sighted, less egoistic outlook upon life and that it was a cowardly, vile act of injustice to send away the man now so scantily equipped, just for the sake of peace and comfort. He had to make a violent effort to bring before his eyes all Kepler's ripe scientific views, his perfectly mature learning, and above all his unexampled success in independent research, and equally the world's acclamation of it, in order to realize that the emotion of parting drove him to underestimate Kepler just as until today he had exaggerated him beyond all measure.

I N   T H E   afternoon Kepler took his departure, provided by Tycho with warm letters of introduction. The solitude which now surrounded Tycho was no longer the impotent, unnatural solitude of the sick room. In the midsummer repose of the park it brought with it some free hours of composure and reflection, and soon a new desire for work by night at the apparatus. Work now proceeded with a real joy, the like of which he had not tasted for a long time. The *theatrum astronomicum*, the totality of the laws governing heaven and earth, began to spread before his eyes its no longer entirely chimerical vault. And nothing could now disturb him. New pupils arrived, some of whom he had already given up for lost, such as Klaus Mule and the Frisian David Fabricius. But neither their acquiescence bred of eagerness for learning, nor their objections drew him as formerly into bypaths. He instructed them with kindness and zeal, but calmly kept his own purpose before him. The most profound emotion with which they inspired him was that of the irretrievable loss of Kepler. Yet even this did not turn him from his course, any more than a malicious rumour that was shortly afterwards disseminated by unfriendly quarters that Kepler and Tycho had separated after a bitter quarrel. This the authors of the rumour naturally accounted for by saying that no one could live peaceably with so unstable, vain, and despotic a man as Tycho. . . . Tycho did not bestow the slightest attention upon this imputation.

Shortly afterwards the news reached Benatky of the death of the imperial court mathematician, Raymarus Ursus. And the rumours at once stopped of themselves. Ursus had thus even upon his death-bed intrigued against Tycho.

Tengnagel's wedding with Elizabeth Brahe was celebrated with great magnificence. Tycho welcomed a whole host of Bohemian barons as his guests for the festivities, such as Hasenburg and the all-powerful Wok of Rosenberg, an enthusiastic alchemist. The turmoil speedily died down. Tycho did not detain any of his noble and learned visitors. He had borne their company with dignity and seemliness and had given all possible pleasure to his daughter on her wedding-day by his joyous and attentive demeanour; but now he would gladly be alone again.

The young couple took up their abode for the immediate future in the castle of Benatky, where Elizabeth awaited her delivery. Little was said regarding subsequent plans. For a space Tengnagel continued to await a reply from the Chancellor Barvitius. But, it appeared, his information against Kepler had simply been laid aside; Hagecius's report must have proved too utterly wanting in content. And Kepler's alleged conspiracy with the Free Cities had revealed itself as a harmless, scientific correspondence with Professor Möstlin and his other friends in Würtemberg. As the answer still failed to appear, Tengnagel became discontented. His thoughts again turned with greater eagerness towards Tycho's patronage, which he wished to call upon for the beginning of a diplomatic career. Tycho promised him with the utmost friendliness everything that he desired. But until the Emperor returned to Prague, there was nothing to be done.

Whether it was due to Tengnagel's temporary impatience or to the spiritual incongruity between the newly-married pair, foreseen by Tycho, from the very beginning their marriage was disturbed by disputes of different degrees of gravity. Tycho sought to trace these disputes to their origin as often as he chanced to hear them; yet it seemed as if it was just in his presence that they were not willing to speak. When he appeared, they fell silent. In the presence of others, on the other hand, they apparently gave full rein to their dissensions. Now it was Christine, now Magdalena, at another time even his sons and his little daughters who reported that they had been summoned by Tengnagel and Elizabeth to arbitrate. Yet even from them he could only gather vague intelligence regarding the real matter at issue. "Some nonsense! Just teasing!" was the answer whenever he inquired about it. Soon the suspicion took root in him that this state of affairs was in some way connected with himself. He now adjured his son-in-law to confide in him. He reminded him that grievous harm had already arisen from keeping matters secret from him. It was all in vain. "Elizabeth wouldn't allow it," was the only answer that he could extract from Tengnagel. He had Elizabeth called. She denied everything. Yet immediately after that a bitter altercation over some quite trifling matter broke out between the couple in his presence, so that one realized how far the estrangement between them had already gone.

"I was aware of it," said Tycho to himself when at night he was setting up the little sextant, his favourite instrument. "If only it could be brought more clearly before me! How powerless I am—with all my good intentions, powerless!" It occurred to him that it was really only now that he had learned to understand the full meaning of his device: "Nor power, nor riches, only the sceptre of the spirit shall prevail." The sceptre of the spirit! Here they were, a couple of staves and an arc. What more did he need to forget all the woe of his heart, to extend his reach to the dark vault of the heaven and to feel the most distant tremor of a star yonder as something of greater moment, as something more intimate, than the restless throbbing of his own blood? Ah, his blood

238

was poured out like the white rippling of the stars over the heavens; there was its real abode, a source of joy to him; there it ran its course, entrusted to the sacred veins of the mighty laws, the indestructible bodies of cosmic space rioting in their youth. Down here it merely quivered on its course through perishable flesh.

In such moments Tycho believed that at least this one joy of science could not be taken from him. He had readily renounced everything of which he could be deprived. It was his proud thought: "No one can rob me of this last thing." But it was just then that the heaviest blows of all fell upon him, as if to take from him this final illusion.

The keen revival of his studies had reminded him very vividly of his great instruments which were still on their way from Hveen and which he urgently needed for decisive points. He wrote to the Imperial Chancellor, and the question was taken up again. But it so happened that tidings of these activities also came to the ears of that stern gentleman Kaspar von Mühlstein, and caused the not entirely unjustifiable anxiety to appear upon his horizon as Kreishauptmann that the arrival of the new astronomical leviathan would entail twice as many breaches of walls and twice as many claims for money. Genuinely concerned to secure the revenues of the Empire and of the Estates, the worthy man took his counter measures. He was so far successful that, simultaneously with the news that the longed-for instruments from Hveen had after two years' wandering reached Prague, Tycho received the other message that these same instruments must now remain in Prague and would in no circumstances be placed at his disposal at Benatky. It was even so; the instruments were installed in Prague in the so-called Belvedere, an enchanting pleasure-castle which the Emperor Ferdinand had had constructed for his wife by excellent Italian architects. It would have been utterly useless

239

for astronomical purposes, even if its principal rooms had not been filled with the Emperor Rudolf's collection of minerals. The apparatus was unpacked in the noble loggias of the Belvedere and set up like curious ornaments or trophies of battle, one between every two pillars. It must be admitted that, with their elegant shapes, mysterious circles, and carefully polished metal rods, they provided a very representative, interesting adornment for the building. For these were great days in Prague, with its cultivated life and love of spectacles. At the beginning only the nobility and professors were admitted to view the instruments; later permission was accorded to the higher-class citizens, whose ranks contained a strong party which, under the pretext of moderation, separated itself from the common sort, with their inconceivably rigid Hussite ideals, and held by one principle only: to rival the nobles in all that concerned an elegant mode of living. For a period it was a mark of good breeding to converse about the new astronomical instruments and to visit them during the afternoon. Tycho became the main topic of conversation; Tycho was positively *à la mode.* Technical astronomical terms were employed according to the user's capacity, and when beautiful, intelligent ladies were present among those surrounding the instruments, there was no end to the hymns of praise in honour of all the elegant screws and ingenious levers. It never occurred to anyone in this joyous, vivacious society to inquire whether the inventor did not need all these fascinating contrivances to put them to some serious use and whether he did not acutely feel their absence.

In the mean time Tycho approached one official after another by letter and even visited Prague in person. No one would take responsibility for the order for the retention of the instruments, but no one on the other hand considered himself authorized to revoke it. The administrative machine had

240

got caught up at some invisible point and was no more to be set in motion. Tycho soon suspected the Hauptmann to be the origin of the impasse. He rode to Brandeis. Kaspar von Mühlstein received him courteously, but with the imperfectly concealed arrogance of the official who for once can let his power be felt and thus clearly show the futility of all resistance against himself, even if proceeding from the most extraordinary and unrivalled of astronomers. "Now you see . . ." and "I could have predicted that to you . . ." were among his remarks, together with others characterized by a like distinguished restraint. Now, it was Tycho's misfortune to be quite unable to restrain himself, but, especially at decisive moments, to yield to the mistaken idea that matters of importance might be discussed openly and without any suppressions as between man and man. He therefore took no notice at all of the evasions of the Kreishauptmann, but, raising his voice to a loud note, explained how the instruments meant for him the bread of life and the beating of the heart, and requested an order instructing their conveyance to the proper place; for he had not constructed them for the jackanapes at Prague. The official was once more ready with his smiling, even amiable manner to refuse this request quite calmly and in all seemliness. At this Tycho lost all patience. "Then I'll fetch them myself," he cried, and dealt the table a thunderous blow with his fist.

His behaviour, alas, did not reach the level of perfection proper to a well-bred Kreishauptmann. Indeed, no one who chanced to break in upon the conversation without a somewhat close acquaintance with its subject would have hesitated before indicating which of the two was the more dignified, the more fully conscious of his responsibility, and the weightier, and which, notwithstanding his occasionally poetic manner of expression, was the profligate and coarse-natured madman.

Even when things went so far that Mühlstein with a seemly gesture showed Tycho the door—was compelled indeed, to show him the door, much as he regretted it and fully as he recognized Tycho's merits—even at this moment the spectator not personally concerned in the matter would naturally have been on the side of the tactful official.

Tycho now proceeded to the most imprudent action which in his position he could possibly have undertaken. Without troubling himself any further about an authorization from Mühlstein he gave instructions for the hiring of a large body of workers and began, even without having the instruments, and as if merely to exasperate the Hauptmann to the highest pitch of irritation, the construction of a fantastically large observatory by the castle. He gave no information in reply to questions, but continued building with crazy haste, sparing neither the imperial forests nor the quarries. Mühlstein now intervened, feeling himself to be completely in the right and knowing, moreover, that public opinion would support him against such senseless excesses. One fine day he had the building-site and the castle occupied by guards. Tycho foamed with rage, distributed weapons to his servants and peasants, and made ready for a *coup de main*. It was now quite clear that Tycho's sons had not on that night of terror, with their wild commotion and their levy of mercenaries, attempted a task altogether alien to their traditions, any more than Elizabeth in her love. Tycho was of course quite unconscious that he was almost imitating his sons. The resemblance impressed itself all the more vividly upon the peaceful peasants and burgesses of the district. Soon complaints poured into Prague that the region, barely recovered from the encounter carried on under the leadership of the sons of this unquiet family, now again beheld its chief occupied with warlike preparations. Tycho was nearly ready to deliver his blow when a letter

242

came from the chancellor Barvitius instructing him to leave Benatky at once and to transfer his family, together with his servants, pupils, books, and instruments, to Prague as a permanent residence. It was subjoined to this letter that the Emperor wished to have the great scholar near his person, as he, too, was returning to Prague.

Tycho's palate was fully sensible of the bitterness underlying the sugar which coated this pill. People had grown weary of his dispute with the Hauptmann, which had actually lasted since his arrival at Benatky; they wished to be rid of it without offending him and yet without pronouncing definitely in his favour. . . . He was wounded in his pride. He had expected that the official would be dismissed. Now he himself was the vanquished party to this quarrel.

It was true that an element of honourable distinction resided in the fact that he was now to make good his title of court astronomer and really to be admitted into the Emperor's immediate circle. But for Tycho, who had hitherto stood almost on a footing of equality with rulers and received their visits in his independent scholar's residence as they received his in their palaces, it was at the same time a diminution of status to be nothing henceforth but an appendage of the court. . . . In his younger days he would not have acquiesced; similar disputes in Denmark had led to his breach with the King. But his defiance, or rather his ill-starred mixture of defiance and over-clever calculation, had throughout the whole of his life brought him so much evil that on this occasion he gave way and bowed to the inevitable. In such circumstances there was no longer any purpose in recovering the building-site by means of armed force. He dismissed the labourers and began preparations on a large scale for an immediate change of residence. Thus he again knew gloomy times. On his arrival in Bohemia he had already been an old and broken man; his misadventures there deprived him of the last powers of resistance, which even now not infrequently flickered up into life.

Even if Tycho succeeded in repressing his anger, the great change was in itself distasteful enough. It entailed giving up the free, beautiful air of the forest and exchanging the habitation which stood in unfettered isolation and yet could be filled with company according to desire, for the turmoil of the capital. In the evening of his life he must accustom himself to professional activities, with all their clamour and intricacies. Tycho had always loved life in the country, never completely abandoning it, so that his habits had formed themselves exclusively under its influence. His childhood years on the estate of Tostrup, his life as a man on the sea-girt island of Hveen, with its salt-laden air—all had been in the open amid unshackled nature, in all respects healthful and well adapted to him. It had been a serene existence amid the movement of the seasons, which had power to cool his frequently excited blood with their peaceful turn and change. And in particular now, at the beginning of autumn, he needed about him the world of plants and trees. This season of the fall, with its first mists and night-frosts, always brought with it melancholy thoughts. He wrestled with nature, as in summer he exulted with her; he felt himself die with every leaf that fell yellowed to the ground. There was a considerable measure of seriousness in the idea which he had once expressed in jest that he would build great hothouses for the deciduous trees, that they might live through the winter. He often quite genuinely felt with overwhelming force that he owed aid and protection even to plants in their life-and-death struggle. The only thing which still used to sustain him in this hypersensitive mood was constant absorption in the contemplation of the trees and the visualized consciousness of their vitality amid all the melancholy. How hard it was, just now in particular, to bid them farewell, to renounce their comfort for ever, and to feel only the destructive elements of the season! The maples gleamed in their airy, attenuated, rustling dress of red gold; beneath them glowed the red hues of the chestnut-trees, a more transient splendour, like the outcome of a moment's intoxication. Tycho passed slowly down the damp avenues of the park, climbed the hill, and stood for a long while by the monument that he had erected over the dwarf's grave.

During these days of leave-taking a letter arrived from Kepler. He, too, had not fared well. The persecutions in Graz had begun again soon after his return. As a Protestant he had been pronounced "expelled and excluded," with a further stipulation that he must leave Styrian territory within forty-five days. The efforts made by his own tutor, Möstlin, and by the Bavarian Chancellor Herwart to find him another sphere of activity in Munich had proved fruitless. He could reasonably ignore the good advice of certain naïve friends to go to Italy and study medicine. All this he recounted in his usual matter-of-fact manner to Tycho and in conclusion asked, without any special profusion of language, as something quite obvious and natural, to be allowed to return to Benatky.

"At last some comfort in all my sorrow," said Tycho in an access of delight when he had finished reading the letter aloud at midday in the presence of his family. He did not hesitate for a minute to answer Kepler in the affirmative. It was as if all the bitterness and the vexations of their relationship were wiped out. Tycho felt just the same longing for Kepler and the same hope as before his first meeting with him. Nothing seemed to be altered. The same law which had formerly so powerfully attracted his heart towards Kepler's youthful star

245

continued to hold sway. "Now my transference to Prague will at least have the one advantage," he said joyously, "that I can unceasingly make my voice heard with the Emperor and his Chancery. Kepler, and no one else, shall receive Ursus's position; I shall make that my business."

From the moment in which Tycho had begun to read the letter, Tengnagel had been whispering angrily with Elizabeth. Now he sprang up in a fury and ran out. Elizabeth hurried after him.

Tycho passed in review all who remained at the table, demanding an explanation. Then he rose resolutely and followed the pair.

Just outside in the passage he encountered the junker, who was running towards him flourishing a paper in his hand. Elizabeth hung upon his flank. He shook her off, while she in her turn caught at his shoulder and arm. She cried out and seemed vainly to desire to hold him back.

But it was now in any case too late. Tycho stood already before them and, taking the paper from Tengnagel's hand, inquired: "What is it?"

"A letter of Kepler's which will enlighten you about the real disposition of your supposed friend."

"A letter to you?"

"No, to his wife. I found it on his writing-table—"

"He stole it," Elizabeth interrupted, "and is not ashamed to make use of it."

Tengnagel looked at her in rebuke. "No, I am not ashamed to do everything for the truth and for my friend and father, Tycho."

"So I used to say formerly," said Tycho gravely, as if talking to himself aloud, "when I was faced with the necessity of defending some piece of meanness before myself. For truth, I used to say, and for friendship—and sought my own

246

gain. But can that be the real truth and true friendship that calls for inequitable methods? Ah, we are very heedless." In deep reflection he had lowered the hand which bore the letter, with no thought of reading it.

"Don't read the letter," coaxed Elizabeth; "give it to me, that I may tear it to pieces."

"Elsa always said that the letter would be dangerous to you," Tengnagel observed. "Now you see; this letter was and is the cause of all the trouble between us two. For I always maintain, on the contrary, that nothing can be so dangerous to you as falsehood."

"That again I must pronounce to be well said," replied Tycho with a laugh. "Yes, Elizabeth has never had much confidence in me. Now, however, we'll put it to the proof, once and for all." He raised the hand bearing the letter.

"No, no, father," cried Elizabeth in acute agony. "Don't read the letter. Franz is hostile to Kepler because—Father, you'll also speak for Franz at the Imperial Chancery, not only for Kepler. You will, won't you?"

"Was it that, then, my son?" Without any reproach in his tone Tycho looked mildly upon the junker. It was as if he read every human fault in the light of his own personality and of his own numerous failings.

At that moment the exact nature of the tie that linked friendship and self-seeking in Tengnagel had revealed itself, without that friendship's thereby forfeiting anything of its reality. "You need have no fear on the score of my intention to speak on behalf of Kepler. I have enough room in my head and in my heart to think of both you and Kepler."

Tengnagel made an involuntary movement as if he would now take the letter away from Tycho.

For the first time Tycho became serious. "Now you, too, would spare me? Is it as bad as that? No, then, I really must see . . ." He read the first lines and turned pale. Suddenly he looked up; flinging a wild look upon the pair, he hastened to his room and shut himself in. . . .

What he held in his hand—and it cut his fingers like a knife—was the first draft of that letter which Kepler had composed for his wife on the morning of his arrival in Benatky, and then not sent. Tycho at once said to himself that the letter was not intended for him; it must be judged by reference to the mentality of the recipient, of whom Kepler was thinking at the time. A certain sharpness and violence of expression must, therefore, certainly be excused. But it was not the expressions that wounded him, not Kepler's small-minded distrust of him, which was perhaps excited only by a mistrust on the woman's part and was an answer to it. It was not even the outburst against banqueting, drinking, waste of time, mishandling of students, and the like. The one thing that dealt him a vital blow was a brief parenthesis in which Kepler described Tycho's system as simply "false." So there it was, black on white, the one thing and the worst that he had really feared the whole time; there it stood with an absence of design and circumstance which made any doubt impossible. . . . Tycho's fear gave way to wild anger. So, at the very moment at which he wished with joyous enthusiasm to render Kepler a marked act of service, at that very moment Kepler was thinking coolly and critically of him. Even more; he had always thought thus; on all those starry nights so drenched with the spirit, he had looked down mutely upon him and had rated all that proceeded from him as false and perhaps ridiculous. And now, supposing it really was false, mused Tycho, or in a large measure false? A precipice opened before him; Tycho covered his eyes with his hands and yet felt himself falling into a fathomless deep, deeper than ever before. . . .

An hour or more may have passed when someone knocked at the door. Elizabeth called him.

Tycho sat with his head and the upper part of his body stretched backwards over the table, in a condition resembling sleep. He answered in gentle tones and asked that he might be left alone for a space. Order began to re-establish itself within him. His doctrine could not be false, but false, misleading elements might be mingled with it, impairing its purity. But even these false passages now possessed significance for Tycho. They were so many rods of chastisement which flogged him through Europe without intermission, rods like Kepler, like Christine and Hagecius and Elizabeth, like everything through which he suffered and which through suffering pointed him to the real truth. "My false doctrine! Ah, is it not given to me as my cross upon my toilsome wanderings, this false doctrine? Has it not been bestowed upon me that I may toil unresting to build myself up upon it and learn to renounce the last delusive happiness, that I may overcome it and shed it from me? Oh, is it not in very truth the false doctrine that is my pathway to God?"

Comforted, he opened the door and rejoined his family. Elizabeth was in tears. Tengnagel sat with gloomy, downcast looks. "Tengnagel was right," said Tycho in joyous tones; "only falsehood can be dangerous to me. I thank him for having pointed out the danger to me."

"And Kepler?" inquired Elizabeth anxiously.

Tycho speedily recovered his self-possession. "The letter was crossed out and never sent. Kepler himself obviously changed his mind."

"So he is coming?"

"If only he would come!" Tengnagel said remorsefully, with a droll air of dejection; "this time I would bid him a warm welcome."

249

Tycho smilingly extended his hands to both. "My feelings towards Kepler are unalterable and, moreover, without importance. Only one thing is of importance: divine truth."

T H E first day which was less rainy was devoted to the transference of books and instruments from the castle of Benatky to Prague. The family had already gone in advance with several pupils and some of the servants. But Tycho would not allow himself to be deprived of personally supervising the transporting of objects so dear to him.

There were five rack-wagons stacked high with baggage which had to make the long journey. Tycho travelled behind them in a closed coach, wishing to avoid the general curiosity. But at every moment he protruded his head, to assure himself that everything was going on in good order. If, for any reason, the convoy came to a standstill, he opened the door and got out for the purpose of once more submitting each of the wagons to a careful inspection during the pause. The progress along the bad, uneven road was slow. Only towards the evening did they arrive at the heights of Potschernitz and Wysotschan. Fatigued and melancholy, Tycho looked down into the dark cauldron of Prague. At the aspect of this crowded mass of houses, over which hovered the stale atmosphere, he was seized with evil forebodings—as if he had come hither, not to live, but in that very spot to die. "So," he murmured, "I now contemplate my last abode on earth." And yet it was now that he had to carry out the most urgent task, that of cleansing his theories from the last errors, which Kepler's letter had lately summoned to a consciousness lively with presage. This letter burned in his mind and unceasingly confronted him with the great task. But even as he reflected upon it, it occurred to him, and the dull chime of the evening bells down in the valley rang in confirmation, that it was

250

prophesied that his own end would speedily follow the death of his dwarf.

As the strange caravan entered the first dark streets, a chilly rain began to fall. A halt had to be made to put on the covering-cloths. The operation was not quite successful, for the metal arcs of the wall-quadrant could not be covered. The delay speedily assembled a large number of people who thereafter accompanied the cavalcade. Attention had been aroused anyway by a growing rumour of Tycho's entry. As the Emperor still held court at Pilsen, no one had thought of simplifying Tycho's labours by appropriate preparations, closing the street or picketing sentinels. It was therefore quite impossible to hold the crowd in check. If the nobility and more distinguished citizens had feasted their eyes on Tycho's apparatus, the common people wished to have their turn and to hold their own fête. Therein they were not behind their betters in either obtrusiveness or inward indifference. Soon the spectators massed together so that the convoy could frequently make no progress at all. Jests were heard, the girls screamed, and Tycho, who thundered imprecations from the coach, was stared at like some monster. The horses became restless. An axle broke on the Steinerne Brücke. It was only now, while the crowd beset the site of the accident, doing nothing, that a few well-intentioned persons appeared who helped the coachman to unpack and procured some hand-carts, on which the luggage of the one unlucky wagon was conveyed for the rest of the journey. A good-natured butcher's lad particularly distinguished himself, taking off his own white coat, as the coverings no longer sufficed for the baggage, now that it was distributed. Without wasting a word he packed an instrument in it. It was Tycho's favourite little sextant. Despite the rain Tycho, too, now went on foot and, together with the strange boy, carried the sextant to the door of the

251

inn. Utterly exhausted with physical as well as spiritual efforts, he leaned uncertainly against the posts. When, after an interval, he looked round to thank the friendly fellow, the latter had long before taken his smock and disappeared.

T Y C H O ' S worst expectations were surpassed by the actualities in Prague. He had been assigned the "Gasthof zum goldenen Greif" for his abode. It was a narrow house in a narrow street, bearing the almost ironical name, "Neue Welt." The meagre vista of the trenches of the imperial deer-park availed nothing to comfort him; on the contrary they painfully reminded him of the paltriness of his present quarters and of the wholesome open country. Soon after his arrival the malignant disease again invaded his enfeebled body. He defied it, but only with difficulty remained on his feet to bring to an end the heavy task of taking up his quarters. Tengnagel helped him gallantly, although now much occupied with his newly-born son and his convalescent wife.

Barvitius, too, proved well-disposed. Indeed, he took a definite step, purchasing the house of the deceased Prochancellor Curtius von Senftenau on the quiet Lorettoplatz and having it fitted up for Tycho. But such work could not be completed in a short time; for the time being, only a couple of servants and a few articles of furniture were installed, so that Tycho continued to endure the annoyance of seeing his establishment divided at one and the same time between four abodes. The family lived with him in the inn; some pupils were still at Benatky; part of the furniture was in the Loretto house, and, what was worst of all, neither in the inn nor in the new building was any suitable place provided for the instruments, so that Tycho had to allow himself to be separated from them and to permit them to join the other unemployable apparatus in the new Belvedere. Fruitful labour was out of

252

the question for the present, even if an unbroken stream of visitors had not continued to pour through the doors of the famous man's house from morning to night. At last they really had him at hand in Prague and need not first undertake a burdensome journey in order to see him. Side by side with welcome friends, like Professor Jessenius, the Rector Bachacek, and the ever charming Baron Hoffmann, there first appeared the intolerable chatterer Hagecius, who seemed entirely to have forgotten Tycho's harsh words. He was followed by a vexatious horde of patronage-seekers, for Tycho's kindness to everyone was well known. The most grievous importunity came from the inquisitive, who would not tolerate the closing of doors and shutters—they even started brawls with the servants on that account—and from their companions, the swarm of adepts, who secured entry into the house by cunning and violence, hunted in every corner for the "great elixir," in order in the end to bring back to their credulous clients a crumbling fragment of a tile in lieu of the divine red powder.

Tycho's spiritual elasticity was no longer equal to the exertions entailed by the constant change in his human surroundings and by the presence of new acquaintances; he lost his inner equilibrium. Sometimes he flung them all out and engaged in a conversation that lasted for hours with some dolt of a student, in order to have rest from the others. On these occasions he could be very sarcastic, when he warmly commended the study of astronomy to the young man and extolled the scholar's happy destiny.

Indeed he had every reason for despair. At the Chancery he had been promised the erection of an observatory to take the place of the castle of Benatky, for any alteration of the Belvedere or of the new house, for astronomical purposes, was out of the question. But as it usually happens that at the beginning such magnificent plans receive, indeed, the most joyous approval and make good progress for a space, but soon meet with delay even on account of trifling obstacles; so this project stood still after the very first steps had been made to carry it out. Finally Barvitius declared that for the time being the idea must be abandoned altogether; there was no more money.

On the evening of this discussion Tycho hastened through the city gate, and in the open fields he gave utterance to his dispute with God. "So I have not yet sweated out all the poison within me, seeing that Thou dost fling me into this last trial? Tell me what Thou wilt do to me, and then I will ask Thee: 'Why, O God, why?' Is the barest necessity to be dragged from me? Wilt Thou cast me back to the beginning of my studies, when I possessed but a hand-globe and no other tool? Am I to be utterly humiliated, naked and unclad as Thou createdst me, standing before Thy heaven? Why torturest Thou me by flaying the skin from my warm body?"

The stars were twinkling and it seemed to him as if they flickered contemptuously upon him. Now he was defenceless against them; his weapons of attack had been taken from him and he could no longer assail them with circles and staves.

With a laugh he spread out his raised fingers, moved them like the legs of a pair of compasses, and sought with this, the most rudimentary of instruments, to measure and compare the distances of the stars. He thrust his feet firmly into the soil, allowing his hands to quiver over the dark expanse of the firmament. There was in his demeanour, lasting for hours, an element of confused and desperate defiance and malevolent revolt.

Some days later the Emperor entered Prague. Tycho at once asked for an audience. He wished to throw himself at his protector's feet and with his tears to beseech him to save him.

254

CHAPTER XI

THE TIDINGS OF the Emperor's return had doubled the concourse in the Hradschin, which at this time was always the liveliest and most important part of the town. Close behind one another the carriages pressed up the narrow, steep Spornergasse, turned the corner, and climbed the long, winding rampart alongside the Rosenberg Palace. Above, the courtyard before the iron railings and the outer court swarmed with humbler conveyances and inquisitive spectators, while the coaches of the higher nobility and of the foreign ambassadors advanced to the second and third court.

The Emperor inhabited the wing running along the deer-park. In his misanthropy he shunned even the aspect of the town and the murmurs that rose from the vast cauldron of the valley. The diplomatic officers all knew almost for certain that they would not succeed in reaching him. None the less never for a single day did they fail to wait upon him, and on each occasion, too, they intentionally displayed the greatest pomp, as if in the name of their governments. The coach of the Spanish ambassador, Don Guillen de San Clemente, who attracted attention with his inscrutable, cunning, raven-like profile, advanced thundering, with its six horses at full gallop, checking only at the imperial portals. Never did Baugy fail in the cut of his doublet to reproduce

255

the last freak of his royal master, Henry IV of France. The deputies of the Hungarian and Moravian Estates, on the other hand, and in like manner the ambassadors of Sigismund Bathory of Transylvania, indifferent to fashion, sported the old gold buckles and clasps of their national attire, which gleamed with a certain defiance. But all those who made up the gaudy, many-coloured picture in the Emperor's antechamber were not there on account of him who had long grown weary of political activities; they were there in order to confront one another in visible power, and at the same time to learn the latest rumours, to stifle harmful reports, and to threaten with tidings of their own invention, to assemble in groups, and, from amid the labyrinth of deliberate deceptions and inaccurate conjecture, to feel their way to the foundation of new alliances. If, for example, the Papal Nuncio approached the envoy of the German Free Cities, it was at once observed. It escaped no one's notice if one of the company drew apart into a certain side-wing in order to have audience with the all-powerful Privy Councillors Trautson and Rumpf.

This daily parade before the Emperor's residence was thus really an excuse for conspiracies. At the same time it constituted a service of strict supervision which the rival powers had established against one another.

When the weather was good, these activities, which uncertainly oscillated between lounging and business, were also carried on in the accessible parts of the imperial gardens. Then distinguished citizens and also priests, sectaries, and commoners mingled with the foreigners and party-leaders. On such occasions the avenues of old acacia-trees, whose green mirrored itself in the arched bronze thighs of the goddesses of De Vries, echoed with the most unpagan strains of fervent religious discourse. Neither the metallic gleams from American birds in the aviary, nor the roaring of magnificent caged lions, nor any other imitation of the joyous abundance of the Italian Renaissance could disguise the fact that here was a thrifty, earnest people, careful no less for its earthly than for its heavenly salvation, making ready for a decisive contest.

At that time Bohemia had become rich from an intermittent peace, lasting for nearly two centuries subsequent to the Hussite disturbances, but this wealth, it seemed, was not yet in steady hands. With uncanny silence the powers contended one against the other in the darkness. Nothing was explicit. With a strict interpretation of the existing laws nine-tenths of the population would have been compelled to forfeit the whole of their property as heretics. So it came about that everyone was on the watch; everyone feared to lose his own, yet everyone also hoped that a bold stroke would win him the privileges enjoyed by others. In general it was a period which forced men to declare themselves before all, to behave turbulently and to defend their claims in every appropriate place; a clamorous time about the silent, invisible Emperor. It was just in the immediate proximity of his repose that the clamour was loudest; for, in fine, he was not really the ruler of the warring powers. He was rather the index which marked the casting of the balance.

Tycho at once took himself to the Belvedere in order again to survey there, as it were, the full extent of his misfortune in the useless exhibition of the instruments. He passed through the park and over the so-called Staubbrücke, to the waiting-rooms. A group of high-born magnates addressed him, Counts Mathias Thurn, Kinsky, and Budowec. Some others approached and a large company of the most distinguished men, all giving evidence of sincere pleasure, surrounded the famous astronomer. Tycho answered but indifferently.

257

The times were long past when such external tokens of honour had gladdened his heart. Now that heart had, with all its wealth of passion, room only for the one essential, for the investigation of the divine law. What profited it that these little gentlemen chattered together in complimentary terms, that some asked childish questions, that others with all the dignity of their polished manner invited him to their castles? What if new hopes unfolded themselves, vague and alluring? Tycho was well aware that he was too old and feeble to follow them up. He knew that he had no more time for such purposeless adventures; all his strength must be bestowed upon the highest aim if ever it was to be reached. For what did those resplendent men know of him? Was he anything more to them than some clever charlatan? Only one man in the whole world knew anything about him and he wrote such letters as we know, containing parentheses about "false theories."

Suddenly Tycho felt himself oppressed in this society, which accorded him honour in plenty, but no field of activity. He bowed and greeted the second, less magnificent group in the waiting-room—the artists.

At this moment they were joined by the young engraver Ägidius Sadeler, red-cheeked and self-satisfied. He recounted that he had the prospect of a commission to portray for the imperial gallery the members of the Muscovite embassy, who were shortly expected at court.

Tycho shook him warmly by the hand. "That is splendid. You are fortunate. You can work."

"Well, I'm not nearly so deserving of envy as you," replied Sadeler in a very unfriendly tone.

Tycho examined him with a long, inquiring look.

Suddenly the lad ejaculated something about the particular favour which Tycho enjoyed at court and among the people.

258

"If only you would see," explained Tycho, controlling himself, "that that is not of so much significance as real work! And I have been deprived even of the possibility of working." He told in detail the story of the instruments; at this moment he attached the greatest importance to making the horror of his position clear to all. "People must help me," he concluded in a tone of lamentation; "it is high time. If not, I shall collapse."

At this Sadeler laughed outright. "Help you, Master Tycho! Pardon me, but I find that really amusing. You need help, you who hold a court like a prince and possess everything in excess? You, the most illustrious man of our time!"

"That is my fate," said Tycho dully to himself, "my curse, that no one will ever help me, ever hold me sufficiently wretched or in need of help, even if I break down utterly. What must I do to give proof of my necessity? Am I to tear the clothes off my body?"

Sadeler had addressed some remarks to another member of the group and now turned back lightly with a smile, which Tycho's eyes interpreted as a grin. "You really are a little too plaintive, master. . . ."

"Yes, too plaintive," burst out Tycho, "and too vain, eh? And too cunning, too clever, too calculating!—You meant to add that, didn't you? Forgive me for having taken the words out of your mouth. Proceed!"

Alarmed at this outburst, the engraver fell back a few paces and said untruthfully: "No, I didn't mean to add anything. . . ."

Once more striving to master himself, Tycho continued: "I know an image of me circulates throughout the world, a nebulous figure made up of prejudices, and that entirely obscures my real personality. I can do nothing without its being misinterpreted. Tell me but one thing, my friend.

259

What further suffering must I endure—in addition to all that has already been heaped upon me—that you may accord me the right to feel pain as a man and not as a whimperer? What must still happen? . . . Do you know, for instance, the game that Herr von Mühlstein has played with me?"

In proportion as Tycho vainly strove to regain his composure, the young man recovered from his alarm. He now wore a sanctimoniously solemn expression, wherein the same smooth absence of discernment could be read as previously in his frivolous smile. "Yes, I have heard it. But, believe me, it is a very good thing for men not to get all they want. It will be a healthful lesson for you."

Tycho turned his back on him in disgust. Moral exhortations from such a superficial, envious boy—that was the last straw! All that he had known amid his most burning griefs and had felt in his very heart's blood, his most inward development towards God, was to be consequentially extolled by this smart little climber and finally, while still in progress, appraised and approved. No, against that everything in him rose in revolt. Better to remain a sinner if virtue is something that commends itself to a Sadeler. . . .

At this supreme moment of his anger Tycho's attention was attracted by three strange-looking figures that emerged from the Emperor's inner reception-room. They were Jews, as might have been seen from their long, simple garments and yellow, wide-brimmed hats: the Rabbi Löwe ben Bezalel and two companions, who had received the unheard-of distinction of being summoned to the Emperor's presence. On the occasion of his first visit to Prague Tycho had been sufficiently free from prejudice to call upon the learned Rabbi of the Commune of Prague in his house. Nor did he now hesitate to approach in all friendliness the old man, who was rapidly drawing near, obviously endeavouring to escape from the sudden silence and manifest contempt of all present. He held out his hand and to everyone's surprise accompanied him to the entrance hall, saying: "I hope you have found favour with His Majesty the Emperor, and wish you all success."

The Rabbi looked about him and drew a breath of relief, as he no longer beheld courtiers. The patches of red upon his cheeks betrayed the fact that for him the last hour had been one of importance, and, as is becoming in great men, he made no effort to conceal his agitation. His long, white beard and the brown eyes, with their tranquil dignity, accorded ill with his hurried utterance. He narrated that Prince Bertier, the Emperor's confidant, had received him with great friendliness and conducted him into a room where, speaking in astonishingly loud tones, he had inquired concerning certain cabbalistic methods. There was a good reason for the loud voice; the Emperor had been concealed behind a curtain and had heard the whole conversation. At the conclusion the curtain had been unexpectedly parted and the Emperor had issued forth. He had himself asked certain questions and had then again withdrawn behind the curtain.

"And that was all?" said Tycho, and he could not withhold a smile.

The Rabbi answered the smile with a sorrowful shake of the head. "I understand you well, Herr de Brahe; we need not exchange many words on the subject. To you it seems a small favour. I, however, thank the Eternal, whose name be praised, that for the first time for centuries one of the powerful of the earth suffers himself to investigate our doctrine. May my oppressed people be raised hereby, for the sake of all men, as it is written: 'The word of the Lord will again go forth from Zion and teaching from Jerusalem.'"

Tycho looked with astonishment at the man upon whom

the people had bestowed the honourable sobriquet of the "modest," but also that of the "august" Rabbi Löwe. He now understood the connexion, and as in his disturbed state of mind he tended to bring everything into relation with himself, he suddenly beheld in this Jew a noble example of firmness and pride in association with external abasement. How naturally did the Rabbi claim on behalf of his despised people the office of teacher for the whole of humanity! This, it is true, seemed somewhat exaggerated to Tycho, but he would gladly have learned more of it. At this moment he once more regretted that he knew so little of Jewish customs and history, although he had frequently associated with Jews and had always interested himself in this peculiar people. He therefore took up the old man's last words and inquired: "Oppressed? Who then oppresses your people with so much harshness?"

"That certainly you cannot easily understand," answered Rabbi Löwe. "The history of the peoples of the earth does not engrave our trials very deeply upon its tablets; they are easily obliterated. We, however, cannot forget what our ancient commune of Prague—we call it 'a mother in Israel' —has endured. Year by year on the Day of Atonement we read the lament of the learned Abigdor Kara, a predecessor in my office—may his merit stand by us in this world and in the next! And what is the cause of his lament? It is that the mob forced its way into the Jewish quarter, 'armed with hatchet and ax, as if to cut down a forest,' as the song has it. And again it runs: 'The inhabitants were with their families and servants in the house of God, and in holy precincts they were destroyed by fire and sword.' And again it is written: 'We weep for the death of the pious Rabbi and for his brother and only son. No sage, no scholar like him will arise. With him dignity and splendour go to the grave! In order to escape certain dishonour the high-minded teacher, the revered of his people, courageously gave his family and himself to death.' "

Tycho listened greedily. And now the Jewish people, homeless and fugitive like himself, the butt of perpetual hostility like himself, like himself misunderstood in their doctrine and yet clinging to it, despoiled and wounded like himself, this people of misfortune, really seemed to him a veritable symbol of his own lot in life. It struck him that he had already once, at some earlier time, compared himself with Ahasuerus, the Wandering Jew. But today the enigma must be solved; that he felt. He had to ask from this Rabbi for instruction regarding the root of his fate and the cause of the failure of all his enterprises. He must question him concerning all the mortifications, insults, and dangers from within and without, which he had suffered for the sake of his learning. He cried out in vehement tones: "But tell me, how is it possible to endure so much suffering? How is it possible to support all this? And all for nothing, for a few letters?"

"It is not at all the question of how we support it," said the old man in gentle tones, which during the conversation had grown ever softer and softer; "we have a doctrine: God is not there for the just to serve and to support Him. The just are there to serve and to support God."

"Does that really occur in your books?" cried Tycho, stirred in his most secret forebodings.

"In many places. Thus it is handed down to us in the treatise of Berachoth that the high-priest once entered the Holy of holies to offer up incense. There he saw the Eternal, praised be His name, seated upon a lofty throne, adorned with His name Akatriel, which is interpreted: 'Crowned throughout all eternity,' and the Eternal spoke and said:

263

'Jishmael, my son, bless Me!' And when the priest had finished blessing Him, God, the Lord of hosts, inclined His head towards him. From this we may learn a twofold lesson: that the Lord held the temple worthy to be His habitation, and that He even held the righteous man worthy to confer upon Him, the Holy One, the benefit of a blessing." Rabbi Löwe had waxed eager and had fallen into that peculiar singing intonation with which the Talmud is recited. His eyes were half closed, as if in ecstasy, and the upper part of his body swayed rhythmically to and fro. His countenance expressed at once spiritual fervour and a power of keen discrimination, which was no vain sophistry, but a joyous solicitude to rise to the level of his august subject. So here in the service of God a dim inward fervour had united with a clear consciousness, those two selfsame opposing tendencies which tore Tycho's soul in twain. They had united to form a living unity, which immediately passed over into Tycho and by the very intonation of the words convinced him of its kinship with him. "Is God, then, not almighty?" asked Tycho in trembling tones. "Does He need our help, our words of blessing?"

Rabbi Löwe continued: "It is just to this that Rabbi Tarfon refers when he quotes the words of scripture: 'Build Me a sanctuary and then I will dwell therein.'—'And then'! That is interpreted: 'Not before the sanctuary is constructed for My service.' But if you prefer it, I should say that what Rabbi Tarfon says is more than what goes before. For from the high-priest but a single blessing was called for, whereas from the whole people the mighty work of building is demanded.—From which, however, it may be seen that the Eternal, praised be His name, not only commands our help, but even complains if it is not rendered. We have the teaching that when the Rabbi Josi was once on a journey and

264

was praying in the ruins of Jerusalem, he heard a *bathkol*, a divine voice, cooing like a dove, and it said: 'By thy life and by the life of thy head!' Not in this hour alone does it speak thus, but day by day and thrice in the day it speaks thus: 'Hail to the King whom they praise in his house. But what is left to the father abandoned by his children?'"

The Rabbi's eyes grew wide. As he uttered these words, they shone with a holy sorrow, filling with tears.

The two men stood confronting one another in silence; there was sympathy between them. At length the Rabbi added, with an imperceptible smile: "Pardon me, it was quite uncalled-for to speak at such a length in your presence, in the presence of a sage. I am an old man and forget what I myself have once written: 'The wisdom of all peoples comes from the Eternal, who has distributed it among them from the perfection of His own wisdom.'"

Tycho pressed his hand. A groom of the chamber had appeared at the door of the gallery, a sign that he must prepare himself for the audience. There was now only time for a brief farewell and expression of thanks. Soon after, Sadeler issued from the Emperor's cabinet, wearing a satisfied expression; he had received the expected commission. As he passed, Tycho looked at the fresh countenance of the young artist, radiant with the moment's happiness; but this momentary happiness was eclipsed by that undying light of reconciliation which for Tycho had poured forth over the whole world from the strife-furrowed features of the aged Rabbi. Such were his emotions as he followed the groom into the Emperor's inner rooms.

In the first chamber two halberdiers, fully armed, wearing upon their heads gilt helmets of a Roman pattern, strode silently up and down. Otherwise the room was empty.

Next came a corridor, with lofty windows shaped like

doors, and numerous mirrors. The walls were stained white and bore silver candlesticks and hunting trophies. This was a passage the shutters of which, according to popular rumour, were always kept open, in order that the people, if ever the Emperor should proceed to the Council of State, might see with their own eyes that he still lived.

Passing through two dark cabinets, in which again guards were on duty, Tycho reached a small chamber, hung all round with red silk. The Emperor entered it immediately from the other side and came towards him. Tycho bowed low. The Emperor took another step, but still remained standing at some distance from him, without holding out his hand. In this position he moved a little in a sidewise direction and, leaning over a table of gleaming agate, inquired in slow, timid tones: "I hope, Professor Brahe, you are already comfortably installed in our Prague."

Tycho again bowed and remained silent for a space, as if he wished to listen to the dying echoes of the gentle voice. That voice, the sideways movement of the sovereign, and his embarrassed motion over the table all reminded him of the Rabbi's words: "How weak God is! We must support Him. Woe to the father abandoned by his children."

It had been Tycho's intention to pour forth all his sorrows before the Emperor in a wild, reckless statement of grievances. All at once he felt that his misfortune was trifling compared with that of the man who had to support and to guide a whole State, a world full of such misfortunes. And this was the man from whom he had wished to demand help, whom he had almost decided to arraign! Suddenly he felt that he had not the courage to give utterance to his trivial woes. He recounted the story of his removal in brief, matter-of-fact terms, merely observing at its conclusion that he still, of course, had some desiderata.

266

With what touching attention the Emperor listened! He did not utter a single word of interruption, but kept his great, melancholy eyes steadily fixed upon Tycho. It was obvious that he forced himself to listen. And again when he said in reply that Tycho should draw up his demands in the form of a memorandum and hand it to the Privy Secretary, Barvitius, his words issued forth as if reluctantly and under constraint from lips shaped for silence. One did not see the smile that usually plays when a request is granted. Those lips had assuredly never smiled. . . . Tycho was overcome and wondered how he could even have ventured to force his way into this sphere of majestic seriousness and world domination. He only felt that his audience was over, and once again bowed to the ground.

But the Emperor had not finished. Advancing gently from behind the table, he said that he would be pleased to cultivate closer acquaintance with the great master of the starry lore. He named certain hours at which Tycho should have daily access unannounced.

While he now spoke in greater detail, Tycho respectfully contemplated the monarch's small but well-built figure. Clad from head to foot in radiant black silk, a short jewelled dagger at the side, his form expressed a natural nobility. His face was devoid of colour, the skin soft as buckskin, and the aspect one of infinite melancholy. The loosely hanging under lip and the prominent chin, with its ample, finely curling beard, held fast an unalterable expression of sympathy and compassion. Tycho, in whose excited brain the imperial figure began more and more to blend with the Rabbi's God in His need of help, was quite enraptured at this clear manifestation of sympathy. Soon he answered with the greatest cordiality and joy. And the Emperor, too, seemed to find pleasure in his company. The conversation grew warmer, and finally Tycho

267

followed a movement of invitation of the Emperor's hand. The discussion continued while they paced slowly through the adjacent rooms.

They found themselves in the famous imperial art gallery, which it had never fallen to the lot of any foreigner to behold. Here for the first time the monarch's face lost its rigid expression. He now behaved with the complacent bearing of the collector who exhibits his treasures. In leisurely tones, as if no ministers and visitors were waiting outside, he interpreted the German, Dutch, and Italian pictures which hung right up to the ceiling and even along columns and pillars. Some were actually placed across the windows. Beneath, in numerous glass cases were massed like sea-foam costly crystal cups, pearls, and silver bowls. The so-called German room, originally intended for state balls, was also filled with *objets d'art* and curiosities. Even the corridors and staircases were radiant with a dense mass of polished, turned, and embossed work, with mosaic and ivory, with the glory of stuffed humming-birds, and with furs, so that at length the silent sheen began to hum in the ears like the sound of a medley of voices.

"No, God is really not almighty." The words passed through Tycho's head as he was reminded by this uncontrollable accumulation of the chaos of the prime. The Emperor, too, in the midst of his treasures, which he had not perhaps surveyed in their mass for a long time, seemed to be alarmed. He shook his head like one weary and soon passed silently back along the exhibits, lacking power to pause by any single object. All this was calculated to intensify in Tycho's reeling brain the interplay between imperial and divine lordship over the world, until at length, giving expression to a doubt which characterized his whole life as an investigator, he inquired in meek but quite unceremonious tones: "Your Majesty, is there some law present in all this or none at all?"

The Emperor stood still. "You ask what law I have observed in my collection? Many have already asked me that, and I have never been able to answer any of them. I know, too, that many of those outside consider it a fault that I live here only for these things and look with loathing upon their disputes. . . ."

"Ah, but they compare you with the Medici princes in Florence, the patrons of the arts," interjected Tycho in genuine admiration. He was filled with understanding of the man through whose majestic, composed tones there trembled an incomprehensible note of weakness.

But Rudolf emphatically repudiated the suggestion. "No, a Medici by no means! They were worldly and found in life itself a meaning which their art was intended merely to adorn. I, however, lock up my art; I keep it pure, for I have found no meaning in life, nothing which must be adorned and honoured. Need I remind you of your coat of arms, Master Brahe: 'Nor power, nor wealth, only the sceptre of the arts'? Some, it is true, come with their religious demands and set them high above everything. Falsehood and deceit! I know my Estates. Freedom of conscience for them is an excuse for extorting liberties of a much coarser sort which have a financial value; they confuse the Holy Spirit with their rubbish. But I—" and here the Emperor raised his head—"I seek perfection in these stones and metals and upon painted canvas, as you seek it in the stars. There is but one thing for the sake of which life is worth living, perfection. . . . There you have the law which governs my collection."

The Emperor had approached a small marble table. It hung over a glass shade which covered a mass of pure gold and indicated that this "alchemical gold" owed its origin to the power of the Pole Sendivoj. The Emperor looked questioningly at Tycho, who maintained an embarrassed silence.

269

Then he continued dejectedly: "Even in the arts we do not often find perfection. I know that I am deceived. That skin you see there was sent me by a Hungarian magnate with a message to the effect that it had fallen from heaven. Herr von Rosenberg has presented me with a stone which grows. I always have the ducal cap of Przemysl and other clumsily forged objects of great rarity. One is taken in; I am well aware of it. In the realm of art it is very much the same as in politics. Thorny is the path of perfection. Ah, if once one could have attained it . . . even as my great-aunt Johanna believed herself to have attained it in her handsome husband!" The Emperor's voice had sunk to a whisper, and Tycho shuddered at the light of madness in his eyes. "Oh, I understand her well. When the perfect dies, the beauty that is irreplaceable, how could one ever forget it? . . . Well might one cause it to be carried about in a glass coffin until the day of one's death. . . ."

They had entered an open gallery. The golden-brown autumnal tops of the acacias in the deer-park brushed against the stone parapet. The chilly odour of decay held Tycho's spirit as in a spell, and the Emperor's confused utterances accorded sorrowfully with this image of decay.

Trembling as in a frosty wind, the Emperor moaned: "I wished to be an example to my subjects. Our time is full of unrest, self-seeking, and vanity. I wished to show that one must observe measure, reflect, live the inward life, be alone rather than amid evil councillors, have but one desire, to discover perfection.— But for that I am too weak."

Too weak!

That was the word for which Tycho had been waiting, and now within him thundered forth a mighty voice: "Yes, God is sick. He is plagued to death; He can do no more.

270

"And the autumn about us—the perishing and the dropping —that is an illness of God, not His ill will.

"Why have I hated autumn and dying and illness? I held them to be God's ill will. But now I see; they are but His fatigue. His love remains eternal.

"Now I have remorse; now I am reconciled with God! In the gloom of this autumn day He will lead me to Him, of that I am certain."

The Emperor touched Tycho on the shoulder, arousing him at this point from his distraction. They returned to the interior of the palace. There in a well-lighted little room they beheld an easel and beside it a tall man about whose head scanty grey locks hovered. It was the court painter, Bartholomäus Spranger, whom Rudolf esteemed so highly that he always allowed him to work close to his private apartments, indeed under his very eye. The Emperor approached the painter with a lively step in order to touch lightly with the handle of a brush certain places which he wished altered, and to praise others. Tycho, too, drew nearer and greeted the painter.

His attire was disorderly. It consisted of an open, smock-like overall, bespattered with paint-stains and without the customary ruff. His fat, pale face, in which the nose alone had colour, argued many a sleepless night; he might have been taken for a decayed debauchee, although, as was well known, he was a solid Kleinseitner citizen. And this old gentleman sat before a canvas on which he had grouped five or six naked girls and brown, muscular boys in the most indecent postures on the pretext of some allegory: "Virtue Conquers Envy and Pride." In all the flower of their youth, white and with red points upon their breasts, the maidens held weapons and trumpets in their hands. A little Eros was occupied

271

in forcing apart the rounded thighs of one who still resisted the importunities of her lover. . . . The picture, with its chilly light-blue tints and its conventional execution, tedious in its complete absence of genuine inspiration and utterly dead, produced upon Tycho a sickly sweet impression, an impression even as of something vicious. What a morbid perversion! The worthy burgess, moderation personified, must assume the mask of immodesty in order to please the virtuous, severe, unsmiling Emperor! The contrast between these frivolous painted figures and the two elderly men who examined and fingered them with the air of connoisseurs produced upon Tycho, as nothing else could, the impression of impotence and senility. Suddenly it seemed to him as if here in the castle there was literally nothing that was young. The dismal chambers which he had just seen, with their precious and ancient lumber, acquired while still fresh in his memory a tone of slackness, decay, the aspect of things shrivelled from age. Did not the caskets totter together like backs bent in despair, and strange white fungus threads twine themselves along the damp walls like some enormous white beard? "Oh, God Himself is a greybeard!" thought Tycho now. "God is incarcerated here in this desolate castle of Hradschin as if in His last refuge. Here He awaits His end. . . ." Tycho hardly observed that he had for a long time been walking with the Emperor through other rooms. Before his eyes God descended ever lower from the clouds towards him. He had already set foot upon the woebegone earth and, somewhat like an old beggar whom he daily encountered opposite the "Greif," stretched towards him, with a look bordering upon utter despair, red, crooked hands. . . .

At length he started in alarm. Following the Emperor, he had entered the same chamber, hung in red, in which the audience had begun. And now he perceived that the audience was really almost at an end. But during the hours that he had

272

passed in the monarch's company, he had not uttered a single word about the matter on account of which he had come. He had passed through the rooms like one lost in heaven-sent dreams. "And yet they say that I am too shrewd," he grumbled to himself. But at the same moment, even as his visions suddenly faded away, the other, the matter-of-fact side of his nature asserted itself, and in well-considered language he reminded the Emperor of his promise regarding an observatory in Prague.

To this, too, the Emperor nodded assent, but not with the decision and friendliness that Tycho had actually expected after so much confidential discussion. The erection of an observatory, said the ruler, was of course in prospect, but for the immediate future the construction of a pyronomic and alchemical laboratory seemed to him more urgently necessary, setting aside the fact that the latter entailed less expense and even offered some prospect of gain. He would, therefore, desire that for the immediate future Tycho should place his services at his disposal to that end. "Rejected, then, a decisive and final failure," thought Tycho to himself bitterly. The ground trembled under his feet. He could hardly hold out any longer against the rapid change of emotions brought about by this momentous afternoon; he had already begun to stagger towards the door. But through all the excitement within his mind his clear sense of duty still toiled on like a ticking clock reminding him of Kepler. "What a good thing it is, particularly for Kepler, that I am so shrewd!" was the thought that occurred to him. "In my place he would certainly have forgotten me, or rather it would never have struck him to attempt anything on my behalf." And at the same time he thought of all the outrages and finally of that letter which Kepler had written. What heartlessness! But, unaffected by the uproar within him, he set before the Emperor the well-founded, carefully-thought-out request that the young astronomer Kepler might join him to aid him in his work, and that he might be appointed to the now vacant office formerly held by the imperial mathematician, Ursus. He added the request that out of regard for the enhancement of prices in Prague the salary might be increased by a hundred gulden a year.

"Kepler," replied the Emperor, and again leaned on his agate table. "I have heard the name. He is the assistant who lived with you at Benatky. The reports about him are not greatly to his credit."

Tycho listened attentively. "What was that? Not to his credit? Kepler, about whom the whole world is enraptured, whom it places above me?" He thought he had not heard aright and involuntarily took a step nearer to the Emperor. The parquet cracked beneath his hasty tread.

The Emperor continued in his drawling tones: "He has even been accused of taking part in a conspiracy against my government. Your own son-in-law—"

"Tengnagel! Yes. The two had some quarrel. The charges are absolutely unfounded."

"Perhaps so. I only ordered a hurried inquiry and quickly let it drop—out of regard for you. I could not believe that you would entertain my enemy as your guest."

Tycho was dumb under the Emperor's suspicious look. Only now did he feel the danger of his position. And once more it would have been Kepler to whom he would have owed this most grievous harm, the *coup de grâce,* the loss of the Emperor's favour. This maddening reflection robbed him of all power of speech.

After a pause the Emperor went on: "But more serious than these presumptions is the report that he has expressed himself in terms of coarse contempt concerning astrology

274

and that he does not practise the art at all. You are too tolerant, Master Tycho, and will never speak ill of anyone. You are solicitous on behalf of your pupils, even when they fall away from you. Listen, I have it from people fully deserving of confidence that this Kepler is more attached to the Copernican fancies than to your own excellent *diataxis mundi*."

Tycho nodded in silence. Was he not to nod? The last sentence which the Emperor had uttered was absolutely correct, was painfully, tormentingly true. Why should he not have nodded? The Emperor's words were correct. There was no doubt that Kepler was Tycho's scientific opponent. And this Kepler, whom all worshipped, was suddenly revealed as not enjoying the Emperor's goodwill. Diabolical fires of malice suddenly flamed up in Tycho. Was not this revenge for all the suffering which Kepler had inflicted upon him, whether consciously or unconsciously, from indifference or from design, in any case so as to penetrate into the most vital part of his whole life's work? In a moment all the good spirits, the vanquishing of self, the triumphs in Tycho's breast, were drowned by a veritable witches' sabbath of loud-voiced temptations. A genuine feeling of voluptuousness had laid hold of him, deep and strong; a burning love of self was kindled within him, gilding everything with its gleams. . . . "A compensation, a compensation for all evil." Tycho exulted. "This, the most exalted moment of my life, compensates me for all the evil that I have suffered. Yes, the whole world pours forth its felicity at Kepler's feet, while I have been overwhelmed with calumnies from the beginning. But as a compensation, out of regard for justice, the highest peak in the world stands out of Kepler's reach and I am welcome there in imperial favour. That, now, is God; that is God's justice; that is the significance of my existence, the justification, the heaven . . . ."

275

"If you insist upon your request," concluded the Emperor, "I will gladly grant it. But from the first this Kepler has not been agreeable to me, and, as I said, I should do it entirely to please you."

Tycho had involuntarily accompanied the Emperor's remark with a genial murmur of joy. "I need do nothing but keep silent," he said, to himself, "I have no need to speak against Kepler. On the contrary, I have done my part and given my recommendation; I could do no more. It would even be dangerous if I were to do more. I can speak no further on his behalf. It would involve me in suspicion myself. No, the Emperor has rejected him—rejected him, moreover, in private conversation; it is no fault of mine. Now it is Kepler's turn to be unlucky. . . ."

The Emperor was really uttering words of farewell. Now he even stretched out his hand. Tycho lightly gripped the white, cold fingers and bent his knee while he kissed them. Then he stepped backwards towards the door, without uttering a single word. The Emperor was already looking down at the shining top of the table, as if Tycho were no longer present in the room. . . .

What now followed was surely something quite contrary to usage. Tycho had already touched the wood of the door when he drew back his hand as if he had laid hold of white-hot steel. At the same moment overwhelming emotion forced him to his knees, so that he fell, weeping, and trembling throughout his whole frame. . . . But in the next instant he had recovered himself; it was just as if he had merely stumbled. With calm aspect and gentle tones he once more approached the Emperor, who raised his eyes in astonishment. "There still remains something that I must set right," wailed Tycho, as if no more master of himself. "I must testify . . . yes, testify."

276

The Emperor drummed impatiently on his lips with two fingers.

"Your Majesty was not well-informed. Kepler is perfect." As if with these words everything was said, Tycho fell silent; more he could not say.

"So you want to have him, if I understand you aright?"

And now Tycho paid no more heed to the Emperor's wrinkled brow, to the possibility that his whole position might be jeopardized, now that he espoused the cause of the obnoxious Kepler with so much warmth. Without a moment's hesitation the words burst from his lips: "Kepler is the most considerable—no, Your Majesty, that is too mild a term—he is the only considerable scholar of the age. He is simply perfection itself, pure, fruitful, inviolable perfection. It is perfection that Your Majesty seeks. Here it offers itself. And so I ask on his behalf still more than the post of mathematician. Everything must be decided. I feel that I have not much longer to live." Tycho's voice trembled. The Emperor seemed only now to notice that something of vital interest to Tycho was at stake, and his morose expression grew gentler. With kindly eyes he regarded the pallid features of the man who strove with himself and adjured him to banish his sorrowful thoughts.

"It isn't a sorrowful thought," said Tycho, "it is my happiest thought, if I may hope that Your Majesty will hear my request. When I die, I would not have my sons, no, nor the junker Tengnagel—they have all indeed studied the starry lore, but they are nothing in comparison with Kepler's genius —I would have Kepler, Kepler and none else, inherit my position and all that I leave behind in manuscript or print, my instruments and all the scientific equipment that Your Majesty in your graciousness has accorded me. Then I will gladly die, for then I shall know that my work is in good hands, the equal of my own. . . ."

"Kepler, then, upholds your theory, and my information is false?" asked the Emperor, full of interest.

"False and not false. There are difficult questions involved. In some we are not in agreement and I, too, have objections to oppose to him. But these are not of the kind that his traducers allege; they are of a kind that could not arise at all unless he were accorded the fullest recognition." Tycho hesitated. Suddenly the inner voice which had already brought him to this point cried: "Now or never is the time to testify, now or never, to testify and to withhold nothing." And so he continued firmly: "As regards the question of astrology, we are of course entirely of one opinion. One must certainly admit the existence of a general affinity and a divine operation within the cosmos, but it is not enshrined in the naïve prophecies of the horoscope—"

"That is my opinion as well," interrupted the Emperor, speaking more vivaciously than at any time during the whole conversation, and a vast surge of confused ideas, of hopes and curiosity, rose quite visibly upon his features like a cloud in the sky. "Tell me about it. But no—you are tired!"

Tycho's alternately pale and blood-red countenance and the deep rings beneath his moist eyes in fact admitted of no other interpretation. "I beg Your Majesty to accord me your gracious leave to withdraw," he said, already speaking with difficulty.

"From this moment onwards Kepler is my court mathematician." The Emperor slightly inclined his head and withdrew with measured tread. "We shall see one another again soon," he said, already on the threshold of the next room.

Tycho passed through the two dark cabinets, the white corridor, and the room where the two halberdiers stood. Suddenly it seemed as if he had passed the whole morning between these two gleaming lance-heads, hemmed in between

278

them and whirled about, so that they alternately clashed together and receded with the rise and fall of his emotions. . . .
He hastened through the ante-rooms, seeing no one. Already
he was in the open air. In his condition of stupor he chose
the road leading in the opposite direction from home, passed
the cathedral along the inner bastions towards the mighty
walls of the fortress. Many acquaintances greeted him in the
courts of the burg. He stumbled on in his semi-conscious
condition, reaching the George Church and the Daliborka.
The autumn rain fell in fine drops. The ivy-stalks, with their
yellow and golden leaves waving in the wind like long pen-
dulums, beat upon the castle walls. Tycho observed nothing.
Only when he had reached the parapet by the castle steps and
saw nothing before him but the grey expanse of the evening
sky, did he start up. His whole tension released itself in one
mighty cry in this lonely place upon the battlements of the
burg.

And now, too, it was also perfectly clear to him that
this—and not the earlier infatuation—was the supreme moment of his life. For he now understood for the first time in
his life the real reason why he was so shrewd, so capable,
and so active, the true significance for him of these seductive
and dangerous gifts. Not for himself should he or might he
be shrewd—that he now realized amid a rapture that knew no
bounds—but in the name of God to establish and redeem the
world.

"Oh, this happiness! I have achieved nothing with the Emperor on my own account, but for Kepler everything that I
had desired. Ah, how pure that is, how perspicuous, how
pregnant with significance: shrewd for others, not for oneself!

"I am upon God's work. I am a servant. I feel the sweet
burden of responsibility for everything that happens.

279

"I am shrewd in the service of God. And to that end it is exceedingly well that I should also feel now how God has heard of my service, how God waits upon me and upon my shrewdness, how He expects sacrifice from me.

"From the clouds on high, God stretches forth His hand, and rising from the earth, I hold my shrewdness high above my head, lifting it up to the aid of my Lord.

"And yet this shrewdness has plagued me throughout my life. It lured me upon false paths, so that I have become weary of it and have learned to curse it.

"Has not shrewdness brought me into insupportable company? Has it not caught me in the toils of weak compliance and compromise? Has it not persuaded me to undertake a thousand useless tasks?

"And yet I have endured it, the evil, the fork-tongued, the poisonous! And yet I have not cast it from me impatiently, like a counterfeit coin. *Nay, I divined that even shrewdness is a sacred thing and that the original nobility of its nature would yet come into prominence! And so I waited and endured amid the tortures that shrewdness inflicted upon me!*

"Oh, praise to the great, eternal shrewdness! Praise to my instinct to bring order to things and to make myself conscious of everything! Praise to my errors and to the right way discovered at long last! For now my shrewdness is in its right place, there where God needs His trusty comrades and can accomplish nothing with such blind Kepler creatures.

"I laud my God. He loves the insensible, but still more those that have within them both impetus and reflection, who would forgo neither and who reach His throne panting under the double burden.

"I laud my God. He has led me to Him, stone of offence that I am; He kisses me upon the face, here, right upon my broken nose!

280

"I laud my God. How could I compare Him with a beggar who supplicates my aid? I do indeed help Him; but who has brought me to His aid if not He Himself?

"Yes, to the governance of the world I lend help with all my strength. But is it my own strength that has made it possible for me to help?

"No, there is God again. God beneath me, who has helped me, even as God above me, whom I help. God everywhere, the powerful no less than the powerless, the helper and he that receives help.

"Hail to myself for that I recognize God is no longer far from me! Alike sublime and needy of help, He stands before me with His tremendous countenance, fierce and gentle, the one eye commanding, while the other seems to entreat or to thank. Ah, how well I know that countenance! How it has accompanied me throughout life until this present moment!"

And suddenly Tycho realized what it was that this countenance reminded him of. Of something quite familiar, even intimate. Of his own father; nay, more, of a particular event, a particular winter evening. For once—Tycho was then a seven-year-old boy on the estate of Tostrup—his father had fallen over some newly-frozen snow, and Tycho, who was smaller even when standing than his gigantic father when kneeling, had held out his hand to help him. And the very same expression with which his father had risen to his feet now shone down upon him from God's halo, an expression which was wrathful and at which one shuddered, an expression which seemed to say: "Help me, you must help me, it is your duty to, and you can't do enough for me," and yet at the same time also: "How fine it is that you do help me! I will never forget it; I rejoice at it, my good son."

"My good son, my son," sobbed Tycho, striving desperately to fight down his emotion and to prepare himself for the sharp contest in the service of God as he now stood before Him. But the idea that God looked down upon him like a beloved child, that God designed no evil against him, despite His mighty and terrible aspect, despite His divine majesty— that God, even in the wondrous manner of a father who, fallen by accident, needs help, looked forth from eyes enraged and yet at the same time gentle, eyes humiliated and yet exalted, eyes sternly expectant and yet filled with a bounteous foreknowledge—this idea was stronger than his composure. Everything began to dissolve, to form itself into new shape. And when Tycho looked down upon the city through the veil of his tears—by the mediation of God, this alien, clamorous, uncomprehending city had also become his friend and confidant. The beautiful river, the pale-hued towers, the streets, and the men—all proceeded from the Father. That life was so hard and joyless to endure among these men, who were by no means merely scoundrels, but also honest, gifted, and earnest people, that injustice should be done to his good intentions by kindly fellow-creatures, deserving of all respect—even this perplexity which caused him so much daily disquiet was now completely banished from him. It was made plain in that paternal aspect which God showed him, in that strange, unfathomable expression which rejected help, blazed up so proudly, and yet expected help with such ardent longing. . . . Quite enraptured, as if fire were streaming through his being, Tycho looked up to the sky. There aloft through the mist, although the sun had not yet gone down, feeble rays forced a path; and then on a sudden—extraordinary, sublime spectacle!—all, all the stars were there! And this time it was no longer a mocking twinkle and glimmer, as in those recent nights, when he had been compelled to contemplate them without instruments. Like great white flakes of snow all the stars stood in the grey heaven. And by virtue of the same power

282

whereby the light pierced through the veil of evening clouds, they now constantly grew in size and sent forth their white, red, and blue light, first in single rays, then in great fans, which again coagulated like sparks and finally with impetuous movement formed themselves into mighty segments of circles. Nay, the stars began to move along those circles just as Tycho had imagined a thousand times when standing before his celestial charts. He held his breath, while a final feeling of warm exaltation passed through him. Now he saw that for which he had longed and toiled in vain so many years, what was more than astronomical learning: the real course of the stars. It was a clear presentation of the divine law in the ordering of the world, a most exalted harmony, an apprehended unity of creation, inscribed in characters of fire. Like a delighted child Tycho gazed about him upon the ever moving, rolling firmament, resounding in sonorous accord. His eyes could not be satiated. There revolved Mars, whose movements in its simple, beautiful, smooth path he had never been able to penetrate. It was like the peaceful rise and fall in the breathing of a sleeping infant. Near by, constellations which had so often confused him met now in the most entrancing groups. They exchanged places, they glided past one another, they seemed to hold each other by the hand, they sported together and returned once more in wondrous order. The heavens opened with a deeper expanse; the Milky Way stretched itself forth, swelling out like a great white cloth in the wind. Worlds whose existence had never been suspected hastened near. Yet another revolution of the whole, another slight tremor through the cosmos, and then all manifoldness had disappeared; the whole standpoint seemed to have changed. Now all the stars circled round, their stations plotted with an indescribable simplicity in one glowing single ring, the diamond axis of the world.

So it was given to Tycho to see with his own eyes a vision to which he could never have attained by means of his most ingenious instruments: reality, the immortal perfection of his system, the genuine *theatrum astronomicum*. And while ultimate matter, ring, and world-axis dissolved away, he was already caught up into a divine aureole, uniting face to face with the Being he had come to know. A mighty voice resounded through the thundering accords of the spheres: "Tycho, My servant." At that he flung out his arms. "Here am I," he cried, and fell unconscious to the ground.

CHAPTER XII

AFTER MIDNIGHT the relief guard found him and brought him home, where his anxious family were sitting up for him. Kepler, with his wife and child, had arrived shortly before and had at once betaken himself to Tycho's abode. To his horror he had now to behold his friend and protector carried in on a stretcher.

Tycho was in a high fever. Hagecius, who appeared that night at the sick-bed, ascribed the critical turn to neglected kidney-disorder. He applied leeches and prescribed cooling remedies. Towards morning Tycho recovered somewhat and looked round with tranquil eyes. He greeted Kepler with a friendly nod.

Kepler had brought with him a present for his host, the long-promised apology of Tycho against Ursus, upon which he had bestowed the whole of his time in Graz. Like everything that proceeded from Kepler's pen it had developed into a work of genius, containing startling new vistas upon the future. In Benatky, amid the wealth of suggestions proceeding from Tycho, he had without any ill intent neglected the apology. Just as naturally in Graz, where he lacked the collected material for original investigation, he had flung himself into this, strictly speaking, historical task. He had in fact produced a work entirely after Tycho's mind and indeed surpassing his expectations. But Tycho only regarded the title-page with a gentle smile. Then his fingers, which had already strayed between the pages of the manuscript, slipped back upon the pillows. His thoughts were travelling in another direction: "Blessed, blessed be this hour! Assuredly I greeted you well, my Kepler, when you came to me for the first time. But that hour was not yet the real blessing. Then I was blinded; then I believed that you were come to be my earthly ally and helper of helpers, and on that account I blessed that hour. Now you have by no means allied yourself with me in earthly matters. On the contrary, you have but increased my suffering. But it is just by that means that you have helped me. Yes, now I recognize it; you were the instrument of God to purify me. Blessed be that hour when you entered my house! Now for the first time can I say it with a whole and thankful heart! Now and only now do I see that you have been my best friend! . . ." Tycho was under the impression that he had actually spoken all these words. In reality he moved his lips powerlessly, without any sound issuing forth. Utter impotence had gained upon his senses. . . .

In the mean time the group of relatives round Tycho's bed had been joined by his more intimate acquaintances, for the report of the great man's unexpected illness had penetrated the city. The consideration in which Tycho's name was held among the people was now for the first time made manifest. By midday the narrow street had become almost impassable; the crowd pressed together in a dense mass far into the neighbouring streets and squares, all waiting anxious and solicitous and whispering in undertones. The courier from the Emperor, who appeared every hour to obtain intelligence for his master, was respectfully allowed to pass; behind him the press closed again its iron barriers.

It was significant of Tycho's popularity that very speedily the rumour circulated that his enemy Raymarus Ursus had

286

poisoned him. Hagecius himself had to appear at the window and calm the people, reminding them that Ursus had been long dead.

Tycho several times recovered consciousness, but felt the end near and desired to take leave of his wife and children. He comforted them with simple words of faith in God. Then he exhorted his sons, Tengnagel, and the few pupils who still remained with him to continue their studies assiduously. . . . This effort seemed to have exhausted all the strength that was left to him; his breath now came irregularly, its movements growing tranquil only with difficulty. He did not speak again. It was with a gesture that he summoned Kepler to his bedside, taking his hand and continuing to hold it. His eyes remained closed and the fever grew in strength. But before his inner eye there appeared once more the vision of the star-set, fiery, agitated heaven as of yesterday. The voice of God resounded in his ear, and the sublime promise was mingled with kindly images, recollections of his childhood and of his days of prosperity on the island of Hveen. Yes, just as formerly he had felt himself happy and at home in but few regions of the vast earth, and those of restricted area, so now the whole world had become a home for him. Intoxicated and set free, his spirit ranged through distant solar systems, and everywhere he beheld Tostrup and the island of Hveen, everywhere laws disposed themselves in order, everywhere new tasks beckoned to him and new results of wondrous beauty. And so a thousand undreamed-of forces stirred within Tycho, while in the eyes of those who stood around him he lay there expiring, almost without any sign of life. All that he had achieved by his labour seemed small and of no account by comparison with that which he now beheld. Standing upon the boundary of two worlds, the finite and the infinite, he once more became courageous, young, and eager for action. When he looked round upon that which remained behind him as the heritage of a scholar, he was exceedingly discontented. And so it was that once more anxiety snatched him from the divine embrace and forced the cry from him: "If only I have not lived in vain!"

The night of the 24th October fell. Throughout the whole night Tycho, rising out of the death agony, several times repeated the cry: *"Ne frustra vixisse videar!"*

All in the room were upon their knees. From the street there rose the murmurs of the praying multitude, the gleam of torches, and the cries of children. In the half-light of the morning Tycho once more had a moment of freedom; the pain had left him. Then he opened his lips, and to Kepler, who had not stirred from his bedside, he made this request: that everything which he should write in the future might be set forth in his system, the system of Tycho, not in that of Copernicus. As he said these words, his features were lighted up by a peculiar smile. He had assuredly left far behind him all vanity, all paltry weighing of success and failure, and so by his system he naturally no longer meant those earthly experiments, but the all-comprehensive, divine certainty of the true law wherein he now felt himself a blissful participant. In this, too, he wished to make Kepler his pupil, even as in many other matters he had shown him the right way. But his strength did not suffice for him to make this clear, and so Kepler inevitably misunderstood his words.

The words were Tycho's last, words which have descended to posterity with the false interpretation which was so obvious. Soon after, he perished in the arms of Kepler and of his elder son.

His remains were buried at Prague in the Teynkirche on the Grosse Ring with great pomp and amid a vast assemblage, drawn alike from the court and from the people. There, close

288

by the high altar, his monument may be seen today, a slab in relief, cut out of red marble, bearing the portrait of Tycho in full knightly armour, his left hand caressing a globe, and his right grasping a sword. The device, too, was not wanting: *"Nec fasces, nec opes, solum artis sceptra perennant."*

H I S T O R I A N S of the science of astronomy are unanimous in holding the encounter of the two great men, which we have sought to depict in these pages not without some freedom, to be one of the most pregnant and auspicious events in the development of its teaching.

As is well known, some years later, on the bases of his own observations and those of Tycho, Kepler deduced those famous laws bearing his name, fraught with such revolutionary consequences. In this connexion the ever fortunate man derived benefit from the fact that during the interval following the death of Tycho the telescope was invented, rendering possible entirely new modes of apprehending nature.

Kepler, whose character in integrity and grandeur did not fall short of his extraordinary intellectual endowments, was always ready to admit with all emphasis his debt to Tycho. Alike in his *Rudolphine Tables* and in the actual work of fundamental importance upon the movements of Mars, and also wherever appropriate in other writings, he never forgot to point to Tycho, whom he styled the "phœnix of astronomy," as his master and as the real pioneer.

Max Brod (1884–1968), born in Prague, was a German-language novelist, poet, and essayist who, after fleeing the Nazis, settled in Palestine and contributed to the foundation of Israeli theater. Among Brod's many works are his widely read biography of Kafka and the novels *Reubeni, Prince of the Jews* and *The Master,* which concerns the life of Jesus.

Stefan Zweig (1881–1942) was born in what was then called the Austro-Hungarian Empire. Before his books were banned by the Nazis, he was among the most famous writers of his time, having published numerous biographies, stories, and the novel *Beware of Pity.*

Felix Warren Crosse (1892–1974) worked in the British Foreign Office and published translations from several languages.

Peter Fenves is the Joan and Sarepta Harrison Professor of Literature at Northwestern University. He is the author of several books, including *Late Kant: Towards Another Law of the Earth.*